SIMON AND HIROKO

Marius Hancu

This is a work of fiction. Names, characters, places, and incidents are either the product of the author's imagination or are used fictitiously. Any resemblance to actual events or locales or persons, living or dead, is entirely coincidental.

This book is dedicated to

Gheorghe and Leucadia Hâncu

my uncle and my aunt

and to

Elena Hâncu

my aunt

It is also dedicated to the loving memory of

Melania Hâncu-Cimponeriu

my aunt

Simon and Hiroko

Simon and Hiroko

Prologue — What it was

He enters their *Sakura* space, looking for her, and goes through separators, walls after walls, entryways, staircases, elevators, escalators, thin high ceilings. There is no shadow here, only a diluted, bright, milky sunlight with no sun, radiating off the surfaces themselves. He bumps into things or pushes on them, weaving along through them, and they move away with no strain on him, replaced smoothly by the next, the neighborly one, as though there is no substance to them.

There is no one, yet he knows they must be somewhere, hiding behind things, probably sneaking off from him.

He knows because he came here desperate to find her, knowing she cried for help. The feeling, the telepathy, still works. Seldom, what with the physical distance, the Pacific in between them, but it does. Someone, somewhere, most probably in America, has been doing horrible things to her, for otherwise she would not have complained — she is so patient.

He has this vision of her surrounded by a traveling rush of water that carries her along and, threatening, more and more present and deafening, rumbling in the distance — this drumming sound. He remembers it from going with his parents to Niagara Falls, from recently watching *The Mission.*

***

She has the feeling of him out there in the real world being down, as on some remote floor, trying to get out from an enclosure — something like a pen even — to break through walls. But she needs to remain in this ethereal *Sakura* space to have any chance at a flimsy communication, at locating him, at helping him evade if this felt reality is confirmed. She needs focus.

But there is this persistent smog cloud, yellow and festering, around Tokyo, where he is. Something already true, in place, or something coming on. And she better be rushing, for there are huge walls of water rushing in at horizon in her vision.

Meeting at Narita

Narita was the place where they had first seen each other, on that afternoon of the beginning of '90s.

His next move out of the luggage area was to have been towards the taxi station, but suddenly horror stories of the prices, in the hundreds of dollars, between the airport and downtown Tokyo, read while in preparation for the trip, lifted their ugly heads from his memory. He switched mental compass and decided that the Narita Express train would just do, even with his five pieces of luggage, including two large suitcases.

And it was at the ticket area for this train, which was in fact a wall set with maps of the transit system and peppered with buttons to punch into machines which would spit the ticket under small plastic windows, that he met her.

Many stations were indicated in English too and some sparse instructions were also available; still, he was confused enough to have created behind him an accumulation of buyers looking at him with the hope of his making quickly a decision and vacating the place for themselves.

When nothing happened in two or, he feared, three minutes, he heard a clear soprano voice, nothing childish to it, closing in on him, asking in English "Do you need help, sir?" He turned, and saw her.

Tall for a Japanese, five-nine or even ten, pink-white-faced, the contours of the chin and the cheeks drawn in round terms, a straight small nose; all surrounded by closely-cropped black hair. Very — he would say 'terribly' later — soft eyes, the countenance a bit shy and embarrassed, but with a helpful question mark superimposed on her forehead just above slightly blushing cheeks. The blushing, later he thought, a matter of interfering with the business of a visitor, of a stranger, of, worse, of a *gaijin*, as she saw it.

"Oh, yes, I think so, Miss. I'd like to get to Shinjuku and I'm not sure at all if this train takes me there."

"No, please get ticket for Tokyo Station. Punch here, please, after you put the money here. From there you take Yamanote-Sen, you know — ring line, I think you call this in English." Her voice stuttered and had a lilt, which may have been, he thought, just how the locals spoke English, but he was able to follow.

"Ah, I remember Yamanote line. Will do that. Thanks."

He bought his ticket and drew his luggage, backing up one or two steps to the side, to make place for the others behind him, mostly Japanese, as far as he could tell. All black-haired, here and there a young girl showing off the artificial brown instead, most of them well-dressed for business, all serious and, to him, difficult to read. They certainly seemed to have their job faces on already for the next week, what with this being the weekend.

The young woman had been the second person in line behind him. Now that she advanced just a bit in front of him for her own transaction, he had time to throw a short glimpse at her while rearranging luggage on his trolley: exquisite — that, to him, meant round and spindly, with a certain softness of contours — but not too long, ankles, standing on medium-high heels; relatively high-placed hips, for a Japanese, not too narrow, on the contrary, intimating the hour-glass. She had a knee-length rainproof light gray coat on, Burberry-style, which impeded the free observation, but this much he had been able to tell with his pro photographer's eye. An umbrella and a shoulder bag. The latter called itself a good name. He had read about that too, status in Japan was a lot. Not that it was less back home, in America.

"Once again, thank you very much, you really saved me," he said, detecting a lively warmth, perhaps interest, in his own voice. "Could you tell me, please, where the platforms are?"

"You're welcome. I'll show you about platforms. I go myself Tokyo Station, to continue on Yamanote, but then I go somewhere not Shinjuku. Follow me, please."

She didn't seem to have any luggage, thus she could not have come with another plane. She must have been at Narita on other business, perhaps with seeing off someone leaving the country. Shadowed, sad, or indifferent eyes, the teeth not shown, short smiles with commas in them, reticence — might well be a lover then, a boyfriend, a husband. However, she seemed too young to be married, perhaps twenty; though, he knew, his experience in detecting age in Japanese persons was null. He also seemed to foggily remember that Asians are thought younger-looking by Caucasians.

They were finding their way now toward the platforms, on and on. He let her walk at the front of their small caravan, on account of his crowded trolley, also to better enjoy the view of her back and ankles swaying over the moderate impact of the heels of her shoes. Moderate in height they were indeed, the heels, but it seemed a very observant eye had made the choice, as the curved convexity of her calves, reminding of a spindle of yarn, was revealed at its best this way, he surmised, and she walked without stress or artificiality.

Weaving her way calmly but quickly ("We only have five minutes until the next… train," she told him with an hesitation, searching for the right English word) through the passages in the station, she turned a bit toward him here and there, so as to see whether he wasn't lost for the cause, her face a bit embarrassed, perhaps with leading an unknown man among those busy crowds. He wasn't trying to speak to her now, as he didn't want to shout — the noise around quite loud from the shuffling and pounding of so many hurrying steps over the imitation marble in this area or the cement in this other. Nor did he want to scare her in some strange way — he might have been the first American ever for her to talk to, even though the Japanese were known to travel quite a lot now. But perhaps she wasn't scared: it had been her who made a first approach, not that it had been personal at all — one unknown, nameless passenger assisting another.

The train wasn't yet at the platform when they arrived.

"Ah, we have to wait a bit." She turned for a second to him, flashing a guilty smile.

"Ah, that's not much. By the way, I'm Simon."

"I am glad to meet you. I — " She had stopped there and her face only sussurated the rest of her reply before turning away. "No use to get acquainted, mister, this is never going to work," would have been the articulation. He was starting to see the Japanese exquisite politeness at work, needling him. He registered a sudden drop of disappointment in his ribs. This was going to be difficult, it seems, if ever.

He was called "The Lucky" in the family since surviving a fall from a twelve-foot-high cherry tree right on his stomach, a saw horse waiting for it. Shamelessly, luck worked for him again: off her shoulder bag, which seemed to have been used as a carry-on on some flights or trips, there dangled something. Sensing his chance, he closed in. She looked up questioningly or perhaps worrying at him, but he stayed there, waiting for an opportunity. It came, just a minute later, when she turned again her head in a definite arc — away from him. A well-focused professional photog's glance told him the writing on the label in the name holder: "Hiroko." He knew this much about Japanese — this couldn't be the family name, but the time for grasping the rest, if that rest ever had been there, never came. The train was already in the station.

They got into the train car. Busy with grabbing a corner place able to accommodate his luggage without too much disturbance for the other passengers, he had lost her for a moment from his view. Then, he saw her seated three meters or so away from him, diagonally. Still able to see each other, but the shoulder bag was too far in order to show anything in any clarity. And the seeing was mostly from the corner of the eye on her part, that is, as she seemed to avoid direct eye contact with him. As though, mission accomplished, you're in the right train, from now on you're on your own, mister, I'm sure you'll do just fine. Simon was confident of just that, but there was something about her that he didn't want to lose for anything in the world but could not have pinpointed, had he been asked about it, something that made him more anxious by the minute, the closer they were of the point of separation, as he was seeing it to be more clearly all the time — Tokyo Station.

The only hope was not in her eyes, still kept away and veering from him at any search from his; it was in her hands. She had them folded in her lap, as she sat on her seat, but there was, at times, finger movement there. He fancied agitation, her being of two minds, perhaps, but couldn't hope for these on account of anything else in her deportment.

They didn't speak at all during the journey to Tokyo Station, only exchanging short eye contact, and on her side it was each time as short as a comma. The rest of the time was spent, he would recapitulate later over and over, absentmindedly contemplating the view out of the windows ghostly running out in the dark. Night by now, seven or eight o'clock it seemed to him, but he hadn't wound his clock forward to local time. He gestured at this time to her, pointing to his wristwatch, a question mark posed on his forehead, and there was another gesture in reply from her, showing her watch. "Seven thirty," she mouthed in English, her eyes looking past his right ear. "Thanks," he mouthed back in agreed-on protocol, but her eyes were apparently not on reception.

One hour later, they were in Tokyo Station. Barely off the train, to his inquiring or perhaps looking-lost face, she came closer shortly and said, pointing to a passage at the end of the large hall, "That's the Yamanote line over there. For you."

"Thanks a lot. By the way, is there *any* chance I could ever see you again? I don't even know your name. Hiroko, perhaps?"

She looked at him for a moment, eyes dilated in surprise, even softer than usual. She blushed, then looked to the side, touched her hair, all while starting to run away with small steps, crying out not too loud just over her shoulder, "Sorry, I'm very busy right now. My train. Bye bye."

The Yakuza tattoo

He was in his forties now, was Kazuhiro Yuasa. Still, at this time, sitting on the craggy mountain ledge making up the edge of the old *onsen*, the rippling muscles of his back were no witness of age, but of the constant punishment of training in the martial arts of samurai long gone.

Fully naked, he kept in his hands only a cloth for brushing and rubbing his skin. The most striking feature on his back was no doubt the huge tattoo showing the faces and parts of the bodies of two men and a woman, in what had to be a replica of a period drawing, the original perhaps three hundred years old. In the center it showed only the face and the kimono open on the chest of the man in awful dishevelment, roaring drunk, lying on his back on the ground, lost, eyes closed, his samurai *katana* luckily still tethered to his side. The man on the right stood spitting on the man in the center of the tattoo, full of despite. Close to Kazuhiro's shoulder, the face of a worried woman was shown in the left upper corner, peeking in on the scene. She seemed, had one had taken into account her habit and her sloppy hairdo, to be a woman of easy virtue in Kyoto or some such.

Kazuhiro was proud in knowing that even a negligent student of the history of Japan could have told you, after the initial shock of finding it in this particular spot, that the scene was tied to the most famous of the samurai stories. The story of the forty-seven *ronin* calling for revenge, three hundred years before, on the court dignitary, Kira Kôtsuké no Suké, who had humiliated their master, Asano Takumi no Kami, and had forced him to commit *seppuku*. However, anyone familiar with Kazuhiko Yuasa's name would just as quickly have told you that it was highly improbable, especially for a negligent student, to ever get this close to Kazuhiro so as to be able to clearly eye the features of the tattoo and still survive the intrusion of his personal space. So the bottom line was that would have been an unfair proposition to be even remotely suggested to anyone.

***

Kira Kôtsuké. The one and only. His presence in the family bloodlines had made Kazuhiro Yuasa's father volunteer for the *zeros* in the war and was the main reason — that and his hot blood — for Kazuhiro himself to get into the Yakuza.

His father wanted to get rid of the shame for the family's sake and he died for it, attacking full bore and frontal an American cruiser during the war. Not enough to wash everything there was to be washed from the damn past that pushed and crawled its way into the future of the whole family, it seems. His eyes might have been spiritualized by death, as the Irish great had said; but it hadn't been enough. Twenty years later, Kazuhiro still felt he couldn't get into any line of honest business. The thing might have been with himself, it might have been with the others around him; it might, worse, have been on both sides. "So, then," he told himself, "turn."

For at the time of the attack on the cruiser, Kazuhiro thought, Yasuhiro, his father, coming broadside and firing with all he had, must have shuddered seeing for a glint of a second the eyes of the American gunner manning *Columbia*'s turret against whom he was dropping sideways, with no return for either of them. And the gun was firing at him those antiaircraft shells that were crisp and shattered the air around him and whizzed by, until one of them caught his tail stabilizer and he knew there was not exit from that trajectory, that the best he would ever achieve while alive was to go for that turret and melt together with that American boy and his mates in the explosion of the ammunition at hand in close storage. And Yasuhiro had read Yeats during his studies at Waseda in Tokyo right before the war broke, and knew the winds for the poet were symbol of vague desires and hope, and also that the Irish had said wind and spirit and vague desire have been associated everywhere. But war came and Yasuhiro had transcended that reading, for the good and the bad, and right now he had only one reading in his head, "I'm coming at you with the Wind of the Gods, American!"

And in he went. The sun was high on that day in the Pacific, there was lots of space around in it, still everyone in that battle knew there wasn't any time left, not for many of them. He channelled the plane in that space in which the azimuth of the turrets was at its most unfavorable as they were looking straight in the sun, and he knew he had to hold the course against tracers and the real AA ammunition flying at him. And he knew the only important thing, the last important thing in his life, was to land on that bridge — dead or alive — where the turrets were and he would have it.

The gunners must have know as much, for were shooting at him steadily and with more and more desperation as he was closing in as a curse, as the *Model 52c zero* refused to disintegrate itself even though apparently meeting multiple hits, so much so that they thought about it as just a sieve coming towards them, any moment now with more holes in it, but ever more dangerous, all hidden behind those propeller blades twirling maddeningly in front of the bird.

He was coming in all right like the wind. He forgot about his wife carrying their first born, asking him during his leave, while both of them were naked on the *tatami* at night and full of the sweat of the love just having been shared, not to ever enroll in the *kamikazes,* for what would I be doing alone without a man to support me and the child coming to us through this mad world, she had said. But he had been consoled within himself that if it were to be a boy, he would certainly be proud of his father. And if it weren't to be a boy, he couldn't care less; another mouth to feed by someone — not him, as he wouldn't be around anyway. Some other man, for sure — his wife was beautiful as a geisha, without being spoiled, and what load off one shoulders that was, her being a natural and straightforward woman.

A willow, she was, Yasuhiro's Matsue, but the roundness in hips and breasts he had been able to make out even under her silk kimono and *obis*, during those tea ceremony parties that he had been well advised by some of the Waseda graduates to attend for socializing. This having been right before the war with America had started and while the one in China was going on for several years now, he knew what this meant — get lucky, meet a nice young lady, marry her with not too many questions asked on either side, and ensure the progeniture before all is aflame around yourselves. But a willow she was, especially in traditional solo dances with the play of the fan, shuffling her feet in just minuscule steps while turning around with the kimono tightly wound around herself, slightly inclined forward from her hips, knees slightly bent and close to each other, managing all the same to throw him a quick look as in "Do we have an understanding here, young man? Then, step in." Which he did, going through the time-agreed steps, simplified for the sake of the war, to ask her parents for her hand. "A future Waseda graduate. If he doesn't survive by the will of Gods, his graft is of good augur for any children to come."

***

Kazuhiro had decorated, or plastered his back with that humongous tattoo right after Makoto Asaye, his fiancée, decided to pull anchor and to vanish from his life, sometime in the sixties. It was mostly in purple and dark blue shades, some of the lines and contours massive. Dark colors, as he hadn't wanted anything not sober enough to be impressed on his person for ever. For ever, as the size of the construction would have made it nigh impossible to contemplate any erasure of it if he didn't want to be skinned alive.

The tattoo master had been brought him from a part of Tokyo in which his own power was dented by the "arrangement." Still, the man was considered an artist and recognized by all the *oyabun*, the capos, and was not reproached for beautifying the competition. Otherwise, the man said, he would go to Hiroshima and start doing something else, go into the fish market or something in which merit was recognized. Oh, no, the bosses said, what a loss that would be, stay here, quiet, and we'll be your customers, no questions asked. Just leave us a phone number where to find you when someone needs a trusted painting of their own body. The general terms agreed, price was no issue. Beauty was not at risk with him, never had been, no contestations of his work have ever existed from neither the more modern nor the classical oriented of his critics.

He was known to use only first-class ink, nothing to poison your body as others have done.

The New Photographer

The Company, located in Mitaka, Tokyo, was small, and had the added benefit of a park, a thing unheard of in those days, when the occupying army of native real-estate developers had taken over the ground of the capital, with the exception of the hallowed historical grounds, surrounded by moats, of the Imperial Palace. To sublimate the pleasure, this was a park endowed with a pond on which a set of white-as-truth swans provided by the Imperial Household glided dream-inspiringly, seconded by ever-hungry red-golden carps, whenever Simon took his lunch break on sunny days with the occasional coworkers present then on the company premises. There were rumors that the Household required reports biweekly on the health of its protegé(e)s and that it had inspectors sent in to check in person on them. Once a royal — or an imperial for that matter in this case — always a royal, it seemed to all concerned.

The Company had successfully dabbled since the Lumière brothers years in film production, and had scored between the wars and even in the fifties some classics, but the times were so tough now in terms of financing any local movie of some magnitude, that greats like Kurosawa had had to go cap in hand to the American studios. At least he, Kurosawa, had been successful, the company rumor mill commented, by getting the funding for "Kagemusha," the huge Middle-Age war movie with horses galore, but many other local creators were left dry on the shores of the mother island, fighting like fish for air. This made for 'creative orientation,' which meant in practice that a lot of the work was these days in photography, a big chunk of it for business advertising. And this is where Simon had been invited to temporarily join the ranks, even though his first projects were more artistic in their aim.

The manner in which things had developed for him had solidified the claims among the Frasers of Simon being the lucky one. What had happened, in fact, was that he had photographed all over the States several celebrated houses, some of them to be presented on a PBS series. His still shots, some of them even black and white, were shown as background in the initial credit area of those documentary movies, even more partly covered by running credit copy, but the stunned viewers were left asking who this damned photographer had been, so well the light, the distance — that secret cousin of space, the lenses, had all been used in order to present the houses, much better than the succeeding edited hour of filming had managed to do. It was the triumph of glimpse over grasp, one of the commentator had said.

That a newcomer to the trade and the art had achieved this much was, to some of the cognoscenti, even more mind-boggling. Instantly, he had become the in-fashion celebrity of the family, putting to shame whatever renown his father might have mastered on Wall Street in his halcyon years.

Compact, the Company's headquarters were; nothing too surprising when one took into account the real-estate bubble in effect at that time in Tokyo and everywhere in Japan, perhaps in the whole world, as it were. While still thinking of themselves as still being in the movie industry, the company bosses didn't see the rationale for advertising too hard for that by spending on studio space in an area which was only half an hour by train from downtown Tokyo, thus going through the roof in terms of prices. Studios were rented or built on an as needed basis, many times on the locations themselves, whenever a major production came around.

However, Simon was lucky, as the photographic labs were on the premises here, which meant he didn't have to shuttle between several places for management meetings, client-related affairs or plain lab work. His laboratory involvement was a major part of this way of doing things. He never allowed anyone to get around to creating his prints, as a lot of his personal view had to do with using the existing technique — cameras, lenses, magnifying sets, or even tripods or chemicals, in a very personally keyed way. Whenever there was any talk about his wallowing so much in this low-level work, as some tended to call it in management jargon, he referred back to Antonioni's *Blow Up* to tell anyone willing to hear and listen that this is, at this very stage of laboratory toil, where, to a large extent, one finds the truth in one's images, that sliver or light or color willing to turn in a new performance. He called his pictures themselves "performances," as he felt the nature — or that segment of it particularly implicated at the time — and himself had to be both at their best in order to harvest the fresh, unadulterated crop able to come out of mounds of clichés to move the eye and the mind in and along a new visual adventure. "Happenings" he didn't like — too much of an element of chance to the meaning of the word.

"Your first project, Fraser-San," Dr. Sugie, the Development Section's manager, told him, "is to find new angles to the two imperial villas to which we have been granted access: Katsura and Shugaku-in in Kyoto. We look forward to your contributions to our upcoming full-scale exhibition of photographic prints on them. We'll, of course, associate books and albums with this event, and the names of our photographers involved in it will be prominently presented, thus we expect you will be satisfied with your name-recognition, at least in Japan, after this. Just a thing: we'll hold, as per our contract, copyrights to your photography performed while working for us, but we are flexible in such matters, should you want to use some of them in collections of your own, to be published in the future.

"After that, I mean, after this project, should both sides be satisfied, we endeavor to do the same for some of the famous castles of Japan: Himeji, Matsumoto, Nagoya and so on. However, let's be successful in our first assignment, I hope you'll agree with that."

Everything was jim-dandy with him. He was provided with IDs, maps of the sites, glossy books about them in Japanese, French and many other languages, as well as two assistants, but he declined the latter, for the moment, he said. Until he got his Japanese feet well under him he preferred to go it alone. He thought he needed elbow-space, and space in general, for reflection, not interference, even helpful and well-intended.

Most of the special lenses he got, some crafted to order by his opticians, were left at his apartment, in one of his suitcases, to be taken with him only when going on assignment, thus not brought to the Company. He was stroppy about people spying on him, it had happened to him in the US and he didn't put the Japanese anywhere above it, even though the initial proceedings had gone exceedingly well here and he felt he was shown all the time the red carpet, notwithstanding his youthful reluctance and bridling at it.

***

But the girl was up there in his thinking layers and he couldn't focus as he normally would have. The label on the name holder, her name. Her ankles. Her soft eyes turning away from him, avoiding contact. The sometimes-lilting stutter in her English. They all added to a snowball going down a slope, threatening to bump full-contact into his body, him right center in the way, exposed, and to tackle him down for the count.

***

He had been woken up the previous night by his mother calling from Connecticut. As though he hadn't explained to her the time-zone difference, she was chirping away with no care in sight for his sleep. Do they always like to listen to themselves, the mothers? For he surely hadn't said much in that conversation, if one could call that monologue a conversation. The hour on his alarm clock was three AM here, and he had been concerned all throughout the call he wouldn't be able to slide back to sleep at the end of it.

"Did you take enough umbrellas with you?" she asked. "I see on TV your weather there and it seems the monsoon has hit home in Tokyo, hasn't it?" This, as though no umbrellas were available in this country, as if he had come not to the second industrialized country in the world, but to some third-world country lost in the jungle bushes, perhaps on another planet, away from civilization.

"We survive, Mother, we survive." Not telling her about arriving at the Company after seventeen-minutes' walks in the morning, all wet from the humidity *and* his own sweat, and about staying in front of some huge fans in the computer room, trying to dry himself up, arms upstretched towards the ceiling, as though surrendering to someone or something. Perhaps to this oppressive humidity. Didn't want to open this line of discussion with her this late in the night, it would never be over, the call, he knew that all too well from — now he realized — close to two decades of telephone conversations with her, mostly her calls, her charges, but that didn't matter to him. On all his trips, camps, his visits to neighbors, visits to friends, visits to his girlfriends. The latter, of course, the one most liable to make him totally furious and despondent. She had this knack of finding him anywhere, even after having being told times innumerable not to call him at all when away from home. Lucky now he had his own place in Connecticut, true, locked down for the time being, while he was in Japan trying to decide for how long. Stepping away from staying with his parents had been one of his best ever decisions, if he was to be concerned only with himself and not with gauging the effect of this on them. For with respect to that, as usual lately, it had been, in not so many words, a disaster, but he had become steeled to that to some extent for a decade now.

Since the start of puberty, no doubt, if he had to assign a historical date to it.

The mood he was in right at that moment wasn't helped an iota by his father recently telling him that his working in Japan was worse, as he saw it, than first, Simon's not going for some serious program at the university, "Not that arts and sciences kitsch, please, Simon, don't serve me that," and second, his not going for an MBA after his bachelor's.

"I mean, I've got a position for you with this damn company anytime you want, I soldiered years for it, and you just throw it away. Shoot.

"Have you forgotten your grandpa died fighting the damn Japs?"

He hadn't. He was, in case they'd forgotten, the one in the family keeping all of Grandpa's pictures, all black and white, curving out of shape and fading fast. Chemicals of the time, he guessed. As well as the letter from the Navy telling them he had died fighting for his country. Their regrets.

On one thing his father and he had agreed: not to go into any military service. Their reasons couldn't have been more different. "There's no honor for *them* any more. Look at Nam and the reaction back home, on TV and in the streets, enough to make you sick," his father's. His was all about not being able to accept discipline except from number one. Not at home, and not outside it. Nor did he like to impose it on others.

"… hopeless, with your 'photography' and all." His father had just banged the door shut on that particular night, getting out of his room at home, clearly signaling the quotation marks to be seen by any rational being out there around Simon's preferred subject.

***

He definitely had to take his wide-angle lenses to Shugaku-in. The imperial villa seemed to be on hilly terrain, lakes or ponds in between. Possibly great vistas.

"Panoramas will be very important there, Fraser-San," Dr. Sugie had told him. "Your talent will serve us well in that respect, I'm sure." He had travelled and studied in the States, Dr. Sugie had. Pittsburgh, it seems to have been for him. He'd mentioned the Cathedral of Learning. His English was much better than that of the un-travelled, stay-at-home-closed-in-on-the-island Japanese. *Good for him and good for both of us, makes for better — shall we say unfettered — understanding.*

***

He had gone in his small backyard garden this morning. The bamboo couldn't have felt better than in this weather with the monsoon around, their shoots a light green, dripping water, their stems pushing toward the sky, still as though undecided whether to really get there, bending in natural arcs, needing companionship from each other and, it seems, from the earth.

That had been the beautiful part. The ugly part had been discovering that his Principe del Marzotto double-breasted suit was in shambles, covered by whitish mold. No chance, it seemed, to buy in Japan anything in his size — the Japanese weren't usually this tall, also they were much slimmer than him, even though he had never been quite a hulk.

Simon gets approval to build I

So in the end they hadn't allowed him to establish his pillar and his perch close to any of the metro stations. It was too much, the dark-blue-clad, belted police of Tokyo said, even for a cosmopolitan city such as theirs was supposed to be. Security reasons and some such.

But Omotesando, in fact Harajuku, might be just fine, they acquiesced. "Just locate yourself on the edge of the park, where each weekend we have the amateur rock bands coming in, and you'll be fine. Under any circumstances, don't make any dirt around your site, whatever you *show* up there. We don't like the municipality to have to clean after people. Also, don't mess up the traffic on the adjacent road or on park alleys."

Omotesando, the super-compact Champs-Elysées Tokyo boasted, the residence of the Armani and Missoni or Miyake fashion stores. Steely and glassy buildings, most of them not higher than four stories though. He liked that kind of size, felt more personal to him, you didn't feel lost inside in a myriad of stores, just three or four in each building. There was a European-style pastry store at the end of it, down in a basement to which he had to get on a conch spiral of a staircase, where he liked to relive the touch, the vanillated-sugar smell and the taste of the European stores of the kind, the Danish ones his preferred.

Simon took what the police told him to mean he was boxed as a performer, for all intents and purposes. *Show?* He had only the pillar and himself for that, and as to himself he didn't have in mind any lubricious exposure. That much he knew from start.

He had spent most of his salary at the laboratory for the last three months in order to pay for the manufacture of his pillar. It should come from the shop in several days, ten feet or so tall, one and a half foot in diameter at the base, with a small platform at the top, allowing him to keep some steady balance, even on one leg only. To ease transportation, there would be a structure of metal tubular bars and beams soldered together in the center, surrounded all around by the outside topping of white polystyrene, meant to help make believe the shape of the style, its tapered Doric column contours. Thus, no stone — he couldn't conceive of it for logistical reasons: how to transport the contraption, how to remove it quickly when he left the spot for anything longer than two hours, as he had been asked by the police? The shop had suggested and, looking with concern at his wads of Yens, he had agreed to have made for him a railing too. Out of thin steel bars, soldered to each other, rising to or about his mid section, this had to be fixed in holes in the platform, just in case balance became a critical issue at any point in time, on account of his using only one leg for support from time to time, as he intended in order to better put forward his message.

Simeon the Stylite might become, in time, proud of him somewhere up in heavens, that was what he was hoping after consulting with some of the priests at the Orthodox Christian cathedral in Tokyo, who didn't quite seem to feel comfortable in his presence after he had made known his intentions of standing on a pillar in downtown Tokyo, proclaiming to the world his hope and despair in love in such outspoken a staging. Thinking Aleppo, fourth century AD, the bone-dry desert, wasn't exactly his thing in this at all, but he would be careful to tell the attending press — and he hoped to have many at his scheduled Meet-the-Presses — that he was doing this in honor of love, not of any gods, Christian, Shinto or Buddhist as they may be.

That might have felt well too demonstrative to some, and his first concern was of course Hiroko, but he needed to do something to get her to open to him, to give him a chance. That much he had decided, as well as not to mention her by name to the press or to anyone not really close to him. And the numbers of those close to him definitely were not legion. Not in the whole world, mind you, but especially not here in Japan.

Now, he was aware that wind might be a concern for a construction that was not of stone. The inherent, though limited, flexibility of steel bars could mean having in store less stability under wind or when a mob might push or stand against it. In this respect, Old Simeon might have an advantage over him, but Simon didn't want to stand there perched for thirty-seven years as the saint had endured back then. Also, against such wind-induced oscillations he thought his Yoga training could come in handy, and planned to do some specialized training on stability platforms at one of the downtown gyms, just to stimulate his ankle proprioceptors.

The plan was to have the whole thingamajig, the support, made in a collapsible shape like an umbrella, with smaller-diameter tubes fitting inside large-diameter ones, a contraption with two wheels at one end and with a hook at the other so as to easily hitch to his bike or to a small truck or trolley. With the crowding on the Yamanote line, there was no hope whatsoever of getting with it into the subway. They would call upon a sumo wrestler, he laughed imagining the scene — he had occasionally seen some in the subway, and it was easy to conjure the image — to evict him out of the car.

"Hiroko, Hiroko, where are you?"

"There must be a Japanese boyfriend out there lurking in some shadows, or perhaps quite obvious, for those friends of hers in the know, I guess," he said to himself, "and you, fool, are mooning around here not able even to pan out an explanation."

From outside in the small bamboo-guarded garden at the back of the house he could hear the remaining drops of the last rain of the night ending their way to the earth in discreet splashes, coming from leaves overhung with a layer of water desperate with gravity. He knew it was humid — his double-breasted suits brought over from the States had been molding, and that was a recent discovery. June, the peak of the monsoon season. The walk to the job in the morning only took him a quarter of an hour, still, at the end of it, he was ready to expose himself, hands high up above the head, sweat pouring down — dressed however, no hanky-panky there — in front of the old-style ventilators in the mainframe computer room, in search of too temporary a relief.

Once in the kitchen, he had gone to the electrical stove to cook scrambled eggs for the breakfast, his staple for years. Toasts, tomato salad, that was it otherwise, his breakfast.

Getting for a moment in the minuscule moquette-floored living-room, he switched on the TV, clicking the remote to NHK, the national television. Always sober and serious. The language programs were on. Today Chinese, so he switched the set off; he had enough troubles as it was, having managed to learn only about four hundred Kanjis over one year and a half, while the requirement for any high-school-educated Japanese would have been of at least two thousand. Dictionary over dictionary lined up his kitchen shelves. This is where he studied, the kitchen — the only place with a reasonable table. Trouble was, it had to be too cold in the winter time, with the tiles on the floor, so he would have to keep the gas stove on at times, heating the air, the only heating units being installed in the *tatami*-floored bedroom and in the living-room. From the kitchen, he also had access to the sepia-pink-tiled bathroom, which contained only a shower without much elbow space. Vertical-stance only for him, at his height.

Hiroko Gets a Portrait

Hiroyasu Aranishi-San, the painter hired by Hiroko's father, was at this time in momentary reflection, suspended somewhere in his work: her preliminary contours were soon to be completed on the canvas.

Kazuhiro Yuasa had insisted on a portrait in a traditional kimono, and on this occasion she had deferred to her family. That hadn't been the case several months before, when she had showed up for one of her tea ceremony dances in a kimono with cubist streaks superimposed ever so delicately over the mainly floral pattern. Quite an upheaval that had been, if one were to consider the reactions of her father and her sister, Michiko.

Hiroko's figure, tall for a Japanese woman, the somewhat narrow hips — still, curved as a violin in their transition to her middle section, and anchoring the straight back — the almond face, the black, short hair, cut around the face, were all there, already suggested, in this version of the portrait. So were the straight, horizontal brows and the small ears, close to the head, as well as the shell-round cheekbones, not very prominent, radiating calm and lack of aggressivity.

What one could not tell so clearly from that portrait, she thought, was the turmoil in her soul. The absence of that in the image in the works might have been caused by master Aranishi's old-school habit of not interviewing his subjects or entertaining them with small talk during their posing for him. You just had to hold your stance still and solid, and that was it with him. He would take it from there and depose you completed, polished and powdered on the altar of art. The art as he saw it. So the old master could not have known what she was about at this time, even though putting on canvas strong emotions wasn't anyway his strong suit or inclination. He would have painted even Toshiro Mifune only if the great actor had agreed to sit still for him — imagine that. Unfortunately, Mifune was away by then in eternal domains.

But turmoil it had been for several weeks now. How stupid she had been, she repeatedly told herself, at Narita, with that young American, breaking off so quickly and really with no reasons, for he seemed a nice man. And, certainly, loaded with luggage, he couldn't have done anything untoward on that night anyway. Brash American he certainly hadn't seemed to be. But there she had been, running away like a scared duck or a bat in mad flutter through the air. It was painful, she felt, to watch now his face slowly fading in the mist — or was it fog, she wondered, in haikus — of time, his heavily curled hair still there, clear and golden-red as a halo around a face that became every day more a product of her imagination. She recalled thinking at the time of the Bee Gees, of a slight touch of old-fashionedness, of back to the sixties — but what did that count, he seemed so young himself — and being fascinated by his small freckles.

In plain straightforward truth, Hiroko wasn't thinking only about him now. Her thoughts also flew to Yujii Kato. It was him whom she had accompanied at Narita on that day of the chance meeting with the young American, Simon, as he said his name was. (No, she didn't have any doubts about the American having told her his truthful name. What reasons could he have had not to have done that? None. It was he who had insisted on keeping in touch and it was she, the poor duck, or bat, who had streaked away.)

On that day back then, Yujii Kato, twenty-two, had been leaving for Carnegie-Mellon University in Pittsburg — Pittsburgh, with its Cathedral of Learning — with his mind set to complete a doctorate in computer science. Only thing was, just a very special god would have known how long such a fancy thing, or exotic animal, would take to complete; precedents showed anything between two to seven years, realistically speaking. Thus, again realistically, they had agreed not to wait for each other so they would not get lonely. At this time, Hiroko didn't remember, nor did she want to rummage in her recall in order to find out who of them two had first suggested this parting of ways. She knew she had not objected to it, from the first it had appeared as a subject of mulling between them. Fairly blocking the history out of her memory seemed now the reasonable thing to do.

Still, now she realized, at the time of talking to the young American (she avoided to call him Simon to herself, better not to glue oneself to illusions), she had acted in part as though she still were Yujii Kato's girlfriend. Why she had so acted, she couldn't tell. The unknown ways of her heart. She wished there were a lot more clarity in herself about how she truly felt about so many things, young men especially.

"Aranishi-San, how long is this sitting going to still take today, please?" She heard herself using one of those sing-song voices that Japanese girls use in the presence of older men, their fathers included, if they want to impress them, or to soften their dryness. Nevertherless, the question was sincere. She had to continue her rehearsals of a new umbrella dance for a *matsuri* to come in Asakusa. The festival organizers had really wanted her as one of the stars for the event. She may have been young, but knew well how rarely such requests came the way of performers her age, so that she accepted immediately, casting concerns aside.

"Oh, Hiroko-San, we need to establish the balance of the main features, before both of us can sleep well. Having only a part of you completed today could generate a kind of frustration and ill will or breeze from the unfinished ones, and such bottled feelings, especially in things so connected with a live person, such as yourself, don't bode well for the rest of the enterprise, I wouldn't think. It might go so far that you could have some troubles, say headaches, yourself. Things can turn against us sometimes, and we should better beware," said the old painter, turning his head left and right in a subdued wobble of disapproval.

Never had Hiroko taken her thoughts about ordinary things that far. She tried to absorb the words of the old master, thinking, right at the same time, that he might be playing a joke on her, or that he had been getting on too much and was on some tangent to reality. But far from her to openly question his doubts, especially as he seemed terribly serious in front of his easel. She couldn't quite resist though, full of the yearning for dancing.

"Just a matter of not upsetting my other gods, the ones of dance, you know, Aranishi-San," she said, smiling modestly.

"I'm sure that Terpsichore, as they call it, is a Greek goddess. The things around us have old all-Japanese soul and roots. I'd say let's think about them first, Hiroko-San, if you don't mind," and he bowed slightly, that bow that is always due clients of long date, and the Yuasa family was certainly of that drawer.

"But my dancing is all Japanese," she observed after two minutes of silence, carefully calibrated to avoid keeling over the ship of politeness in its journey to an elder.

In silence, as though unmoved by what she'd affirmed, the painter continued his work for another ten minutes, at the end of which he stepped back from his work and peered at it through his glasses and half-open eyes. It must have been that he liked what he saw, as he told Hiroko, with a barely hidden smile:

"Well, we're done for today, Hiroko-San, but we must see you here in two days, at the same appointed hour."

In two days, again. This is getting to be more and more like work. But she didn't articulate the thought. Obviously, the old man was just doing his job the best he could. It wasn't with him that she had quarrel, but with her father for having asked for this portrait. On the other side, in all reasonableness, any father could demand of a daughter of maturity age such a portrait, it was just something to stay with them while you took your flight into life.

Only thing was, Kazuhiro had never lived for too long with his daughter. It was just vacations, and even that didn't happen too frequently in the last years, since he moved up to the highest ranks, *saiko-kanbu*, senior executive and *kumi-cho*, godfather, in the Yakuza. Really, she had been entrusted to her mother. Not only that, but her parents had never really married. Not for her sake, not for the sake of her sister, Michiko, and, one could see that, not for each other's sake either, and the latter, Hiroko thought, was the worst. For how long they had lived separately, she didn't quite remember, but it had been kindergarten time for her then. On the other side, thinking about how her parents couldn't these days sit in the same room with each other, even look at each other, or talk about each other, all without being upset, she wondered if it wasn't for the good of everyone involved that they weren't together. It was like fire against fire. But the fire one of them possessed was so very different from the one of the other.

Simon gets approval to build II

Back in a mind of his mind, the sky was red. He was thinking about her.

***

He was now ready to climb atop his pillar, on its platform, in Harajuku.

Several slots away from him on the blacktop of the boulevard closed off for the weekend was this punk rock band, all in studded black leather, blowing and banging their stuff with hourly precision, assaulted by teenager girls during the breaks, girls who, while the gigs were on, were jumping up and down, all in sync, with one arm raised to the vertical, index fingers pouncing the sky in some affirmation of something. He had never seen this syncing back in the States. Something quite Japanese for sure — affirmation of being in common in spirit or some such — he thought. The guys had to have hundreds of watts in the sound setup. He was concerned with being totally swamped by it in terms of focus and made perhaps to lose balance on his platform, yet not with their sound volume per se, as he didn't have to speak forth to the masses.

This was the beginning of summer, the mauve sharp in irises in full bloom in the imperial and other gardens around Tokyo. Sunny day, the wind barely felt here and there in the space and waves of the light air.

The pillar came behind him, its top side tethered to the rack mounted over the back wheel of his bicycle with pieces of medium-thick cord, while its bottom rested on a improvised three-foot wide carriage using itself two bike wheels connected via an axle. All over ten feet in length, the contraption at his back slowed him down considerably and he had to pace himself during the hour-long bicycle ride from Ueno.

It took him a while to lift it in place, what with the crowd of onlookers and passers-by, trying to avoid hitting any of them with the long legs of the platform. After pushing and shoving hard at it, he had it now in place, vertical and seemingly stable enough. He had tried to place it to a side, so that should it fall with him on top there would be less risk for hurting anyone around it at the time, at least in one direction. The transparent white of the leg topping made it conspicuous, but not strident, he hoped, even though in Harajuku being discrete didn't score any merit points for you. Blowing your horn was much more the thing at the time.

The Japanese around him looked curiously at this *gaijin* bracing himself up to raise and install it, for it was apparent that the thing was relatively heavy, even though the good shape he was in was also obvious. However, no one tried to offer help, as this must have seemed to them to be just one of those strange things *gaijin* always did once landed in Japan, where they must be left in peace to do them to their heart's desire. Here and there at times, when he seemed on the edge of losing balance and of falling to the ground with it all in his arms, a collective sigh and individualized aahs went out from some of the onlookers, but other than that, there was only silence around him. As luck would have it, on this day the closest rock band was several places away, as several buskers and bike showmen had imperturbably wedged themselves — first-come-first-served — in the space between him and the rockers. He knew this would make quite a difference in terms of the noise level he was to be exposed to, and was glad at the concurrence of the fates.

First things first, was the idea. After raising and propping a bit the pillar under its legs with small stones for stability, he placed a small white tablet having just

HIROKO

Please call Simon (222 xxx xxx 2767)

in black printed *romaji* at the basis of the platform, right in front to where his feet were to be located. He thought he would post more tablets on the other sides as need be, trusting more the power of luck than that of real hustling for someone who might perhaps know her and her whereabouts.

Then, using the small rungs located on one of the legs of the pillar, he clambered to the top of the platform, placed first his knees on it, then gradually and with the caution of amateur Sunday acrobats raised himself from his crouch to a tentative standing stance. "Wow," he said to himself, "this is much higher than what I've been used until now." Everybody else in the park was under his station. What position was he supposed to take? This had been quite a matter of reflection for him and he had decided to start gradually, with simple plain standing stances, in order to get familiar with the sight in front and under him and to familiarize his ankle proprioceptors to the relative instability of the platform, so they would strengthen and start compensating for its wobbling, which was just natural for that, kind of light, structure.

What he hoped was that someone would get their pair of names, Hiroko and Simon, to the media, and this way the exposure would be increased ten-fold. He didn't have the connections to get on TV by himself, someone needed to do it for him, be it out of a sense of charity or of curiosity for this strange way of transacting business pursued, or as it were, muddled, by the foreigners. Not only that, but going to the press in person and asking for help didn't feel quite right in Japan, not from what he knew. This was more the roundabout, the indirect route, which seemed to be preferred here for fear of not bumping the other too hard in his or her ego, comfort and/or discretion of living.

Not a hustler, he. Was this laziness? Perhaps not. Still, he laughed to himself remembering an instance where he had been supposed to peddle t-shirts on a street in Seattle at two dollars a piece. Ten-years-old, he had been then. The going had been tough and slow, what with his loudly advertising his wares and the sun beaming down on him on hot asphalt. So, he'd decided to be for once generous — right, not *his* money, that — and pushed them one for one for free into the hands of incoming passers-by, until finished off. It meant being fired from that job, no question, but he had just had enough with hawking on that day, that had been it.

He didn't expect to speak forth asking for help from above his pillar.

Walking by, were they. Some had already started to come up to the pillar.

"*Mistah*, who is Hiroko?"

He bent down to reply. "Oh, she is a girl I would like to date."

"She is Tokyo?"

"I think she lives in Tokyo, yes, but there's no guarantee. Perhaps she lied to me when I talked to her."

"If she lied, why do you want to meet her?"

"Question bugs me too. Don't know. Guess this is just the way I feel. Isn't this enough for you fellows in Japan?"

"Perhaps not. Do you know her long?" The guy had in fact said something like *perhapsoo*.

"Let me think. I met her two months ago, I'd say."

"Are you Simon? Indeed?" another one interspersed, tentatively. To Simon, it sounded a bit like *indeedo.*

"What do you think? That I'm doing this for others? Come on!" He first had wanted to say 'pimping or touting for others,' but then, just in time, realized these verbs might be too strong or badly understood in this place, what with many of the Japanese not fully versed in the American vernacular.

"Are you gonna preach to us?" This one, in his twenties, perhaps a well-travelled student, seemed to master English quite well, for a change.

"Should I? No way. Why would I do that?"

"Well, you Americans like to fight and preach, this is what I know."

"Wrong on this American."

"Fine. Good luck to you."

"And a very good day to you too, sir." Nice fellow, and perceptive too. He smiled to him, funneling and holding him in the eddies of his sight for several moments, while that particular Japanese man left the area. But then others came, the milling around uninterrupted, it seemed, in Harajuku on such a day, and now he had to enter his concentration time, rock bands booming or not booming nearby.

***

Whether it might all seem funny to some of the onlookers was of no concern to him. He thought of keeping up the spirit of the original Simon. That, he had promised to those kindly Eastern-Orthodox priests at the cathedral, and he didn't want to make a joke of it all, just play-acting the Simon the Stylites.

"Tentative in our sliding toward our goals we are in our solitude," father Dimitri, the Russian — the church was subordinated hierarchically to the Patriarchy in Moscow, a thing Simon had felt strange at first, but there seemed to be several of such things here — had told him. "We ask God that your endeavor be in the same spirit as that of our saint father Simon," he had added before continuing.

"My son, drawing heed to spiritual concentration is accepted in Japan and is not something considered flimsy or unworthy, or 'showy,' as you young people are calling it today. They partake of this concentration in Shinto, they search for it eternally, as it were, in Zen. One can find a common ground with the Japanese just by being sincere on that particular issue. Whether this might help you in your search for your beloved we don't know, and it is less of our concern as we don't quite want to intrude in personal matters, even though finding the right pairing in spirit and body is a blessed care for all those surveyed by our father in heaven." .

***

Trying to dismiss the public moving in light — and quiet, for the time being — waves around him, he set himself up in the Yoga tree pose, standing on his left leg, his most stable. There was a temporary hush, people stopping their pacing about and their talk and looking up toward him. His right foot was now on the inside of his left thigh, the arms with the palms together straight above his head, piercing the sky in an arrow. The hush was over now, still everything, voices, shuffling of steps, seemed to be kept very low. It was as though anything Yoga or Zen, anything with a shell of the spiritual, was able to jerk these Japanese into respect or at least silence. He was curious how long he would able to stand in this pose on the platform on top the pillar. Soon enough, he knew he would be able to mark half of the time he had recorded on safe ground.

It was easy, as he didn't have to think of something so ethereal as God, as the original Simon had had in his thirty-seven, years back on that Syrian mountain slope, sixteen hundred years or thereabouts before. He had Hiroko to think about. He didn't feel blasphemous in not imitating, beholding, the same exact object of adoration; he never had been a hard believer, and the priests here seemed to have clearly been understanding about it. This was his thing, his pillar and his pillar time.

It was easy then, and he had already mentally singled out one image of their first meeting, at Narita, and cut out of it the sight of the name tag affixed to her travelling bag right in front of his eyes, with her first name, *Hiroko*, at no distance at all. He tried to aim on it, as it was easier to keep focused with just one view in the mind's eye. Her face wasn't present, and he tried not to bring it in, which wasn't the easiest of things. He knew that switching his mental peek at it would mean to get troubled, and he wanted to keep concentration high at such times. The crowd of people around him had sensed he didn't want to be disturbed any more for now, and had stopped questioning him. They just passed by or milled around, talking quietly to each other under their breath or contemplating him and his pillar by themselves. Some of them wrote down the message on his pillar on small agendas or pieces of paper found crumpled in their pockets, others just the phone number, others tried instead to memorize it by looking just a bit at it, still others seemed they could have cared less, going straight for the rockers or the clowns and dismissing what they thought was just another show, and not one spectacular at all in itself.

He had decided to close his eyes during each concentration phase or interval. Still, the tips of his ears sensed a change of compass and a fading in the wind, which was brushing now on them differently, as though it had decided to avoid the area and had gone to rustle and flutter the leaves of summer in more far away areas of the neighboring Yoyogi park. Not quite believing in such personifications and still avoiding any godlike interference, he said to himself this was just him being more separated from his surroundings, and nothing preternatural.

After half an hour or so in several static Yoga positions, he felt the strain sneak-snaking into his legs

(I've lost my Yoga training, gone down the river)

and decided to take a break by walking slowly, with diminutive steps, in the very small circles allowed to by the size of the platform and its trepidations. It was not very far from simply whirling in place, he laughed at himself. The flying dervish. Now that he had opened his eyes to make sure he wasn't falling over the railing, the visual contact with the passers-by happened naturally now and then, even though he kept his eyes skidding mostly above the heads — on the whole and unrelentedly black-haired, with some punk and tourist exceptions — of the crowd.

Kyoto, Shugaku-in

He has been at Kyoto now for two days, in Shugaku-in, the imperial villa, his first assignment with the Company. Nothing like the brick-like solidity of Western villas, it's all about being in, with and of nature, light and breezy, just another leaf to be flown about and into eternity. Tea pavilions so light you would really think they are just a skin left behind them by their princely inhabitants when going off on their way as dragons or serpents would, but quietly, with no roar, as humiliated by nature into sneaking around to unknown endeavors at horizon or to the dust of time.

By the time he had left Tokyo he didn't have any news that might help him locate her. Something tells him she must have been here, in this very place, once. At times uncertain, but recent in the grand scheme of time, as the local things, instantiations, of the nature were so soft and beautiful and most assuredly of interest to her. Or so he thinks. But then, so are to him, or so it seems, so many places in Japan. What and how much is the exotic, and what is the real, honest surprise in himself, he wonders at times. Where is that thin membrane of separation, and where in our minds is it really placed? Should we care, if the wonderment is there, what its source is? *Divide and impera.* No, divide and you might be vanquished, that's what he's afraid of, at least in his work. He goes for unity.

Three times already he's made the roughly triangular journey between the three villas — the Lower, the Middle and the Upper — and their gardens. The large pond, Yokuryuchi, The Pond of the Bathing Dragon, close to the upper villa, has impressed him the most, its calm mirror offered to the myriad of leaves suspended in the trees on the banks. It's mostly about the *shakkei*, that cocooning of the villa by design in the mountains around and its being in tune in their background.

"And it is capturing that *shakkei,* the borrowing of the outside scene in the frame, Fraser-San, that we are most concerned with in our assignment and in which we really would appreciate your help," Dr. Sugie told him. "I think you are one of the best in the world at making your picture frame flexible, and that is our hope here."

He knows that, but he wants to think about it, to do it his way.

There is something he has already seen, an angle. Right when you go down to the level of the water in the lake and you look along its foil, as skittering on it, there is this reflection of the leaves, Japanese pines, Japanese maples, cypresses, whatever they are, on the margins, that paint and throw a ring of green all around the surface, paralleling the banks. He can imagine that being the fiery rusty red of the autumn. But it's only summer now, July. With a fish-eye or a really wide angle lens he could get it all in, he expects. He places a tripod — he's got authorization for it, he chuckles to himself — settles the camera on it, snaps on one of the bulkier lenses and looks in the viewfinder. It seems all there, but there's not enough of the sky, just its reflection in water. How to get both, the water and the sky, into the frame, might be the whole deal. The sky, light blue at this time of the day, sun hidden behind some transparent clouds, seems to be willing enough: it has already given part of itself for its reflections in water.

Another series of shots would show the sky and the horizon as barely seen through the hedges leading atop, where the Upper Villa is. These are made up of shrubs with differently shaped leaves, so they don't allow the light and the view carried by it to penetrate too early in the climb in the eyes of the observer, to keep the surprise for the final shock when you suddenly *have* to turn around, and see the great panorama of the mountains around framing the view of the seeing domain of the villa itself. Obturated light, leaves in conflict with it, as though placed in front of the observer, in front of his nose, that'd be it.

Then there's the view towards the lake at the Upper Villa from the edge of the small Bansho island in the middle of it. It would again show the limits of the lake with reflections from the trees around it. The trees and the water, but this time with the lens in the middle of the oval of the lake.

Groups of visitors are passing by, some of them looking at him, not quite used to the Caucasian-looking professional spreading all his accessories around him on grass in such a hallowed Japanese setting as this one. They know the access to the site is quite restricted, especially to pros interested in making a quick buck on it, and wonder perhaps how this one could get through their own bureaucracy.

In the group passing by him right now, there are two American college girls, by the looks of them. They both sneak obvious peeks to this wiry, athletic man, with the dark-blonde curls around his head. Both close to his age or thereabouts, perhaps two or three years younger. He's a graduate now, they breathe that collegiality found in those still students. But then, they might be graduate students, for all he can tell.

"American?" one asks, stepping closer and obviously generating jealousy, or perhaps the envy and disappointment generated by one's own inaction, right then and there in the other one, who sniffs and looks away, keeping her own distance.

"Yes. And where are you from?" He turns several degrees towards her, trying to keep his focus on his dealings with the nature around him. He's down on his knees on grass, trying to vet a camera angle.

"Cornell."

"You don't tell me. Thomas Pynchon country, isn't it?"

"Haven't heard of him. Who's he?"

"Come on, Jennifer, the writer, don't you know," says the other girl, obviously having overheard the discussion and trying to one-up her friend, still keeping turned away from him.

"That's right. 'Gravity's Rainbow,'" he telegraphs from the side of his mouth, returning to his work. Even if they were looking, there'd be no point in showing too much interest, that much he knows. The less you do, the more women will come to you if the balance of obvious sexual power is on your side. He's not too interested to find out how things stand in this case, not too much, not having been impressed yet with anything special. Average size, average looks, both artificially blonde, that much he has been able to tell in the flash of a look. There's a distinction in one having long hair, while the other is closely-cropped. Pretty squarish, might be playing soccer or hockey, if anything.

"And which university are *you* from?" the girl's asking.

"Columbia. Recent grad," he telegraphs back.

She circles nonchalantly around him at a distance of several feet, while he continues his work at comparing views from different angles and heights, without even looking at her.

"Did anyone mention you and David in the same breath, I mean the hair?" she asks.

"Which David?"

"Michelangelo's, 'course."

"They might've, but they didn't survive the ridicule," he says, "so I've forgotten the incident."

But now their group — mostly Japanese people with a Japanese guide speaking Japanese, so he wonders if the two understand anything — is away along the gravel path, and the girls run after the others, one of them passing to him under her breath right before taking off, "Come tonight by our place, Fukudaya Riokan, say eight, it's in the book, in Kyoto, if you don't have anything to do. Ask for Jennifer and Annie," adding the crucial information at the end, "I'm Jennifer."

Now, hours later, he finds he doesn't have anything to do tonight, with work done by this time, the prints of the day good enough, hanging in a laboratory in downtown Kyoto where he has been provided with contacts with his bosses.

So he goes to the party. The girls are in their room, and it seems their plans for the day don't include as yet any going out in Kyoto, as they're presently sharing between them a bottle of sake and two other bottles wait patiently their turn on the *tatami* of their small *ryokan* room, lit only by a small-globe table lamp which is, however, on the floor. It's a pale violet, that light, and he believes for a moment that the outside might be the same at this late hour of the day, as the contours of the window are violet too from reflections. But it couldn't be that, it's just the mind, more comfortable with the indoors at this time of evening, trying to impose its characteristics on the world outside. An undesirable carry over, he thinks.

There's susurration of water dripping coming from the outside. Though, no rain for today yet.

"Come over here," the long-haired one, Jennifer, entices, right after he's put his light summer jacket on the floor, making him sit on a blanket, closer to her. How the Japanese survive without so much of the Western furniture is a mystery to him. There are no chairs, no table, just the *tatami* and the knapsacks of the girls, so Western and modern looking on the *tatami* — out of *tatami*'s place and time, really — some of their contents already randomly arrayed or, as it were, splashed around the room. Several hangers are suspended on nails on the walls.

All three of them sit on the floor. His feet are in his cotton socks that he usually wears with his sneakers, but the sneakers are now behind the door, on the corridor. That much he's already learned here. The girls are in jeans, with nothing on their feet.

The other girl, the short-haired one, her eyes brightening into his, comes shuffling on her knees and shins, close to sitting *seiza*, Japanese style, and gives him a glass full of sake.

"How's that? *Kampai*, I think," the long-haired says, not losing a step to the competition. They clink glasses. The girls' eyes go fuzzier for one moment, looking aside from him, to hide the burning produced by the sake down their gullets. He's still sharp enough not to need that maneuver yet. They all say, in one form or another, "Ahrr." It's a hard sake.

The short-haired one goes back to the place where she had been moments ago. She seems the more reserved, he thinks.

"So-o, what are you ladies majoring in?" he ventures.

"Oh, let's not, not that serious, will yah," the longer-haired complains, lilting, while reaching and softly touching his biceps that is closer to her with the nail of her index finger, small-massaging.

"How, then?" He prefers to let them run whatever drift is out there. He doesn't yet see the light at the end of the tunnel for himself for tonight.

"This is how." The same one shuffles on knees to the other girl, only three steps away, reaches and lifts the hair on the back of her neck and then bends down her own head and deep-kisses the uncovered spot on the other. She does it twice, and each time thereafter, sneering, sneaks a peak to him from the side of her eyes.

The other moans and closes her eyes the while. Then the one having gone away says something into the ear of the short-haired, covering her own mouth in a funnel of hands. They giggle, shuffle on knees towards him, both of them. They somehow sandwich him between them, both still on their knees, and bend down to him who's still seated on the floor, and start kissing his face on opposite sides, ruffling his hair with their fingers, playing touch-and-leave and piano with his back, pulling at the muscles that, he's thinking now, they should find sparse on him. *I've never been a hulk, sorry, sisters.*

He continues not to reach and grab anything and this only seems to kindle them.

But soon he's had enough.

"Whoa, I need to take a break, girls. It's not fair, I can't really be on the field tonight. Sorry to not quite make it for you."

He reconfirms for himself the light is low, light violet and shooting up towards the window.

"Why don't you have another shot of this?" The long-haired slithers herself along the *tatami* to the bottle, to pour some more sake into his glass.

"Oh, it's not that, you know." He stands up, not too brusquely, so as not to hurt their feelings, paces around them into the small room, as though thinking, and perhaps really thinking, chin low in one hand, so low a ceiling he might touch it with his extended hand above his head at any time. Stops at the window, looking out. It's just the courtyard of an old Japanese ryokan, a fountain showing water pouring into a inclined wooden V-shaped trough or open pipe that guides the water into the quiet, waiting surface of a small basin walled by old stones covered by moss. The girls clink with each other and look to each other, questions now on their faces as to where this all goes.

He knows what this is all about. It's that flash of the face of the Japanese girl at the airport — again. Going through his mind now and then, enough to concern or upset him, as it is her that — now he knows it — he wants.

One of the girls, that should be Annie, sneaks behind him at the window, hugs him around his middle with hands clasped on each other and feeling his six-pack, and murmurs "You don't have to play big enamored Romeo for us tonight, you know that, don't you, Simon?" He's told them his name when coming in, felt it to be just basic manners, and now they're using it against him as a gas pedal, or so it seems to him. He feels her breasts pressing on his back and they seem globulous and firm, not to be neglected, and she knows that, of course.

"I've never said that I would, ladies." He's not doing anything to free himself.

"Make that 'girls.' It'd be friendlier," she says and snickers.

He feels his erection has been well in order for the situation for several minutes now, but it's just that hands and mind don't want to move tonight, don't want to feel and grasp these girls and to make love to them in smaller or in larger ways, as though they were in another room or on altogether another plane of reality, not intersecting at all with the one cutting, passing, here.

Finally, he makes his move, slowly, gets away from her, goes and picks up his jacket from the floor, passes by each of the girls, pecks them on their cheeks, pats them on their shoulders, telling them, "Sorry for tonight. Too tired, I guess," and leaves.

At his own hotel, he takes a long shower, and it's a really cold one at the end. July. Even more now, Hiroko's back with him, in his mind. He wants to apologize. *Sumimasen.*

First Signs

"Well, Fraser-San, my wife and I saw you last night on the NHK," Dr. Sugie mentioned first thing, eyes sparkling questions, the morning after Simon's return from Kyoto and Shugaku-in.

"When was that?" Simon was flabbergasted. He wasn't aware of having talked to any reporters, especially someone from the national state broadcaster. Unless …

"Imagine that, we were watching the weekly national lottery draw results. My wife is a long-standing fan, I can't get her away from the TV during this show. And I sit there myself watching, most of the times. Spousal solidarity, I'm afraid it's called."

"And? Did they mention me during the draw?" Simon was skipping on hot coals by now.

"Not quite. That's a very boring piece of entertainment, a good-looking young lady makes the draw and announces the numbers. Public titillation, you know, nothing more, nothing less. Not that I'm telling my wife any of the kind. That would mean a riot in the family. No, it was in the late night news bulletin after that. They can't usually have more than ten-minutes worth of news, clips from Tokyo and the whole of Japan, nothing international usually at that time, which I guess is about 11:25 at night."

"Are you telling me, Dr. Sugie, that they had a clip with me at that time of night? On NHK, the national broadcaster?" He couldn't quite fathom the news.

"Well, there was nothing initially on your name, and the video was kind of white and grainy, perhaps an amateur recording in Harajuku. You know, sometimes even the national broadcasters are using such clips." Dr. Sugie laughed.

Simon instantly knew: someone must have filmed him on the pillar, in Harajuku, on one of the weekends. At least now he knew how bad the situation presented itself, so he could improvise an eventual line of defense. It was embarrassing. Still, nothing could have implicated his employers. Thus things weren't so bad, overall. It was his personal, private thing. How private, only now was he able to find.

"And?" he asked.

"Well," said Dr. Sugie, "what we initially saw didn't make sense at all. A kind of a platform, a ladder, a pair of first names, one Japanese, the other English or American, on a board. Or do you call that a plank? The American name I recognized instantly. It was yours, Fraser-San, even though I assume there are many Simons these days in Japan," he continued, enjoying the surprise, but without malice, in good humor. "It seemed to me the American gentleman wanted to find a Japanese lady, and provided his phone number. I wrote the message down. I think it was this something like this." And Dr. Sugie read it from a piece of paper.

"Yes, it's mine." Simon felt being red-faced. "Did they show me in person?"

"Only a flashing shot of someone who looked like you. I thought at the time you were in some meditation or something like this, standing, eyes closed, on that platform. It was very short, but it was definitely you, I thought at the time. They said Harajuku … "

"Then it was me, Doctor Sugie, most probably." No reason to hide. "I can explain," he fumbled the starting line.

"Fraser-San, we in Japan know what's private. I'm not asking anything. I've just told you what I saw, and that I thought it was you. I didn't see any mention of the Company, thus I'm not treading into this in any formal capacity, believe me. I just thought it might be of interest to you having been mentioned in an NHK broadcast, that's all. Some Japanese wait their entire lives for something like that. I don't, but haven't been mentioned either." He laughed.

Simon was glad to see the take Dr. Sugie had put on the event, or incident, but wanted to settle things on an even more clear ground.

"I'm just trying to find someone I met in passing."

"Small country, many people." And with that Dr. Sugie seemed to close the conversation, and Simon didn't feel any incentive to pursue the discussion.

He switched to business. "Would you have time to review some of the pictures from Kyoto? I've just processed them in the lab."

"Let's do that tomorrow morning at ten, Fraser-san."

Simon felt this was a further concession to discretion by Dr. Sugie, who seemingly didn't want to make, not even inadvertently, a connection between the two issues by stringing one after the other in their conversation or their daily schedule. So be it. The outcome satisfied him.

***

He was at his home. This particular call came in at midnight and seemed to be made from one of those bars in Roppongi. He heard party sounds in the background.

"Simon, this is Hiro-ooko." The first voice, a singing one, was clearly male. It seemed American. It went on "And I want you. Oh, I so-oh want you. Oh, yeah."

"And we want in too, you weakling motherfucker, we want in too," another voice sneaked squealing in, garroted for the sake of fun, from the same group. "We can't bear the wait, you funny face." The line went down.

"Har-rooh, Simon *desu ka*? Simon there-ah? Are you-uu *Saimonu*?" Simon became atttentive, as this one seemed to be a young Japanese woman's voice, lilting. Calling around nine o'clock in the evening, it took him out of his kitchen routine.

"Yes, Simon here. What can I do for you?"

"Hiroko *desu. Kurabu kara.* From a club. *Intiristidu* in fun? *Seksii*? No-oh?" By now he knew this couldn't be Hiroko.

"No, thank you very much." He cut the call. Couldn't be anything of interest, he thought. Some wet-trade club in Kabukichō, most probably, trying to rally things for the night. A hostess trying her hardest. "You may well be a Hiroko, but you're not *my* Hiroko. But nice try," he mentioned to the caller in his mind.

***

"Hello, mate," an Australian came up to him at the bar counter of the disco club on a night out in Shibuya. "Don't I know you from somewhere? No, don't tell me, I'll remember you." Several seconds later, he came up good on it. "Harajuku, that's it. Saw you over there two or three weekends ago."

There was no point in denying it, but Simon didn't want to be explicit. He asked back, "What took you to Harajuku?"

"Selling knick-knacks for the Israeli small-item chains. There's many of us camped out along Omotesando: glass or wrought metal jewels, jade statuettes, small Barbie Dolls in oriental fashions, stuff like this. Don't tell me you don't know about them, the Israelis. Crowds of them in this city. They and the Iranians, they are in numbers here, but those others are piss poor."

"Can't say I've ever bought anything on Omotesando yet, except ice cream from the corner kiosks. Ah, no, I bought some cheap kimono from one of those souvenir stores. Sent them home to friends."

"Israeli-owned too, I know that one. What kimono could you have for thirty to sixty dollars? Only a joke. Anyway. But let's not forget about you, mate. What were you doing in Harajuku hiked up on that contraption? The most ridiculous thing I've ever perceived in Tokyo parks, mind you."

"Just trying to find a Japanese girl I met in Narita."

"Any catch? Just curious, from a *gaijin* to another?" Laughing, the Australian showed sparkling teeth.

"Nothing yet," Simon had to sheepishly admit.

"And you think advertising or praying for her would help in any way? Pffft," the Aussie said.

"Well, it's not so much praying as meditation. And, well, I'm trying. Anything's better than not trying, don't you think?"

"You must be really caught up hard to just get out in the open and advertise it. As the Japanese put it: only a *gaijin* would go for it this way. But, hey, that's you Americans, this is why the world has fun with you, and you've fun with it." And the Australian reached to hob and nob with the beer of the moment, the Danish Faxe. "Cheers!" Simon liked it for its lightness.

***

The pictures taken by him at Shugaku-in were, some of them, hung on a wall of Dr. Sugie's office with some clever Japanese clips he had never seen in America, compact and tight in their grip, nickel-plated shiny. The rest were in an well-ordered pile on Dr. Sugie's desk.

"Great work, Fraser-San, there's no doubt about that. You've caught reflections in the pond at Shugaku-in that I've never seen anywhere else, and the *shakkei* is shown extremely well, with a depth of perspective that made me look for minutes at a time at some of them, hoping to see more details behind the first appearance, and behind the second one, and so forth, such was the trompe l'oeil. Also, speaking of colors, the combination of browns and blues is really outstanding.

"I have the impression that the Imperial Household management will be very satisfied with it, when we make the presentation to them before the public exhibition, as we are due to do out of deference.

"And, who knows, they might reach higher." In the coded Japanese manner of speech, showing through even though Dr. Sugie was always speaking English to him, Simon knew that would mean the imperial family itself.

"But we must look forward, past this exhibition, I mean. I have in mind to employ your kind services in photographically exploring another avenue of Japanese life, and that is traditional dancing. All the way from the festivals, the *matsuris*, to the *kabuki* and *buto*.

"I've already obtained a calendar with the major matsuris, both in Tokyo and throughout Japan, and some information on the *kabuki* and *buto* theaters to see.

"It would be very recommended for you to start to have a much better familiarity with these. Feasible, would you think?"

Simon couldn't see anything to the contrary.

Hiroko in dance training; Matsuri

Hiroko was turning clockwise in a circle using the slowest of steps she had in her repertory, a succession of barely advancing moves. Knees slightly flexed under the kimono, the motion mostly from the hips. The shoes sliding, as in permanent contact with the ground, still their friction inaudible. The focus on her fan, vibrating lightly in suggestion of cherry blossom falling over a crude and awakening world in spring, the eyes following the fall from the trees to the earth, then coming back into the same cycle to go again with the ethereal loss of beauty for the future heaviness of fruit.

Her point she made with the eyes and the mouth. The eyes were wide open in wonder and awe at the passing, the mouth as though in breathing movement with an infinitesimal pucker advancing and retiring in its stress at the cruelty of the nature not able to keep around its beauties. The face, slightly upwards, continuing a spine and hips that were back from the vertical just a touch, didn't fall into resignation. In the inalterable sequence of seasons, this just wasn't the time for such feelings.

The shamisen player stopped for a moment, and so did she. They needed a break after two hours non-stop of practice. She went to an adjacent room, disrobed herself of the kimono and the *nagajuban* long chemise, hung them on a support, remaining in the white *hadajuban* inner layer of underwear, then washed her armpits with a towel with water from a small basin, and rubbed her thighs.

In a small paper bag, she found her lunch in a *bento*; she sat down on the *tatami* and started to eat the sushi pieces with the chopsticks in the box. She found the soy sauce just a tad weak for her taste.

The thoughts about the nice young man at Narita came back to her. Several months had passed. He might well have forgotten all about their encounter. From the States, there had been just one postcard with the Cathedral of Learning, nothing else to follow, and she hadn't pushed things either. Let that other river flow as agreed.

***

The *Sanja matsuri* is in full blow now in Asakusa, and Simon is in the full maelstrom of it. The portable shrine, the *mikoshi*, several tons in weight, with tens of loin-clothed, white-bandannaed men carrying it, is coming right now among and along the river of people making place in its middle for *mikoshi's* lulling, rhythmic advancement. Here they are right in front of Simon, in the small plaza in front of the great shrine, starting to whirl around the allegoric house of the god, sweating, mostly naked — except for the white *fundoshis* around their loins — male bodies pushing into one another and supporting the others, hushing the crowd with their growls of encouragement to each other. "Y-yah, y-yah, hurr, hurr" they go. And the small house of the god is all in gold leaf with the Phoenix on the top, shining under the sun, a square structure supported by those long beams under which tens of men travel in circles or spirals. And it wobbles sideways and up-down; Simon feels its human energy going to the skies and taking up even now, in its deliriant maelstrom ripples, godly shapes.

A couple of American tourists in blue-jeans sneak their way through the mostly Japanese crowd, moving slowly past Simon. She's a redhead, thick circular glasses, heavily freckled, squinting half of the time at the sun to find the best sights for taking pictures. She talks all the time to her partner under her palm, in what she thinks is low voice.

"John Paul, come quick here to see this angle. Come on, climb and stand on this rock. There's a better view through these two things. Yes, columns, but they're wood." Then, lips fish-mouthed, going to her man's ear, still loud enough for Simon or for any living, breathing American, for that matter, to harken, she says, "This is all crazy, so sexual, I'd've never thought about it this way before, the way the thing bobbles up and down, then turns around in place, carried by them."

The man — large apple-shaped cheeks — seems comfortable in his roundness, not the least perhaps on account of his being tall. He allows her to close in and whispers back "How about their groaning and hushing, or whatever they do with that sound of theirs?"

Simon moves his camera around all the time, gets another, then another shot. *Wait till March next year, ma'am, when you could go see the Honen Matsuri at Komaki. That giant phallus on display. That'd move you for sure. Yes, ma'am. Funny thing, why would they have it on March 15? That's the Ides of March to me. Better to stay home then, perhaps, so as not to meet a woman like Sada Abe there, able to cut one's member off. That'd be a personal Ides of March truly to avoid.*

He has come earlier; he is in a higher, more advantageous position than them, on a small stoop in front of one of the buildings facing the great shrine. He isn't jealous of the competition, never has been, and these are clearly amateurs anyway. There's a pie big enough for everyone, you just need your own vision, he remembers sometimes the commentary from one of his profs in visual arts at Columbia, Mircea Bodea, a Romanian refugee.

He triggers his F4 and it fires several salvos. Unsatisfied with the current angle and his closeness to the real players, he leaves his temporary cradle, gets down in the street, weaves around a policeman and comes to face several of the *mikoshi's* carriers, running towards him in their rotation, nine-inch-thick pole on their backs, bracing them together. Simon backs off just in time and just enough to let them pass, conscious he would otherwise be trampled to the ground with no hesitation, in their fugue. No question about that — their faces are tense to the job and sweaty, no room for intruders. He skips sideways around their rotating spiral, shooting all the time, changing film in rushes. Doing all that between the crowd and the carriers, the poles of the portable shrine coming now and then right at him, threatening to run him down.

After circling them one time, while they rotate in the other direction, he feels this might be just it from this distance and decides to run to another vantage point, perhaps thirty meters away from the carriers, on the greened-gray stone edge of an old fountain at a side of the plaza. Just one minute ago, there had been another man there, but he too had wanted change and no one else had clambered back in his place.

Simon likes it here and it's all in the depth of the perspective. No doubt, he has the layers he's so much after: in the center, the men with the *mikoshi*, milling around; around them, the crowd waving in its movement around them like corn; the old buildings surrounding the plaza, old lacquered tiles on their peaked roofs converging into old eaves that let the time pour on rainy days to ground; and back of all this, the sky opening wide up and sideways in all blueness. And atop it all, not directly present in this line of sight at this hour of the high noon, the sun, inundating everything in light and heat that make the houses, the people, the images, lose definition in their contours.

The milling of the *mikoshi* carriers gradually slows down. The men soon stop their rotation and disappear in a courtyard, apparently to store their precious load, as they issue one by one or in small groups, most of them now in small three-quarter cotton shirts — *happi* coats — with the sign of the neighborhood on their backs and shorts, belted around their mid-sections. They group together again and, to the sounds of a small band of drums and peeping shakuhachis, start the parade of the neighborhood on one of the main streets nearby. It's so hot they continuously pour in good fun water from small barrels and other containers over each other and, with feints and in mimicked surprise as to their own actions, they throw it on the spectators jumping up in shock at the touch of it.

Six steps away from Simon, an American matron on a tourist visa cries out "Come on, this wasn't part of the deal!" ready to escalate to indignation, when the water reaches and licks her two toddlers stationed on the curb, watching innocently. She's right away tempered by hubby motioning to the sun "It dries out in two minutes, hon, will you?" She won't find support either around in the crowd excited by the sun and the music and the bandannaed *odori* dancers jumping and skipping on toes in circles and spirals as they advance with the parade. They just want, Japanese and tourists alike, to partake of this ritualistic proceeding crazed out of bounds, to keep it as unruly as they can for their memories. For they know, most of all — it won't come back soon for their eyes to behold it. Once a year, that's it, *Sanja Matsuri* is around, the greatest in Tokyo, and who knows where they might be at the same time next year.

Simon's now after some of the *odori* dancers on the parade track around the neighborhood. He's got a photographer's ID dangling from his neck, which helps him whenever the police become too concerned with him running in front of the formations or floats, skipping as a fly among the dancers, letting them pass, shooting from high up above his head and down from the waist, or crouched down on the asphalt. Whenever a float comes around and looks approachable, he quickly apologizes with a *Sumimasen*, using to advantage the stunned takes of the attendants, most of them not used to foreigners speaking to them in Japanese, or flattered by it, and climbs up for two-three minutes on the front, the sides or the back flanks of it and shoots dancers and crowd alike in fast, sweeping series of takes. He's changed several film cartridges by now, perhaps half of the day's stock.

There are improvised stages set up everywhere, in parks or patches of parks along the way, in the large courtyards of some old inns or of some newer restaurants, where dancers and singers, buskers, mostly Japanese, but also the odd *gaijin,* offer their wares. He looks in, pops in here and there, but mainly tries to stay with the parade for the time being; for him, this is the day of the large groups.

While he passes by, from a park, through verdant trees of this May and through the people massed around, a plangent shamisen and several small *taiko*s and perhaps timpani are making themselves heard, weaker perhaps for the rarefied air of the midday. *Nihon buyon*, it seems to him, something for the stage. "Let's move on. But clearly I need to come back here. If not today, then on one of the two remaining days of the *Sanja*. To do: look closer at the dancers here; shoot in this and other off-the-mainroad spots around the parade route."

***

She knows this part is closer to *butoh* and to Tatsumi Hijikata than some of those in her audience might be comfortable with after the traditional piece dance of a *maiko*. The music — more syncopated, broken at times by unexpected waits, then rushing again like a cat wanting to get quick grabs and scratches at the time.

She dances *The heat and the rain*, one of her own pieces. She's now in above-the-knee white shorts, dark blue *happi* coat, it too of rough cotton but with the sign of Denpoin-dori street in Asakusa large on its back, the straw conical paddy hat of the rice laborers tied under her chin with a thin band. No shoes at all. The happy coat open, its belt hanging from one of her hands.

The heat is on. The music is slow, and she moves along with a long gait, lunges in fact, feet rolling through long contacts with the ground from heels to toes. At times, exhausted with the heat, she stops on one foot, the other leg raised in the air, flexed at the knee, testing the fluid with sharp knocks and bumps: is it still there? She's not steady when she stops. Still, again she advances, head wobbling from one side to another, barely articulated at the neck.

Suddenly, there's a *taiko* drum roll, and the rain is falling now in sheets around her. The relief is here; she frolics with quick jumpy steps, but crouches down with fear at each thunder clap. The head bobs up, neck crane-extended, then down to chest level in at times hysterical joy at the break in the heat.

She knows this is the kind of dancing her father had fumed about years ago when he refused to allow her to take dancing lessons. "Stubborn and fickle as you are, I bet you won't be able to respect traditional Japanese dancing, and I don't want our name to be damaged further. Your grandfather died to avoid something like this happening again. It was enough for our tree to be spoiled just once, three hundred years ago, for us all to have to pay for generations."

"Well, yes, he still pretends he entered the Yakuza because no honest work was open to him," her mother mumbled as for herself, when hearing that. By that time, her parents were separated and she lived with her mom. "But don't listen to him, he had other reasons for that," she said with a higher tone, as openly speaking to her daughter. And Hiroko didn't listen to him on the matter of dancing either — that was one advantage of having your parents separated, she thought, you could ignore whomever you wanted, and be guaranteed the support of the other.

It took about ten years for her father to accept the fact of her having gone and taken dance lessons without his permission — nor his money, in fact, as that that had been paid for by her mother. But it would take forever for him to accept her dancing that other way of her, the *butoh.* That, to him, was close to sacrilege. Still, after seeing her in one of the more traditional dances, he'd asked for her portrait to be done for him. *At least that*, she had contemplated the situation with some equanimity.

Found

He had come back to the courtyard in the small park two hours later, back from his tracking the parade.

By that time, there weren't any spectators or artists left, but he went on in front to the stage, in the hope of finding a schedule with the upcoming shows to take place during the festival, as he wanted to be better prepared for the remaining two days. There were, as he understood the pictures, several announcements of instrumental music and traditional dancing, all nailed or tacked to an unpainted side wooden wall. He didn't have such luck in figuring out the text — he had barely advanced to the *katakana* in his Japanese-language work at home, and the copy here was replete of full-power *kanjis* totally opaque to him. Under each poster, there were small open-mouthed wooden boxes in which flyers describing some of the shows were available for the curious to take home. He quickly assembled a collection, placed it in his knapsack and inched to leave, when on a poster placed to a side he saw *her*. Months after meeting her.

She's a dancer! OK, perhaps not a professional one, she seems very young, but she must be dancing well enough.

It couldn't have been anyone else, that he was sure of. Above the poster, it was written *honjitsu-wa* . This much he knew — today. The box underneath had no fliers left.

He looked around, scanning for people who might be able to translate the contents to him. He soon found a young couple, seemingly college students, loafing hand in hand around the park, and went straight for them.

"Hi. Sorry, I don't know Japanese. Would you please come over there and translate a bit of one of those posters to me? I'd really appreciate it."

"We can try," the man said, and both went after Simon, who was rushing back.

"Is this show today?" he asked, pointing at the poster.

"Early. One o'clock. Not later."

He had missed it. Something very heavy had dropped into his stomach and was pulling him down.

"And not on any of the other days left in the *matsuri*?"

"No, sorry. Name — Hiroko Yuasa. She quite good. A bit modern style."

Hiroko! The name glimpsed at Narita was right! He tried to keep his cool against legs still of molasses, and asked "Yuasa, you said?"

"Yes: Yu-a-sa."

"Do you know where she normally shows her work?"

"No, sorry, but sometimes even TV. But rare. Seldom." Then they spoke briefly in Japanese to each other and the young guy corrected himself. "We think."

"Thanks a lot."

For a moment after they left, Simon considered ripping or just detaching the poster from the wall and taking it with him. Then he thought that might not rhyme too well in Japan, where even the street machines didn't deliver beer after midnight, so in the end he decided to just get close-ups of it, which he did, the light still good enough at this hour of the afternoon for him to do it without any flash.

Now that he had it on film, he could relax and really look at her on that color poster. *The feeling of seeing her in some shape or form for the first time in months.*

She stood there, in the kimono and the sophisticated hairdo with several large hairpins of a *maiko*, facing at a forty-five degree angle, the arm holding the open fan extending to a side, the other hand lifting a bit the kimono off the ground on the other, lips tight as per the tradition, eyes peering half-ironically at him from the powdered face. So heavily powdered, in fact, that now he was surprised at having recognized her. Still, the eyes and the contour of the face couldn't have been taken to belong to anyone else, he thought, all the while patting himself on the back.

***

He went the following Monday to Dr. Sugie's office during the lunch break.

"Ah, how was your *Sanja Matsuri,* Fraser-San?" his boss asked.

Simon delicately closed the door behind him.

"Couldn't have been any better, Dr. Sugie. Especially-," and he lowered his voice to signal an appeal to discretion, "especially as I think I've caught a link to the young lady we've talked about."

"You mean the one you advertised for?" Dr. Sugie asked, half laughing.

"I guess I can agree with that," Simon laughed back.

"So then, did you meet her in person?"

"Only in a poster showing her. Here you are, pictures of it."

Dr. Sugie stood, took the pictures, riffled them over his desk as a set of cards. There was a pause, he raised his sight, looked at Simon carefully, as though he really wanted to say the words required by a situation ponderous in meaning.

"Hiroko Yuasa. Yes, I certainly know the young lady from TV, something like a Japanese traditional dance show, four or five months ago. Exquisite dancing. Now, in what concerns you, this might be difficult."

"Sorry, I'm not quite getting your meaning."

His boss pondered again, looking back at the pictures, then again at him.

"I'm not sure how advisable it would be for you to proceed."

"You mean, to pursue her?"

"Well, yes, something of the manner of things you young men do these days in similar situations. She seems to be, from what I heard or overheard, how could I say it, protected."

Simon considered the meaning of the rejoiner, looked out the window, paused, sighed, then asked, "Do you mean, Dr. Sugie, that she's involved with an older rich man?"

Demuring. His boss was certainly demurring. "I don't think *involved* is the right word. This is someone one calls, I believe, a

Maecenas in the western culture." And after another break. "He's her father."

Simon was relieved, "Ah, her father. Then — " *Where's the problem?*

"A special father. He's reputed to be one of the local bosses of what you might call in America a syndicate."

The young man couldn't take it any more and blurted out "A crime syndicate? I'm sorry, you mean he's a *Yakuza* boss? I guess that's how you call it here."

"That's what it is. The nature of the thing."

From the way Dr. Sugie looked at him, he realized he had done well to have closed the door — his boss wasn't comfortable with the discussion any more.

"Well, thank you very much for telling me this, Dr. Sugie. I'll see what I can do." He added, barely controlling the heat in his voice, "Sons, or daughters for that matter, aren't necessarily molded the same as the parents. Not as far as I know." He wanted to believe that not farther than in his own case.

"Sure. You're welcome." Dr. Sugie seemed to come up with something on a rebound, after several seconds. "You may want to talk to some of the Tokyo dance associations. They should know something about locals, I mean places where one shows up."

Simon instantly detected the switch to the impersonal pronoun in the last sentence. Dr. Sugie knew his English, no doubt about that — years in American universities do that for you. There was distance and neutrality in there, and he decided to pay heed to that and to retire for now. He'd learned more than he cared to bear, for the time being, and for this he should be grateful. Being warned wins half the battle sometimes, he thought. At least you can rearrange the cards or, should he say, the pieces of artillery.

***

Two days later, he brought Dr. Sugie to the photo lab, to see some of the *Sanja Matsuri* shots. They were layed out all around on tables or pinned on wall boards. Mostly color, but he had done some on black and white film too.

"Quite a collection!" said Dr. Sugie, moving from one to another, drawing in his face to some of them, stepping back in front of others, eyes larger than usual in obvious interest and surprise under his glasses.

"Well, we might have only a quarter of my film here. It was a good day, weather-wise, thus I was able to take lots of them."

"From what I can see, you performed lots of gymnastics!"

"I simply had to, in order to have all the angles that seemed interesting at the time."

"For myself, I like the most the close-ups to the *mikoshi* and the ones here from this higher position."

"Yes, there was this vantage point on the edge of a fountain which I caught free for one instant. Lucky to have gotten there at all, with so much of a crowd."

"Interesting, you seem to have obtained your deepest views here. Your layered perspectives at work again, and I must say quite impressive. Different colors and nuances on each layer, light falling differently on each."

"Thank you. It's just a matter of the right lens in the right position, you know."

"I have no doubts it's much more than that, or otherwise we wouldn't have had to invite you to come to us all the way from America, Fraser-San. I think it's mostly having the right eye behind the visor, or the lens. Let's not mechanize things, or over-mechanize them, at least."

Simon couldn't agree more, but preferred not to articulate himself.

Several of the pictures showed the *mikoshi* carriers from only several feet away, it seemed, in their full all-for-it-movement, totally absent to the sweat, to the public, to the weight on their shoulders, focusing only on the other men around them, all in their twenties and thirties, and on their breathing and chanting, so as to stay in step with them. They were so close, the pores on their faces were visible, the drops of sweat on their brows and cheeks rivers under the heat, the mouths open, groaning and moaning in fraternal strain.

"Ah, but these are definitely some of the best I've seen of a festival!" Dr. Sugie pointed to a series of shots made with a long exposure time, allowing the carriers to appear superimposed on themselves in their movement, light contour echoing light contour in succession. It was the full *mikoshi* in rotation in one, from above, while in the other, Simon must have been with the camera at the knee level of the carriers, so in this case it was the ankles that were superimposed on themselves, tens of them in rapping sequence. To emphasize and separate just the movement, Simon had used only black-and-white film at the time.

***

In his dream of last night, the sky had been red again. He had to find her quickly, he had to agree with that part of himself who told him he had already lost too much time. Then, only god knew how things would develop, but everything seemed good to him in comparison with this treading of waters — mostly forced by circumstances, he rushed to his own defense.

Hiroko gets in touch

That call came to her mother's house on a Thursday afternoon and fortunately Hiroko was there to answer it herself. They wanted to tell her a young American man had called the Kokubunji dance association to inquire about her, whether they knew her and her whereabouts. Naturally, they hadn't given away any information, but he had left a telephone number, kindly asking for it to be passed to her, should she by any chance get in touch with them. Also, just in case there would be any surprise on her part, he mentioned having met each other at Narita several months ago. Naturally again, the lady in Kokubunji, who seemed to be middle-aged and a bit tired toward this end of day, hadn't asked him for any details and wasn't asking Hiroko for any either. It was obvious she was just passing the word between two young people, with no intent whatsoever on her part to help them too much, nor to impede them in whatever they decided to go along with in this matter. If they wanted it, they had to go ahead under their own sails, or by their own muscle and oars as it were.

So then. That number facing her, a plain sequence of digits with a magic power of attraction and fear. Just as the young man at whatever length of them, still in that vision tethered to them or perhaps watching their vibrations from a distance. Only thing missing: watching each other's reactions.

***

The black, and, she thought, cowardly fear. All she had to do to summon that was to think of her father's reaction four years ago when finding her reading some American art albums: "What is this?

American? Japan's occupiers? Do you forget Okinawa and those bases are still theirs? Japanese land under their heel. Their heel, do you hear that? That's rape, not what you women and your ilk think." Eyes more furious than ever Mifune had shown on screen, a deep, deep furrow on his brow just above his fuming nose. He took the book and threw it out the window on the rough rainwashed gravel of the courtyard of her mother's home, where he was visiting. Her mother had felt best to leave before he came around. Lest he would blow up even more, Hiroko forced herself to wait for his leaving to recover the book and repair it the best she could. And she had felt like a coward after that, for not even opening her mouth during the whole scene. But never had she felt able to talk back to either of her parents.

"You've forgotten grandfather died fighting them. With honor. And now you want to turn to some foreign dragons as if those here aren't handsome enough for you any more," he went on boiling, sweeping with his arm towards the walls of the room, covered with modest reproductions of old Japanese art, some of them pointedly showing reared-up dragons. None of those prints had been bought by him, that much she knew.

"And, of course, you care to think least of all about what we have to wash away for centuries now. That's nothing to you, small fare, I guess." She had just nodded sideways for "No." She knew all that all too well. The original dirt and blot on family's history, Kira Kôtsuké no Suké's, whose blood hadn't been good enough to pay more than a drop in the sea of guilt, the way many Japanese saw it.

She had heard her father all too well. Since then, hiding things from him had become a priority with her. As hiding her interest in *butoh*, something that could have him bristle and rear up on the spot as fearsome as any of those dragons and so much more real and touchy to her. She didn't call him any more to report on her dancing, steps, costumes and everything, as many times now she wasn't doing just the traditional. Books and pictures she was keeping away, open only when he wasn't around to see them or check them out.

And she took up something that could have upset him even more, terribly more, even though she couldn't be sure about it, as she would fall sick even at the thought of telling him that. Each year for the last three now, she had been making a trip to the Sengaku-ji temple in Minato-ku in Tokyo to pay respects at and to lay flowers on the grave of the forty-seven *ronin* forced to commit *seppuku* after killing Kira Kôtsuké no Suké, her own forebear, and thus revenging the death of their beloved master. Even her mother didn't know about this, though she was in on the *butoh* and the realignment in her dancing stuff, and she acquiesced to it, perhaps as a payback to her separated husband, perhaps as something that was in line with her own rebellious nature.

On that day four years ago, maybe four hours after her father's blow up, by the time he had long left, her mother came home. Upon coming in the kitchen, she looked at her daughter's face and saw traces of tears and trouble.

"What did your father tell you?" she asked. It was rare for her to ask so plainly, and anyway Hiroko didn't feel comfortable sharing.

"History," Hiroko just said, knowing that after an initial attempt, her mother wouldn't insist, knowing better than to torture her by letting her feel between the hammer and the anvil. Still, this time it was true, it had been history.

"Well, you're old enough now, so I might as well tell you one thing or another. Your father's great on history and bad at today's things, that one's for sure. Never, ever, do that, live in other ages. Don't live for the dead, live for yourself. And, yes, he needs a mirror too, before going about telling others what to do. Preaching, that's how I'd call it. But enough for today about him."

She often thought of her parents as a tiger and a tigress, ready to bare their fangs and claws, to growl horribly and rear up on their hind legs and claw the air in front of each other, even though at the rate they were sometimes going at it, she could have said they were clawing at the very fur, flesh and bones of the other.

***

During the Kobubunji lady's call, she had uttered respectfully just "Yes" and "No," not much else, while writing down the number on the inside of her left palm. Thus her mother, just steps away in their kitchen, had no reason to assume this was any matter involving young men, even more, a foreign one. She wasn't quite sure how her mother would have dealt with it, and decided she'd better not risk anything, especially as, first and foremost, she wasn't sure about *herself.*

***

The attraction. This is something she has been locking horns about with herself for several months now, whenever her thoughts went back to the young American. But too frequently those thoughts have gone there, for her to have doubts on board that she at least wanted to have a stab at meeting him again.

You never know what might happen. She really shivers now at the thought.

A nice pair of shoulders and some long, straight legs she thinks he had, even though she would first think of him as quite thin, the body moving in all its details as one, with nothing unsharp on it, it had seemed to her then at Narita. Longer shins than the Japanese men legs, higher hips perhaps too.

But mostly, she pops the question to herself in the mirror, was it those curled blond locks she remembers seeing in reproductions of Michelangelo's *David* in Japan, the hair thick, blond-red, as streaked with golden flakes, long, a la Bee-Gees, she thought, a bit old-fashioned, naturally curled, but with long loops or curls? Nothing too frizzy as she had seen on some Black males in Roppongi on her rare bar-hopping nights with other girls.

No, that neither, she fesses up to the truth. It's that smile under blue-green eyes. Large, but sharp and firm, darker when transiently concentrating on something, eyes. The smile that created long lineaments above this wide mouth on expanses of skin so pink-reddish, so sprinkled with orange-brown small freckles that she had wanted to laugh with surprise at times at Narita, but hadn't wanted to seem ill-mannered.

That, and the elastic, bobbing, loping step that was moving him forward so quickly as though the balls of his feet were touching fire even when he had been loaded up by luggage, back at Narita and at Tokyo Station.

***

This morning, she was up with the awareness that she would do it on this day — would call him. Somewhere in the afternoon of this Saturday, when Mother would be out shopping in Shibuya and Shinjuku downtown Tokyo. The feeling that has swelled up gradually in her over the last two weeks through nights of candle-like-burning curiosity and excitement over what would happen then is come to a crest.

She has refused any food at lunch, pretending a stomach ache. In truth, something was there, but different, more as a sharp feeling that she has to be clean and pure for this to work out this afternoon, as though the ordinariness of usual days would not be good enough for something so special.

It is 4 p.m., the appointed hour. She checks out first — mother's not home yet. She goes with small steps — she's in her kimono, dressed for the occasion, but no shoes — to the *tatami* room to the back of the house facing the small garden and looks out the floor-to-close-to-ceiling window. The air is still pierced by wide swaths of sun light, passing by the clouds. This looks propitious enough.

She goes to the handbag, in which she has kept the number, transcribed from the inside of her palm to a gray piece of paper, which suddenly seems inappropriate for the occasion. But she has to do it now, everything else looks in alignment and she isn't sure when will she be able to muster again this strength.

The phone is in her hand and she nervously punches the numbers.

"Yes, please." A man's voice, a relief for her.

"*Moshi-moshi, Konichi-wa. Hiroko desu.* I think someone give me this number, sorry." Just in case it isn't him, she's just though it better not to give out her family's name for now.

"Hiroko — ?" The voice at the end of the line seems stunned and pauses for several long seconds. "Yes, Hiroko, Hiroko-San, of course! This is Simon Fraser. This is amazing! I've been trying to find you for several months already after our meeting at Narita."

"Narita, yes." She still has doubts whether this is the right person. "Fraser-San, you make pictures? I mean photographs?"

"Yes, yes, I am a photographer. Don't you remember all the luggage I had, the tripod and so forth, at Narita?"

"I remember well, I think, but your voice different, perhaps telephone."

"Of course it's the telephone. I don't think I've changed that much. And I'd still very much like to see each other again."

"Ah, each other?" she says. She isn't sure of the appropriate words, something that wouldn't seem too forward in English. "Mmm- Interesting. Possible, I think. But when?"

"Well, now that I've found you, Hiroko-San, again, I don't have to go tomorrow at Harajuku to ask people around about you, do I?" he says, laughing. "How about tomorrow, Sunday? I think today might be too late perhaps for you."

"Harajuku?" She isn't sure what he really wanted to say with that. Still, she finds she likes to hear him laughing. "But today difficult, yes, so - …" She thinks about her mother coming back and not having any news about her, should she leave now. "Sunday, tomorrow, noon, Omotesando? Omotesando close to Harajuku, same station. Good?"

"Perfect with me. But where in Omotesando? Do you have any ideas?"

"You know Apollo Fashion Center?" she finds herself asking after several moments of thinking. She says *Sentaa*.

"I think I know it. I might even have been there. But don't worry, I'll find it. Shall we say on the street level, right at the entrance?"

"Entrance? Ah, main door. Street. OK. Twelve o'clock tomorrow, yes?"

"That's exactly it." He confirms slowly: "Noon, tomorrow, Sunday, Apollo Fashion Center. I think and hope both of us have it right. I'll wear a red jacket."

"Ah, to recognize? No problem, I think," she says.

"Just in case my hair has grown bigger during these months, which I think it has, even though I had it cut once." His voice seems to her to be skipping over laughter now.

"Cut? Perhaps pity," she enters her repartee, and she smiles to herself. "Then, *Soredewa mata ashita*, tomorrow, bye bye."

"I'm *very* grateful to you for this call, Hiroko-San. See you tomorrow, definitely. *Sayonara*."

She feels he's put something special, something mellifluous, in saying her name this time, different from the tone used for the rest of the words in that sentence. Perhaps. "Fancy thoughts," she gives herself the heat a minute later. "Let us first see him again face to face. Then, we might have to teach him how to really use *Sayonara*."

Face to face again I

His 6:15 a.m. He's up. Hasn't been sleeping well, going time and again late into the night over their meeting at Narita, then over the image of her on the dance poster. Even just between these two instances there have been observable differences in her face, some of them, no doubt, caused by her in-role persona into which the poster allowed a peek. How, then, would she be now? Would she be reserved once again? Perhaps, now that she took a first step by calling him, she might be more relaxed. Certainly that might have taken some true grit on her part, to call a foreigner at his residence, someone who might not even have been him. He has a new-found respect for her since she did so. God, how many other months of legwork saved! That he is lucky!

"I mean," he thinks, now under the shower in the minuscule bathroom which is able to contain only that, the very shower, "she could have just said 'another freak or perv! Wants *me* to call him' and dropped the whole bit entirely. She could've, no buts about it. But didn't."

***

Her 5:40 a.m. She read *haikus* well into the night, before finally being able to sleep. Focusing her mind on a small number of words always helps. She wonders if the mind takes the words for yoyos to be swung slowly in front of the guardian of wakefulness until he crumbles down and is done and over it for the night.

Her mind has recalled the image of her father, but she knows a bit now how to compartmentalize things and forces it to keep it away for the time being. She knows he wouldn't like it. Well, in no uncertain words, he would hate it — her having for friend an American. And that doesn't mean a boyfriend, for she doesn't like herself even to go there in her thinking. So remote a thought of everything she has imagined about herself and boys, now about men. She could all too easily imagine her father's ramblings and interdictions on the subject. She's eighteen now, but he could still read her the riot act and impose a curfew again on her, the way he did two, three years ago. Ridiculous in this day and age, but he isn't sometimes of today, he belongs to times past, is surrounded by ghosts past, her mother tells her, and she can't but agree. Not in terms of money, her mother sometimes adds, there he uses the latest tricks in the book. This, she doesn't know anything about, and has learned it's no point to speculate on your own parents. Let them be and you'll find soon enough what they're about on one matter or another. The real goods.

***

His 8:15 a.m. He's in the kitchen, going through half a cup of yoghurt and a brown bread toast. No one yet passing by in the small asphalt-covered street in front of the house, except for the odd old woman going to the shrine to burn a stick of incense for memento mori this early in the day — people usually like their Sundays comfortable these days in Japan.

On TV, the NHK is buzzing what seems to be sumo news, short flashes of some of the *yokozunas* and *ozekis* in *dohyo-iri* salute. He only half-listens and peeks now and then to the set through the open sliding doors between the kitchen and the minuscule living room. He opens the latest Japan Times that he has, but only to put it aside on the square table he has in the kitchen and to look again absentmindedly to the street. Should he take some of his recent photographs with him? His camera, perhaps, to make some pictures together today? Finally, he decides against a portfolio, he doesn't like to appear to be boasting, nor to show up loaded by stuff, and cram the conversation with talk about it. It's him and her, that's where it's at. Also, the camera: perhaps she doesn't like to get in the picture on a first date. For this is what this is — their first date.

Just last night, there was this call from his mother — Father never calls while Simon's away from home. It's her who's tasked or who tasks herself to the cause of "bringing Simon back in line," as his father has called it for four years now, since the time he entered Columbia in an undesirable field, the way George Julian Fraser II, American, 56, saw it. "Arts and Sciences? What's that, the most undefined thing on the surface of the earth, or what? Wouldn't open any doors, not to mention horizons — as you call them in your 'photography' — with any self-respecting company, son." And 'photography' had come accompanied by question marks, of course.

Figuratively even, best not to take to this date: his family, or he might scare her away for ever. And he's seen that done to others of his acquaintances, no matter how cinched or in the bag the things had seemed at the outset.

***

Her 7:45 a.m. The kimono: this is her biggest question for the day. Should she get it on or not? Have it on, and she might be seen by him as too traditional. Don't take it, and she might lose one of the most important bargaining chips a Japanese woman might have.

She feels stifled for several minutes by the question, until she remembers her mother's one time advice. "A Japanese lady *cannot* look bad in a kimono. She might be in fact old, she may have the lineaments of meanness engraved on her face, she may be stupid and wide-eyed, or, god forbid, even one-eyed, but she will *not* look bad in a kimono. Ever. Consider this whenever in doubt." And she has been in doubt now and just goes for it, for the kimono.

She might need two hours more for the preparation, especially if she wants to have the appropriately combed and pinned hairdo. But there won't be any makeup. An expert by now, with playing and dancing so many *maikos*, she doesn't want any inkling of a *maiko* on her face. She is going to be herself. In her most Japanese dress, if not the most Japanese incarnation in what *that* would involve — she doesn't expect them to talk too much in Japanese, with his apparent lack of facility in it. "Take it easy on him on that. And hope that he, in exchange, will be patient with us on our English," she tells herself.

***

It's 11:30 a.m. and he's already on Omotesando. Looks around for a flower shop and finds one but decides to buy just one red rose — he doesn't want to load her up with an armful of them, especially as he doesn't know yet where they might go and whether they might have to stand a lot.

At 11:45 a.m., he does what he feels is the polite thing and shows up in front of the fashion building. There's a large Issey Miyake couture store on the main floor, overlooking the promenade through huge windows. He feels a bit exposed, standing by himself on the flat black-stone terrace in front of the building, three steps up from the pedestrian walk, the rose at his back in crinkling cellophane cover. But then, he is supposed to man the barricades at this time, he's telling himself.

He walks slowly back and forth on the terrace for several minutes. He likes to think he's being calm, but he knows he's far from it.

On his left side when facing the street, he's screened by a leafy potted tree somehow left to live on the hard expanse of stone and concrete.

To suddenly see Hiroko walk smiling towards him on the sidewalk from that side develops into a full visual grenade blowing up into his face.

She must have dropped off from a taxi something like twenty meters away. "How absentminded I have been!" he tells himself ruefully, but there's no time to go on rambling — he rushes down the steps to greet her. She looks to be literally pink with pleasure. Whether it's the sight of him or the small line-of-sight trick she's just played to her advantage and surprise, that he doesn't quite know and won't debate now. He feels at a loss for words at her sight, but senses right away it would be polite to bubble away at least something in Japanese.

"Hiroko-San! *Konnichi-wa!* I'm *very* glad to see you again," he's able to articulate in front of her, stopping just in time from what must have been, he vaguely realizes, a quite headlong climbing down of the steps and walk towards her. He extends the rose while bowing slightly and a bit awkwardly with a "This is for you." His face is burning red, so much so he guesses his freckles are invisible now.

"*Konnichi wa*, Fraser-San! *Domo arigato gozaimashita!* Thank you very much. Beautiful flower. Thank you."

She bows back to him and takes the flower, smiling openly, looking back up into his eyes just several degrees away from the direct line of his sight. Would that be Japanese or women's reserve? Or her particular kind of reserve or coquetry? He doesn't feel he has enough experience to separate, nor does he feel inclined to do so for the time being. What he knows is that his stunning has been achieved at least in part thanks to that light red kimono with long but thin floral motifs on her, which offers her head up as a magnificent flower from within its folds. Only now is he able to have it, the kimono, more clearly within the periphery of his sight, his eyes not having released her face from their grip for several long moments already, as though in sharp fear of losing her again.

"Please call me Simon, Hiroko-San!"

"Mmm- , then me Hiroko for you, yes?"

"I think we have a deal."

"A deal? I don't understand." She seems flummoxed.

He rephrases patiently, "It only means we have an agreement to call each other Hiroko and Simon. Said otherwise, we'll be on a first-name basis."

"First-name basis? I think I understand. First time this too. My English is poor and slow. I apologize."

"Well, now you'll have an opportunity to practice." He laughs.

"Yes, I can see that already. *Already*, yes?" she smiles back, a slight question mark on her forehead.

"Yes, *already* was good there. Shall we walk a bit? Are you comfortable walking in the kimono and your shoes? Aren't they too tight on you?" He demonstrates the 'tight' on his hips by clamping his palms on them.

"No, for Omotesando this is OK," she says. "But where on Omotesando?"

"Well, I assume you and I aren't interested in shopping today, thus why not walk toward Aoyama-dori? There's a nice Danish tea, coffee and pastry shop there, right beside the intersection."

"Ah, I know. I was there. Once, two years ago. Perhaps. Nice, I think."

He feels the first difficult moments are over, that something more relaxed is flowing and settling between them. The boulevard, narrow and intimate as it is, really not much alike in grandeur with the Champs-Elyseés to which it's sometimes compared, is full of people anxious to enjoy their Sunday out on sunny day by shopping, window and people gazing, and just walking and talking. Being surrounded by people eases both of up them up.

He paces himself after her, keenly aware his long legs at a full stretch are much too much for the delicate walk with minute steps allowed by the kimono dress. At times, he shuffles shortly behind her and changes from her right to her left side. After the first switch, when she looks surprised at his disappearing for a moment from the expected side, she seems to accept this dance and to be amused by it.

"So, you're a professional dancer, right?" he asks.

"Dancing for many years, yes. But a professional lives from that, I think."

"Yes, she or he survives on that only. I'm a professional photographer, at least I like to think that."

"Not so sure about 'she survives on that *only*' my case." She laughs, catching quickly his idiom and stressing *only*. "Good, bad weeks, must say. Summer is better, more *matsuri*, you see. Invitations, right?"

"Yes, that's the perfect word, invitations. Invitations to dance."

"Ah, English grammar. Purpose: *to* dance. Now I remember," she laughs. Under the small nose, the teeth are moderate in size and very white; also, they're exposed much less than an American girl's would be, he thinks. And the mouth is closed back down on itself quicker. Sometimes, she brings one hand in front of the mouth, as though to hide the laugh behind some physical discretion. This seems to be a right thing to do for young girls here.

But now she springs a question on him. "Harajuku, you said. What did you do, Harajuku?

There's no point in hiding this. He says, "In Harajuku? Nothing special: I was trying to find you."

"Find *me*?" she laughs, cheeks suddenly pink-red, looking at him sideways up, head turned to a side in disbelief but also in obvious pleasure. "But how? No name!"

"Ah, not so fast," he laughs back, "I knew you *might* be Hiroko, that is, your first name might be it."

"But I did not tell?!"

"No, don't worry, you never told me. Your memory serves you well, Miss," he laughs. "But I saw at Narita, just for one moment, 'Hiroko' written on the label of your shoulder bag."

She wobbles her head from left to right in disbelief. Her eyes are opening wide, but the mouth's still laughing.

Good sign.

"Very fast eyes. Yes, photographer!" she says. "But many Hiroko in Tokyo, I think."

"Right on. However, I signed my poster with my name, Simon, and put in my telephone number. There aren't many Hirokos in Tokyo who know a Simon, I thought. Well, not a real poster, mostly a small notice board."

"Poster? In Harajuku?" Her eyes were popping out in surprise, "Mm- Interesting idea. Courage. Many, many Japanese girls called, yes?"

"Well, not many, in fact, and not of the right kind, I'm afraid. Night clubs, you know. And that's just daring on my part, not courage. But now it's all for the better, now that I've … now that we've found each other."

"Night clubs?" she laughs, a bit ironical. Then she changes tone, and a shadow passes quickly over her face, "Night clubs not good, I think."

The change on her face has been eye-bat long, but it has registered with him. He decides he won't tell her for the time being about the mobile platform, it might be too much, she might think he has a screw loose.

She still has something important to ask him and he watches her articulating, treading it with care:

"Then, how could you to find me?"

He perceives a worry in the way she says it, as though saying that it might not have happened, their meeting again, for reasons only accessible to fate itself and its associated gods or semi-gods. Her eyes and her forehead convey it — choppy waters under sun. The sun of having gone past the worries already. And he suddenly feels so much the need of quieting her worries, that nothing more important exists.

"Well, going out and putting that information on display in Harajuku seemed to have helped. The NHK itself seems to have reported on it on TV."

"On television? You?" She smiles and looks concerned at the same time.

"Well, yes and no. They showed my notice board and me in Harajuku, but they never identified me. They never said who I really was and they didn't interview me. Nor did I see myself on TV, it was others who reported it to me. I think NHK reported about it late at night, and I'm not watching TV that late," he's trying to explain to her. "Then, the company I'm working for here wanted me to photogragh several *matsuris*."

"*Matsuris*? But why?"

"Well, I guess they liked the series of photographs I had made in Kyoto, at the Shugaku-in imperial villa."

"*Honto?* Really? *Shugaku-in?* "

"Yes, I was for several days there." *And couldn't help thinking about you.*

"Then? What happened?"

"Well, what happened was that I went out and took pictures of the *Sanja Matsuri* here in Tokyo. This is where I saw your posters, luckily with your pictures, otherwise I wouldn't have stopped to have a look at them. I found your name and I was told you are one of the up and coming traditional dancers in Tokyo. Then I started to call all the dance associations in Tokyo and someone must've called you with my phone number, I guess."

"Yes, they also said Narita." Her eyes are relaxed now. She inhales deeply, as after a treacherous trek, saying "Then I believed was true and you." She takes a very long look at him, a new look, eyebrows raised as in some wonderment or amazement, as though all this story has put him on a higher something in her eyes. Perhaps his stubbornness in going at it, he doesn't know.

Face to face again II

At the Danish coffee shop, she points in front of her and lets him go down first on the narrow spiral staircase leading to the basement, taking the support he offers by slightly reaching with one of her hands, while her other hand, on her thigh, takes care of the iffy business of making sure the kimono stays tight to her body and doesn't get entangled anywhere so as to bring both of them down.

There are ten or so small tables there, all high, with high bar stools. It's a more quiet area than the main floor. She likes it that way; this is why she suggested it on the way here.

They find a free table. Simon asks "May I?"

She doesn't quite understand "What, please?"

He explains, smiling, "May I help you climb and sit on this high chair? I'm concerned about the, shall I say, the effects of the tight kimono." To make sure she understands, he makes a vague gesture towards the elegant, but simple, dress.

"Yes, but how?" She is really surprised at the question.

Her forearms are horizontal, holding the handbag. This seems to make his job only easier.

"Excuse me," he says, while already proceeding. He's placed his hands under her elbows, cups and grasps them gently, and in one swing, heaves and deposits her carefully upon the chair. "*Voilà!* There you are! This is how."

Hiroko hasn't had time to react until now. Her skin suddenly paints a red contour underneath her hair, to its very roots. She realizes that during the process of conveying her to her new location he's exercised just enough delicate control not to touch her upper body, just her arms, but this has been close and her pulse is up. *Strong and impetuous — and why do I like this.*

"Ah, thank you! American strength, perhaps," she laughs. "*Voilà!* Indeed."

He feigns modesty, cracking back at her "No, no big deal. I think it's just like in the old saying: 'the quickness of the hand deceives the eye.'"

They're both seated now, and rearranging themselves after the walk. She places her handbag on the table and daintily puts the rose above it in a tight balance, as the flower has a very long stem. He puts his shoulder bag on the floor.

"What can I get you?" he asks her.

"One Danish cake and a tea, please."

"Fine. Be back in five minutes."

He brings everything on a metal tray covered with thin silk paper in Japanese patterns, miniature geishas and scowling samurais.

"Ah, Japanese drawings," she says. "Danish drawings — better for this place."

"Perhaps they might, but then we wouldn't be in Tokyo, Japan." Both of them laugh and look at each other at some length, the first time, she thinks, they've done so today. The last time might have been on the train from Narita to Tokyo Station, but then, she clearly remembers it, she kind of avoided his look.

"I don't think I've told you yet," he takes up the conversation again, and looks into her eyes, "you look very nice in this kimono."

"Ah, thank you very much." She feels that for a moment, her eyes might be playing up on her, becoming too soft while meeting his regard, with his words flickering, fluttering and lingering around. She doesn't want to look like one of those Nara deer. She knows she could have asked 'Only in this kimono?' but doesn't want either to play the coquette or to complain. He might get bad ideas about her. *Mother knows best — a Japanese lady can't look bad in a kimono. Good idea this has been, putting it on.*

"You also," smilingly she tells him, "seem in good shape." This can't commit her too much, she fancies.

"Well, thank you. I'm doing my best to keep up with my tennis and swimming."

"Tennis? Swimming? Where can you do that?"

"At the Company, in Mitaka. We have some good tennis courts. Funny surface, if you ask me: artificial grass, covered by a thin layer of sand. But works out quite good; it plays similar to clay. There's also a small indoor swimming pool. I'm doing morning laps there, after tennis."

"*Spoiled*, yes?" Upon getting the nod from him that this is a good English word, she continues, "You are spoiled there. You know that things like that, difficult in Tokyo, yes?"

"Oh, I know, difficult to find and expensive, this much I've learnt already. So, I *am* grateful."

"But why Japan, for you?" she's asking.

"That's simple: someone at a company here saw some of my photography, and they decided they wanted me to come over to apply some of it to Japanese landscapes and scenes."

"Ah, special invitation. I am *glad* for you." She spells the words out carefully, with earnestness, with longer breaks than natural, meaning them and stressing that *glad*. "And did you like to go from America, United States?"

"Well, let me put it this way to you: I had special reasons to leave for a while. I'll tell you more some other time, if you don't mind."

She sees something has changed on his face, it's tighter, less welcoming. "Some other time OK," she says quickly, nodding, and looks away to avoid the embarrassment of putting him somehow on the spot for reasons unknown and of indisposing him.

He munches at his cake and asks after swallowing and drinking some water: "Why don't you tell me about your dancing? Are you doing it for a long time now?"

"Perhaps five-years. Five-years-old," she corrects itself and smiles.

"Since the time you were five-years-old? You must be a professional then."

"No professional, no full time. Training was only now and then, when I have time. High-school, you know, until last year."

"You mean, you're only eighteen, nineteen, then?" He seems flabbergasted.

"You not far," she plays around it. "But *I* don't like ask age and blood type. *Other* Japanese girls like it."

"Oh, that's fine with me, sorry about it. I can understand that. But me, I'm twenty-two," he says smiling broadly.

"Oh, congratulations." She smiles back, without taking the bite. She's relieved, that was a long word.

"But I'm not giving you my blood type," he chuckles, and she laughs back at it. She likes this casual, friendly bantering. *I feel OK.*

"I not asked for it," she says. "But I ask for something else, perhaps a secret also."

"What would that be? Perhaps I can accommodate your wishes."

"Accommodate me?" She's suddenly confused and red-faced. "But I live with my mother."

"Ah, that's another English idiom. Accommodate *someone's wishes* "he says, stressing the important words, "means to satisfy a request, a wish, not living at or with someone," he laughs off the situation.

"I see. That is OK." She's breathing easier. She then puts on for a moment the face of a spoiled *maiko*. "Then, may I ask how do you keep your hair so- ?" She hesitates, and makes the sign of rolling up something around a finger with fingers of the other hand, and smiles while at it.

"How do I keep it this curly, you mean?" he asks.

"Yes, curly — the word," she nods.

"Oh, that," he laughs. "I'd say it's mostly genetics — I mean, parents. My mother has it this way too, even though the color comes mainly from my father. Once you're there, and *I'm* there" he smiles, "it's quite easy, I just have to wash regularly with a special shampoo and dry it up, and it comes up this way, nothing secret to it. I mean, not something that I can think of at this time."

"For us, Japanese people, that not possible. We have straight hair. All. And black."

"Ah, but things change even here, I can tell. I think there are many hairdressers in Japan these days making good money by changing hair color or by making it curly, aren't there?" he asks.

"Yes, you right," she says. "But not the same." She fancies touching his hair, but feels she doesn't have the courage to ask. *We're not there yet.* Then she looks at his wristwatch — she has it in her handbag, she didn't want to wear it with her kimono; not appropriate, she had thought.

"I think I need go home now, sorry," she says.

"Why so early already?" he asks, and looks distressed.

"You know, my mother."

"Is she strict with you?"

"Strict?"

"I mean, does she want you to do things exactly as she says?"

"Ah, not that," she says, "she very good. But careful, like mothers."

"So, how do you want to go? Taxi again?" he laughs.

"No, let's go to Harajuku Station by walk and then we take each subway."

"Sure I can't accompany to your home or in the subway?"

"No, better this way," she says.

"All right then. Are you ready?"

"Ready?" She makes a questioning face and really has no idea what he's about.

"Ready for me to get you down from the chair," he laughs.

"Ah, this time I think easier with the kimono," she smiles.

Yet, when he comes up close to her high chair, she picks up her handbag from the table, tucks in willingly the elbows to her body, and steadies herself for being picked up from under the elbows again and landed in a single swoop safely and delicately on the floor, standing.

"Thank you. You're fast," she tells him, looking up from a side at him with a full, dimply smile, still with a touch of irony, the long hairpins blackslick with the fluorescent light.

Strange Happenings

Michiko knows there is a need to visit the old place. On this Sunday morning, she's already got the voice of her sister at the other end of the line.

"*Hiroko-chan!* Your portrait for Father seems something out of this world, if I happen to listen to Mother." Michiko knows Hiroko is going to get the old sarcasm oozing through the lines, but can't help herself. "When can I see it?"

"Well, anytime before he picks it up, I guess. You may have a problem to find it after that; he's in so many places these days, or so I hear. Moving things along with him too. But as to that portrait, don't put your hopes too high — you know the original." Hiroko laughed lightly. "Why don't you show up today at eleven at Mother's place to see it? We could then go out, say downtown, to do some shopping at Shibuya or Shinjuku. Touch on some of the best places, you know."

Michiko moved out of the parental house two years ago. "This is getting too crowded for three women," she would say after a flare-up of temper, and she might as well have been right. Anyway, going to any place that ranked other than "best" in her view, was out of discussion.

"All right, then," she says.

Michiko knows that shopping together wouldn't be Hiroko's first choice in the great scheme of things. But both know it's still the best bet for them these days to suffer each other gracefully while doing something together. And there's always that difficulty of saying "no" to an elder sister, especially so when she doesn't live in the same place with you anymore, when being fed up with each other isn't that much of a worry, supplanted by strange yearnings for tightness lost.

***

Three hours later, just twenty minutes late, Michiko is in.

"Ah, this portrait really makes you beautiful. That old painter knows this job. I need one for myself too — perhaps another copy for father too, if he insists. Where's Mother?"

"At the shrine, as on every Sunday," Hiroko answers.

"OK. We two have better things to do. Are you ready?"

"Five minutes, please. I need to go to the washroom."

Michiko walks and turns through the living room, waiting. On the table in a corner, left open, is her sister's handbag. She closes in, makes sure the sound of water rushing is still heard from the bathroom, then takes a peek and a quick fingering through the contents of the handbag. Quite in view, there's this corner of a photograph. Delicately pulled out, it reveals a blond guy, smiling from under a spectacular crown of hair. After some lightning-fast doing, she replaces it carefully, then puts her flash camera back in her bag. *Ready for shopping, now. We are.*

***

Kazuhiro Yuasa is fifty meters under the surface of downtown Tokyo, in a bunker vacated by the Japanese Defense Forces decades after the World War II, also years after the big atomic scares of the fifties and sixties — the Russians are coming or bombing, the Chinese are coming — were over. It had been sold to the highest bidder, a construction company, just a front for the branch of Yakuza led by him.

The bunker has been brought up to date in terms of facilities after the purchase, and the only unpleasant thing is really the want of natural light, should claustrophobia be of no concern. High-speed elevators bring him to the surface, full air-conditioning systems make him breathe purer air than most of the other denizens of Tokyo.

Kazuhiro is still there because he isn't sold on the news, not the big political news. As far as he is concerned, the cursed war could start at any time. And the worst thing is, it could start anytime with America, of all powers. They, the Americans, could well still bloody decide anytime there is too much juice that Japan has again, and that also goes for fanning hard stuff or shroom on its own to the local customers. And don't tell him the American Mafia couldn't have itself a hand in it. So, logically, a Hiroshima or a Nagasaki could be blown again off the face of the earth at any time. One had better be prepared, and the deeper under the ground the better.

But you couldn't catch Kazuhiro at any of the peaceniks' marches. "Left-wing — bad for business," that's his call on the matter. "Leaders don't mix with the crowds, except if they are the worst of the worst — politicians still running for office."

Yukio Imashita has just been shown in boss' office. Yukio's in his thirties, razor thin, yet tall and very nimble. Delicate matters touching on magic go to him as a matter of course. Placing things in certain places of a sudden, or making them disappear just as mind-blowingly, is his domain. Making the competition lose their suits in patches to the ground, the getups suddenly having become thread-less at some critical junctures right in the middle of an important business meeting, say with a local mayor or a chief of police, is his competence too.

"This a matter that needs to stay between you and me."

"*Hai*, understood, boss. It's gonna stay that way." The bodyguards have been temporarily removed just outside the door of the huge office, and Yukio understands there are special stakes here.

"You better make sure." Yukio understands parts of him might become considerably shorter if he flubs this. He just nods and deeply bows, hands aligned with his outer part of his pants legs.

"This is the man." The boss pushes towards him a grainy picture of a Caucasian. "The name is Fraser."

"American, boss?"

"Seems so. Civilian though, so I don't expect troubles. Works in Mitaka, at the Company. For the time being, just make him jittery. No real damage."

"Pics, boss?"

"Only if he's alone. You get the go ahead and collect information, but nothing gets scribed here. Everything stays crowded in your slim brain, in case I'm asking, understood?"

"Yes, boss. Bugging the phone line?"

"Not yet."

Five minutes after Yukio has left, the lithe Kayoe Kuriyama is let in. Massage time.

She busies herself with one of the toilet commodes, dabbling at finding and opening oil and cream bottles and receptacles in the many drawers of the multi-storied piece of furniture, flexing her strong fingers, one palm against the other, right until Kazuhiro feels in mood for it and calls her from the massage table set up in the bedroom. He has already directed and locked-in his sight to the TV home theater with its panoramic screen, but Kayoe knows better than making any assumptions at this point in time, and has read well her Sada Abe book. This, the way she sees it, is but a journey in patience.

***

When something tripped Simon in the men's clothing department of Isetan at Shinjuku, no one around realized who, if anyone, had done it, nor was Simon initially aware of anything intentional at work. At first, he thought he had just tripped himself over his own shoelaces.

There had been this feeling of slightly snagging something with his feet. He didn't go down entirely, having recovered — quads pushing hard, feet skipping fast on toes — when his nose was just half a meter above the carpeted floor.

However, soon though, his peace was punctured when he saw to a side a broadly and pityingly-smiling Japanese man in his thirties looking straight at him for a flash, then taking his sight to a window case carrying luxury watches. The distance between them at this time was large enough to preclude any direct physical interaction having taken place, but Simon thought he knew enough about life to exclude happenstance coincidences. Still, he decided to go on on his way, what with no one around him apparently having seen the matter to be used for a witness, also, to boot, the smiley Japanese having volatilized himself by now in a whiff of time.

Frisbee in Harajuku

By one o'clock, she has to be at Harajuku station on the Yamanote line. She and Simon agreed on it two days ago. Luckily enough, for she's running quite late, there's no kimono planned for this time. It's mostly Frisbee today; surely, the traditional dress wouldn't help at all. She wiggles herself into a pair of gray knee-length tights, places a short skirt over them, arranges her bra, then pulls over her head a white T-shirt with red flying kites on its front. That should do it for Frisbee.

There have been two calls from Michiko this morning complaining about the way her own portrait has been advancing with the old painter.

"I've no idea, *Hiroko-chan*, how you were able to put up with him. First, he's a procrastinator. Then, I don't see myself at all in it, as though it's someone else, a girl picked from the street or a pachinko parlor; no connection with me whatsoever."

"Perhaps it's just his preliminary stuff. Be patient, *Michiko-chan*. He might be trying to get you on one of your better days, so he muddles away the posing hours until the day comes when you're fresh as an opening flower," Hiroko said, trying to sisterly placate her. Michiko at odds with world's view of herself — that was definitely no news.

"Certainly wish that were true, but I'm afraid it isn't," Michiko said sourly. Then, after a break and a change of course that Hiroko found eerily significant, her sister went on. "Wonder if it weren't better to have made a large photograph of myself for Father instead. D'you happen to know anyone reliable in that business?"

"I might, but I'd have to find their spots somewhere in my rolodex. I'll tell you if I find any." A photographer, of all people. Hiroko shuddered, wondering if someone else except her mother knew about Simon, especially someone connected with her father. Sooner or later, her mother had to learn about Simon, what with so many phone calls in English going on around their place, sometimes at inordinate hours, for the past month. "Just a young American man, Mother" had been her only explanation by now, as though young American men were a daily occurrence in their household. Nonetheless, her mother carried a large question mark on her face, especially on those occasions when Hiroko initiated the call. And Hiroko knew — her own world would come apart if that happened — it couldn't have been her mother talking about it.

No. Since losing Shuji Miyamoto, her lover, to a single horrendous *katana* slash never assigned by police to anyone, Makoto Asaye, their mother, has seemingly embraced the value of discretion. That blow had practically separated Shuji's trunk from the lower part of his body. For the seventeen years following, Hiroko and their mother have been inseparable. It has been only Michiko who has gone from the father to the mother, swung to and fro by Michiko's own or by their father's wishes at the time; wishes as changeable, on both sides, as the sea.

***

Second date for them at Yoyogi Park, again for Frisbee. Both of them are in sneakers. Quite tall grass, dark green with dried up tops; it doesn't seem to have been cut in quite a while. It could be the rains, too.

This sunny Saturday afternoon has brought out three parties of throwers, including them. The other two groups are of three and four people. Bottom line: there's space enough for everyone. Hiroko likes it — more space for her errors.

"I'm just a beginner," she tells Simon after each missed through or catch.

"I think you've told me that very recently," he says, laughing, "and I think we've agreed on it, haven't we?" He's in worn-out knee-length jeans shorts, a red cotton tank top, and white cotton socks cut low to the level of the edge of the white "Rod Laver" tennis shoes, which seem to have pretty thick soles. They make his feet, Hiroko thinks, bigger than they are.

Their Frisbee is red, average size, bought here in Tokyo. Just in case he decides to show her some nail delay tricks and needs less surface friction, Simon has brought in his knapsack a small bottle with silicone oil. For the time being it's just warm-up, casual throws from one to the other. He's not using any tricks yet and she's glad, because she needs a good, simple model to follow, nothing sophisticated.

Still, to raise the stake for her, he intentionally sails it at times a bit to a side, so she needs to follow, by walking or running, its curving flight, to make a good catch. Sometimes, she feels rushed and then she is upset with herself for not focusing on the tricky flying object right from its takeoff from his hand. At those moments, she feels the disk behaves like an Australian boomerang, which in fact she has seen only on TV, going off of its own mind on a very nasty trajectory.

"I'm going to throw it to you from both the left and the right hand now, for you to get acquainted with the different curvatures in the path of flight," he says, and challenges her with a smile.

"OK, I'm ready," she says, but when the Frisbee comes dangerously close, she panics now and then and misses the catch. Then, her face becomes an intense red, and she feels that red washing down on her, her arms and legs becoming red too. Just a moment later, just by looking at him, she calms down each time. His face is so relaxed and he doesn't seem fazed by her failures. His calves are in evidence, very strong, every muscle lined up there, lineaments upon lineaments, and she likes to look at them. A wide red-and-white-striped bandanna holds his hair in place, pushing it in fact upwards in a raised crown-like tussle of rebel curls that grabs as a glue so much her attention at times that she forgets what she's supposed to do in the normal sequence of not-absentminded life.

Their Frisbee goes off its intended path and bumps in the air into their neighbors'. Both disks are crashing to ground. "The pilots have successfully ejected," one the others says in Japanese. Everyone is having a laugh. She translates it for Simon and he laughs too. She hopes at the end they might talk to some of these people. She likes people, making friends or just acquaintances. Last time, someone recognized her here in *Yoyogi Goen* as a dancer, and she was pleased. Always, though, there's in the back of her mind that desire that it not reach her father, her showing up in the world with an American, even as handsome as Simon. Her father might become even more furious and concerned because Simon is handsome, seeing her at a greater risk of being grabbed in proverbial seducer's clutches.

The air is the hot and dry one of beginning of August in Tokyo. The sun is set up high in the sky, and doesn't seem to want to relinquish its position at noon. Its heat stays around in columns that extend themselves, tall, to the sky, and one can find relief from it only under the trees on the periphery of the grass meadow, but then there it's where all the other visitors of the park are navigating too along the pedestrian walks. At least the place where they are, in the center, under the sun now slashing, is recognized in unspoken ways as Frisbee heaven in the area during weekends, and no one really bothers them.

"Now that we've warmed up, I'm going to try to show you one of Brothers Velasquez' tricks, a nail delay with an under-the-leg jumping pass," Simon tells her, " but let me first do some simple nail delays, no leg action involved."

With quick deft moves, he applies some silicone oil to both sides of the disk with a rag, then throws it in rotation above his head and catches it on his right-hand pointer-finger nail. To Hiroko, it seems the disk speeds up its rotation once it touches his nail. He pops it up delicately and catches it deftly on the other's hand pointer finger nail. Sometimes, he tangentially touches its periphery with his fingers while it's free up in the air, in a brushing motion, to keep it in rotation and speed it up again.

"They call this an airbrush in freestyle Frisbee," he tells her. She understands the meaning of these words, and she's glowing with pride at having such a knowledgeable friend. At times, she applies the brakes on such a pride, deeming it un-Japanese, but lets something warm build up inside her. That, she would not slow down or put a stopper on no matter what, as she feels it's good for her and part of her now.

His freckles are obvious now; he must be very hot.

"OK, let me try one of those Velasquez moves. I saw them in Central Park in New York."

He starts the Frisbee in rotation, brings it in a nail delay lower to his side, then suddenly breaks into a scissors jump in place and passes it under his right leg in the air to his left hand nail.

"Woo-hoo, I did it, man," he says and there's a sparkle of joy in his blue-green eyes that, she sees it, look at her, seemingly for her glad recognition.

Hiroko applauds with the small, delicate hand flutter of Japanese ladies. Others are coming closer to watch, and amid some failures, he manages other four or five such passes. There's light applause from some of the others too, and Hiroko feels the sun generously beaming down on them all.

"Lunch, let's have, yes?" she suggests five minutes later.

"I'm more than ready. In fact, I am very hungry, so hungry I might become a cannibal. Be careful," he says, and she laughs at him.

They go to a corner under a tree now and sit on the grass. She opens two of the *bentos* she has brought for the occasion. Mostly sushi. She knows by now he likes sushi very much, as they've been together to several sushi places in Shibuya, Shinjuku and elsewhere in Tokyo. He says "Abracadabra!" and conjures, with a spectacular play of hands, out from his knapsack, three bottles of fruit juice and two glasses of white polystyrene, which he joins on the towel spread out on the grass to the *bento* boxes.

Hakone I

They've been at Hakone up in the mountains for two days, for both sightseeing and photography. Still in separate rooms at the hotel. However, while walking along the gravel-covered alleys, she now allows handholding, and at times she's playfully pushing into him from hips or elbows to take him out of balance. Her hands are very hot when touching his; his touch is cooler and more nervous: it's as though he needs to keep moving his fingers over her hand, at times as in making bread, at times as in playing the piano. Now and then, she presses his hand, signaling he stop the fiddling, just stay in place. He likes it then in other ways, as there's osmosis between their skins at the points of contact.

Simon's moving around her with the camera and the tripod on the alleys and on the grass, measuring the light from different angles, stopping her at times from her dance, whenever he feels there is a good view for a shot, even though the music goes on and they have to restart it, as they have no assistant while doing this. As she is in her full dance regalia, she must be very attentive on this uneven ground, but it's as though she has a special sense in her feet, only rarely losing balance.

In other runs, he lets her perform a full dance with no interruption, shooting as she moves. He varies the exposure times with the intent of getting some blur and overlap effects. Some of that will have to be done at dusk, with and without flash, as the results are more striking; yet then there's loss of color too.

They've been to the open-air museum of modern art here and up in the mountains several times. He's been upset a bit at all the copies from Western masters presented in natural size,

Michelangelo's *David* comes to his mind most frequently, thinking this might make some of the visitors take these as originals and/or give up on ever trying to see those originals at their places of residence. "On the other hand, this is better than nothing," he tells Hiroko.

Right now, she's dancing several of her parasol and fan dances outside the open-air museum, on a stony platform covered with the very short and sparse grass of the mountains at that altitude, in an isolated area far from the entrance to the museum, so as to avoid most of the other people come for a day visit. As there are hardly any trees on that slope, the sun isn't screened at all, even in late afternoon. For sound they use a ghetto blaster of average size, a squarish thing in a metallic, silvery cover that he has recently purchased in Akihabara in Tokyo and is very proud of, as it is really one of the first things bought in Japan from his own salary and bonuses.

The flowers on her pale-golden kimono are irises with long green stems rising from the lower hem. The *obi* is just a paler golden, so wide that he's been concerned about her breathing. "No problem, don't worry," she told him with an easy laugh when asked. *I have to believe that's true, or she wouldn't be doing what she's doing.*

"And-now-you-know-you-gonna-*stop*" he speaks in rhythm with the music, and stresses the last word to signal to her.

She stops. The top of her parasol is tilted from the horizontal, and the actress in her peeks from under it at her presumptive suitor, and she herself, Hiroko, might as well peek at him, with a smile that is all a challenge. "Are you going to take me, to love me with my kimono and all, or are you going to pussyfoot around the issue? Please tell me now," she seems to say. And he is just as worried as any full-blooded man would be, because he feels he with his species is bound to jump in the ocean-like fray, irrespective of the outcome, ready to swim in this ocean opening in front of them, and — right after — closing behind them.

Still, he needs to stay in the here and now of it all, so he goes to her in her frozen stance, places delicately his pointer finger under her oval chin and lifts it an idea, enough to open her face more to the sun.

"There!" he says. She might have just widened or brightened her smile more on the inside, but nothing is visible to him, as the original smile brought on her face by the music stays on.

"Are we having a pro here, or what?" he says loudly, and again she takes it in with no external change in demeanor.

He's glad at times to be behind the camera, so intense it seems, as though coming and going in pangs, the visual rapport establishing itself between them, eye gobbling on eye.

***

On their first day here, close to each other in the sky-lift open throughout the summer, going up suspended above the mountain, both sitting on one of the benches, he had put his hand around her shoulders, her shoulders that were just a bit lower than his. Twenty or so passengers in all, but she hadn't minded the others' presence; she had smiled and looked into his eyes with eyes dilated just a bit, lacquered with a special film of wetness and brilliance for that moment of physical togetherness. Then she had placed her open palm on his thigh closest to her, feeling his muscles for the first time ever.

Crystal crisp in its coolness, the air, penetrated in slashes and sheets of light here and there by a stubborn sun, notwithstanding a whitish cover of clouds.

He viewed and considered for an instant, aware at his own pleasant shudder, the so-transient show offered by layers of pink and light red brought up to the surface of her face, usually so white, from layers of blood and energy unknown and secret.

His heart boiling over, he felt he had to tell her about it in some way. Turning a bit towards her, he put his free hand over hers on his thigh. "I have the feeling your pictures will come out particularly beautiful here. Just from the way you look now."

"Thank you," she said, and from her short lilting laugh and the dimples just outside the up-curving ends of her mouth he knew she had fully taken in the compliment.

They marveled from up above at the dry face of the mountain puckered with geysers spread all over the place, pluming vapor whenever they cared from their mouths.

"Look, another one's breathing!" he would say.

"No, look over there!" she would counter with a different offer.

"Would you like us to walk among them?" he asked her at one time.

"I am not sure if they smell. Perhaps sulfur you call that. But let's try a bit sometime. Could be-" She had stumbled over the word.

"Interesting? Exciting?" he suggested.

"Exciting. Closest."

"Or, you could say, 'Exciting is the closest to what I had in mind.'"

***

There's now and then, coming up in their talking, but also in their practical day-to-day doings, this inkling of a difference. It's as though they come through different pathways to climb a mountain. He wonders if this the truth, this mountain, but doesn't want to go philosophical about it. The Northern Face of Everest, he remembers it. She much more goes about it on principle, on form. He thinks all the time about the experience to be lived in attempting the thing. Little by little, he feels she's much more anchored in the past than him, that he fumbles more into the future, willing, even eager, to do so. How this difference between them would work itself out is anybody's guess, he feels. *It's all fun and dandy with myself. We'll just survive.*

Sometimes, he thinks this is the Japanese manner versus the American manner of doing things. Just one moment later, he feels going about it this way is too much getting into generalizations, into dry, abstract notions.

He has no qualms to tell her about it.

"You see, when I'm taking a picture, I tend to think about how I am going to feel, by looking at it, about the thing frozen in it, how the eventual viewers or spectators of it are going to feel about it. Once again, 'by looking at it,' I said."

"Yes, I think I know," she says. "I think more about the thing before you take that picture. Looking at food, I think how *soba* or *udon* were made."

"I think about how they're going to taste in my mouth. Perhaps I'm the egoist," he laughs. "I like to anticipate, I tend to forget about everything that went before me, before this moment even. I mean, this moment for all of us, not just for me."

"Egoist?" she asks. "But this is something bad, isn't it? I don't think you're bad. At all." She's looking half-amused, half-concerned at him.

"Ah, perhaps not the baddest of them all." He laughs. "But I think all of us carry a small piece of the bad in us. Not of the very bad, which is the evil. And not, of course, you," he quips at her.

"Oh, I think I have bad in me too. I remember with my sister, we had-"

"Fights? Quarrels?"

"Right, quarrels. And sometimes it was me."

"Who started it?" he finishes the thought.

"Yes. It was me who started it. So I don't like to think me very good."

"'Think about myself as being very good.' Tell me what you could have done to start such fights. I can't really believe this thing about you. You seem so peaceful," he says.

"Yes, but you know proverb: Peaceful lakes are deep. I think I know *haiku* too about this. Or, more than one *haiku*."

"Hiroko, you should say 'You know *the* proverb' You need to stick an article, a 'the,' there to say you think about a specific, or known thing, or a thing that you have talked about before. Then, 'I know *a* haiku,'" because this is the first time you've talked about it. Thus, non-specific wants non-definite article. One of many things, that is."

"Ah, but *specific* difficult for me," she complains.

"When you focus your mind on it, and it's one of many things that you select, it's specific, definite. But let's not forget where we've started." He looks at her intently, smiling.

"Yes?" she asks.

"I've asked you to show me ways in which you could have been bad, even once, to your sister. I can't quite believe that, I've told you."

"Was, I'm sorry, more than once. Bad. You know chess?"

"Sure, I heard about chess, the game. Now, if you want to talk about playing chess, that may not be my best suit. I think I'm quite bad at it. Anyway, what happened about chess and your sister? I am all ears." He smiled.

"Well, I with my sister, we played chess many times, perhaps since I five."

"'Since I was five-years old.'"

"Right. Both very ambitious, I think. So, the bad thing was I bought chess books for me and I kept them."

"You kept them hidden from her?"

"You always guess me very well!" She laughed. "Yes, I kept them. Studied. A lot. But never give them to her. Hidden."

"And? And what was the result? Did you beat her?"

"Many times. But then, she asked Father for a chess teacher. Only for her. She nine-years old then, I seven. Later she beat me again."

"She got better at it herself?"

"*Hai, so deshita.* Also, then I was interested only dance."

"I can see this was a serious crime: hiding books and reading them for your own exclusive good," he said and then laughed. "I agree that you were a tiny bit bad."

"Thanks for only 'tiny bit.' Generous." She smiled and bowed, ironically.

"'Generous of you.' Or 'You are generous.'"

Hakone II

"I'd like to paint a frieze with you dancing. You know what a frieze is: walls upon walls with paintings or sculptures on them. Here, of course, photographs, not paint, but you've got the gist of it. Gist, I mean essence, what's important," he says. "Then, we could have an exhibition with that. Imagine all the walls covered with yourself. Would that confuse you?" He smiles, tempting her to answer, as she hasn't shown a reaction yet.

"Not modest, me everywhere, I think" she suggests, nodding doubts from side to side. *What would Father say?*

"Immodest? Perhaps if one thinks in the traditional Japanese way, I don't know. I'll let you decide that. But I'd worry about it only after seeing the reaction from the viewers. You may be pleasantly surprised, and you may forget for once about tradition. Now that I remember, I saw snapshots of your *butoh* dancing; pretty modern to me. Isn't it modern, the *butoh*?"

"Twenty years or so," she says.

"But that's nothing, when one thinks Nara, Kamakura, and so on, here in Japan, I'd think."

"Still, people could say it's *immodest*, the word you said."

"Yes, but think about an exhibition built as an imperial villa, two or three pavilions, hallways or just walks in between them out on the sand or pebble, and all the inner walls covered with full-size pictures of yourself, in rotation during a dance. People passing by, peeking in. I think that would look wonderful, going from an angle and instance in the dance to the next one. Strobe by strobe. That is, flash after flash."

"Thank you for your-, your confidence," she said and opened two moonlike dimples, smiling, yet right at the same time readjusting her bottom on the *tatami* of the restaurant room, as though wrought between some discomfort over the idea and some budding excitement.

"I'll let you think about the idea."

"OK."

"However, it may be better to think it over some real pictures, so we could go ahead immediately when you feel like it. Here in Hakone."

"Ah, time enough in three days?"

"Let's try just several series of shots. And when that's done and we have the prints, natural size as I've told you, I'll talk to Doctor Sugie about the exhibition. It's better to show than tell. Not that I think they would manage to use one of the very imperial villas, but why not, they seem to have some contacts high up there? They have visitors like everywhere else, the villas, and why not photographs instead of paintings on silk or wood, whatever?" he says and lifts his hands to the sides, as in wonderment at such a question, and she can tell this is honest wonderment, as though facing a crowd of doubtful.

***

The *onsen* is set up, really carved in, in a huge ledge overhanging one of the slopes of the grey stone mountain. Five pools, close to each other, range from piping hot to shrinking cold, the stone edge in some of the colder ones covered with green moss facing itself immodestly in the reflections of the water and changing its black hue possessed by lack of direct sunlight. There's a bamboo booth for the men and another for women, each with benches to sit and with wall shelves hooks to leave your bathrobe on in wicker baskets, but the pools are shared even though you're not supposed to carry more than a small cotton rag in one of your hands in order to protect your modesty while getting in the water or getting out of it through the staircases carved in rough stone. Hiroko's already in the water for her first time. This is a rare *onsen* that allows both sexes in the same area. Submerged but for her head and shoulders, dressed in a bikini, she hangs in place on a hand alongside one of the pool edges, casually moving the other in the water on and around herself, using it as an advanced spy to the temperature and the feel of the water.

She's waiting for Simon to come in, to stay together with him while they take in the heat. There he is, descending the steps into the water from the men's side, and this is the first time she has had a view of his body, naked except for the swimming trunks, required here as this is a mixed *onsen*, and this is past the Meiji restauration, the Western-inspired prudishness in place. He is hairy enough for the color of his skin to be perceived at first sight as darker than the one on his face, even though she knows those hairs on his body are golden in the right light. She's fascinated by the look of his long limbs, the thighs arcing down from hips set higher than those of the typical Japanese male, the arms swinging quite low, by the bones so visible in their structure in knees, shoulders, elbows and hips. There's then that contrast between his wide shoulders and his narrow hips that she has always guessed under his clothing, but now she has just glimpsed the flatness of his stomach and the sharp pectorals. He seems to be set more in bones than in muscles, the latter lacking roundness but projecting a fibery definition, line cut under line. One of the things she likes about his bones and muscles is their being setup in a vertical, straight, unbent, dignified, but not massive, figure. A body that moves around with unexpectedly agitated spunk at times, speeding up some of the connecting segments of his trajectory in space in quirky ways. An arm that takes off, a leg that pushes away on the balance of a second. You wouldn't able to predict from his present position where exactly he will be next, the next increment, the next differential. This perpetual 'find me now' mesmerizes her, without finding it tiresome, as it's obvious he isn't courting attention: he doesn't look back at you to see whether you've been following him, he just moves ahead mercury-live.

"Wow, this is hot!" he exclaims when he gets close to the place she's ensconced in at the periphery of the pool.

"Go in colder ones first, get used to temperature," she says.

"Nah, too late this time, I've already managed to scald away five layers off my skin, I guess," he says, laughing. "How do you feel in it?"

"Oh, for me fine. Doing it many years. I like it very much, relaxes me a lot. When back in the city, I'll be better, I know this. Like, stress goes."

"But can you think about anything else in it? The only thing on my mind right now is, This is hot."

They are not alone: there's another couple, much older. They must be in their fifties, both Japanese, eying the young couple, perhaps strange for them in its obvious mix — his blondness. Everybody has left their small towels on the margin of the pool. There are strict restrictions on not bringing outside dirt in here, as people may have been using these same towels for their washing at the showers under which one sits in the indoor entry area. The *onsen* itself is just for one's soaking pleasure.

"So, what are we supposed to do here and now?" Simon asks.

"Very simple. Let the water go into you. Don't do nothing."

"Ah, you mean just soak in. Fine, I'll put my mind to it, if you say so." He laughs and crouches down in the water, so it reaches now his neck. His face is suddenly much ruddier than Hiroko knows it on a normal day, and drops of sweat pop up on this face as an yet-unapplied, transparent make up, growing in size by the minute. But soon he seems to settle in, and flashes his old wide smile to her.

"OK, it seems I've just come to again. I might even be able to hold an intelligent conversation, but don't hold me to it too roughly," he says. "I like your hair, the way you've caught it so high above your head."

"Ah, anything good about me is intelligent," she quips. "And thank you." She has taken half an hour at the mirror in her room to build that towery construction.

They are half-facing each other at arm's length. There's this yearning in her and, as though in response, he reaches with his right hand and passes his palm over her forehead, carrying it as delicately as a cloud on her skin. She doesn't look surprised, even though this may well be the first time he has ever touched her face. There's something very hot welling up inside her.

She knows enough about herself to assume there's no telling what she might do next, and she finds herself catching his fingers over her forehead with a slow but purposeful motion of her left arm and hand, moving them next across her own face, over her cheeks, her nose, her lips, in one single brushing arc. She then twists her fingers among his, slowly drops their united arms in the water between them, and closes her eyes.

She also knows him well enough already to feel quite assured he won't say anything for now in his respect for her and for being not familiar with the surroundings, and that is fine by her. For the time being, this physical connection between them, made secret by the water, it's all she feels she really wants.

She likes the feeling of sharing this medium, the water, with him, in so close.

Later, seconds or minutes later, when she reopens her eyes, she's aware of his regard fixed on her face while his carries a smile.

"Welcome back among us!"

She knows she hasn't slept, as the whole time she has been aware of their holding hands in water. Water and their hands together. She tells herself she could well put up with a life with just these two things around for subsistence.

She sees his eyes leaving her for the adjacent lake, separated from the *onsen* proper by a dam of huge granite boulders moved undoubtedly in place by unknown giants in time immemorial.

"Look at those birds taking off and coming in. Aren't they *amazing*?" he asks and tightens for a moment his half of the grip over her hand to stress the final word. His eyes are back on her face and her jealousy directed at the flying witness of their being together fades away in another moment.

Kazuhiro aboard boat

Kazuhiro Yuasa was at the helm of his all-yellow Honda powerspeedboat wallowing in place out in the ocean waters off the Yokohama harbor. Waves chopping thinly, sun already up by this ten o'clock on an open, blue sky, free of any cloud. Great setup on a normal day, but he hadn't had one nor recognized one in years now. Boat yellow to tell of his presence in waters nearby. To avoid accidents. Warn police off unwanted interference. Generally, make him feel better about himself. Matter of fact, he liked bright colors and he had several light cotton and linen summer suits or just pants or swimming trunks in a similar fluorescent yellow.

"Not modest, me," he would tell family and business associates on any occasion, and there wasn't any reason to doubt his words. He'd also add "Yellow's just fine for hardy men," for the ears of his bodyguards, who still knew better than to try to carbon copy him and thus compete for any attention. Dark, preferably black suits were the just kit for them, and two guards were presently in evidence on the bench at the aft of the boat.

Yukio Imashita came aboard from another powerboat that had swept in and pulled up alongside. The two muscle men had to move for the duration of his conversation with their boss onto the other boat. Nothing doing, standing orders.

"The American is getting chummier with Hiroko-san," Yukio opened the real juice.

"And vice versa?" asked Kazuhiro.

A double take back to him. Out among regular people, this would have been a sigh. "Yes, *oyabun*."

"Go on. What went on last?"

"Hakone drill. Separate rooms at the hotel."

"This part I like," Kazuhiro said.

"Yes, but mixed-sex *onsen* after."

"Less good."

"I know that, *oyabun*, but- There's worse news: they seemed close. Touching. No kissing though. No pics, as you asked."

"I remember what I've asked. What else?"

"The *gaijin*'s been taking lots of pictures of Hiroko-san dancing at some distance from the museum."

"Dancing? What museum? You know damn well I never go to things like that."

"Sculpture museum, boss. You know, the one with lots of sculptures out in the grass, and some large pieces inside."

"Ah, the abstract garbage. I know someone got her into it, so much so it's even in some of her dancing. Spit, any idea what the pictures would be for?"

"Can't tell for sure, as I haven't been allowed to bug him yet. I've no talk from them two."

"Know that too, but can't you think for yourself? I mean, you moved in that there museum, I guess?"

"Yes, boss, I did. Thinking I have tells me it might be for some exhibition about her dancing."

"Wouldn't be the worst. Not that I like all that *butoh* stuff she does sometimes. All that jumping, the jerking, the violent stuff. Nonsense. Can tell it's not Japanese."

"What I've seen outside the museum, she must have also that kind of dancing, the jerking you said, caught by him."

"Anything coming up with her, posted in the dance sheets? Shouts, events, whatchamacallit with her?"

"Nothing yet, based on my tuning in. But had to keep remote, as you've asked."

Kazuhiro, The Capitulation, Kabukicho

The signing ceremony on the *Missouri*: he had been a small bug then — not even two — too insignificant in the grand scheme of things to be able to see it at the time, not even in movie theatres, not that many of those were left standing at the end of WWII in Japan. However, since he had been six and seven and looked at pictures, the memory of MacArthur imperiously looking at the Japanese high command signing the capitulation was seared in his memory.

He had that picture plastered in his underground office and his internal cry to it was "Never again." Never again should real Japanese men surrender to bloody Yanks the way it had been back then. Yanks insolent enough in their victory to bring with them that old banner of theirs since the time of Commodore Perry's forced opening of Japan to the Americans and their business. 1854. Good thing MacArthur wasn't around anymore, what with some of the weaker Japanese making him into a *Kami* or something of the kind. That's where one gets when giving up on home-grown Shinto.

Pictures he *didn't* want around him were of Hiroshima and Nagasaki. They could weaken the spirit, provide an explanation for the capitulation, and that, that he could never take in. True inner power doesn't bow or bend to power.

Hiroshima and Nagasaki. Still, on the other side, they could help glue people together against the Yanks. People who still had spines. *How many left?*

Another picture in his office was Yukio Mishima's, *hachimaki* with the Rising Sun and the samurai slogan "Serve the Nation for Seven Lives" around his forehead, the eyes intent on doing things, piercing at you. The man who had told the emperor had been too weak in renouncing divine essence. Too bad the guy was into men, but at least there had been some burning courage there. That young intellectuals' rebellion now already twenty years back. The *seppukus*. Water down the river, but these are still some of the more recent props we need, he thought. The pictures of *Kamikaze* pilots looked old even to him now, even though all had been and looked young at the time of their life being crunched from under them, even though the one in the center, big, life-size, all grainy and gray, was his father's, before one of his last sorties in the Pacific. Already knowing by then that a final mission was to be in the cards soon, a mission on the wind of death. Already knowing or hoping that he, his son, would sometime look at his picture, searching back across time, trying to find him.

***

He's out in the Kabukicho tonight, visiting a pleasure spot which has been off the charts lately in all the Tokyo men's magazines. The girls in this S&M imitation place are all dressed in dark, wide-lapelled, cutout business suits, not leaving the eye much to desire. Cutouts at the knees, cutouts at the bosoms, cutouts at the hips, cutouts on the asses; still the flesh isn't putting itself forward unfiltered, but through silk and nylon membranes right on top of the skin. The music is disco and reggae, flowing freely from large loudspeakers hidden behind false walls.

Cordoned off on the outside by his men, there's no one inside but the girls and three hulks on his payroll. The madam is only forty-five or so, but they know each other better than both of them would like it, for whenever a real man has such a longstanding association with a woman, he's bound to also entertain the memory of his failures to come up to the task.

There are no *tatami* rooms in this place, all is western business furniture adapted for intimate enjoyment. On the desks or the chairs, the girls prance in high heels to the music. Massage tables open down from the walls and chains, collars and manacles issue similarly from niches hidden in the ceiling or the walls. The businessmen coming here know full well there's no flopping onto comfortable sofas or heavy, upholstered chairs. You either behave or you're smacked or tethered. And, of course, there are private rooms with similar accoutrements for those more guarded about their image.

"We have all the books open to your inspection, Kazuhiro-san," the madam cries out to him from her room at the back. For there's this important point with him of having accountants sent in right the next day after his visits, during morning hours, when the customers are at home or at their offices, recovering from hangovers, to check up on the ledger books and assess the tithe.

"I didn't expect anything less," he shouts back, sneaking in his right hand through one of the knee cutouts of the blonde, generously-endowed American girl twirling on the closest table, stopping her from her giration and going up under her business pants to finger her sweets to the point of juicing up. The time of this is well attended to by the madam, as she's supposed to let her best girl on the day leave with Kazuhiro in his limo, to reggae the bulk of the show in his underground office. The girls find the latter place damned freakish and aren't comfortable with going there, but a job is a job even be it a blowjob or a handjob, madam Kitta tells them. And Kazuhiro getting the better of American girls is known to be one of his preferred games, so don't let's be surprised by it, she tells them. Thanks gods, he's still in great shape with all his *Kendo* training, so the least you can do is enjoy the sustenance and further it.

The Mizuage Auction

"*Oyabun*, can I go ahead with the auction now?" asked his personal assistant, Yuji, from the interphone's mouth set in a black lacquered box with ivory incrustations on his desk.

"You mean, it's not over *yet*?" Kazuhiro felt he might go through the roof any time now. He pushed himself down in the chair for it not to happen, matter of setting the normish to the trigger-happy in the gang.

"Sorry. No, boss. Things have gotten simpler, unfortunately so, if I may say that, as we might not be able to pump up things so high. Of the three stalking horses left, Yojiro-san had to retire this afternoon as his wife didn't want to hear about him getting involved in something like this. I mean, getting involved again. I called the *ochiya* mistress and told her about it, so she wouldn't be too kerflemixed about it." The *ochiya* was the geisha household to which the maiko belonged.

"Heck, look at this modern world now! Wives starting to throw monkey wrenches in *mizuage* auctions. Jealousy: not that they ever were virgin themselves. So, who are we left with in this competish?"

"It's the real-estate guy, Kunetori-san, and the car dealership guy, Yasunori-san," Yuji clarified.

"How high's the water?"

"Four million for now, boss. I 'spect it to end up at about six. Kuneko's a top *maiko*; that nose and those lips of hers, not to talk about that hip action when she dances, might snatch it higher. The two guys left are really into her and they've lost to each other in the past, so, you know, them being worked up plays in our favor."

Kazuhiro knew forty percent was *gumi's*, the rest to slosh to the *okiya* and a bit to the ryokan where the winner would take the girl to enjoy the spoils.

"OK, keep me on it the whole under-the-hammer. Flash them from start that if they don't come up whirling as expected, we're leaving camp and they will have to kiss our sweet behinds, not Kuneko's."

***

Just four months ago, in April, he had been in Kyoto at the Ichiriki teahouse, perhaps the most famous of Japan, at the time *The Dances of the Old Capital* were being staged in Gion at the Kaburenjo Theater. He had been there to meet with other Yakuza bosses from all over Japan, and the entertainment from their *gumi's* side had been provided by Kuneko, even though she was, as it were, a Tokyo geisha.

One may have quickly understood Kazuhiro's bent for setting the meeting up at the Ichiriki, had they recalled is was right there at Ichiriki that the sworn family enemy of three hundred years ago, the head of the forty-seven samurai gang, Oishi Yoshio, had spent untold hours of frolicsome revelry in the company of geishas, sake and great food, just to put to sleep the suspicions of Kira Kôtsuké no Suké, Kazuhiro's ancestor. And put to sleep those suspicions Oishi had managed, enough to convince Kira that those *ronin* were just riff-raff bent on drunkeness, not loyal retainers bent on mortal revenge for the humiliation and death of their master, Asano Takumi no Kami, which they proved themselves in the end to be, killing Kira. Thus, in what he certainly saw as an eye-for-an-eye unending story, Kazuhiro understood to pay part of his family's debt by showing up himself there, re-establishing the balance of attendance at Ichiriki, this time in his and his family's favor. You go back and beat the opponent on the very battle grounds where he had once beaten you to oblivion. You beat him in women, you beat him in sake, if these were once his chosen weapons; you beat him on the same *tatami* mats, be they only the descendents of the original mats in some *tatami* mattingdom.

The *obi* in heavy brocade, with twisting sunflower patterns on a sky blue background, as well as the charcoal black kimono, had cost the *okiya* a pretty yen, and he had been forced to contribute, in order to uphold face in front of the other *Oyabuns*, the honchos.

That he remembered well, together with having called Hiroko from Kyoto the day after that party, to tell her he wanted her to see Kumeko dance upon their return in Tokyo, as Kumeko had a new great piece now. The party had been strictly entertainment, as geishas, as good they are in terms of keeping mum, weren't still to be trusted with words about deep business.

Hiroko hadn't been too forthcoming, "I think I've told you already, Father, what your geishas are dancing and what I'm doing are different dishes, like those with freshwater fish and those with saltwater fish." He hadn't liked the comparisons with fishes and dishes. It had been as though she felt he wouldn't quite get it otherwise.

"Yeah, yeah, I know, these days you're all *modern*. But if my memory still serves me, you still have something traditional in your dances, haven't you? So you might as well get some ideas from Kumeko," he had said.

"OK, please tell her ochiya's mistress I'm going to call for a dinner appointment, where Kuneko could show me that dance," Hiroko had replied. He had felt it was mostly her desire to end the conversation that forced her to agree to something right then and there. These children today can't even see when you wish the best for them; or if they see it, they won't jump up in gratefulness.

The worst had been, as on other recent occasions, that damn feeling that she was, in some way or another, ashamed of him. "That comes all from her mother spewing dirt against me for years. Women can't understand this is a business just like any other," he raged to himself.

"Well, how did you feel about it?" he'd asked her a month later.

"Too submissive," the curt reply had been.

"What in the gods' name you mean by 'too submissive'? Some of this new-fangled feministic stuff?"

"Well, if you have time and patience I might tell you, Father."

"Go ahead. I might have just now that kind of time for the youngest of my daughters."

"First, she looks only to the audience, which is to say the men there, of course. Second, not even by chance does she stop to contemplate the nature around her — the sky, the grass, the cherry blossoms, that kind of stuff — heaven forbid. Third, she presses her toes and her knees together something unbelievable, which looks a bit prudish or full of shame to me. Now, mind you, Kuneko-chan has a great sense of music and makes all this pleasurable and nice to look at, but in the end the way she's doing it isn't quite my cup of tea. But then, I don't have to pour drinks for anyone or to make them feel great about themselves with clever, I-am-submissive talk, and for that some think I should be grateful," Hiroko had said, making him huff even now, upon his recalling their talk back then.

"So, that means you really don't think you could find anything worthwhile in her dance; is that what you mean to say to me?" he had asked.

"Oh, no. You don't get me, Father. The song, for that matter, *The yellow sun above the blossoms of that spring,* is great. Also, some of her steps might be of use here and there to other dancers. But if you think your daughter here might dance it in the same way, even remotely, you're sorrily mistaken," she said, laughing ironically at him over the line.

"Well, at least you've found something in it." And that, partial and fraught with dissatisfaction as it was, was quite something at the time between father and the younger daughter.

***

First, when Kazuhiro was ten, eight-years-old after the war, there was this dilapidated rickshaw gotten from a market where it had been left by its owner and driver, too tired of repairing it and perhaps of schlepping it around with people in it too. The boy fixed the wheels, shortened the shafts, too heavy for him, and started to use it initially to carry fish and vegetables from the markets to the people in the neighborhood where his mother and he lived at the time. When he got strong enough the supports were extended back to their normal length and poor ladies but later also geishas could be seen being carried back and forth about Asakusa by him. He kind of avoided the men, they were too heavy, and able to punch him in case of wrangling over a fare.

Yamanaki-san, a steady customer, had shown him first how an mature lady's *obi* had to be properly unfastened and put back in place after your visit to a healthy widow's home was nearing its end. She had also warned she had to bite into his shoulders in order to retain the noises that would have agitated the neighbourhood in the middle of the afternoon. "Your eel is too wide and lively for me to withstand it and give back to it otherwise," she'd say.

Then, when he was sixteen, and police would find less reasons to complain about a license, as he was strong like a bull, but compact, by now, easily looking twenty, he upgraded himself to an old Yamaha scooter for the repair of which he paid over several weeks the mechanics in produce given to him by the fruit and vegetable mongers for having brought customers to their stalls.

This is where teenage girls started to be seen with him on the back of the scooter, some from the good families around them, some of them right in their private school uniforms, being driven to and from the cramming school or to parties, at a time when it was public knowledge he had left school for years already.

It was always women for customers. He was less trusting of men. His father having left his family on the wings of Kamikaze during the war hadn't helped. His figure loomed large in Kazuhiro's life, but there wasn't warmth to it, mostly a dry awe.

***

He was seventeen now. On this day, he took his scooter around Tokyo Station and around the Imperial Palace nearby. The sun was terribly bright, so he put on his goggles on which, in the upper part, he had glued a dark but transparent film, his own invention at the time, so he wouldn't have to squint on a day like this.

He was making rounds around the moat of the palace, being now perhaps in the tenth of such rounds. He liked to do it for fun, he knew the police were on the watch around the place and he wanted to play cat and mouse with them. Sometimes he was flagged down from one of the police cars on the edge of the avenues, sometimes a policeman on a motorbike would rush to catch him from behind to tell him to go away. But there were all new rules after the war, and he knew no one really could have legally forbidden him to drive in that area. They would tell him he was driving too fast, or that his exhaust was too noisy, or nonsense of the kind.

However, what this time had appeared all of a while behind him as looked in his side mirror was not a police car, but a long, black, American-style limousine as not many could be seen on the cramped streets of 1960 Tokyo, whose driver was savagely boxing his horn to create space in front of him, even though the Hibiya-dori Avenue was wide enough to allow several cars in parallel, without care for a bike.

Upset with this show of force, Kazuhiro started to zig-zag in front of the car approaching from behind, dashing and breaking here, waving them along there with signs of "Pass me!" with his left hand continued to himself with *If you can, suckers!*, speeding forward and slowing back like a piston.

The driver came abreast with his car and starting to crowd Kazuhiro's scooter to a side, swerving now and then toward him, making as though trying to hit him with his front fender. Whenever the black monster was on the point of hitting him, Kazuhiro pressed wildly the metal, yanking himself another ten meters in front, teasing him.

By now, they had completed together in this dog race a fifth of the circle around the palace and entered the straightaway Hibiya Avenue running along the moats of the palace with just the narrow space for the pedestrians in between them and the moat.

The side window of the car went down and the driver stuck his head, face all-congested, out the right window of the automobile, cursing loud and wildly at Kazuhiro, taking his right hand off the wheel to threaten him with a closed fist. The engine was turning higher and in a heavier groan, the car pushed forward with a jerk toward him, swerving to its right.

Kazuhiro let them close in, this time not losing any time with replying in kind to the driver, but at the very last moment, when the car was just a half foot from pushing him into the pedestrian curb, sneaked ahead with the last push of energy of his small engine, which unknowingly to his competition was provided with abundant help in terms of fuel injection from his racing contacts.

The heavy car, in its all inertia, wasn't able to change trajectory with the same nimbleness and madness, continued its run to the right, bumped over the pedestrian curve, crossed the pedestrian walkway, bumped into the short wall on the right side, and hitting a segment in it which was not all concrete, penetrated it fully and stopped hung on its rear wheels, with the front wheels and the bonnet precipitously close to the water of the moat.

Kazuhiro didn't wait to see what really happened, as he heard the sirens of the police cars coming in from the distance.

The second day, most of the dailies of Tokyo were splashing the news "Car close to trespassing Imperial Palace property!" together with pictures of the automobile dangerously dangling from the edge of the moat-wall. Never minding that the car owners were never mentioned, as if it were a mystery story, Kazuhiro was upset the writers never touched on the involvement of a motorbike in the incident. Feeling neglected was not what he wanted from life.

Two days later still, that feeling changed when, returning to his scooter from one of his errands, he was confronted by two huge guys, black suits, black ties, black sunglasses on, who might just well have been retired sumo wrestlers, barring his access to his vehicle. He also detected a black limousine, shadowing them all, just like the one who had pursued him.

"You coming with us, boy" one the the mountain-sized people told him.

"What for?"

"Our boss wants to talk to you."

There was excitement in him, the smell of opportunity high in the air if he ever had sensed it, but he didn't want to make it too easy for them. "And who could that be, your boss, if you don't mind?"

"We don't mind, but he does. Cut the chatter and come with us."

Crisply said, so Kazuhiro compared sizes, escape paths, the risk of having the motorbike disappear if he himself did that, and decided to do just what the tools requested him to do.

The car was equipped with two-way radio and on it he heard his conveyors reporting to their boss their coming in, with him, "the hot dogging kid," among them, as a wished-for prize. Being identified even so vaguely made him feel safer, for reasons unknown.

Upon arrival at the putative destination, he recognized Shinjuku and Kabukicho around them. The presumably retired wrestlers took him with no words spoken up one flight of stairs, to the second floor of a gray three-story concrete building. He had decided to move with them, and there had been talk about a boss, so he decided to ask him further questions, not these fleshy underlings.

Kazuhiro, The Scooter Network

"Well," asked the dour man with penetrating eyes, lounging behind the huge desk in a tall armchair covered in gaudy white leather, "d'you know who I am?" He wore a red tie to a dark, gray double-breasted suit. On the front part of the desk was a *katana*, old by the look of scabbard and handle, on black supports with golden inlays.

"If these guys who brought me here don't lie, you must be the *oyabun*," Kazuhiro replied. It was midday, and the smell of recently opened *bentos* remained in the room, merging in his senses with the blinding light coming through the huge windows. He considered the fact that he himself hadn't had lunch and felt an inner irritation on that issue, not having been invited even to sit.

"That's right. Don't you want to know more about me?" The face asking this wasn't welcoming.

"Why should I? You'd still be the boss, so what's in it for me? Knowing names can put one in hot water," Kazuhiro answered looking straight at him.

"I like that 'tude. Thing is, you're here for a reason: you seem to know a fair bit about driving and engines, at least for bikes."

Kazuhiro saw an opening and immediately went into offensive. "Says who?"

"Says one of our former drivers."

"Ah, the guy who tangled with the moat at the Imperial Palace?" Kazuhiro sneered. *Don't leave the whole say-so with them.*

"That one. He's in a different line of work now, and I'm of the mind we'd better hire you for that job."

Kazuhiro shifted legs. "Just for your scoop, boss: I'm only seventeen, and I don't have a license for driving cars."

"We have our own layouts, the police won't bother you. I mean, not every day," said the man.

"Fine, but should that happen, I'm sure as hell lined up for the slammer. Tough odds to take."

"We got good shysters too."

Kazuhiro felt the need to cover this angle. "Well, perhaps they're like your drivers. A mix-up in court, and my skin gets hung inside to dry. What would I do then?"

The man's fingers drubbed the table impatiently. "You'd get double salary for any day inside and your mother'd get each and every sen of it on the first of each month, until you'd get out. And no worries, I think we might be using you more as a motorbike driver for now, which is exactly your niche."

"What for?"

"Small package dropping. Something screamin' fast, up to snuff to get into the narrowest places in Tokyo, even where cars really don't help."

Yes, that'd be my line. Still, raise the odds and cover all angles. "What exactly would they bag inside, those packages?"

"Choke up, kiddo. You must be first in the *gumi* to get to ask such questions."

***

The old story with Kira Kôtsuké helped just in time when they wanted some kind of a dope sheet on him. Someone with that kind of skeleton in the pantry would be just the thing, it seemed; the right hang-up one would like to have. The dusty past seemed to have serious pull on them.

Even before he became a brother, and that took time and ceremony, it didn't take him long to figure out the thing they were after was just a proposish to push the junk, the shit, the narky, the uppers and downers, the cap and the dynamite stuff throughout the city.

So what he cooked up was something like a baseball game played all through the place. The pitchers and the catchers, that's what they would be. Only the players would be all juniors, all fifteen at most. The pitched thingies would be most of the time real baseball balls, but they could be dailies rolled and caught in rubber bands for the throw like the morning delivery, or apples ready for the cut to unveil the jazzy cores.

The catchers would be all in tagged, fingered places: courtyards, trees in bloom in a *Goen*, pillars in front of a beer or tea automaton, ducking outta sight at the mouth of a passageway between two old houses of a hood. Lolling and lounging and cutting the time in thin slivers with not a care.

Then the pitcher would come and sometimes he would be the driver, sometimes the guy on the back seat. The bike would stop short, or turn on a dime, or just pass by full hog, and the pitcher would grab the thingy and he would arc it nicely on the fixed-to trajectory. And the catcher would be there with dark glasses for protection against the sun and stinks looking on, and would grab it in a flash and he would disappear just as fast as though swallowed by some hole opening and closing in the ground. The catchers would most of the time come into existence at their designated plates with real baseball gloves, for the serious game hadn't been invented and practiced for nothing, and this was just another 'plication.

***

Today was bagging day. His personal headquarters were in Shinjuku, the place where his twenty or so team lead-off boys, all younger than he was, all on scooters, were supposed to bring in at the beginning of the evening the pickings from their hoods for the three previous days.

His setup for this particular thing had its pit stop in an adjoining underground parking spot. One of the exit charge boxes had been handily reserved for his racket and several of his boys were posted to detour any cars or motorbikes not tied up to them to other exits.

There was double spotting at the entrance and at the exit. At the entrance, to make sure you were the known quantity expected for each team. At the exit, after the booth, in the short tunnel leading out to the street, to have your brains blown off if you had just done same to the man in the booth, instead of handing over your bag, or if the pickings were seriously not on the level with what he had on his sheet for the latest stuff drops. One never knows, but the first had happened only once. Small diffs in the scores — well, that was just some solid kendo strokes on your back for warning. The sheet would be updated and the checking and the doing would go on the next week.

Beef Sukiyaki

This is the end of their second day in Hakone. During the afternoon, which has been virgin-like cloudless and brilliantly sunny, Simon has shuffled in irregular circles around her and has made her move a considerable bit, while taking pictures of her dancing, as planned in that brainstorming talk they had about the intended exhibition. All the movement and the exposure to the elements has made both of them tired and glad to take a break in a restaurant before retiring for the day.

"You know, I think that exhibition might not be that far-fetched, in the end," he's saying, while waiting for their waiter to materialize with the order. "I'm quite sure we have already some very nice tableaux — you know, like large wall paintings — that can be assembled from individual shots. It's mostly editing work, I'd say. I expect you to be in the lab with me for that, you know. Consider yourself warned." He smiles.

The *tatami* room in which they sit is closed off on all sides by sliding doors, with no natural light, but he doesn't regret it, as it's late in the day. She sits on her heels on the floor, in *seiza*. He can't quite do that yet without pain in his joints, lack of flexibility, he has decided, thus he just sits with this bottom straight on the floor, knees in front, not underneath, as she does.

"Tomorrow rain, you know?" she asks.

"How do you know it?"

"People talking about at breakfast. This morning. Hard rain."

He thinks about it. He doesn't like to stay inside for a whole day. Not in separate rooms or in the lobby of the hotel. But he wouldn't want to tell her that. They aren't there yet.

"Do you think we may be able to walk out tomorrow with the rain?" he asks.

"In mountains, dangerous. Slippery on stone, you know. Also light crashes."

He laughs. "You mean, lightning?" Then, an idea. His eyes open up in pleasant surprise at himself. He has stubbornly just come back to the thought of doing something outdoors the next day, even though from a different angle.

"Would you mind dancing in the rain?"

"No Gene Kelly, but I try." She beams a modest smile at him, which seems to say something else too. He's not sure what, but he feels better and his face lights up in response. "OK, it's settled then. Same music, same kimono, or whatever you want. Just rain for a change."

She demurs a bit, a slight sideways wobbling of her head. "You know, some modern music and a simple cotton kimono better. I have music and other kimono here. Simpler. I'll try dance *butoh* under rain with it."

"And that, ladies and gentlemen, is our program for tomorrow," Simon proclaims and takes a bow for an imaginary audience.

She applauds in the Japanese women's style, with small beats of the palms.

The food is here, the first dish, *udon* soup for both of them. She knows by now he prefers it to *soba* noodle soup, which seems to him much rougher.

"Do you know, I can cook *udon* soup for you?" she asks all of a sudden.

"*Honto?* How did we get here?" he asks and laughs.

She flushes. "Not only in restaurants can eat well."

From time to time, grammar is a good diversion and Hiroko doesn't seem to be flustered by being flagged down, so he goes for it. "Not only in restaurants *can one*, or *can you*, eat well, you mean."

"You're not slurping well enough *udon* soup," she observes, making a serious, professorial face.

"Why?" He thinks he's quite skilled by now at using the sticks, thus this remark of hers comes out of nowhere to him.

"Because you're not noisy. Japanese men are noisy when slurping." She laughs at him, a sign that it's a made up concern, a repartee for his remark on her English grammar.

"Ah, that? *That*, I can improve right away," he jokes, "if that's what you want."

"No, please. You just fine." She shakes her head and smiles.

"Then you agree my eating of *udon* soup is just OK, or, on the contrary, shall we say, spectacular?"

"Yes, that was joke. And I give up."

"Oh, you shouldn't give up so easily, just after challenging me. That's not a good mental habit," he says.

"But I don't want quarrel with you."

"But you like ribbing me?"

"Ribbing?" She raises question marks with her eyebrows.

"To be sarcastic to someone, to tease, that's what it means."

By this time she has found the word in her dictionary in her handbag. "Ah, *wakarismashita*, I understand."

He's finished with the soup. "What have you ordered for the main dish?"

"Come, you already forgotten? Beef sukiyaki, of course. Your preferred dish." It was also the reason the waiter had moved them to a traditional Japanese room, with *tatami* and small tables for serving.

"Let's see that! I'm hungry," he proclaims, looking for the waiter with the air of a Kabuki dragon ready to eat everything offered to him.

"Let's forget food then, it's gonna be easier for you." she suggests. "Change subject. What is your favorite Japanese movie?"

"Good question!" he muses. "On life, *Ikiru.* On history, *Kagemusha*."

"Both Kurosawa?" Her black eyebrows unite above her nose in an effort at breaking through to his possible reasons, while the surprise is conveyed in their outside corners, lifted.

"Why not? What can I do if the old man is so good? How about yourself? What's your favorite movie made in the West?"

"You have two, I have two." She laughs. "*Lawrence of Arabia* and *Romeo and Juliet.*"

"Which *Romeo and Juliet*? Zefirelli's?"

"I think that's his name. Italian director, perhaps."

"It must be him, then."

"I liked music in it. In *Lawrence*, I liked the desert and Peter O'Toole's eyes," Hiroko explains, adding a shrug and a bright flicker of the eyes for the excuse perhaps required by the latter.

She moves her hand like a fan around her head, suggesting, he thinks, how much her mind was turned on and bowled over by it. Simon is aware by now that many times she likes to suggest dance motions with her hands whenever trying to find a reference, a comparison or a metaphor for something that doesn't have anything to do with dancing. *I might be doing the same with photography.*

The sukiyaki setup has been brought in and set on an adjacent table. He moves the small cooking burner in front of them, lights it under the pan and fills the latter with soy-sauce based soup. She then starts adding the vegetables and the marbled beef to the simmering whole. This is a live cooking show that both seem to enjoy, the pleasure in one's face mirrored. Glowing at each other, they take turns at flipping the beef until it changes color to a touch of brown, the signal it's done, then serve each other and themselves.

"There are worse things in life, I think, than this food," he says. He always finds this beef great tasting and wonders why. It's as though all that whitish fat marbling when raw softens it while cooking just right, to the lean and mean one likes. Perhaps the vegetables and the sauces play into it too. And the rice cleans the taste buds to freshness again and again.

"Worse?" A moment later, she gets it. "Ah, for sure," she says, palm in front of her mouth to hide the action of her mouth and part of her smile and laugh.

Matter of the local politeness. "Great rice, eh?" he asks. "Cooked just perfect, nothing watery to it."

"And look at it, so white," she answers. "This is a good place."

"If you approve of it, what can I say?" he says, adding after a pause, looking into her eyes, "I like being alone with you here in this room. No interference. Quiet."

She doesn't take away her sight, smiling back. "'Just the wind going through the screens.' A haiku, you know." She pours him sake from the vial and he reciprocates. He likes this custom — there's both respect and sharing to it.

"*Kampai!* Cheers!" they both say, clinking lightly the small, lacquered tumblers.

Just at the time she was taking her second sip, Simon sees her face jerk a forty-five degree to her right, her eyes bulging as in a blank scare, putting her right hand over her mouth as though to stop the awesome fright opening it.

"What happened?" he rushes his question.

She can't talk, she just points behind him with her left hand. He wheels, sitting, to his left, and sees from the corner of the eye the screen making up the room on that side sliding shut, followed by a quick succession of thuds as if someone were coming down some stairs.

Simon jumps up, slides open with both hands the screens on that side, but there's nothing or nobody in the hallway, so he runs to the staircase. A shade at the very bottom, one floor down, disappears into the dark. Seconds later, after a rush down jumping three stairs and more at a time, he's himself in the hallway on the bottom floor of the restaurant, looking into the courtyard facing that staircase, but there's no one out there and all is silent.

He comes back into their dining room on the second floor in a mad rush to calm Hiroko down. She looks with a pale face towards him coming back into the room, and he instantly realizes it might not have been a great thing on his part to have left her there alone.

"What did you see? Was there really someone out there?" he asks.

"A man, Kabuki mask, I think, but not sure."

"You mean, wearing a Kabuki mask here? How strange."

"Yes. This is why I was so scared. And on his hands white gloves."

"Sorry to have left the room for a moment." She shakes her head in understanding. Simon continues. "Couldn't catch up with whoever or whatever that was, but I saw a shadow moving out off the lower end of the staircase. Thus must have been something material, not a ghost, except if that was the shadow of a ghost," he jokes.

It's lucky they've practically eaten the beef sukiyaki, as there's clearly no appetite left in any of them.

"Do you think it could have been someone crazy just trying to peek at random people in a restaurant, perhaps to surprise them in compromising situations? A voyeur, I mean?" he asks.

She doesn't seem to know the word, but has understood. "No, I think someone who knows me. The mask had smile."

"What smile?"

"Like he knows me and wants to laugh at me."

"Like he knew me…" he starts from reflex, but stops. He doesn't want to sit on this unpleasant subject. "Let's just pay and leave. I'm glad we finished the sukiyaki before that happening."

She calls for the waiter, who comes after two minutes. Simon pays and asks Hiroko: "Can you ask her in Japanese if people in other rooms were disturbed by a visitor wearing a mask?"

Hiroko talks in Japanese to the young waitress, who seemingly isn't surprised by the question. "She says he passed and looked several rooms, on both floors. People complained. But first time, she says, man with mask."

"OK, let's just leave, then," he says.

First Night

In Hakone, they have not been staying at a ryokan, but at a four-story Western-style hotel close to Lake Ashi, with great views toward Mount Fuji, nothing too fancy though. "This way, you can rest better," she had told him when making the reservations. "I'm more used to both Japanese and Western-style beds than you, so . . . "

In the dim light of the evening, all along the way back to the hotel from that restaurant, they have talked about the strange apparition and Simon is not convinced he has been able to placate Hiroko about it. He also feels it's as though she senses or even knows more than she has told him by now, things she isn't quite comfortable mentioning to him.

She shuffles along beside him on her *getas*, and he likes to look while talking at the small steps of her feet, the small lifts in her hips under the kimono and the *obi*, the white neck and forearms, the frame tall and flexible, still powerful in its slimness, as he has learned from her dances.

"Perhaps he wasn't targeting us," he says. "As the waitress mentioned, he seems to have peeked in other rooms too, both on the first and on the second floor."

A sudden patch of light appears in front of them, as the screen of pine trees that accompanies them opens up for a moment to the moon. Her face seems calmer under it.

"You're right," she says. "But mouth under mask smiled as if glad to find me, as if knew me. Perhaps looked everywhere for me, for us." Notwithstanding her words, Simon likes it that at least she holds her head high, looking at him when trying to make a point, not watching the ground. Even though she's now, as always when dressed in kimono, in *getas*, those most unstable of shoes, as they lift her up from the ground, protecting the hem of the garment.

"Ah, you mean, he was glad to find *us* after all his search? Perhaps, that's always a possibility."

Her hand tries for his hand, while walking, and finds it. He's taken a bit by surprise. He likes the feeling of her skin, the confidence implied by the gesture, and after the bath at the *onsen* he expects things like that from her. But this time it also rings as a need for help, as if she's still truly scared. Yet he would take this mixture anytime.

At the hotel, they decide not to wait for the elevator, and climb the stairs instead, as their rooms are only on the second floor. He offers — in what is a first — his arm and feels hers stealing underneath his elbow and pressing on his forearm, bent now at the elbow for support. Whatever this thing at the restaurant might have been, he's grateful in some strange way.

The light along these passages is subdued, the walls are pale stucco interrupted on the hallways by the brown veneer of the room doors and the glint of the door handles. There are deep plush burgundy carpets all over the hallways and the stairs; he feels his own legs shuffling and slogging through them, in witness of a long day.

They've reached the space in front of her room's door, adjacent to his, and are facing each other, arms and hands separated by now, even more so in his awareness.

"Well, I guess I'll have to tell you good night," he says.

She looks up into his face and delays her reply, as though she has to explore his face with her eyes right here and now. There's an opening of the features in her face, a relaxation, and an intriguing, guilty-looking smile.

"Can I sleep in your room tonight? You know, with all this ... " she asks, making a gesture showing an awful mess in the air.

"Oh, sure." He hasn't expected this, and it must be on his face, but he keeps his emotion in check, opens the door, holds it open with one hand, enters to feel the light switch on the wall with the other, to turn the light on. But right at this time, there's a commotion. Without waiting for him to advance more into the entryway that continues past the bathroom door to the center of his room itself and to make space for her to comfortably step in, she rushes in with a tremendously worried look, wheels around and pushes the door shut behind her forcefully with two hands, virtually yanking it from his hand.

She turns an agitated face, closes in to him and murmurs into his ear “There’s someone watching us,” urging, immediately after, “Don’t open, please!”

“Out there in the corridor, you mean?” he asks in a low voice to her ear, then in an instant tiptoes to the door and bolts it as quietly as he can.

“Yes, there was a mirror,” she tells him when he’s back and leads her gently into the center of the room by her elbow. The room, luckily for their mood, is brightly lit from the ceiling lamp and from two wall lamps.

“A mirror?” He’s flabbergasted.

“Yes, I saw a mirror like this.” She shows her palm open to form a small mirror, as issued from her wrist or attached to it.

“Where was it?”

“At the corner.” He understands it was at the corner of the hallway behind her, where it turns by ninety degrees.

“But no face?”

“No, but I think he was, how to say that? … Spying.”

“Spying on us in the mirror?” he asks.

“Yes, this way,” and she shows again her palm and he figures someone watching along the corridor by facing that small mirror towards it and looking into its reflection. He gets it immediately.

“Are you sure you saw it?” *That couldn’t have been more than a flash, so short was the time she remained behind outside. Are we on firm ground here?*

“Yes, but please do not open to check,” she prays.

“OK, relax now, I won’t leave you.” He passes the fingers of his right hand over her forehead, just one pass from left to right. Something feels right to her, as she takes his hand and applies it again herself to her forehead, holding it there as if to help calm her down, to blot away worries.

“I’m sorry,” she tells him.

“What for?”

"For problems."

"But it's not your fault," he tries to reason.

"I'm not sure," she says and looks long into his eyes with a serious face. "Perhaps it's for me."

"What do you mean?" He stands back a half step, as though to have a better look at her, to reply to the concern in her eyes with a bit of calm and perspective. But it's also a half-instinctive response to the surprise contained in her words.

"My father, perhaps."

All of a sudden, he grasps her meaning, remembers the talk several months ago with Dr. Sugie, the not-so-hidden, still obscure, warning.

Underworld.

Could that be? He's not sure he should go on a limb on that assumption. Couldn't it just be that she's an oversensitive girl seeing something else trembling around her than the motions of reality? Still, a ghostly play of ninja warriors sneaking around settles itself in some hidden corners of his mind, and he knows it will take some doings of the very reality in order to remove it from there.

He needs a break from all this and a solid grounding: all this has been thinking in overdrive.

"OK, let's unpack for the time being, Hiroko, OK?" he says. He knows she likes his calling her name and hopes it has the effect of drawing her attention to something else.

They have been both out in Hakone with backpacks today. She looks back at him, seemingly welcoming the idea of changing tack. "OK."

The room is Western style, carpeted, relatively high bed.

"Please put all your stuff you need on the table. I'm going to put mine inside my travel bag and on a towel on the floor, all right?"

She nods and takes out from the backpack a cotton top and a pair of tights, both black. Perhaps for the sleep tonight, he thinks. She's still in one of her best kimono, which she put on this morning in preparation for the shooting.

She turns her back to him and murmurs, "Can you help me? The *obi*, please?" As usually here in Hakone, she needs his help with untying the *obi* knot at the back. They have been doing this in her room until tonight. At other times, at home or somewhere else, it's her mother or other dancers helping with it. There are funny small bustles or pillows, strings, small clamps and tie-ins involved, he knows. Still, her dancer's setup is much simpler than the one used with the kimono of an apprentice geisha, a *maiko.*

The skin of her neck is pale under the light in the room, still there are touches of the sun having caught up with it during the last days in several spots under the area where her lustrous black hair starts rising into a simplified rendition of a geisha hairdo at the back of the head. "I can't wear that hair style," she has told him, she would need to sleep on a *takamakura*. "I would do that only for a very traditional show, and I'd have to go to a hairdresser; it's not something that I could do or arrange by myself."

"Slowly does it. I'm getting to it; you should soon be free again," he says laughing, fumbling with the knot of the *obi* and the maze of strings, pins and catches around it. Thanks God, the material is not the heavy brocade used by geisha apprentices, nor is her *obi* quite of the same length. This means the knot doesn't rise really to the blades of her shoulders, nor is the *obi* as a whole so ponderous.

Having extracted, untied and unfastened, he's done with the knot itself. Now she turns in place, smiling, her arms extended up above her head, while he takes up in his hands the full length of the *obi* and gradually folds it in a temporary fashion.

Her kimono is draped straight down from her shoulders now, as a toga, freed from the strangulation, or is it embrace, of the *obi.*

Now free, she takes hold of one of the ends of the *obi*. He does the same with the other end; they go to two diagonally-opposed corners of the room, the *obi* extended between them, and she does the proper folding herself coming towards him.

After putting the packed *obi* on the table, she looks at him. "Could you? Your shower now, please?" He gets this is about needing some privacy to change herself from the kimono, the underrobe and the *hadajuban*. With no direct comment or reply, as though to avoid breaking something fragile and shameful, or perhaps not to trouble waters which seem to his liking, he takes his pajama from his travel bag and goes into the bathroom, which holds more or less just a standard standing-room-only shower and a toilet sink with a tall mirror above it.

All through his shower, he flashes back to their closeness in the water of the onset, on how her body revealed itself to him there, white and full and chiseled round everywhere in its slimness.

When he's back, she's in her top and her tights, sitting on her knees Japanese-style in *seiza* on the floor carpet.

"Come on, why didn't you sit on the bed?" he asks her. "It's not too clean down there. This is not a *tatami* room, you know."

"Oh, I know, but I too need a shower before that." She shrugs, smiling, and sneaks past him into the shower, a clean towel of his and a piece of soap in her hands.

"You sure you don't want to me to go over and bring you something from your room, a pajama or something?" he asks through the door of the shower.

"No, I just fine," her answer comes back.

When she returns, he's on the small two-seat sofa beside the table flipping through his films of the day, checking out he's not missing anything, that everything is clearly labeled and boxed in, but loses focus instantly, as she's again filling his space. It must be that full-bloodied oh-so-oval face, the eyes warm and bright under eyebrows now lifted in relaxation, the cheeks sharper in their tones of pink, also higher, or those breasts daringly pushing the top, the calves so intriguing in their elastic roundness under the tights.

Transfixed as by a sudden apparition, it's only now he is aware she has come out of the bathroom and, seemingly without hesitation, perhaps with full premeditation, has gone and lain herself down, materializing full length on her side on half of his bed, face sideways propped on her palm, arm raised at the elbow.

She taps the other half of the bed in front of her. "Come here, enough space."

"I'll sleep on this sofa," he says. "Enough space, perhaps, but enough danger too," he adds with a mischivious smile.

She laughs. "Me danger or you danger?"

"Ah, your English is sweet in its ambiguity. That could mean 'I'm the danger or you're the danger,' or 'I'm in danger and you're are in danger.' Which one did you have in mind?'

"I think both." She drums playfully the bed cover with her fingers.

"Ah, that's the critical mass danger. You put two things or people together and ... You know, like in the A-bomb," he says, makes a magician's gesture with the arms of something being blown up, and instantly regrets it. Japan is not the place where you can make this connection easily.

But she's another generation, as he is, so just a flash of a shadow passes over her face and she says, lively again just one moment later, "Ah, yes, big pooff." She shakes her head. "Perhaps something better, for us. Come here, you tired over there on sofa. We are friends, yes?" She taps again the cover on the bed.

"That's exactly what I mean," he says, but comes over and lies down on the other half of the bed, facing her, propping his head too. *Two odalisques facing each other.*

For a long time, they gaze into each other's eyes.

"What now?" he asks next, when coming up for air.

"For me, this," she says. Her left hand, the free one, goes up and reaches for his blond rebel hair, separates as vines and tendrils with her fingers some of his large curls out of the dense mass of it, slowly massages them, playing with them, releasing and retaking them under control, swinging them, brushing hairs against hairs, feeling them in their thick consistency.

"This is something I've wanted myself to do for a while," he says looking into her eyes, smiling, going for her hair now, but more carefully, what with her hairdo, so he just takes in his hand some of the free-hanging thin tresses above her forehead and at the back of her head and passes them slowly through his fingers. He traces with the same fingers the sides of her neck; she closes her eyes and moans barely audibly. He sits up in the bed, then, crouching, plunges down to one of her ankles, kissing hungrily and long a spot issuing so white from under the black tights.

Under his touch, her ankle shudders first, then shivers. Time oozes between them. She sits up in her turn, reaches to his bent back and caresses it and his neck with both hands now, then calls quietly, "Come here," and, when he sits up again, she embraces him, her hands holding his shoulders, hiding the side of her head in the crook of his neck, skin on skin. He responds hugging her back just above her midsection. Their bodies are now at an angle to each other; had they been asked about it, their spines would have called this an awkward stance under any other circumstances.

It's as though now neither of them wants to detach oneself from the other anymore. All the waiting, all the questions, all the doubts — they must have been worthwhile.

Kazuhiro escalates

"What took you so damn long?" This is the question Yukio Imashita is dealt right away by his boss.

Yukio shuffles double speed his large feet over the Persian carpet of his boss' room in the bunker and pulls up, breathing hard, in front of the huge desk. "Crowded on Aoyama-dori, boss. Couldn't move a whit. Bumper to bumper."

Traffic in Tokyo isn't what the boss knew when he had his scooter network. He could say that and risk his neck. Or just swallow it and wait for the water of anger to ebb out of the docks so his ship would be on dry and safe land. The latter — he'd go for the safe thing at any time with his boss.

"And where are we?" His boss cuts to the quick.

"The parties of interest have shared overnight sleeping quarters, boss. Last night only, that is."

"And? Cut to the chase, you idiot."

"Can't tell. Didn't go on the inside, boss. No go-ahead. "

"Certainly didn't give you any. This much I know, you don't have to open your talk trap to tell me that."

Then what is axed of me? Can't say this loud either. "The farthest I went was face them with a mask at a restaurant."

"What did you do that for?"

"Hoped it would scare them. They left pretty soon after that."

"And?"

"Perhaps it did." Yukio doesn't mention his seeing Hiroko looking back at his mirror, nor the fact that that restaurant visit of his might have lead to the first night together of the subjects. There is a limit on how much one can get in trouble with a boss such as Yuasa-san. Too much, and you may hang snug as a bug in a rug with meat hooks into your back, sweet prey to them flies.

"Boss, I thought I'd better ask. Strategy issue."

"Strategy, you dummer? Let's hear it."

The boss seems amused, still the thing hangs heavy in the balance, Yukio thinks.

"You know, boss, they might figure someone is on to them. And the worst is yet to come, boss."

"Spit it now."

"They might figure out who that someone acts for. No concern with that, boss?"

"Certainly that American punk wouldn't be able to get the picture by himself."

"But he's not alone, boss. Not alone in Japan. Meets people, talks to them. Can ask questions. Can receive answers. Then, there's the other party … " Yukio couldn't have been more careful in spelling this issue. No names, nothing. He thinks he was good to himself, really considerate of himself.

"Well, what about the other party?" Obviously to Yukio now, Kazuhiro accepts to play his little game of names.

"The other party might be in on the whole thing."

"How would that be, *usunoro*?"

"Personal history. Being already onto that kind of thing, that is. What has been cooking in their lives. The people who might be keen on catching up to the latest in their story can't be that many."

"So what? Let them get the dawn, let them get it through their thick heads. There are things to know and to do in this life, no matter the others know about you being up to those things, no matter they get it, it is you in that *udon* soup under their very eyes and no other.

"Don't you know that haiku about the moon and the people back here on earth?"

"No, boss, truly don't."

"Well, *kiremono*, is that the moon knows about us earthlings peeking into her ass with our scopes each and every night, but you know what, she still shows her naked bottom up there in the sky as though there's nothing going on; nor down here, nor nowhere else."

"This is rich, boss. It truly is. And to call that a haiku!" Yukio bows in respect, holding his ribs from made-up laughing.

A shadow passes over Kazuhiro's face, and Yukio knows better than to say anything until that is over. Chair now turned to the window, it is as if his boss is concocting something, and everybody around him knows it is bad thinking to interrupt his inner brainstorming. He never likes to involve others in his cooking, as he calls it. "Many ladles do not a bouillabaisse cook make."

After five minutes or so of this reflection, Kazuhiro wheels around in his chair and proclaims, "I'll tell you now what the new line is."

In the Lab

They are both at the Company, in the laboratory, knocking about ideas for the first series of prints for the exhibition. There's no one else around — it's a Saturday afternoon — and they like it. There's coffee on the flat square table in front of which both of them stand talking. Only artificial light — this is, in the end, a dark room.

"So, we should have the main prints for your seven seas ready soon," he tells Hiroko. She's wearing her hair in new chignon he doesn't recognize, pulled back from her face, making it even more oval by its absence, more pure. Her whole face seems larger this way and whiter, perhaps as there's less black of the hair to contrast upon, the skin more transparent in a touch of pink here and there.

"Sorry, roll slowly. Seven Seas. Explain. What is that?" she asks. Suddenly, she looks lost and uncomfortable, and that's only the beginning, so he thinks to himself he'd better do it properly right from the start.

He laughs impishly. "I've just dreamed up this scheme where the tableaux for the exhibition are divided in seven main scenes and I've called them your seas. You are navigating through them, or from one to another, in dance, dancing, sort of, like a captain in your grand ship. Don't like the comparison? I could've called them rooms, spaces, whatever." He looks into her black eyes, explaining. "Being that Japan is really an archipelago, this might fit, but it's really your call. Mind, it's something important: we might decide to use it, 'seas' I mean, in the title of the exhibition. It suggests slash forces a mental suggestion, a hint, in the mind of the prospective viewer."

She thinks about it for quite a while. "You know, we dancers mostly about earth, ground, not sea, water" she says cautiously, but then her face lights up, she does a pirouette in place, jumps up and throws her arms onto his neck, hugging him. "I cannot reject, too good, you are."

He likes the feeling of her firm, pointy breasts pushing into his chest. In a quick but felt motion, he caresses her spine in one long sweep with two of the fingers of his right hand, then breaks off pushing gently away, making a mock stern professorial face.

"Back to work, princess."

"OK, Professor Higgins."

"Oh, you know *that*."

"Of course. Audrey Hepburn huge star in Japan."

There was something Japanese about Audrey, no doubt. I mean, even photographically speaking. "I can believe you.

"I've thought these prints today are the ones supposedly introducing the visitor to each of the areas." He walks around her through the room, around the table, holding his chin in one hand, thinking and explaining aloud, peeking now and then at her, to see her reaction. "Like a headline would. I'd still call them main prints for the sake of our discussion, all right?" He likes what he sees in her eyes, there's glimmering understanding there.

And it is sharp. "No objection. How about different from each other? Say other color, or shade?"

"That's exactly what I was going to suggest. Let's have them done each with a different filter, perhaps something that would give the effect of mist, like a ship that is barely visible at the horizon, a Fata Morgana in the desert, or a girl just visible on the other side of a plaza, in which one becomes suddenly interested."

She is bucking up, laughing. "You talking girls, or talking theme now?"

"That's the glorious word I was missing in my messing around, Miss: theme. Yes, they would kind of establish a theme for that section of the expo."

"How about each section or series in a different color?"

She's clever. He likes ping-ponging back and forth ideas with her. "That's what we wanted to suggest just now, princess. A different background color and different main color for each section."

"How about unity?" She looks concerned.

He's flabbergasted for a moment. "Familiar with Aristotle too? Gosh, you're something, Miss." Flashes of his Columbia years through his head, libraries, professors. He sits on a chair for several seconds, stands, moves around the room, searching for a solution. *That's a damn serious good point for her to make.* The photographer in him swims back to the surface soon enough and grabs what looks like a saving straw.

"I know what we'll do for your darling unity."

"What, please?" she asks pushing her finger playfully to his forehead, curving it back onto itself.

"Yes, it just so happens that poor me has another idea. But don't push too hard, I'm going to serve it free to you," he says and smiles back at her. "How about using the same family of colors for the whole exhibition, say all hues or tints of red, or of orange, or red and orange, whatever. There would be a wider palette, of course, but I'm talking about the main colors, the ones giving the tone of a picture. Say I wake you up at five a.m. and ask you the color of that picture, you'd say, 'I think, perhaps or mostly, red'."

She admonishes him like an annoyed teacher, "But you had better not wake me up at hours like that, or no guarantees about what happens."

Yes, her English contractions aren't quite there. I'd have to tell her sentences look longer and fussier because of that.

***

She is at home with her mother, relishing their time alone together after lunch, in the dining cum kitchen room. "Family time," this is what all those brainy new-fangled relationship shows on TV call it. If she's at home, her mother knows Hiroko always plays the nice daughter and helps with washing, drying and stowing away the cutlery and the plates after each meal. Sincerely playing, that is. You won't catch Michiko doing that. "As if I had had them with two different men, or the water in Tokyo had changed at the time" their mother runs on to herself or to visiting neighbors. The dining room is traditional, with low serving tables, and sitting on the mats. At this time of the day, the yellow-brown horizontal blinds are flipped closed so the sun doesn't have a chance to get in to them except via the heat in the walls.

In a nonchalant voice, as this is the right time to add commentary to their daily kitchen routine, while cleaning up the table, her mother mentions, "Just in case you don't know it already: your father came over yesterday."

"What for?" Hiroko asks, putting on the none-too-interested-daughter facade. She knows that with their parents being who they are and with where they are in their relationship, an outward display of affection, or just plain interest, for the other one isn't too highly-regarded and can easily disrupt the balance as they see it, whether the other party be present or not. Truth is, this time she really wanted to know why father's Bentley had come around, with him in it at that.

"He tried to sell me on the rumor that one of our daughters is mixed-up with an American. Would you, by any chance, know that as being true?" Her mother's face is as deadpan as they make them as she rolls on. "And, should you know, would you tell your poor old mother about it? On the assumption that, if asked, said old mother would not tell said old father?"

"Nah," Hiroko says, laughing. "I think I'd let said parents to wallow in uncertainty: first, if that is true; second, about the particular daughter concerned."

"Your call," her mother said shaking her head and shrugging shoulders. "However, I shouldn't have to tell *you* that things said in this kitchen don't go flying out the window and either taken by the wind into the big world," her mother said, and Hiroko couldn't tell if Mother was happy about her cooperation or not. "Especially as," the continuation came and there was a tone of earnest warning in it, "there might be much less pleasant locations out there in the big world where said questions could arise, and where answers would have to be provided."

"Are we talking about Father's bunker, Mother?"

"Some such. You know I haven't been to all places to which you've been invited by your father. Not that there wasn't an invitation extended *to me too* to some of those places."

***

In fact, Hiroko knows for sure her mother would never go to the place in question, that it is, in fact, anathema to her. Furthermore, Hiroko doesn't want to remember her own visit: it had been done of all times during the *Saitansai*, the New Year's day ritual, or on the *Shunbun no Ohi*, or *Higan no Chu-Nichi* , on the day of the vernal echinox, and the intent, her father had said on those days, "was for them two to remember together the true heroes, those of yesteryear Japan, especially her grandpa, fallen during times of war fighting for his country, which was hopefully also the country of his nieces and nephews, notwithstanding," and the latter word had brought along with its heaviness both a shadow and an ecstatic light on her father's face, "notwithstanding the way, he, Grandfather, understood it hanging in the universe with, for and by the Gods."

What Hiroko also doesn't want to remember is the side catacomb to which he had taken her. It was an eerie and somber underground shrine, Shinto perhaps, but perhaps more of war and death and not having anything to do with any religion but with past history and its dusty noose around one's still shamefully alive and contemporary neck.

In the dusk underground light of emergency shelters lamps encased in metal grilles, row upon row of rust-colored pictures of Kamikaze pilots, with their bandannas pointed by the Rising Star emblem centered upon their foreheads, hung upon the rough gray concrete walls that were roughly white-plastered just here and there.

War flags, proudly carrying the centered *Hinomaru* with sunbeams, were affixed in full extension to the walls and, her father had told her, were all from real and true former fighting units. Flags found after painstaking search and purchased sometimes at large expense after difficult arrangements and negotiations with former commanders, their families or museums that kept them.

Also, in a corner niche setup as an alcove, there was this picture of her own grandfather, larger than anyone's around, framed in dark lacquered wood surrounded by black mourning bands, as those around the portrait of a recently passed-away person presented in a Shinto shrine for the family, friends and colleagues at work to come and say their sad farewells. Still, non-fluttering, hung the bands in the underground silence, so much so that she, scared out of her wits, had wanted out right away.

***

For now though, Hiroko leaves the kitchen. Five minutes later, she's out the house in apparent rush. Her mother's question will just have to wait. She needs to take in some fresh air.

***

Two days after the brainstorming session, on a Monday morning, Simon and Hiroko are supposed to meet in Mitaka at the laboratory to see the first life-size prints.

Just around eight a.m., he calls her at her home. As luck has it, she takes the call in the kitchen, her mother still sleeping.

"Hiroko, good morning. Sorry to call this early." Hiroko must have sensed trouble immediately, he thinks: his voice is heavy and rushed, he feels it himself.

"Good morning. No problem, I *like* to hear you." Still, her voice is so calming. However, he needs to break this mood.

"Unfortunately, something very bad has happened."

"Are you OK? Please tell me quicker! What is it?" Her voice is suddenly very hot.

"I am fine. But there's something which definitely isn't all right. And it touches on both of us. Reason I'm calling. Overnight, the whole set of prints I processed yesterday in the lab, letting them to dry hanging, has disappeared. No trace of them. No trace of forced entry either. I haven't reported the thing yet to the security here. Also missing: all the original negatives I made with your dancing in Hanoke. I had placed them on some shelves in the lab."

At his end of the line, it's as though she delays her answer. She must have a tough time taking all of this in. Then she says quickly, "My copy. How about it?"

"Yes, I've immediately thought about using the duplicates I made for you. Question is: do you still have them?"

"Let me see." Her voice sounds worried, the same tone and vibrations, to him, as on the night of the intrusion of that masked face at the restaurant.

She comes back three minutes later, breathing hard on the phone from probably having climbed and descended the stairs to the first floor of her mother's house.

"Yes, I have them with me here."

"Oh, we got lucky." He makes a break in speaking, to calm down and to let her recover. "Let's meet as soon as you can. I need them in order to make two other copies: one for the laboratory, to be able to go on with the work, and another for the bank."

"Which *bank*?" They have never discussed money matters among them, thus he understands this word coming as a surprise for her.

"Mine. I'll open a safety deposit box to store another copy there. Too many things seem to happen in Japan: fires, earthquakes, break ins. We'd better be prepared."

"You sure California is different than Japan?"

He feels some irritation in her reply, and there is a twinge in himself that any just semi-patriotic American might have reacted the same to a similarly over-reaching comment about the States.

"OK, I apologize for my stupid remark. Let's just meet and do what I've just suggested. When can you make it?"

"Ten a.m. in Mitaka station would be fine with me."

"OK. The platform of your incoming train. I'll wait there. I can make it, for sure. Being in Mitaka, I mean." He laughs lightly, hoping this breaks this ill spell, not just of happenings but also of a thin line of discord between them. Their nerves seem to have become frazzled just a little bit.

Meeting at Mitaka Station

After a quick walk from the Company, Simon has arrived fifteen minutes before the train is expected to come at the Mitaka Station. He's hyper, and being aware of it doesn't make it any easier, still he forces himself to stop from walking around on the waiting platform. He doesn't like to draw attention to himself by moving around; being a Caucasian, thus in such a minority, is reason enough for being observed, at least from the corner of the eye, in this place. Also, the Japanese don't seem to be doing it too much, this aimless walking; they prefer, it seems, a stance of resigned waiting in place, with a stoic face on — why make everybody around you antsy when you are so? To him, this is just a sign of civilization. Further, we wants to put a calm face on for Hiroko; he doesn't want to scare her too much. The latest goings on are tough enough; peppering them with the wrong behavior would not help them overcome whatever this might show up to be in the end.

Autumn is here. Some of the trees just across the station are changing color, leaves agitated by the small day breeze of a sunny, clear day.

Somewhere at the middle of the train, he sees Hiroko descend among the first passengers from her car. It looks like she might have been stationed close to the door, impatient to meet him and to have the latest news. She's in gray tight pants that leave the ankles free and a gray-white wind jacket, a blue small stewardess cap smartily at an angle on her head, an umbrella and a plastic bag in her right hand, looking keenly from the distance for his face and his eyes as for something that would help her in this crowd of people. When seeing him, she rushes up with small steps, but stops right in front of him for them to greet each other.

"Ohayoo gozaimasu, Hiroko."

"Ohayoo gozaimasu."

Both of them bow lightly. Tradition's too strong to do otherwise in Japan; he respects this anyway. There's that glimmer in their eyes of seeing each other again.

They share a light friendly hug, nothing more than that in public yet. What with the reserved Japan, he doesn't feel like pushing things for a kiss in public, even though he's looking forward to a change in the nature of things sometime soon.

"Do you have them?" he asks, trying to calm down his voice.

"Yes, of course," she says, on a much lower tone.

"Let's go to the park nearby to talk and make the transfer. Too many people in this place. That OK with you?" Simon realizes his voice has issued this time lower, as by itself.

"Let's do it," she answers.

They turn toward the exit from the station and start walking. He finds her hand at her side and takes it in his; she gives in reply a quick short press with her fingers to his palm, smiling up at him, at a time mysterious and quizzical. *She might be not that scared in the end. She might be of a tougher stuff than I've imagined her. Lucky me.* They stroll along the Tamagawa Josui canal to the Inokashira Park for a quarter of an hour, and walking in step with each other and swinging their arms together would seem to an outside viewer the most vivid concerns they presently share.

The day is bright enough, thus she might regret taking her umbrella, but that is never too much of a precaution in Tokyo. The sun, screened in spots by a lacy curtain of thin whitish clouds, beams at times more and more vertical flashes that, coming with suddenness and reflected by the waterworks, dazzle them, flashes that make them giggle, and at times even laugh with no apparent reason to each other, when closing or sighting away their eyes to duck them. The air is fresh and today there aren't too many people in the streets yet, not at this morning hour when many people are toiling away at work.

Even at this autumnal moment, the park is still dominantly green. Green the cypresses, green the grass; still, drying up here and there as though losing water.

Barely past the entrance gate, Hiroko pulls her hand away from his and springs off into a madcap, childish sprint along the alley, veering soon to the wide expanse of grass to their right, crying back at him, laughing:

"Catch me if you can!"

He's still in part prisoner to the surprise of her rushing away and to his concerns about the recent happenings, but it takes him only a short moment to break away from them and he starts running with short then with gradually longer strides after her. She takes avoiding action, ducks under his attempts at catching her, looks back, giggling and breathing hard, veers in a half-circle, but is finally caught under a old tree at a side of the grass meadow. For several minutes, they just stand, hugging each other tight.

Just before they separate from their embrace, she asks him murmuring, "You know why I've run, yes?"

He takes a double take at her. "You won't tell me all that was premeditated?"

"Tried to see *them*. Running and running in circles. Easier when running, you know."

He takes another look at her, then puts both his hands over her shoulders, holding her at arm's length, scrutinizing into her eyes, a wide, crooked smile opening all over his face. "Forcing them out in the open to catch up with us? Whoever you are, young lady, you never told me this Hiroko is so clever. We don't need any Agatha Christie here no more, ma'am," he says. She has a short laugh and shrugs.

There's a cracked wooden bench nearby and they take refuge to it. The sun has already made it quite warm.

"All right," he says, "first things first. May I have your copies?" He makes a serious face saying this, and sounds to himself like a doctor in a psycho ward when he continues, "We need to bring back some normalcy to all this."

She rummages into her plastic bag and feels there ten small black film cartridges with gray caps, but before getting to the stage of taking them out, he places his hand over hers and stops her movement. He talks with his other hand over his mouth. It's as though he's thought better of something.

"Wait a moment, please. Let's not show them out in the open. You never know, there might be a telelens around out there in some distant bushes. They might be even be able to pick up on our lips — words, conversation. That's why my hand's at my mouth. If you don't have anything else in that bag, just put it between us and I'll pick it all up when leaving. If they're there, perhaps they didn't notice who brought it in."

She moves her hand slowly as in a trance and drops the bag where he wants it.

"So, not showing film, yes?" she asks discreetly under her breath.

"Yes. We shouldn't give them any ideas we have more copies. No free lunches for them," he murmurs, sneering at those unknown foes. "They might figure it out by themselves, but that's something else."

"By the way," she asks, "did you have any troubles at work because of this?"

"No. I've already informed my boss and security and it has been decided that until this exhibition is over, I'll have access to other rooms, kept secret except for my boss and a selected few. They'll also go looking for better electronic locks and will install hidden cameras in the areas where I work at this project." He isn't telling her that in fact his entire photo lab is to be moved today into such a secret room, one that doesn't show up in any map of the company even. This is something that Dr. Sugie extracted from him as a promise not to tell anyone. Dr. Sugie told him that the company doesn't want to get into anything open with those who might be behind this, just strongly deny them access and interference.

Having put this aside, it's as though the hard part of the day has been shifted away beyond the horizon, and they may turn now to themselves.

"Ah, so I am not to show how I feel about you in those places, if I come again." She puckers her mouth in discontent.

"You know, this is a perfect place for something like this. You're more than welcome, in fact," he smiles, curving his arm around her shoulders.

Carefully and with shy gentleness, she places her palm, her fingers over his lips, then moves them around his face, velvet-like feeling its contours and caressing at the same time, finally resting them on his chest, on one of his pectorals, which she feels contentedly through his thin woolen pullover.

Then she comments with a slight sarcasm on his latest, “Don’t you know it! This is correct English, right?”

“And how fit to the moment! Course it is. Just tell me, is it about this being the perfect place or about your being more than welcome to, you know, to …” he wickedly smiles.

She doesn’t go on that, just adding, casually, “I dreamed about you the whole night, and when I woke up I continued to think about you,” in a tone of fake complaint.

“Then I am exactly where I want to be, reaching where I hope to get,” he laughs.

“I have to believe you.” Her hand takes off and rambles over his chest, then settles back where it had been.

“Why do you *have to*?”

“I think because I cannot know what is in your mind.”

“Do you think I’m lying?” His eyebrows are very high, but his smile says they are not yet on very dangerous territory.

“Not at all, but I am not you, I am me.”

“So, you trust me, but perhaps you can’t believe me, because my mind is not your mind?”

“Something like that, but also words, they may be not exact,” she says.

“You’re saying that I might use not the most exact words to tell my feelings about my reality and my dreams?”

“Perhaps. But also psycho, so subjective, isn’t it?” she asks. “Words exact perhaps, but how to get what soul really feels? ”

“It’s *the psyche*. Only then would we be able to express it correctly, is that what you mean?” he says.

“I think so, I never went to university; you did.” She laughs. “When I dance, I think perhaps I show more than I can in words … about my soul.”

“*Articulate*, there’s a good English verb for putting things in words. Yes, they talked of layers, in the courses I took at Columbia. Layers in the personality, layers in the speech. I don’t know too much about it myself. Certainly didn’t major in psychology, but in Visual Arts and Photography.” He wants to break this path in the conversation, to return to the original, good, warm source. “But I like you dreamed about me. I think a lot about you, too, even though I don't dream too much." Now that he says that, he realizes he hasn't dreamed at all in the last months. However, he doesn't want to say it; it might show him in a bad, dull light. And with Hiroko he feels romantic — dreams or no dreams. It's part of the good thing she does to him, that she has been doing from the very beginning. Like that pillar in Harajuku. He himself can't quite believe having done all that, having the pillar designed and manufactured, standing on it, exposing himself — God forbid, not in *that* sense — that's language to you — to so many people, in a foreign country, in Japan of all places.

He looks at her and tries to unriddle a question that has floated in his mind for quite a while: What color are her eyes exactly? They are of a dark brown going to black, perhaps with the dense black hair crowning her head, yet from this close the white in them turns misty-blue at times, depending on the sunlight playing reflections on the objects nearby. Not to forget though: looking at you in anger or excitement, they are liable to turn violet — or so he thinks.

What he has longed to do for quite a while he does now: passing his fingers up and down through her long hair, which today is released low from its usual chignon, simple or complicated, of other days, in its full unadorned blackness going down close to her lower ribs. He holds his fingers in a soft, gentle comb and she responds to his movement with more pointed pressure on her fingers, still finding themselves on his chest and with her eyes mirroring his and, as he sees it, changing colors.

Breaking the silence, she's asking now, "What are we going to do now, Simon?" She has turned her face fully towards him, and he knows the sweet silence of moments just passed is gone for now like the toll of a bell and he needs to face it. There are very fine wrinkles now on her forehead between her eyebrows, making her nose seem a bit thinner. Her cheeks have nigh suddenly lost a bit of their relaxation and of that pretty central dimpleness.

"Continue to live normally, that's what. I'll make copies of those films, put one of them at the bank, go on with preparing the exposition. Let's just take these as 'difficulties of life' that hit on everybody, not just us."

She listens patiently to his waxing philosophical, and her face seems to lose a bit of its tension, but just after several moments she comes up with a continuation. “Yes, but why us?” she wonders and he can’t say her question is off-base, but he sees no point in bruising her ego now even more, asking questions on her family. *Let time solve some of them by just flowing with us in it.*

“Asking about destiny is a sure recipe for messing ourselves up. Let’s just duck as much as we can those parts of it that we see coming in time. Broken ice coming down over the river, that’s what they are.” He’s of course heard somewhere, be it chess or football, that the best defense is offense, but in this case the obscurity and ghostliness of it all doesn’t help him for now to think of any clear-cut way of grappling with it. Just avoidance. He’s glad that none of them has gone ballistic at any time yet, where there might have been plenty of occasions for it.

She doesn’t let him brood for too long, standing up from the bench, catching his hand and pulling him up.

“Let’s walk a bit in the grass. Perhaps last time this year. Autumn’s here,” she says with a permeating sadness. She takes off her white shoes and carries them in a hand, the other hand in his. No cotton socks nor pantyhose on her today, thus, pink-white, the skin emerges indiscretely and openly above the low pumps to where the pants start, mat, but crossed by blue-purple veins. The pants are quite tight, helping his eyes, hungry to watch in motion the round contours of her hips and of her compact bottom, the tight knees swinging, the round ankles and calves in elastic step, gliding along and bouncing.

The tableaux; Shinjuku Gyoen I

"Tomorrow afternoon, five o'clock. All seven are there." Sent via a fly-by-night courier, a boy from his neighborhood, this message told her to come over to the Company in Mitaka to review the seven main prints with Simon.

Initially, Hiroko thought to put on a kimono, a modest one though, nothing flashy, flickers in her mind of better immersion in the mood, the purity of it, then decided against it; the feeling of strangeness and clashing with the place: modern company, old dress. The distance in looking at herself brought on by something more businesslike might be just the thing.

In the end, she has settled for a simple skirt extending itself to the knees, pumps on medium heels and a wind-jacket over the whitest long-sleeved silk blouse among those that she owned, with a small, flattish flounce on the chest starting right under the neck. It has no collar, ending right under and around the neck. This, she thinks, makes the neck seem longer, an advantage when one thinks that people always seem to like to buy long-stemmed flowers, reasons unknown.

Simon comes quickly to the gate when her arrival when the porter calls him on her behalf. She likes to look at him walking at a distance: the long strides, the joints so flexible — knees, hips, ankles — the hair blowing around him, the feel of energy he injects in his surroundings by his very presence. Even though at times he seems lost in dreaming, she knows there's something ticking strongly in him, an undercurrent of hidden brainstorming. He seems so alive when he comes up with ideas. And she likes the way his eyes brighten up when seeing her for the first time on the day. Every time.

Once inside the new, secret laboratory, he apologizes. "Sorry for the lack of windows. We chose one of the inner rooms for this temporary role, in order to minimize any chance of interference from the outside."

The seven large panels for her coming exposition hung half a meter above them on two of the long wall. All in black and white for the time being, and as tall as she is, they are, in the intended sequence: "The Kimono," "The Maiko," "The Older Geisha," "The Fan," "The Umbrella," "The Feet" and "The Rain." They chose the names on her previous visit at the lab. To compensate for the lack of natural lighting in this room, tall pillar lamps are positioned in the center of the room and small point lamps hung just above each panel.

In "The Kimono," she is coming to the audience wearing a very rich kimono of an apprentice geisha with nothing in the hands, except for the huge hanging sleeves rolled on the forearms in the manner of maiko. The face serious, the afternoon sun at her back, it's as though she's coming from a large door in the sky to face us in this world of ours.

Hiroko touches it lightly. "But this is very rough, this surface!"

"Don't worry," Simon tells her, "people won't touch them in the exhibition, they are only going to look at them, and that's the only thing that's going to count in their impressions. I used a high-granularity paper just this once, since I didn't have anything better for the black-and-white version. Also, I wanted to see what the effect of such a paper would be. I think that for the final version, in color, we'll be using an average grain, which is much finer in the end, as well a glossier paper."

She looks around to all of them slowly, then closes in to each in turn. It's as though a revelation grows inside her, the more she goes around, and it appears in a flushing of her face and neck. It's the first time that she sees herself portrayed in such a large size, and the effect is astonishing, as though another sister of hers, but not Michiko, would dance out there, someone wild and serious at the same time.

"Am I so serious?"

"A lot of it might be the black and white, and its psychological effect. Still, yes, you are serious at times, and I like it," he tells her touching her forearm, to calm her. "But look at 'The Rain,' you're not serious there, or not only serious."

In that panel, she dances under sheets of rain, her hands defending her head, her face, feet splashing left and right in a pool of water — the *geta* long lost — fighting back the rain hopelessly. Still, with definitely no gain against the elements, her face is opening in a huge devilish-child smile showing the mouth open, the tongue out to a side, as though in tasting the river coming down from the sky in a mad play.

"I think I like that most, but all look amazing. Thank you very much, Simon. You've made me look much better than I really am." She goes to him and gives him a deep bow, to which he, equally touched, issues an awkward reply in kind. She then gives him a huge friendly hug, throwing her arms around his shoulders that seem to her so wide for her arms, gently pressing her hands on his back. Not forgetting where she is, she doesn't feel comfortable with externalizing anything else right now, still her face is very warm with emotion, her eyes filmed.

He comes close and tells her in a low voice at the ear, "We are in the bank right now," and she understands enough copies have been made to be on the safe, or safer, side.

***

"It would be nice to see each other this Saturday," she had told him, looking up at him, with a special glimmer in her eyes, while walking along Omotesando Dori. At the time, he had ceased walking, letting her go on ahead until she stopped too after five or seven steps, all the while looking at her from under his mane of blond curls with a certain sudden hunger and fixity in magnified eyes. Everything counterpointed by his toothy, relaxed smile that was enough to make her comfortable and safe at any time. There was in some shadowed background the symbol of the male on the prowl that she had started to recognize in her teens, now however tinged inside her in something that made her be dry in the mouth and hungry.

Together in the Shinjuku Gyoen, walking arm in arm, and it is Saturday afternoon; the sky is devoid of clouds and the air of significant breeze. There are many people come to see the park on this day.

Just five minutes into their stroll, Hiroko is called out to in Japanese by a young man passing, "Hiroko-san! We haven't seen you in quite a while!"

A young couple, a tall, thin man in his early twenties and a bubbly woman of Hiroko's age, both Japanese, he in a jeans jacket and pants, she in a frumpy, but lively colored knee-length skirt and a black long-sleeved blouse, come up to them, and bows and introductions are exchanged all around. Hiroko keeps her hand in Simon's all the way through. The man seems a bit flabbergasted by Simon being present at the side of Hiroko, sweeps his sight several times from one to the other, but doesn't seem to be able to get himself to put forward any clarifying questions. He might well consider them indelicate, Hiroko considers quietly.

He just asks, "You American?" and the question seems directed to both Simon and Hiroko, the way his face is oriented, as if he feels uncomfortable talking only to Simon.

"Yes, I'm from New York City," says Simon.

Hiroko rushes in to add, "He's a professional photographer."

The girl has badly formed front teeth, but her face is all smiles and the eyes curious.

"Ah," she says, speaking a quite fluent English, and looking more open and friendlier than her partner, "Toshiaki here is also fond of photography, but he's an engineer. Perhaps you two can get together to talk about it."

"Yes, sure," Simon replies, friendly but non-committal, the way Hiroko feels it.

The Japanese guy says, "Let's see when we have time." "I'm very busy," he adds, a bit gruff now. "You still at the same number, Hiroko?"

"Yes."

"Then, when I have some time, I will call you."

Hiroko pulls Simon's hand imperceptibly for the others, enough to signal him a bit of impatience, and says, "Yes, of course."

There's half a minute of stopped conversation and then all decide to take their good byes.

Simon asks, with obvious piqued curiosity, "Could you tell me what happened just now, what was in the air? The guy seemed quite uncomfortable."

Hiroko looks away for a moment, as if searching back in time, then looks straight at him.

"He's my former boyfriend's best friend. We haven't seen each other, I mean Toshiaki and me, in one year."

"Your *former* boyfriend?" He seems perplexed, as confronted with something or with someone he has never considered of the equation, or surprised by his own surprise at having neglected things.

"Yes, he's in America now, for studies. We decided to separate before he left. Toshiaki doesn't seem to know that," she says.

"And?"

"Well," she says, and she feels she looks concerned and frazzled, "we've stayed separated. No contact since then."

"So, Toshiaki's attitude was him somehow defending your former boyfriend's territory?"

"Perhaps that's too much. Perhaps just surprise."

"At what?"

"That I have a *gaijin* friend now. Not too common here, though more common in Tokyo than in the countryside, of course."

He looks at her; a deep look, as though truth is being fathomed. Then, as though satisfied by his findings, he relaxes, tightens his grip over her hand and says, "Let's go on walking. This is a nice day, isn't it?"

Finding their way among the throngs of people around them, many of them couples, families with small children in baby strollers, looking at the flowers — purple azaleas, chrysanthemums, tuberous begonias — through to the Japanese traditional garden part of the park, they are both silent for several minutes. She feels she has to do something about it, this moment where everything among them seems in suspense: she's afraid now of losing it all like dust sliding through one's fingers. Still, she feels terrific in this place, with the nature so beautifully showing around them in Himalayan cedars, tulip trees, cypresses, large expanses of grass, beds of flowers, the bushes, beautiful ponds among them, the pavilions with tile roofs with pointing ends, *shibi*, on their ridgepoles, small bridges, the sky — so benevolent and clear today.

She pulls gently on his hand and draws him to a halt. "You know, special program for the garden today: open until six-thirty."

"Yes, and?" Simon asks for a logical continuation, it seems.

"How about staying until the stars are on? I'd like us to look at them together from this place."

He considers the idea, a devilish smile showing up on his face. "You know this isn't quite kosher?"

"Kosher?"

"I mean it isn't quite OK. Certainly forbidden by the rules and regulations of the park, established no doubt by the Imperial Household itself. Enforced, perhaps, by night-time wardens." He continues mockingly, "Am I right in detecting a decidedly un-Japanese streak to your character?"

"Now you're talking like my father," she says with a small pout, and a shadow passes over her face.

"OK, sorry, I take that back," he says, and seems truly regretful about the remark, or about upsetting her. After two minutes, he seems to have run that by once more time. "Let's go for it, if you think it worthwhile. I mean viewing the sky from here at this time of the year. Granted, it's a great day, visibility might be very good for the night too. Point is, first, we would need to hide somewhere — I'm pretty sure they're urging everybody out toward the closing hour. Second, we'd have to jump over the closure when leaving. I mean," he says laughing, "I doubt you really want us to stay the whole night here."

"That long? Too much, indeed. We would get bored," she says with an impish smile. "But we could hide behind that pavilion over there, it has large trees and shadow behind it," she says, pointing towards one of the tea pavilions.

"Ah, fast eyes, young lady, fast eyes. Well, let's peek inside and behind it and see how much cover the trees and the building itself provide and what are the dangerous angles from which we could be glommed if getting in there," he says. "Also, after closing time, they might have guardians checking up on all nooks and crannies — that is all small places. So, we'll need to observe very carefully what is going on around us at that time, be very vigilant."

"Also, let's have another look at the height of the closure," she says, "let's see if we need something to climb it."

"Let's, then," he laughs, and they go through a serious perusal of the local configuration, watching out for each other while they go behind that building for a quick look in, at the end of which the exploit seems more feasible than initially thought. Also, gardening ladders in another corner seem just the thing they might need to scale the metallic fence with no complications. Considering some of the last trains and subways are scheduled around midnight, they agree that leaving the place by eleven o'clock would be highly recommended.

As the closing time nears, most of the visitor populace exits by itself. The stragglers are pushed out by persistent staff checking some of the places but not the hideout of Simon and Hiroko. Things are simpler than expected for the time being. However, just twenty minutes later, another wave of personnel, these clad in all-orange overalls, comes in for a cleanup of the place, and these, armed with pointed sticks and large vacuum-cleaner machines for the alleys and large mowers for the grass, take a tight look at the surroundings and work pieces of them. So tight is this sweep, that Simon and Hiroko have to sneak, skip and run around the hiding place, from behind a tree or bush to behind another one, lest they be seen, but really no one goes in the back of that pavilion tonight. All is to the good at the end. Blessed hiding place have they found.

It's already eight at night, Shinjuku Gyoen in blue, then violet, then in black darkness and in deepening silence. There's only the distant buzz and hum of the great city around, and even that barely penetrates a space where only they are now.

"Let's go to the pond," Hiroko urges.

"Where? You mean, to stand in the open? It might still be risky," he comments.

"No, inside the bushes close to the water. See there?"

"OK." Hand in hand, with the longest strides they manage while still on tiptoe, there they go and sit down. Surrounded by bushes towering beside them, still leaving the sky wide free to the view, they let themselves on their backs on the grass, one beside the other. The sky is the only lighted space around them, the moon — a large mat-white disk shadowed by spots tonight — low and silent in a corner, the stars twinkling infinite distances in beautiful coldness.

Hiroko squirms in place, as under the strain of something trying to get through to the surface of said things, finally turning toward him, lying on her side. "I'm happy I'm here with you," she says, stressing one moment later, "*Very* happy." She shudders saying it, and a flush, undetected in the dark, comes powerful as a warm tide from her chest to her neck to her face, in sweet shame.

He's still on his back, but turns toward her slowly as if considering the whole situation, then suddenly, decidedly forward, places his freer hand on her hip, and swinging back in one quick motion, a motion wanted gentle and managing to feel so, brings her on top of him.

He places his hands on her back and presses down in one long, extended, yearning motion, as though hurting to feel one with her. Still a prisoner of his hold, her breasts burning, feeling as if ready to explode with inner and outer pressure, and longing against his chest felt through garments, she raises her hands toward his head, and ruffles his hair with her fingers, recognizing to herself it has been a long-held desire — this. Then, right at the time he weakens his hold, she wriggles upward on top of him until they are level, face to face. It is dark, but the light from the stars and the moon makes it a transparent, iridescent dark, and they travel the whole imensity of it to see the contours of each other's faces, the burning eyes.

Just one moment into this contemplation, their mouths hungrily become each other and enter a kiss that dulls and sweeps away the ache of long months of searching and waiting for the other, of uncertainty, and that wall of darkness around them does away with anything else except for the vegetal, tannined breeze of the grass, trees, bushes and flowers, except for the glimmer of the lake nearby, in deep, autumnal, resigned silence.

They roll sideways on top of each other, hugging and clasping each other, in that exhilaration that so naturally issues from togetherness, back and forth they roll in the grass, until they tire in doing it and laugh in the ears of the other, in heavy breathing, gasping and even hiccuping with emotion.

As though there were a proscription of words in the world they've just stepped into, they don't say anything for now, as if the physicality of it all should cross easier over than their languages.

Several long minutes later, they've separated from their embrace and lie extended on their backs, just looking at the sky, one hand into the other's closest.

"We're like open to the sky now, no?" she asks, whispering.

He thinks for a moment. "You mean, in frontal exposure to space?" He laughs at his own terms.

She nods, then, unsure if he has been able to see her gesture, she says, "Yes."

"We are as open as a huge radar antenna could be, as large as an radio-astronomer's," he starts to free verse, his head levitating full of the matter of the simple poetry of the moment, then continues his recitation, inviting, "We are. Space! We're here! Ready to communicate; if anyone's out there … Roger us!"

She smiles. She knows he can't see it now, but she does. "Do you think they see us together? I hope so," she says.

"There's no doubt about that," he says, pressing her palm with his fingers. "Not a single slim sliver of doubt about seeing us as a single, unique dot somewhere this side of the mirror."

Shinjuku Gyoen II

"Do you know anything about the stars, Simon?" Hiroko asks him, while they are still on their backs with the sky in their sights.

From the tone of the question, in this darkness, he isn't able to tell if she knows a lot about the matter. *Am I doing so badly? Anyway, no reason to boast.*

"Astronomy was never my strong suit. You may as well add to that sciences in general," he says. "I don't know much more than Orion, the Evening and Morning Star, and the Great Bear, and don't count on me for showing them to you," he answers, and chuckles. "I know Neil Armstrong was the first man on the moon, but don't ask me much more about that subject either."

Through the darkness, he thinks he sees her shaking her head a bit. She gently takes his hand and points it towards the sky. "Do you see the Great Bear there now?" she asks, guiding his hand to draw the contour of the constellation in the air.

Now that she is pointing it out to him, he's able to recognize the milky-white contour of points once seen, he thinks, in long-forgotten storybooks that his mother might have stored away back home for future generations of Frasers at the time of his entering the university.

"How about a short walk through Shinjuku Gyoen at night?" she asks. It's already past ten, there's absolutely no sound nor sight of any other humans in the park at this time against the organic silence, against the organic darkness.

"If this is an offer, Miss, I'll take you up on it," he says, chortles good-humoredly, and shows a bow with a hand. "And, yes, if that's what you mean, I agree the risk of being seen or apprehended is pretty negligible at this hour," he chuckles.

The night is clear and in it the silhouettes of the trees are clearly traced in black silver against the diffuse light coming from the sky, even though they can't distinguish branches, leaves, colors.

She picks two pink chrysanthemums from a bed of flowers and places one of them into her buttonhole and the other into his.

"Now the police are bound to know where we're coming from!" he whispers with a low guffaw.

"Knock on wood. I think this is how you say it in English, isn't it?" she asks.

"Right on. And let me find the wood straight away; that shouldn't be a problem in Shinjuku Gyoen," he says, cackling. He taps lightly on the trunk of a huge tree nearby — he thinks, from the labels read during the day, a Himalayan cedar.

She looks a bit worried, but right then she closes to him, rises on her toes, puckers her lips and asks in a small, childish voice, which he hasn't heard yet from her, "Kiss?"

So she was just anxious for a kiss? Difficult to read, the ladies.

He bends down to her, only too happy to oblige, and this is a long, hot kiss, hands walking hungrily over their backs, to grasp the other and feel each other's sensual incarnations longing to be felt, to feel each other's heat.

Then, he places his right hand around her shoulders as for protection, she looks up at him in what he takes for gratitude expressed, and, still following the corridors of shadow accompanying the trees, they step out again into the open from their hiding. The ponds glimmer to one side, under drying water lilies of an autumn; they walk towards the large, empty meadow of the English Garden that creates a huge void in the darkness, then toward the long double rows of the spare, tall plane trees of the French Formal Garden cutting black with strangely-formed branches into the dark, violet sky lucent with the light put out by the moon as a discrete background reflector.

"Aren't you cold, Hiroko?" he asks, caressing her hair, freed now from the chignon, let to fall on her shoulders and down the back. It feels so dense, firm and silky, her hair.

She likes him to call her by her name. She likes him to play with her hair too. She likes to see him occupied, preoccupied as well, with minutiae of her life. She likes that feeling of a small island lapped by the great sea — this is just the haiku she had in mind last night. She told him all of this two days ago, he remembers it now.

When he wakes up from this short bout of half-dreaming, she answers his question, "No, I am not cold, Simon. How about yourself?"

"Don't you already know I can't possibly be cold while you're in my immediate vicinity?" he whispers with a low giggle. "Still, it might be a good idea to get the last subway. It's ten-thirty already."

"Do you remember where the ladders were?"

"I think so. Let's go over there."

Weaving their way through the park, trying to stay in shadow most of the time, they reach the storage shed. He knows even this transparent, pale moonlight could be enough to show them to an eventual vigilant night watchman.

Only the ladders aren't any more in the place they saw them hours ago. For one moment, they look open-mouthed to each other. Part of the shed is now locked, which it wasn't before, and the door doesn't move when pushed.

After two minutes of careful inspection and rummaging around the place, Simon says, "We'll have to scale the fence, there aren't two ways about it, if we don't want to remain here for the night. And I don't think we want."

"No, it's already too cold. Autumn," Hiroko says.

"All right, then. Let's find a part of the fence that is less exposed to the light from the outside, and perhaps lower, or easier for one reason or another to climb or cross."

What they are facing is a typical chain-link fence, supported by thin metal pillars fixed in the concrete base, with no spikes at the top, still over two and a half meters high.

"Look, the holes are quite large," she says. "Perhaps we can climb, with no shoes, just in socks or barefooted."

"Yes, but woe to our toes after that."

"Well, once in a lifetime," she says, shrugging and smiling.

"OK, you'll have to use me as a ladder first. Then, I push you higher. Once at the top of the fence, you'll have to jump down.

Make sure you soften your landing, so you don't break anything of your porcelain riches," he chuckles, but looking concerned.

"I know how to do that, I did a bit of karate and judo," she says, tapping on his arm to reassure him.

"There you are then! The martial arts practitioner! Now seriously, leave your jacket and the shoulder bag here, I'll throw them to you when you're over. We need to avoid your catching on something with all this wire. You'll have to step on my thigh first, then climb on to my shoulders," he says.

"How about yourself?" She looks worried at him.

"Shouldn't be any problem to climb over it, I think. Worst case, you lose me here for the night," he shrugs, a bit uneasily though. He hopes he's still in good shape. At Columbia, this would've have been a cinch with his condition then.

"OK, let's go," he says, decisively. There's no point in waiting.

"Fine, I'm ready," she says.

She's a tough girl. He turns to face the fence, puts his hands on it and crouches a bit.

"OK," he gives the signal. "Start climbing, keeping your hands on the fence for support at all times. I'll try to remain stable as much as I can."

Her face more set that he remembers to have ever seen it, she scrambles in two quick moves from his thigh to his shoulders.

"You stable there?" he asks.

"Yes, Simon, I'm ready."

"Careful now, I'm lifting." He rises from the crouch to full standing extension. "Now, I'm going to put my hands on my shoulders, a new platform for you. You'll need to step on them, so I'll be able to push you up." She steps onto his palms facing up.

"Ready again? I'll push. You try to pull yourself up as much as you can over the top of the fence, then jump down carefully."

He's lucky she isn't too heavy, he thinks. However, she isn't any small Japanese lady either, so his arms strain a lot pushing her up, but her arms do a good pulling to help his action. She's now on top of the fence.

"Now, look down carefully to see the ground and jump when've got the faith baby. Sorry, I mean when you're confident."

"Well, not too confident here, but I go … now!" she says and jumps down. Everything seems to have been OK, but her ankles are a bit sore, it seems, as she massages them with her hands.

"Are you fine, Hiroko?" he asks, not seeing her too well from inside the park.

"Nothing broken, I think. Please send my stuff," she says.

He throws her jacket, shoes and shoulder bag over the fence.

Suddenly, she whispers with trepidation in her voice, "There's someone coming!"

He hides behind a bush, looking out through its branches. A couple passes by on the pedestrian walk, throwing a wide-eyed look at Hiroko, who's alone and stepping into her shoes in the most natural of manners, then moves away from the space until they disappear from sight at the closest road cross. Then, she runs back and looks around.

"Simon! Come! Now!" she whispers.

He shows up from his hiding, comes to the fence and sends over it his wind-jacket and his shoes.

"Got them?" he asks.

"Of course. Come!"

"I need to do this slowly, but not too slowly, if I don't want to cut my toes in this wire," he says.

He starts his own clambering now, hands pulling, then toes and legs pushing, then hands again. Somewhere in the middle, a toe slips, then his hands give, and he finds himself on the same side of the fence, crumpled on the ground.

"Wow, this was one rough go," he says and touches himself over knees and hips, as if to see they're whole.

"Are you fine? Can you do it?"

"I certainly have to, or otherwise I'll need to stay until tomorrow here," he says and smiles crookedly to her, shrugging.

He hedges his bets with more care on the second attempt so as not to advance any of the four limbs until full support of the other three is in place, secure. He's up now on the fence with his upper body; one final swing brings his legs over and he's a cat landing.

"Well, wasn't too bad, but my feet and toes are zinged, oh, God!" he says, breathing heavily. Quickly, he slips into his shoes and his jacket.

Hiroko has been watching the area around them the whole time. She rushes with small steps over and kisses him on his cheek.

"You know, I was really afraid something strange might happen to us there. This is why I didn't want to stay," she acknowledges only now.

"Well, let's go toward the subway to head out for the barn as fast as we can, and we'll talk later," he says, though looking inquiringly at her as to what she really means. "By the way, I'll take you home first, OK?" he says.

She looks at him for a moment, then says haltingly, looking at him a bit sideways, "Simon, may I come to your place tonight? Late already — for you to go to two places … lots of time. But not only that. I'd like to be with you this whole weekend." Then she adds, as an excuse, "I don't know your place. I'm curious, you know."

She seems to be hanging upon his lips for his answer, still, she doesn't seem to want to give that away. To him, her face at this very moment is being as unreadable as she can probably make it. *Women, never liking to be left out on a limb. Is that it?*

He tries to breeze in as cool as possible as well. "But of course, and this is a very good idea too," he says. However, she presses the palm of her hand, and then she passes a sneaky, ashamed smile to him from a side. *Hey, we just might be talking about the same riff. You're not kidding, man.*

At his home

She feels his hands around her, and she wouldn't want anything else. It is close to two a.m., Sunday morning, at his place, the indoor light dim, the moonlight and the light of the stars flickering pale-silvery through the partly curtained window, bringing in suspended greenblack particles of the shadows intimate to the bamboo garden at the back. In that, their night hasn't changed from Shinjuku Gyoen to this crammed Tokyo flat, but how much less of an opening to this night, to the sky, there is here. However, they don't need nor want it. They are too tired, too overwhelmed by the impressions of the past day and evening, and all they want now is to turn to each other. They have had their separate showers in the narrow standing-room-only bathroom. Both of them are wearing differently colored pajama sets of his, he a dark green one, she a gray one, greatly oversized, rolled up on her hands and ankles: she has not taken anything with her for the night.

She is crouched-cocooned in the low bed, knees at her mouth, on her side. He envelops her, his long arms covering her arms and shoulders, he too lying on a side, at her back. She likes this oozing comfort of human Matryoshka dolls, warm shells wrapping warm shells. In the darkness, she feels at times the blond long hairs on his forearms and his shins touch her skin. Tickling, minuscule electric discharges that make her shudder.

"Are you sleepy?" she murmurs.

"With you here and in my arms? Are you joking?"

"We could also sleep in this position!"

"Not exactly what I have in mind at this time," he whispers into her ear.

"*What*?" she giggles.

"Well, that would first entail undressing."

"Entail?"

"Sorry to have been so idiot to use that word. It's 'require,' 'demands.'" He continues, "Have you ever been naked with a man?"

She finds herself surprised he has never asked this particular question until now, exactly at the time when she realizes this question is probably secondary to the one that must be burning in his mind at this time.

"Never this way. Only at an *onsen*, in water, you know, with other people, as in Hakone."

"And … you never went further than that?" he presses with a hesitation the second question.

Men are men everywhere, she thinks. They automatically go for this button, whether they be good or bad.

She weighs his latest question for several long moments, and comes on the side of the truth. First, because he is Simon. Second, because she doesn't like lying about things like this. Third, because there's really nothing to be lying about.

"No, we stopped. Neither of us knew too much. I was seventeen then. People around in the water, at *onsen* … " She isn't sure if this wouldn't cast her as a dummy or a prig in his eyes. She really hasn't known too much about American boys. Not until this particular one.

"Seventeen? That means last year."

"Yes, that's when it happened."

"Thanks for telling me. Just wanted to know how comfortable are you with the idea … " he says.

"Of being naked? Hm, I have to think," she says and she rolls to her other side, all the way through still in his arms, in the bed, to face him now in the velvet darkness. "With you and for you ... " she says, instinctly sensing this time it would be her hot-burning face that made the continuation for him now that her lips, searching for his, too busy in their quest, wouldn't.

Her face, her nose, are met by his scorching hot breath and the strange, tempting scent that comes from the locks of his long hair, which for unknown reasons seems to smell like burning incense. Through this tantalizingly marked space of darkness her head moves in closer to his, and they fall and lose themselves into a deep, searching kiss, whereby mouth opens and closes on mouth, teeth gently bite on lips, tongues probe and soft and wet push each other.

Under their kiss, she feels and hears his hands shaking and fumbling with the buttons of her pajama shirt, opening it, then she catches herself lifting by her own arms over her head to help it pass and free her from it. His palms and mouth then descend, caressing her breasts in repeated and broken spirals, which she discovers pushing forward in response and yearning.

She finds herself in imitation, removing his pajama shirt. She is flooded, rushed, by the touch of his skin — its smoothness, the touch of his muscles — their tautness, in his back and of his spine, as her hands travel over his back and pull him tight towards her, both still on their sides, facing each other, now in full-length, extended contact.

He then raises himself on his knees and goes backward on them in the low bed, and the wide pajama pants are being pulled down from her gradually and smoothly, with no rush, as she curves and lifts herself, and wriggles herself out of them to help. Then she hears a similar sound but nothing slides over her skin, and she knows these are his pajama pants being taken off. In the dark, there's a shadow being thrown away from the bed.

Michiko visits

This is a Sunday and Michiko Yuasa has decided to drop by their mother's. She has this eerie feeling that things have recently cropped up there that might require her being up-to-date. How long could it be, three weeks perhaps, since she crashed the place? It seems so. And it seems droll, but she hasn't recently been able to get hold of Hiroko, her sister, over the telephone. To add to that, inquiries to their mother are met with what can't be but dead air or evasive disquisitions on today's young generation. Once such addled, lookie-lou concerns are put to rest in one way or another, there are hours enough left in the day to make a good thing of a visit to dear old Mitsukoshi in Nihonbashi after that.

She knows full well, Michiko does, that such visits in Nihonbashi and Ginza are accomplished in the best of moods when her bank account has been recently buttressed by her father. In related matters: there was this call from him just three days ago asking for updates on her sister's general well-being.

"You know, Michiko-chan, I can't really ask your mother such questions," he growled. She bet a double shot of whiskey was being served at this time in his underground headquarters.

"But, father, me either, I don't get any replies to them when I'm calling Mother. I really have to go over and be face to face with her to get anything out of her."

"Then, please do, please do. There's no point in my getting addled here about what your dear sister does or intends to do in her life. I'd rather someone waved a red flag at me before it happens."

"Winds are such now, that my going over doesn't guarantee having a lock on getting anything from Mother. Sometimes, she's not up on the latest herself. These days, Hiroko-chan goes in strange ways about life — to say nothing about dancing and fashion." Here

Michiko could hear their father snarling and buzzing with agreement.

It's now time to leave for the hour-long train and subway journey, and she calls right before that. Better not to give too much notice.

"Mother! I thought this should make a great day to come over and see you and Hiroko-chan."

"Hiroko, Michiko?" Her mother hesitates for several moments, then continues, "I'm not sure whether Hiroko-chan will be here by the time you arrive."

"But where's she going? I wanted us two to go to Mitsukoshi in the afternoon." Michiko fully knows such intentions have never existed — not on her side, that's for sure — but blabbing the elders away is always a good way of edging them at least a bit on your side, and one never knows when that could be of splendid use.

"I don't know, dear." A hesitation, a break, and just one moment later, her mother came back on the line. "Well, I think I've just heard her leaving now. Guess she didn't want to bother me."

"Well, I'll come out just as well." She'd better inspect the premises just in case. Something — a genuine article — for father might be in order again, just like that photograph of that American, or whoever he is, young man, that had been so appreciated. That might just cool her father down — or perhaps not. But matter over mind, as the philosophers said; she will have something pulling for her there. Better than nothing.

One hour later, she's in that area of Ueno where Makoto Asaye had lived for over twenty years. Her mother never really wanted to reside, or for that matter spend time, in Asakusa, where their father would have preferred to stay in those years back then when they were together. Too much *mizu shobai* around.

Today, Michiko is dressed in a splendid autumn-yellow kimono, with a light-silvery-gray *obi*, for when going to Mitsukoshi one never knows when one meets some older gentlemen, and many of them would go most of the time, if the choice were theirs, for a traditional woman. Mind, one should leave them this illusion that the choice was theirs. For rhyming with it, her handbag is made from the same silk brocade as the *obi*. Her lips are highly alluring in their rich hot-red rouge.

Michiko walks in a fussy manner, with very small steps, in her *geta*, through the small vegetable garden, collecting three splendid tomatoes and placing them in her shopping bag. One can't rely any more on those supermarkets for true vitamins these days. She enters the kitchen, goes straight to the fridge and picks up a *Sapporo* beer can. Good to have at night. Then she turns to her mother, there in a corner, and bows, not too deeply, as there's no point here in overdoing it, they know each other so well, don't they?

"Good morning, Mother. And how are we today?"

"Good morning, Michiko-chan. I'm fine. As I've told you, Hiroko-chan has just left."

Something in the tone of this doesn't hit right with Michiko, so she says, "I'm going upstairs. Hiroko-chan might have left something for me in her room, a message, perhaps. And she promised me a book too. It might be there."

Her mother's face doesn't change expression, but her ears seem to have just grown redder, a sure sign of embarrassment with her. She just nods, barely.

Michiko has left her *geta* right at the entrance of the house, thus it's in her *tabi* that she rushes up the stairs and enters her sister's *tatami*-style bedroom. The whole bedding set is there, laid out on the *tatami*, prepared for the night, ready for the body to tuck itself in. She turns a corner of the coverlet over, looks at the sheet: clean, flat, starched, fresh, virginal, most probably undisturbed by anyone during the night. Also, her sister doesn't suffer to leave the bedding on the *tatami* during the day, she stows it away as soon as she's standing on her feet. Michiko has an inkling and looks around for a confirmation. And there it is on the wall: the calendar still shows Saturday, and this is already Sunday. Hiroko is so darn picky-picky about time, she always turns calendar pages first thing in the morning. *She hasn't slept here. Couldn't have.*

Michiko doesn't need anything more material than that. Still, she picks up one of the several volumes of the huge English-language edition of "Shogun," left on a corner of the low table, and goes back down into the kitchen. She shows off the book, just in case. "Found the book, Mother. Now, if you'll excuse me, I have to go. Lots of shopping still to do."

"Won't you at least stay for lunch, Michiko-chan?"

"I'm too rushed today, Mother." *And I don't want to be served any more lies.*

The book finds its rightful place in a garbage can, right at the entrance in the Ueno station. Michiko will never ever want to read such long, boring — and, to boot, American — stuff.

***

Having arrived at Mitsukoshi, just before having another look at the magnificent statue of *Magokoro*, the goddess of sincerity, carved out of a five-hundred-year-old *Hinoki* Japanese cypress, she decides to call her father, from a pay phone outside the store, with some news. It's difficult to get to him on a Sunday, but this time he's working overtime at the headquarters, it seems. "Perhaps," Michiko rights herself, "a nice dame or two are around for rejuvenating company. Massage and some such."

"Hello, Father. Nice to find you there."

"Hello, Michiko-chan. What can I do for you on this Sunday?"

"Oh, nothing really, Father. I'm in Nihonbashi. Just wanted to tell you I've passed the old place. Talked a bit to Mother, then I left."

"How about Hiroko? Wasn't she around? I can't believe you didn't talk to her. You sisters are keeping too much distance between you two, as though you have a beef with each other."

"Oh, father, you know how things are! We're both busy." She pauses in reflection, then she continues, "But somehow I have the feeling she didn't sleep at home last night. Even though Mother seemed to be of another opinion. But you know how Mother is sometimes in such situations, weaving a cocoon around sweet, sensitive Hiroko. It's as though she were a kid forever."

"All right, all right. Let's snag the details. Is Hiroko in Tokyo or, again, she's left for Hakone or I don't know for where?" Kazuhiro Yuasa asks.

"She seems to be around. It's just that she didn't sleep at home last night. With friends somewhere, I guess." She decided to leave it at that. From the rumbling, huffing and puffing on the line, Michiko can just imagine what is going on at the other end, her father mad as a hornet already, walking in the room with the telephone in his hands. There is no need of extra fuel.

"OK, thanks for having this conversation with me," her father says. She knows he never likes to name the crime. "I hope you'll enjoy your shopping today in Nihonbashi and Ginza. By the way, your account will get some loving attention these days." The latter part, he has been able to tell her in a smooth, cool voice. She knows and fears this instant control he is able to deliver at will, as if throwing huge blocks of ice over fire.

"Thank you for your care, Father. It's been a pleasure talking and doing business again with you, as you can imagine," she says, making sure there is no trace of sarcasm in her voice.

***

She is now in the department of Horlogerie of Mitsukoshi. Funny to see the French name, perhaps related to the glory of the Swiss clocks made for Napoleon, present in these whereabouts from time to time in replicas worth tens of thousands of dollars using no doubt just as much gold as the originals sold in auctions at Sotheby's in London or here in Tokyo.

These are large clocks, some of them real towers as tall as a grown person, when one counts the base cast in marble or in expensive, rare wood, clocks which are encasing their precious mechanisms in gold-, silver- or platinum-plated structures shown through crystal windows as clear as a haiku.

The formally dressed clerks know her by sight, and bow and nod to her, acknowledging her oh-so-discreetly. Her favorite departments are this and the one of modern furniture, where she is a frequent visitor. She likes them for putting forth two precious commodities in Japan: time and space. Time, because, to her, time so luxuriously displayed seems to slow down its crowded incarnation normally clinging to the locals. Space, because one really needs an unusually large home or apartment in order to accommodate such voluminous pieces of furniture, resonating more with a Western home, than with one found in this Asian metropolis, as modern as it wants to seem to be and really is. Thus they must be well-established.

It is here she met Yukio Nakashima, a gentleman in his fifties and a lover of fine luxuries, one year ago. Their tryst had taken them to several *rabu hoteru.* These days, however, Michiko looks for something more. Perhaps a separate apartment somewhere around Tokyo or the surrounding areas within reasonable distance, perhaps a monthly attention or gift of substance, perhaps being favorably mentioned in a will. Yes, more like a home run is what she wants these days.

Kazuhiro in his car shop

On his back under his Bentley in his garage, in one of his underground residences, this one a huge, gray-painted cave in Shinjuku, Kazuhiro Yuasa went on sucker-punching Yukio Imashita, who, though he didn't share his boss' mechanical hobby, had to share the position and stay put, in order to avoid the escalation. At least here, underneath the car, the limitation of space was telling in the smaller swing his boss was able to take in any of his swipes at him.

"She is with him. That's the only thing you can tell me. What did you do the whole afternoon and evening yesterday in Shinjuku Gyoen? Bet on dog races?"

Ducking another blow, Yukio managed to say, "No, boss. I was able … I was able, boss, to take the ladder from where it was, close to the shed where they were, and hide it somewhere else."

"So what, did that stop them from disappearing from the park?"

"No, boss. Honest to God, I've no idea how they managed to do it. That's a high fence."

"Honesty and you. Hark! That! By using their noggins, that's how they did it, you fuddle-head. I'm not paying you not to know. For that, a slug would be enough." This came with a mean dig in the ribs from a wrench, followed by a kick with a heavy-duty boot toe into the side of the shin. "And hold that flange straight and up, for heaven's sake! I need to screw it back, and I can't do anything with you dithering like this. Girlie-man! You're all girlie-men! What a puke, this harvest of mankind."

Kazuhiro wriggled out from under the car, mumbling, "We need a hydraulic lift here," then dusted his overalls off. Imashita scrambled to do the same. However, having not anticipated his boss' move, he was bound to be late. No overalls for him. His suit had taken a beating and Yuasa looked disapprovingly at him.

"Worse than a garbage man, that's how you look. Mind, you ask all the time for a pay raise. What for? Making a bad name for me? That?"

Yukio didn't reply. He seemed to know he couldn't win at this game; that'd be messing up his current situation even more. Waiting at attention so that his boss's anger would peter off, Yukio's hands were lined down as though along some trouser stripes, and he was frozen. What would follow? Anything could follow, if his history with his boss was any guidance.

In dumb silence, he helped Kazuhiro Yuasa take off his overalls and slip back into his navy-blue suit, left on a chair in the corner of the garage.

"A glass of water!" his boss demanded. He gulped it down quickly, then made his way in a rush to the metallic door leading to his office at his location. Yukio followed him down the long corridor, lighted by bulbs protected in wire-mesh, on a par with Armaggedon-type fixtures left from the times after the war when this place was the property of the Japanese Self-Defense Forces, a refuge against the Bomb among many spread around Tokyo.

Plopped into his high-backed armchair, Kazuhiro Yuasa was thinking hard.

"We must strike at the very pipeline through which all this yackety-yack goes on, all this huddling," he finally said.

"Pipeline, boss?"

"Communications, idiot! We must strike at this *gaijin's* telephone, but good, so that the damn guys from NTT won't be able to fix it quick."

"Will do, boss." Yukio Imashita had in mind 'pipeline,' and a plan. Next Monday, in the morning, yet late enough to guarantee that Simon had left home, he went over, in a Nippon Telegraph and Telephone repairman uniform, and found the duct through which the phone connection to the house was brought in. Then he took out a pair of scissors mounted at the end of a meter-long pole and remotely activated by a wire. He inserted the contraption down the pipeline, fumbled around, pulled hard on the wire and cut the connection at about half a meter from the opening of the duct. *Good enough to mess up the NTT guys for at least a week.*

***

I could let the whole thing build up as if nothing were going on, Kazuhiro thought. In due time, I'd be served with nephews who wouldn't go to no Shinto shrine, for which all my collections of artifacts would be nothing but the tails of a sick mind (that is, mine). Even worse, I'd be left with just a daughter when Hiroko decided she had enough of cherry blossoms and Japan and took off with hubby to efficient Amerika, taking said nephews with her. Now, efficient Amerika I don't need in my business, not now that MacArthur and his grace that sickened me is long gone. I can easily suck in my smokes and dopes through my pipelines from Thailand or Vietnam, worse case Afghanistan. Nor do I need now the Russians. Nineteen oh-five was good enough to take care of the bloody Russians; why did we have to change history after that?

***

In a disquieting wind, the field of chrysanthemums fluttered wide and white in front of him. In this dream that lately came and came back to Kazuhiro, as though his mind was playing an ugly trick on him, he would go to the center of that field, there would be no clear, exposed sun, and the sky would suspend itself above the world, all flushed in light gray clouds as if cobwebbed, the only light really coming up from those flowers. He would stay there, dressed in his most formal kimono, waiting for hours for the sun to appear. But that would not happen, the wind would not become less troubling either, the chrysanthemums would still remain submissive to it and would in wide swipes be ravaged by it. He would stay for hours out there. He would come back with despair in his soul and the next day would be for him like walking with naked soles over shark teeth thrown upon the ground. His people, aware of it, would avoid him from afar.

***

Then, where would he be, Kazuhiro rhetorically inquired, if all of Tokyo, underground and above ground, would cull through the grapevine that his own daughter is in cahoots with an American, who, listen to this, photographs her? Photographs her! Then the next question would be, does he photograph her with any clothes still on? Coz we've all heard about that magazine *Playboy*, coz we all know who has brought the smut into this country. Not that he's not himself making a huge killing from it. But when this kind of question would be asked, everyone and his mother would assume he treats his own daughter just the way he treats the girls in his many bars and funny places. In Japan, family is Family. That would be the end of him: not being able to lean on his own family. He might just as well hire Mitsuko and Hiroko as hostesses. The worst thing is that no one except Makoto knows that these two girls would rather kill him first before agreeing to work for him in any shape and form, even as office clerks. Michiko for laziness', Hiroko for pride's sake. So he would not go out on a limb on that. However, this doesn't mean he shouldn't be in the driver's seat in all dealings with them, and with Makoto too.

Not having to deal with Americans had been his main why and wherefore for getting rid of his whole setup in Roppongi: too many Americans or *gaijin* in general over there, each and every night, in each place over there, bar, disco, in the whole *mizu-shobai.* Divesting of undesirable assets — that was what it had been, the moniker put on it by his shysters.

The bosses of the other families in Tokyo had thought Kazuhiro had become crazier than a bedbug to sell off such property. But he wanted it for his own peace of mind. And now *this*? He sure wouldn't have all his marbles if he didn't do something about it.

No phone

Hiroko had left his place on Monday morning. Their parting had been hot, distressing and sweet, as though neither of them wanted to say their goodbyes, not even for several hours.

Trying to speak to her upon returning from the Company, around seven p.m., Simon discovered his phone line was dead. He slammed the receiver down — this wasn't the surprise he needed right then, right before fixing dinner for himself, and being as he was quite bushed by the long day. Then, mumbling to himself for being forced to put on his jacket and his shoes again, he at once went to a pay phone nearby, for he had important news. Glad it was Hiroko who replied, not her mother, he knew he wanted to get as soon as possible to the very matter, even while having the feeling of somehow barging in with the rush of words brought forth by his feeling constricted in the booth and by other people milling about, seemingly waiting on him to finish.

"I'm calling from a public phone. My line is down," he said.

"That's too bad. Have you called NTT to fix it?" she asked.

"No, and this, in fact, is only the second of my issues. Now, could you please call them, I mean NTT, tomorrow morning, on my behalf? My Japanese isn't good enough to go past the initial questions of the customer service rep."

"They may want you to be at home when the technician comes," she said.

"Right on. Could you ask them to come Wednesday morning, after eight am? I'll be waiting for them. If not Wednesday, then Thursday. If not again, Friday, same time, and so on, until you get a firm appointment for them to come over. Then, please call me at the Company to tell me about it. Sorry to involve you in this." They usually avoided using the Company lines for private matters, for he had been indoctrinated on it at his starting with the Company. This, he thought, was a justified exception.

"No problem, I'll do that. But what was the first of your *issues*?" She stressed the word with a jingle of a laugh in her voice, and this made him happy it hadn't been too difficult a word for her English, as well that, as shown by her sarcasm about it, she was aware of its formality. She was steadily improving.

"The first, for a change, was good news — an announcement I wanted to make to you. Some of my pictures with Shugaku-in might make it to the National Museum here in Tokyo, for a personal exhibition, under my name, this coming January. Nothing big in terms of size: one or two halls should be enough for their selection."

"But this is great news!" she said. "The National Museum is big deal here in Japan for anything linked to tradition or history."

"Well, they seem to have liked my new perspective on the imperial villas. Two professors from Waseda, one in history, the other in multimedia, called to congratulate me on it. And do you know the *really* big news?" He could see on the faces of the people waiting outside that this had been a long call, but he decided to go on.

"More big news?" She laughed.

"We might be invited to exhibit the pictures of your dancing in either one of the imperial villas or at the National Museum. There is some ongoing pow-wowing — sorry, discussions — between my boss and the guys at those places. Nothing official yet though. They, I mean the Company, must decide first what face they want to put on their interest in your work. OK, I need to leave now. I'm hungry. Sorry. By the way, should you want to talk to me or see me in the coming days, you may have to come over. As you see, phoning isn't one of the options anymore."

"This isn't so bad: I mean, being forced to see you frequently." She giggled.

"OK, I really need to hang up now," he said with a huff only half-faked, "or I may be killed by the people waiting outside this booth. Bye."

She laughed. "Take good care of yourself, then. Bye."

***

"It can't be that. That's too remote to even consider," Simon was telling her. "It can't be your father who's behind all this."

"I've been thinking about these troubles for three weeks and it's the only possibility I was able to have," Hiroko said.

"You mean, the only possibility you were able *to come up with.*" He danced his finger in the air along the stressed words.

"Yes, thanks for the correction," she smiled, shrugging. *Sorry, can't do any better for the time being. English is so tough.* She didn't want to openly complain, she'd rather work at it silently.

They had barely sat for tea and cakes in this pastel-painted Shibuya pastry shop when she told him, "You know, the repairman from the NTT called me at home to talk about your line."

Still carrying a smile on his face, he did a double take at her. "You don't tell me! What was it about?"

"He said he didn't want to call you, as this was impossible to him to put in English."

"This I can believe." Simon smiled. "He wasn't a talker, and even when he was, he was mumbling mainly to himself in Japanese. And perhaps just as well, it took him over two hours to fix it."

"Yes, but to me he mentioned right from the start it seemed to be a strange and delicate matter, *henna mono.*"

"You got me here. Why would that be? A phone line is a phone line, no ifs, buts and maybes." His face was long in surprise and his smile had worn off.

"Well, the line had been definitely cut off."

"You mean, physically cut?" he asked, flabbergasted.

"Yes, half a meter inside the pipe bringing it into the house from one of the street — how do you call them? — pillars. There were sharp edges as of specialized scissors, he said."

"But who could have come with such specialized tools to damage my line? And what for?" Simon asked, his face all amazement.

"He didn't say, but he seemed truly concerned about your safety, Simon. He said that from his experience sometimes very strange things happen after someone's phone line is cut off."

"What do you mean?"

"Sometimes, the house is broken."

"You mean, the house is broken *into*?"

"Indeed, thanks. Or they are attacked by some enemies. Rivals," Hiroko said, searching for words.

"Rivals? What rivals? No one really knows me here in Tokyo, or in the whole of Japan, for that matter!"

"Yes, but *I* may have. And we've been seen together for a while," she said.

"Rivals? You? You're … you're such a good person." He still looked flabbergasted, but she saw on his face that tide of concentration coming up that she had seen first while watching him work in the photo laboratory or doing a tricky move with the Frisbee. "Someone from dancing? Competition, you mean?"

"I thought about it," she said, "but I don't think so."

"Why not?"

"Because they would have — how do you say that? — they would have given me a hard time directly, not to you. Also, the people in dancing who know me don't know too much about you," Hiroko continued her thinking out loud.

"I get your point here. That seems true: I haven't met too many of your fellow dancers. Perhaps I should; in fact, many of them should be great looking girls too." He laughed, trying to strike a lighter note.

But Hiroko didn't want their focus to waver. "I thought, since that appearance in the restaurant in Hakone, on our last day there."

"You mean to say *I've been doing some real thinking*. Use the progressive, as this seems to have taken quite a while, thus a continuous verb is better," he intoned didactically, then refocusing, "Well, should you see any connected points out there in this maze, or whatever we call it, let us hear about it. Coz, honestly, I don't."

She let several heavy moments pass, then added, "I think I had an idea about it, and I think I've told you about it," and she moved uncomfortably in her chair, close to squirming.

He frowned, in an effort to remember, then did a double take at her, and this time he looked really amazed. "You mean, your father? You cannot be serious!"

She said, with a sad smile, "Well, I know John McEnroe says *You cannot be serious!*, but I'm very serious here." Hiroko saw his face instantly following her words with deep, clouding concern in his eyes.

He passed his fingers through his rebel hair, so brightly and temptingly lustrous to her on that day that she wanted to pass her fingers through it every other minute, from the back of the head to the forehead and the crest of the head and around. "But you can't mean your own father is your rival or enemy? What kind of man would act against his own daughter? That happens very rarely in the real life I know. Not that it doesn't, but it sounds like a bad story in some rag — I mean newspaper."

"Well, perhaps I was not right about the word. Not rival or enemy. Just someone who thinks evil at times. Can you give me a better English word for it?" she asked.

"Not necessarily. Even a rival or an enemy can have better or worse days for his hate. And that hate, as you, the target of it, sees it, might be exactly the very thinking and acting of evil that you've just mentioned. However, let's not split words. *Acts* have been committed that we feel uncomfortable about. So let's talk just about the strange facts of our situation as plainly as we can."

"Well, let's do that," she agreed.

"So, where did it all start? Was it at that restaurant serving beef sukiyaki in Hakone?"

"Yes, and on the same night at the hotel there, do you remember?" she asked.

"Yes, I remember you mentioning something about someone in the hallway peeking at us through a mirror. Then, I think it was the problem at my lab, when I asked for your copies of the film to make others. Right, right, and when I opened that deposit box at the bank, to protect one set of copies."

"Was there something else?" she asked.

He sat looking at her, thinking, then suddenly continued, "Well, now that you asked, I've had the strange feeling once or twice lately that someone threw a strange, perhaps even sarcastic, regard in my direction, only to be followed moments later by my tripping. I once remember such a strange occurrence in Shinjuku, at Isetan, when I was really close to falling to the ground. But I've never considered these as part of a string of events, not until this talk. I remember these, for very rarely someone notices me in Japan, and especially makes visual contact with me."

"Well, we're too busy," she said.

"And polite," he said and smiled, and put his hands atop her right hand, on the table.

"If you say so." Embarrassed, she smiled back at him, and shrugged.

"Don't worry, I'm not accusing the entire Japanese nation of not giving my precious person due visual consideration." He laughed, then he seized himself. "OK, let's go back to our muttons, as Rabelais would say; I mean, to our matters. What made you believe what you … seem to believe, then?"

"That my father … ?"

"Yes, that he may be involved in all this. I mean, you mentioned in passing in Hakone that things there might be connected to him, but this is too much."

"I will try to say facts only," Hiroko said, frowning a bit, "to keep cool heads."

"Both highly recommended too." He laughed.

"I told you in Hakone something about my father, that the visit we got there was perhaps because of him. I didn't want to say more then. Now, things have changed, and we must talk.

"He seems to know about us. Worse, he doesn't like Americans. Sorry, I've not told you this before," she said.

"We seem to be on equal footing on this issue: my father isn't too partial to Japanese. Lovely families we have, haven't we?" He snorted, then sighed and shrugged.

Hiroko wanted to continue as though to shake off a heavy, crushing load. "But there's something even more important about my father. I didn't tell you about it because I was afraid you may run away from me. He's a Yakuza boss, a *oyabun*. You know about Yakuza, of course?"

"Yes, your Mafia. But I knew about this, Hiroko, for quite a while — I mean, that he's a Yakuza. I didn't want to mention it. I didn't want you to believe this has any bearing on what's between you and me, that's all," he said. "It would have been too late anyway: I was in love with you since Narita. No escape for me." He laughed.

Since Hakone, no escape for me either. She put her hands over his on the table; she felt her face red and hot. They spent several moments fathoming into each other's eyes, taking in everything they found. As though spurred by an electric shock, they suddenly stood and hugged across the small table, then sat back. Smiling, people looked at them.

"How did you learn about him?" she asked, wishing to continue, arranging her hair, troubled by the sight of others focusing on them.

"Let's just say you and your father seem to be well known in this city, Hiroko. You, for your dancing, among the dance lovers, … " He checked himself from stepping into the continuation, and smiled softly.

She felt he wasn't comfortable with saying more, and decided not to press.

"Still, you haven't yet told me yet why you think all this might be tied to him," he continued. Then, as hit by a late truth, said, "Ah, I see, he doesn't like Americans — so he doesn't like the idea of you and I … being together. But I still don't see what you promised: the facts. The facts that have made you believe he has acted on this. For there's a very long path between ideas and follow-through, young lady. Between unpleasure or even hate, on one side, and action, on the other side. There's no smoking gun; not as far as I see."

"Facts, then," she said. "The mask, first. The man 'visiting' us at the restaurant in Hakone had a mask that looked like one of the masks in my father's collection. I've known his collection since I was a child. I even borrowed some of the pieces for my dance shows."

"This collection — where is it right now?"

"Oh, he keeps it in a very strange place, a tunnel where he is a lot these days."

"Meaning, he works and sleeps there? Is this tunnel underground? In Tokyo?"

"Yes, he even sleeps there. And yes, under the ground in Tokyo, this is where it is."

"Did he have it dug for him, this tunnel? Is it large?"

She laughed the first idea off. "No, too expensive for him to dig it. It was built in the '50s for the army, for defense against the A-

Bomb, I think. Sold some years ago, at a very low price. It's huge. Wide and tall. In some areas, I think you could go with a tank through it. And it's tunnels from tunnels, you understand?"

"Ah, a network of tunnels, then," he concluded.

"Or a maze. I always lose myself in there," she said.

"No windows, no natural light, I guess?"

"No, only electrical light. Bulbs, but he's added something like this here," Hiroko pointed to the ceiling of the coffee shop.

"Fluorescent lighting panels. And this mask, did it have something special? Did you recognize it?"

"I sure remember seeing it. It's a sad man's face, from Kabuki. Also, quite rare: it has some lines of gold painted close to the ears. A very special design. This is why, I think, it was in his collection."

"But you don't think it was he himself under it on that night?" Simon asked.

"Oh, no. I know him too well, the way he holds his head. And he always uses some of the people in his company for messengers and other stuff."

"Ah, he likes to *delegate*. A company? A front company for Yakuza?"

"Yes, I think this is how it's called in English."

"Still, even if this was someone else, why use a mask that could have been recognized by you?"

"Oh, this was not by chance, no," she said sarcastically. "He likes psychology, in family even. Not much with my mother, who doesn't like this and cuts him short, but with my sister and especially with me. A lot."

"He plays mind games on you? Give me an example," he said, and Hiroko saw Simon's youthful, pink-reddish face had suddenly become crinkled in spots by displeasure and discomfort, and his freckles had darkened. He didn't like people playing such tricks on others, this much was obvious to her — and this made him even more dear to her, so much so that momentarily there was a bird's flutter in her chest and a rush of blood to her neck. She pressed her hand gently again over his on the table.

"Mind games? Say 'domination': he always enters first in a room, when he's with us. Or he curses us if we interrupt or contradict him. Say 'neglect': whenever I go to his underground place, his tunnel, as you call it, he removes my portrait in advance from his office. And this portrait, a large one, was done by a painter, to his special request. My sister tells me it's there all the time when she goes to visit him, but not hers. So there, I think you say it in English." She smiled with sadness. "So using this mask was just a warning to tell me he knows about you and me."

"And I think that the worst mind game," Hiroko continued, "is playing my sister against me. This brings my second idea it is him."

"Your second hunch."

"Yes. Now, do you recognize this person?" She smiled jokingly, opened her handbag and took out a small picture of Simon himself.

"I suppose I do," he laughed back at her.

"Well, my mother tells me she has received in mail an envelope with a copy of it, labeled 'Hiroko's new friend'."

"Why would this be your sister?"

"Because she's unfortunately the only person who knows how to open the lock, OK, as you're saying, the clasp to the secret inner pocket of my handbag and to put it back; even more, she's the only one who knows that this pocket exists. She has herself an identical handbag: a gift from our father, just like mine. This photograph was in this pocket; I made no copies of it. I'm quite sure she was asked by my father to find who is the person keeping me company these days. And she used the occasion to make sure my mother knew too. Also because she's lately making lots of jokes about blond athletic Americans I'm seen with," Hiroko finished, looking into his blue eyes as though she wanted to disappear in them for a moment, to forget about this all.

Father and daughter

"Hiroko," her father was telling her over the phone, "I'd like to see you soonest."

"I'm glad we seem to agree on this, Father. This is just what I was trying to suggest. Where and when would that be? Could we go somewhere outside, in a park or something like this? Autumn is with us, and there's not much left of it either. Let's enjoy the good weather while we can."

After a gentle beginning, his voice was back to its usual roughness, as though he had more chips on the table with her now agreeing to a meeting. "I'm too busy, and I don't like others not minding their bees-wax. I have only time for a talk, not for the rest of the goings-on coming with it. Why don't you come to my office?"

This time she found in her the energy to drive a small bargain. "All right, I'll come, but I'd like to see how my portrait you ordered looks in its new place. Could you show it to me? I need to take care of myself, even if it's just a painting." She laughed easily, to oil the wheeling and dealing with some levity.

One could have taken the cough that followed as his procrastinating for a decision. "All right, all right," he said coming back gruffly on the line, "I'll show it to you. It's in one of the nicest places I have here, don't you worry."

Several minutes more and the time of their father-and-daughter encounter had been set and, knowing their habits, she was very confident that both would accurately stick to it.

***

Two days later, she was in the elevator going down to the ground-minus-ten level at which her father's main office was. Huge, blackly burnished, metallic doors opened noiselessly. She knew she had been under observation from the entrance to the elevators. Hidden in the walls, perhaps suspended in the air, made invisible, were eyes and ears — but she had been accustomed to this thought for several years now. Her step was not more tentative for it.

She knew too well her father's preference for her to come visit him dressed in a traditional kimono. However, she had decided that on this particular occasion she couldn't abide this preference if she wanted to deal with him on a level ground, so she wore a gray business suit, as simple as she had been able to find in her closet. Selected gray for its neutrality, it carried now at its *boutonnière*, upright as a flag, freshly cut from her and her mother's garden, a white chrysanthemum. Not any chrysanthemum, but the rare kind that had been planted there by her mother, a kind which Hiroko knew her father would instantly recognize with some irritation, as it had replaced years ago all the chrysanthemums he had given her mother for planting before their separation. Medium-high-heel shoes of a darker gray supported her perky entrance past two secretaries and three bodyguards located in the antechamber, all of which stood and bowed deeply to their boss's younger daughter, for you never knew this day and age in Japan how a will was written, and in whose favor.

As she had guessed — and this must have been definitely for her sake and attention — her father was in a sober men's kimono of a much darker gray than her suit, tailored in the traditional way, with wide, straight shoulders much wider than those of the bearer's, also wide in the *hakama* pants. The dress was ringed tight around his narrow middle section by a black silk *obi* making two trapezes from his upper body and his lower body, joined on their small bases, one atop the other.

From the middle of the huge room, which naturally, being underground, didn't have any windows and always succeeded in making her feel claustrophobic, she bowed silently to her father, who nodded back to her, waved her to advance and rudely dismissed with a swing of the back of his hand a fashionable, pin-thin, young male underling who stood close to his office, at frozen attention.

"Come in, come in, Hiroko-chan!" he said, continuously waving at her to advance and sit in front of his desk.

"Father! So glad to see you again." On most occasions, this would have been true — Hiroko thought she still loved her father, even with all his strange ideas, with his behavior, which could really get naughty at times, enough to send her, not to speak of her mother, a-flutter. She bowed to him, then sat down, and he formally bent to her from the waist while sitting. She placed her handbag in her lap. All his kimono-clad splendor made her feel being — as no doubt his intention was — in an audience at one of those high-ranked warlords portrayed in Kurosawa's historical movies, so she tapped and pressed her thighs under her handbag with nervous fingers, to recover the feeling of reality.

"And how are you these days, Hiroko?" her father asked from under bushy, imperious eyebrows, joined together above his flattened nose of an aggressive martial arts practitioner.

"I'm healthy, fine, Father, couldn't be better. Just so we won't forget, could you show me, please, the arrangement you set up here for my portrait?" She wasn't sure for how long she was going to be able to sit in front of his desk, decorated as it was in a corner by a regal cobra coiled to strike. The snake was reputed to have been shot by her father himself in India, right before it was to strike him, in a mano-a-mano confrontation. Lucky for her, the dead snake looked now towards him, but she was able to see the fangs.

Her father fixed her with his sharply focused sight for a moment. His face reddened, as if caught by un unpleasant surprise at her repartee, but his power of self-control seemed to get the upper hand, and he finally replied, in a casual tone, "But of course. Why don't we go over to my bedroom area?"

Having to face eyeball-to-eyeball one or several of his lovers walking around in a bikini or substantially less, which could always happen when dropping into his private quarters here, wasn't something that Hiroko was looking forward to, but she stayed her compass. Still, this time she needed to keep the initiative, as she had agreed with Simon. "Er— I thought it was somewhere else, in your museum. That's what Michiko told me last time. But OK, let's go then. Hope we're not disturbing *anything*, are we?"

"Michiko talks too much. And no, we're alone, if that's what you mean." Her father sneered, roguishly acting the part of the uncaught Lothario. Hiroko knew he thoroughly enjoyed their reporting back to their mother on his latest vamps. He heaved himself from his presidential high-back, black-leather-covered chair and swept in full kimono glory towards the door leading to his private chambers.

In her imagined horror, she was looking from her portrait on the wide waterbed in the bedroom and the goings on there.

Things weren't so bad though. Her sister's and her own portraits had been placed in their father's fitness room, right above a large mat seemingly intended for Yoga and Zen meditation. May be a resettlement of sorts, as compared with the place last reported to her by her sister.

"There you are, you two. Looking beautiful, I'd say. Satisfied now?" He drummed the fingers of one hand against the breast of his kimono, looking ready to turn around in a jiffy and return to his office.

"Well, I'm glad we're both well lit." She smiled with a bit of sarcasm. "Especially here, ten levels down from sunlight. I was concerned Michiko's and my look-alikes might become anemic, if you know what I mean, Father."

"All right now, you've had your druthers, Hiroko-chan. Let me have mine."

They were still in the fitness room. Utilitarian, it was at least a bit more intimate, in comparison with the hollowed, vertical immensity of the office itself, which she in a hyperbole thought couldn't have been used decades before by the Army except for detonating explosive charges or for a inner cathedral definitely with no bells, totally silent.

"Do you think we could manage to go on here? Cobras don't quite inspire me, Father, even those that have been killed by you."

And there, among barbells and mats, Nautilus machines, stationary bicycles and treadmills, they slowly walked around in circles, absorbed in their conversation, barely avoiding to bump here and there into one or another piece of equipment.

They had been trailed step by step from the office by Kazuhiro's huge, dark, gray-golden-black German shepherd, a sight to behold, who either sat on his haunches, unmoved as a boulder, whenever they stopped, or came up to them and pushed the side of his head or his huge muzzle into their legs. Hiroko was used to him and enjoyed passing her fingers through his thick fur, but rumor had it he was a worrisome devil with people unknown to him.

"Tora-Tora, sit!" Her father displayed a shadow of impatience over his face. "I need to talk to Hiroko-chan now." He turned to her and spoke slowly, "And I do need that. That's why I called you."

"Yes, Father. This is why I am here," Hiroko replied, in a neutral tone. She thought she knew the subject to come, but was always piqued and curious to see her father's approach to steering boats or more abstract things, for he was an original in his every thrust and move, even in the awkward ones.

"Word is out you're pretty tight with some *gaijin* types," he said, his eyes piercing her.

"'Word,' would that mean Michiko, Father?"

"Definitely not," he answered. "That much you should trust me: I've had several pigeons coming in to me on this."

She wasn't surprised — he always took painstaking care to cover all his traces and to avoid disclosing any sources. As well, she didn't feel it necessary to stoke the fire under him, thus she didn't comment on his boast. *Another verb. Pigeons returning, in fact, to him. All his own.*

"I have friends. Not a crime, in my book," she answered, shrugging.

"But *what kind of* friends those are always matters, in mine. I mean, Russians and Americans I wouldn't touch with a pole. We had wars with them. Do you understand that? Wars. We lost family to them. Understand, family?"

"The last war was over twenty years before I was born. Isn't that enough?"

"For some things, enough is never. Our family carries our shame for three hundred years now." He inhaled noisily, shoulders rising as under a load, brow stricken as with saber wounds.

"No one except you, Father, told me about it. No one ever bullied me or put me down on it. But it's true, I don't talk to members of *Nihon Komintō*."

Her father went on as though he hadn't heard her. "History is no cat to make it purr when you want, it is what it was and what it is."

"Nor is it a Tora-Tora to be afraid of, I think," she ribbed him slightly, to lighten the tenor of the conversation. The dog growled deeply, as though not liking the reference.

"So, I guess," Kazuhiro continued, growling himself now, "you'd willingly go to any peacenik meeting, walk any peace march, weep anytime over Hiroshima and Nagasaki, but you'd forget with just one stroke that it was the bloomy Americans who dropped the Bomb on us? Just because you have the hots for a pretty face? Turn the other cheek, you would, after having your own grandfather killed by them, wouldn't you?".

"As far as I know," she answered, "Grandfather volunteered for that mission, fully aware of its outcome. On both sides, it was giving and receiving death, Father. Tit for tat. An eye for an eye. I'm just saying: could we be excused from all this past, Father, if you don't mind? Could we have our own lives for ourselves?"

"Ah," he signaled dismissively with his hand, "I bet many of you younger people would do just that, push the past under some rags, together with the memories of your ancestors, even recent ones as Grandfather," her father said, his face as though pinched by acid, sneering out his sarcasm.

"You know this isn't true, Father. You aren't being fair." Hiroko wasn't going to take all this, but she said this as level as she could.

"Not true? Are you willing then to come with me to see Grandfather and pray for him?"

Hiroko knew this meant going to his private underground museum, and she cringed, and shivers went through her, for this really meant replaying or invoking death. True, the death of others, generations removed; still, Death. However, where they were in their discussion didn't amount to any progress. She wanted to make at least some baby steps, so she pushed herself up to his challenge.

"Now?"

"When do I get you here? Yes, now."

"Fine, then. Let's go." She shuddered as she agreed, and immediately read on her father's wary face a badly disguised surprise at her reaction.

They inched forward, gathering their thoughts for something that both knew would be hard on them, out of the exercise room up a dim long hallway, and entered a large hall illuminated discreetly in pale *chiaroscuro* from hidden lighting fixtures.

The rough walls were covered to chest level in black velvet that continued to the height of about three meters with pale white silk. Hundreds of grainy, discolored portraits of young men of another world, of a lost generation, hung along the room, for tens of meters in length. *Kamikaze.* To the side of each, their names, their unit, their last day and the kills or the misses. In the middle of them all, the Rear Admiral Arima who had started the wave and the death frenzy. Up in one corner, a Shinto alcove with one picture only — her grandfather. She wondered sometimes whether he was one of the lost, restless souls, the *muenbotoke*, who cannot get respite and salvation, so much was he torturing her father.

They knelt on the small steps in front of it, clapped their hands and said the *norito*, their Shinto prayers, quietly.

Each time she looked at this picture, Hiroko was amazed at how much of her grandfather was showing in her father: the long face, the sharp eyes, drilling into you, the high cheekbones, the dismissive smile, faded above a strong, wide chin. She sometimes wondered how her father felt being so much of a replica of someone whom he had never known. Did he feel smaller on account of that, lacking originality in eternity?

They rose, backed away from the shrine, and at some distance from it, looked again at the face trying to get at them from the depth of time with that derisive smile. And the funny thing was, she felt reverently about that distant man.

"He knew his enemies, your grandfather," Kazuhiro Yuasa said. "Those who wanted to stop Japan, put her to her knees, rob her of her God-given power."

"Power to her, weakness and humility to all her neighbors, Father, was that it? How long could this work? Hitler wanted it for a thousand years. Same for us, perhaps?"

They were close now to his office.

"'Carry a big stick!' Ask your American friends about it," her father said. "They always do that — state policy from Roosevelt the old. How's that different from what we did, tell me, please? How's Hollywood taking over the cinemas all over the world? How's Presley taking over the music all over the world?" Then he exploded, "How's them American punks trying to dictate my business?"

"Which business, Father?" She knew perfectly well it was the junk, but wanted to hear it from his mouth.

"Well, why should I tell you? Your clever mother never liked my line of work, and surely she taught you to fly the same way."

She realized he wouldn't open to her on this, not now, perhaps not ever; and she wasn't really interested in digging about it. His hiding behind words was enough. So she changed tack.

"My friends … my friends are helping me." She'd just decided to stay in the plural; to mention Simon directly just didn't seem to her a great idea at this time. "They are helping me in my work."

"Are they somehow dancing with you?"

"No, Father. They are preparing an exhibition about my work."

"Rather, I'd say they want to ride the coattails of a naïve Japanese girl to get a foot into the Japanese market, also into what you young people might call Japanese society, nothing else. It pays well to be here for all these *gaijin*. Nights in Roppongi with Japanese girls, days to collect their dough in *kaisha*. No ifs, buts or maybes about it. As the Christian punks say, *Amen* to that."

"Father, I'm not going to sit here while my friends are badmouthed. Would you perhaps agree to meet them face-to-face, to see how they are really?"

"There's no need for that," her father said. "I don't want to pollute my sight with their view."

Her voice trembled. "Can I at least hope that they won't be bothered by you, that *we* won't be followed by your people?"

He didn't look at her, but put his hand on Tora-Tora and patted his back, and mentioned as in passing, "Something like this never happened, it's only your fancy. I don't know them, and I never bothered about them. Only thing, I would've liked not to have to hear my own daughter is mixed up with them. I s'pose that's what you in your clever, highbrow world of yours call artistic license."

"All right, Father. Let's call it a day for now." There was no point in her staying around. She bowed, left his office and went to the elevators for the outside world.

At the National Museum

"The attendance to your exhibition at the Tokyo National Museum is as good as when national treasures are brought over from Nara or Kyoto, once in forty years," the reporter from *The Japan Times* was telling Simon over the phone, prodding him for an exclusive interview.

January was around Tokyo. The exhibition was going on for one month now, with another month left. *Not bad at all. This might help with Hiroko's exhibition too.*

"How about having the interview at the museum, in two, three days?" Simon asked. "It's easier to speak to you surrounded by the subjects of the talk, I mean the pictures of the imperial villas."

"No, sir," the reporter countered. "With due respect, it is you who are the subject of the interview; you and your vision of landscape photography, in particular, and photography in general."

"I'm not sure I can talk in general terms about myself. I've never had an interview yet, and talking about oneself requires not only a good deal of immodesty, but also a good deal of thinking. I'm not sure I've arrived there," Simon said, hoping the self-deprecation was well received at the other end of the line.

The reporter seemed to have detected in Simon a difficult subject; he backtracked. He didn't want to lose him. "OK, we'll start talking about specific pictures, some of which will accompany the article. Perhaps this will in turn open your appetite about some more general issues; let's hope you'll make us then some confidences. We'll be just by happenstance there, ready to record them."

Simon laughed. "I have no secrets. If you can get me talking, and my babbling makes any sense to you or your readers, so much the better."

***

Both Hiroko and Simon were on this day at the exhibition, but she seemed to have decided to disappear discreetly into the other hall, to avoid any distraction for Simon during the interview.

The girl in the brilliant turquoise kimono was running forever around both Simon and the reporter in the first. She had to be seven or so. Luckily for them, she hadn't managed to engage other children in her play. Also luckily, she was constricted in her skipping and frolicking by the tubular nature of the kimono itself. In the adult world above her head, the interview went ahead.

People were standing and shuffling three-deep in front of the human-size pictures and there was a long lineup on the staircase leading to the entrance to the museum.

"Do you have any explanation for this influx of public?" the reporter was asking Simon.

"I think I should volley back this question to where it came from," Simon joked.

The reporter expounded. "We assume it's because of the veneration of the Japanese people for the imperial villas. Many of them have visited both Shugaku-in and Katsura in Kyoto, and have fallen in love with them, especially with their placement, cocooning, in their natural setting. Also, many of them might have visited them a long time ago, thus nostalgia comes to bear too."

"You might be right," Simon said. "I have no way of knowing. Many of the people who have talked to me during the exhibition have been older people, perhaps looking back, hanging to some happy moment in time in their lives. Some told me they went to Kyoto from Tokyo on their honeymoons years ago and that coming here was for them an occasion to bring to their mind those moments long past and to re-visit those places in some form."

"What could you tell us about your approach to showing *shakkei*, that embedding of the villas by design in the natural background?

Critics, as well as ordinary people, tell us this is what most impresses them in your pictures."

"Well, depth and perspective are permanent issues for any good photographer. It took me quite a while to roam around the grounds of the villas before I discovered some advantageous angles. Off the record: I'm embarrassed, but I think at Shugaku-in I had to make this tour more than three times. On the record, again. Once one is there, the rest isn't something that complicated — just a matter of lens and camera choice, as well as, naturally, waiting for the most propitious moments in terms of light. I was really lucky with the weather during my stay in Kyoto for the photo shoot-out. And —"

An intense *ssshhtt*-like hissing sound interrupted him. It had come from the ceiling of the exhibition hall. Next thing everybody knew, violent, non-discriminating, crude, wide streams of water from the sprinkler system positioned in the ceilings were inundating the two halls of the exhibition, the walls, the floors, the people rushing for cover bumping into each other at the doors. Panic ensued, parents calling, shouting to their children, children crying or answering back, everybody all of a sudden dripping wet.

Simon told the reporter, "Sorry, we'll have to —" looked around, didn't see any fire, but saw with the corner of his eye several of his panels crinkled, crumpled or plainly crushed under the weight of the water. *A lost cause there.*

He saw the young girl in the turquoise kimono — she had been knocked down to the floor by the crowding people, just meters away from them — and rushed to her. He took her in his arms, and made his way to the large hallway outside the exhibition, engulfed himself in the mass of people going with a panicked shuffle through the tall doors luckily opened wide. There, he stood the girl on her feet and told her "*Matte, kudasai*" to wait in place, while he started to look around the hallway for Hiroko. The parents of the girl soon emerged from inside and found her. She pointed to him and said something to them, and they all came to him and thanked him profusely, bowing several times. On her score he was thus able to relax.

By now, the museum's volunteer firefighters were already in full force at the door of the exhibition in ugly dark-blueish uniforms, prohibiting reentry, ordering the people in the hallway to exit in order out of the museum, to the courtyard, as quickly as possible.

The sirens of the professional firefighters came on in too at this time. Their red trucks unloaded men and equipment right outside the building.

Finally, Hiroko herself came out through the doors of the exhibition, carried through by another wave of people. Her hair and the top of her kimono were drenched, her face streaked by sadness. Simon rushed to her, hugged her head shortly to his chest, took off his jacket and covered her shoulders, then gave her his handkerchief to dry herself up.

"What about you?" she asked, skipping lightly in place to warm herself up. "You're just as wet." Only now did he have a look over himself, felt himself. He was wet everywhere, from his black corduroy pants to the back of his neck, in most places to the skin. He tapped Hiroko's back and she did the same with his own to squish away some of the water before going out in the chilly January day. It was good to see through the hallway windows that the sky had dumped only five centimeters of snow on the ground outside since the morning.

He was trying to think and it didn't come easily; he felt tempted to smash something into the wall.

"Do you feel like waiting around to talk to the management of the museum?" he asked Hiroko.

"No," she said. "I think we should go home now. With the firefighters, this could take two hours, as they start their inquiry. And, sorry to say, but there's nothing to be saved from your things in the second room, where I was." She set her hand over his forearm, and tapped lightly to appease his disappointment.

"The situation wasn't much better about the exhibits in the first room," he conceded, feeling the need to take a huge intake of air.

She asked, "There's another month left in the schedule of the exhibition. Any chance you could prepare another series of prints for them to show?"

He thought for one moment. "It would take me three days at the most to have another series of prints ready, and to make a new installation here. The walls should dry up quickly and even if stained by water here and there, the exhibition could take place. I assume the public isn't that fussy. This is only feasible if they, the museum, want it, and if the company agrees to fund the work, I mean pay —

for the materials, not for my time. However, both these parties might not want to have anything to do with this unlucky exhibition."

"I guess, Hiroko said, "it depends on what the press says. Talk to everyone tomorrow. Let's get out of this crowd and go to our places to dry out and change."

"You're sure don't want to come over to my place for that?" he asked.

"No, I'd better go to my home straight to see if anything can be saved from my poor kimono. It's expensive. Perhaps if my mother and I wash it soon enough there won't be any traces of water left, when it dries out. Plus, I need *tabi*, *geta* changes and underwear," she said blushing.

***

Having had an interested and thoroughly soaked reporter on premises at the time of the incident, *The Japan Times* had, of course, the inside track, and came up first with a detailed report the next day.

Its title was *False Fire Alarm and Sprinkler Malfunction Lead to Flooding of Great Photography Exhibition at the Tokyo National Museum.*

The adjective "Great" had been inserted in the title by *The Times* editors under pressure from the reporter himself, who had included parts of the unfinished interview with Simon together with his own enthusiastic take on the exhibition.

Conspicuously missing were any photographs taken after the inundation.

Also missing were details of the firefighters' inquiry report mentioning the evidence of sabotage: the electrical output signal from the fire and smoke detectors had been bypassed, and replaced by timer mechanisms which had started the false alarm and the sprinkler action at the same predetermined time in both halls. The small timers had not destroyed themselves after the deed and had been descovered *in situ* by the explosives experts called in by the firefighters upon finding the bypassing circuitry.

However, both The Company and Simon had been informed about the suspicions of sabotage, after being sworn to confidentiality.

The Japan Times article continued by promising on the part of the "organizers of the exhibition" swift action for rebuilding the exhibition "within the next days, for the pleasure of the appreciative public, who has patronized the exhibition in great numbers." It finished, "Please stay tuned."

All the major Japanese-language Tokyo newspapers, as well as the TV channels, announced the incident, praising the quick action of the firefighters that had led to no one being seriously hurt, and made quick reference to *The Japan Times* exclusive.

***

For a day and a half, they had both stood guard by the huge drying machine with calenders at the Company, to get the prints out as fast as they could. Simon and Hiroko were now ready to go with a covered minitruck hired by the Company to the National Museum, carrying with them in a large flat metalic travel trunk all the prints, separated from each other by special sheeting.

"You look very tired. You need some rest," she was telling him.

He looked at her drawn face, eyes ready to close, and answered, "You too. And lots of it."

"Let's get these prints to the museum first," she said, nodding sadly, stubborness still setting her small chin. "Then," she said, "they can do the installation themselves — it's their job and they are experts at it."

"Fine, let's do it. We still have two hours until they close the museum for the day."

They climbed as fast as they could in the back of the truck, and sat on the small bench there, in order to keep an eye on their precious cargo during the trip to downtown Tokyo. Simon tapped the driver's cabin to start off. The man was ready, and took off right away.

Simon thought this was as good a time as any to broach the subject they hadn't touched since the alarm and the flooding.

"Do you ever ask yourself why this has happened to us?" he asked.

"Well, they told you about the sabotage, didn't they?" she answered, shrugging. "And you told me." She trailed her words, looking tired and disappointed. "It's like my visit to Father hasn't achieved anything."

"Do you really think he bothers that much about us?"

She looked with some blue strangeness in her face at him. "Too bad you haven't yet visited his underground place. That would open your eyes to some things. He's a very stubborn man — if not fanatical — on some issues."

Simon put a hand around her back, grasped her shoulder and pressed her to himself. He looked to her, not speaking until he was convinced she was again with him, back from a spell of tiredness.

"This might be just him telling you that he loves you and doesn't want to lose you. It happens to many fathers when daughters reach your age," he said, slowly.

"All this — all this is just too much for me to believe that," she answered hesitantly. "This is more than jealousy. This is very close to hate, if it's him."

"Perhaps, but I think it is directed toward me," he shrugged.

"Perhaps, but doesn't he know we're *so together* now?" she asked with some desperation in her words, letting her head drop on his shoulder.

All the way to the National Museum, he was glad to see her drowse.

The Professor

Frowning, Professor Kuriyama from Waseda University wanted a confirmation.

"Are you sure about the date?" he asked Yukio Imashita. "Could you double check it was indeed the 29th of January 1945?"

Yukio looked again at the file in his briefcase, and shrugged. "That's what the person of import told me. That must be it: he's so very keen about that day."

"No less than thirty-five heroes went down on that day in that single area of the Pacific. A very unfortunate moment in our history," said the historian, his white-haired head swaying with sadness. "It makes the separation and identification much more difficult."

"We know you are our last hope. We also know that you are using some of the latest ways," said Imashita. "And I'm prepared to cover all expenses, plus a very generous fee."

"I'll do my best," continued the professor. "However, many times historical records are missing, and confusion may well reign. Generous fees and my willingness won't make documents appear as the Phoenix bird. That was — if the person who sent you doesn't know it, or doubts it — a full-scale war. Places like Hiroshima were totally wiped out. We were not in such a bad shape in Tokyo; very serious bombing occurred here notwithstanding."

What bird is he talking about? What gobbledygook is that? Boss didn't blabber 'bout no bird. These profs are sometimes light in the head by a score.

"And the name is Yasuhiro Yuasa, right?"

Yukio was on more solid ground on this one. "For that I can guarantee. On the other hand, we know that the dates of death are on thin ice. It seems the *Dai-Nippon Teikoku Kaigun* didn't always have the right information to convey to the families."

"I'd have to agree with you about this last item," the professor said. "The cruiser the pilots seem to have had as target on that day — it was *Columbia*, right?"

"This is what had been communicated during the war to the family by the Imperial Navy," said Imashitta.

"I'll check up on that, don't worry." The professor ended the conversation abruptly by first ruffling, then gathering all of his notes, then again placing them in his attaché case, finally leaving with a sigh the wooden bench in front of the Yasukuni Shrine where they had had the conversation, with just a slight bow. He had a preoccupied mien. Yukio barely had the time to stand up and begin the motions of a summary reply in kind.

Strange bird the professor, but then, not my money.

***

The professor culled most of what had presumedly passed on that fatidic day in the Pacific from the reports of Yasuhiro Yuasa's two wing men, Masafumi Ogawa and Kiyoshi Araki. They hadn't been sworn in as *Kamikaze* pilots at the time and were thus consigned to do their best to return to their aircraft carrier alive. They managed this, even though they were left with only five-minutes' worth of fuel.

Yasuhiro had been ordered to take most of the scalp of a Cleveland class cruiser and to add to the injury by hurtling his Nakajima B5N torpedo bomber — after the launch of a type 91 torpedo — into the second-bow Mark 16/1 triple 6-inch /47 gun turret of the enemy, which was supposed to be manned by about fifty-five men. Just the lives of these men would have been something precious to take with him into the netherworld, but this was not to be the end of it. Each of the three 6-inch rifle barrels were about seven meters long. The turret itself sat and rotated on a barbette, a deep well built several decks into the ship. Close to a thousand projectiles were stored in the lower end of the barbette and underneath all that that went the powder, stored in powder canisters. All this mammoth of a turret weighed seventy tons.

The plan designed by Yasuhiro's superiors was to get a direct hit against the turret, thereby starting a conflagration that would rush like a viper downward to the powder stores. The ensuing explosion was hoped to break apart the guts of the USS *Columbia* and doom it to the floor of the ocean with all her twelve hundred men.

The Nakajima B5N torpedo bomber had been especially modified in order to employ only a pilot — himself — instead of the regular crew of three. No need for a rear gunner or a commander on such a one-way mission. The Imperial Navy believed there was no need to lose more pilots than necessary, as there was quite a shortage of them even for *kamikaze tokubetsu kōgeki tai* missions.

Four months earlier, their unit had been visited by Rear Admiral Masafumi Arima, the very man who who had come up with the idea of *Kamikaze*, who would die himself by personally leading a large such attack during the October of 1944. When visiting home for the last time, Yasuhiro told Matsue, his wife, about this visit that had strengthened him. She would later tell her still-to-be born son that this had been the time that she knew from the grey glint in his eyes that there was no way of stopping Yasuhiro from going on that mission.

He had decided to separate from his wing members and attack alone from the port side of the ship, in order not to direct the AA fire against them too. However, by this time the ship had turned around for evasion purposes, offering a small profile, thus he thought better to add a ninety-degree arc to his trajectory executed at the very last moment. The six-inch guns of the turrets would not fire against him, as they were designed for sending their 130-pound projectiles against much larger land or sea targets covered in up to five-inch-thick armor plates, and were anyhow too heavy to follow his movements. His main opposition was to come from the ship's AA guns, much nimbler devils, he knew all too well, after having lost many friends to similar guns on other American ships.

Only one Cleveland class cruiser was embedded in this enemy task group. This would years later help professor Kuriyama in the tricky identification of the name of the ship. The Japanese knew Kazuhiro's plane had hit a Cleveland class cruiser, and the

Americans reported after the war that the only such ship in the area on that day had been USS *Columbia*. The Yankees also reported the damage suffered by the ship, and this matched what Kazuhiro's Yuasa wing members had reported in kind.

***

"I've got some bad news for us. The National Museum has passed to the Company — unofficially, of course — that 'regretfully there seems to be a shortage of space' with regard to their scheduling of new exhibitions for the coming months. They didn't say it explicitly, but this was, of course, about hosting my pictures of your dancing." Two weeks after the flooding, Simon was in bed, passing his hand over Hiroko's back, which arched under his touch. In the room, the light was diffuse, coming only from a lamp on the night table, palely inviting to calm and tolerance. "We should look elsewhere, and immediately."

"Why am I not surprised?" She turned on her side toward him, tapped his hand as for a reality check, and showed a tight smile. "I'm glad that at least they went on with your exhibition on Shugaku-in for the remaining month." *Someone must have found who my father is, put two and two together, and made some of the very assumptions that went through our own heads. Or perhaps a well-intended message — a word of caution — had somehow found its way to the museum.* She didn't want to trouble Simon too much by uttering all this, but considered the continuation neutral enough. "Perhaps they thought about money: lots of people came during the first month. It's mainly subsidized by the government, the museum, so I guess they appreciate any source of extra income …"

"Perhaps. They'd be fools not to appreciate that. Still, it seems only a one-time show of courage for the benefit of the perpetrators has appeared to be OK to them, but not a repeat. I might have become too hot a potato to handle. Sorry for that." He laughed with some sarcasm, his fingers playing at the back of her neck with swathes of dense, hard, long hair.

"But what were you saying?" he said, the joker rippling in his voice, and in one swift, powerful, and deft motion, grasped her middle section with both his hands, turned himself from lying on his side to his back and swung her above him, his arms outstretched, her suspended on the bones of her hips on the platform offered by them. Laughing, she tensed her back to straighten herself into a suspended acrobat, mimicking a swim in the air with her arms and legs.

"Let me down, Simon!" she said, guffawing.

"Only if you say 'please'!"

"Never! You started it!" She continued to flounce and try at the air.

"Fine, then." He went on holding her up. She sensed her breathing was becoming more labored by the second with the effort of maintaining herself horizontal, his two palms the only points of support.

All of a sudden, she saw him losing focus too, his eyes switching to her breasts. Next moment, she felt herself lowered onto him, her head higher than his head on the bed, her breasts in his hot mouth going at them as famishedly as to a ripe cluster of grapes.

***

"I can't remember what I wanted to tell you," Kazuhiro Yuasa told Yukio Imashita. "But it wasn't to thank you for services on the museum job. The eggheads there are as sure as death and taxes someone did a number on them. What the hell, traces of your wiring were found in the mess-up. Can't you clean up after yourself anymore?"

"Boss, I hate to see you think that. Me and the boys left the stuff in there to make their poor asses burn with cold creeps. Bottom line: they won't have any other exhibition of the guy in our cross-hairs, there. If you want it, I have the lick, sorry, the taping, of the bugged lines to prove it."

"Nah, what's shitty work stays shitty through oceans of words," Kazuhiro closed the interview. "Take him to area 347 and let his sorry ass rot there with those Sutra chanters until his mind clocks faster, which I think won't happen too soon," he ordered his bodyguards.

So Yukio was taken on a kilometer-long trek through much narrower, broken-stone-strewn tunnels, until a new wide area opened in front of them. He never entertained the idea of running away from his guards: he knew perfectly well his head was at serious risk. He was supposed to just take his punishment in silence.

About a hundred believers Yukio didn't know what of, all clothed as Buddhist monks would be, in long yellow robes mostly with no sleeves, all shaved on their heads and faces, sat on a wide wooden platform in front of an altar-like contraption. They mumbled and recited in low voices Sutras after Sutras in scary stubborness, all the while slowly bowing and bending from their waist to the altar wall. Some were known to sleep in these underground premises; Yukio didn't know where, in what burrows.

He knew many made guys had returned from this crowd to the family, *gumi*, bonkers in the konkers, but this was his best choice at the time. "Re-education through prayer with our friends the *Delta's,*" his boss called it, and seemed always in cloud-nine land mentioning it. This was supposed to help focus and historical feeling, Kazuhiro hotly contended. Yukio, he had enough trouble figuring out the dang words themselves. Historical feeling, my foot.

The Lotus Flower

He felt lost, Yukio Imashita, he truly did. In this subterranean cave, surrounded by hundreds of faces unknown, not too friendly either, he failed to see any meaning in them. To top it off, at any attempt at a conversation, those faces froze even more — if that had been at all possible — or, worse, their owners just moved away from him.

He could tell he was not appropriately dressed, for everybody around him was wrapped in yellow or orange robes of cheap silk or cotton, while he wore uncomfortably tight navy-blue denim pants and jacket. He did not know or chant the proper mantras, in lieu of which he mumbled something that at least in his view was damn similar. He did not know why he was in the place, except that his boss wanted him there to "observe" and "insert himself," while everybody else around him seemed to be running on some divinely-inspired gas or conviction.

The *butsudan*, the altar, was wood shellacked white, shaped as a huge open scallop shell, all covered in pearls. He was to learn in time that just two generations ago, many of these people had been pearl *ama* divers in places in the Izu Peninsula. The women had kept at it at least in terms of having unusually thin bodies and a sight that went everywhere. Here on solid ground, they made for a disquieting presence. Whatever power worked over them, it had them fully in its grasp and they didn't spy for themselves, they spied for it and passed the word from one to another, in murmur or low whisper, until it reached the higher-ups and then, he has heard, it exploded in blowups, actions and counteractions, all secret — for these people would never try to attract attention to themselves.

He was supposed to stick with those who had sponsored him in joining the community, which meant sitting close to them during prayer, eating with them, walking along with them when visiting other sites. For the sect had several sites for pray and assembly spread in underground Tokyo, in the same subterranean city of years past. So there was this mass migration from one site to another, kind of a rotation system, where one group, regularly in the hundreds, took over the site of others, and so on.

"What is the purpose of all this going to other sites and of moving around?" he had asked soon into his initiation.

"The lotus flower has several petals, and the beauty lies in their being together. The brothers and sisters in other places pray to other incarnations of the Supreme Being," Hiroshige Tanaguchi, the senior member of his group, told him. "And we must submit reverently to all those incarnations, for in unity lies the force. The lotus flower lies on water, and the water is the world around us that it commands, and the plate of the world itself is supported by the huge elephants that the spirit of the lotus flower keeps in its service too."

Yukio knew it was his boss that had recommended him to Tanaguchi-San, he just didn't know how had that been done in detail, but he didn't want to play the nosy, so that was the end of it. He also knew that Kazuhiro Yuasa's syndicate was the only one in all *gumi* that had this underground location. In fact rumor had it the cult, the *Shinrikyo,* had bought their properties from him. Yukio thought his own presence there was only a sign of his boss still watching over his partners in that past transaction. What for, he didn't know, but he knew he had better keep wide open eyes and ears.

Her Father and Simon

Hiroko had waited and postponed, waited and postponed, and now, after two months, the candle of her patience was burning very low. She knew she really had to talk to her father. As Kazuhiro Yuasa was someone who didn't usually wake up on the right side of the bed, she gave the thumb down to any mornings. She knew she had to call in the evening, aiming for a one-on-one with her father on another evening. Just a matter of having his bristles dulled down by the exertions of the day.

The subject of their conversation touching on Simon, she had arranged to call from her mother's kitchen, so as to have the privacy that a call from any of the dancing venues she appeared at couldn't have provided. Just as well, her mother wasn't at home at the time — not happenstance, just proper logistics.

Problem was, she didn't like going through his bodyguards, and his secretary worked only until five p.m. or thereabouts. So she had to call close to that hour, and at that time the secretary was sometimes just a touch antsy, even toward her. But on that day Yamashita-San was agreeable, and Hiroko was lucky enough to get her father on the line right away.

"Ah, Hiroko, I'm so glad to talk to you."

"Me too, Father."

"Do you remember that time I took you and Michiko and climbed Fuji-san to the half of its height?" he asked, his voice fading just a moment, right on 'Fuji-san.'

She was taken aback for a moment by his mood, but it was perhaps just what she needed on that occasion, thus after she remembered the scene, she sensed the need to reply warmly, and said, "Yes, and what a rain caught us there! We stopped, but we had a wonderful rainbow just at the end of climbing down."

"I guess you were twelve then, but strong already, especially strong legs. You didn't have any problems in keeping pace with your elder sister and me; on the contrary, you ran in front of us all the time, you small bee! Remember I was calling you my dancing bee in those days?" he asked, his voice sounding unusually warm.

Father might be just in the right disposition. Let's go on for a while.

"I hope I am still your bee, father. Only my bee suit might be just a tad small these days." She laughed.

"Ah, that's why you're calling? A shopping expedition in Ginza or in Hong Kong, I guess? Can I help?"

During her teens, Hiroko had taught him with some difficulty to ask for what he called with some irritation 'daughterly permission' before giving her money and even gifts: she didn't like to feel force fed. She knew Michiko didn't have such scruples, but imitating Michiko had never been her priority, not in shopping matters, nor in others. Hiroko accepted gratefully some of his gifts — some of those kimono she danced in she would never have been able to buy herself, as they were collector's items — but she wanted to keep her own ways.

"Not at all, Father. No shopping. It's about what daughters are supposed to do sooner or later, if they are true and faithful to their parents — introduce their own friends to their fathers." She said "parents" to bring in the equation some invisible boosting from her mother, just so her father would feel the obvious constraints of their situation and behave less self-centeredly.

"Ah," he replied after a short pause, a rasping touch now in his voice, "the friends helping you with that exhibition of yours you mentioned last time?" His memory was sharp as ever. "And how many are they?"

"For the time being, I want to introduce to you one of them." Playing with the plural might help shield Simon from too much focus on the part of her father, she thought.

"And, if what I thought I learned matches the truth, they're *gaijin*, right?"

"Yes, Simon Fraser is American," she conceded, and expected the worst, but she couldn't do anything about it. His name was out, for better or worse.

"Well … " The answer came after a short break, and was measured enough, as though her father was sipping coffee in the meanwhile, "I am doing business with Americans. I guess, if need be, I can face your friends too."

Even though I don't like it, nor do I like them. Surely he thought that way.

She knew she would never get more than that. "Would a restaurant meal be good for you?" she asked, concerned. He might suggest his underground office or even his museum, and that would be a dead-end in all respects, that much she could guarantee.

"Well, why not, as long we're not forced to drink from the same cup," he said, and he must have sneered upon saying this. "I'll arrange something in two weeks from now, on an evening. Would you consider having Michiko or even your mother with us?"

"Not yet, father, let it be just the three of us on this occasion."

She knew down pat her mother would never meet her father in a restaurant these days, alone or with their daughters present: that would, to her, mean an out-and-out lie. "If he couldn't live with us, why accommodate him with fake merry-making? I can't take that, you know, it would sicken me," she would have said at any hour of day and night, probably under torture too, Hiroko said to herself, laughing half-sad in her mind.

As for Michoko, she would stir something up, play the coquette and try to steal Simon away just for kicks.

No, thank you.

***

As the one most versed in both languages, Hiroko knew she would have to do the translation honors on this occasion. That might help assuage some of the petulance in her father's language. And she liked the restaurant at first sight, a tea-house on Aoyama-Dori, quiet and old-fashioned with an old style roof with thick ceramic tiles glinting dark-brown under the February moon. Their room was on the second floor, a *tatami* room with no windows, its only opening the sliding screen-door toward the passage. She had tried to make sure she and Simon would arrive there first to avoid upsetting her father. She looked around while they entered and climbed up the stairs — no bodyguards indeed. *This is good.* Perhaps her father hadn't come, or they were unusually discrete — not quite their habit.

At the top of the stairs the tea-house owner, welcoming them with deep bows in her simpler gray kimono of an older woman, confirmed her father hadn't arrived yet, and pulled open the slide door to let them in. Hiroko and Simon left their shoes at the entrance to the hallway and placed their long coats on hangers on the walls. She was left in white *tabi* and he in black socks.

She liked to see Simon in his dark navy-blue Principe del Marzotto suit. *Thank God he saved it from all that mould last summer.* Double-breasted, wide-lapelled, it outlined well his wide shoulders and narrow middle section. Still, it looked wide enough on him to show him comfortable in it. He would need that here, she laughed to herself, as they had to sit down on the floor. He wore the dark burgundy Tino Cosma tie with thin stripes she had bought him on Omotesando-Dori, in one of those Italian boutiques, and a plain white long-sleeved shirt with a collar the cut of which she liked very much. Not too small, not too large, the right thing, letting the tie emerge nicely from under it.

This was the first time Simon had seen her in this kimono, and she enjoyed to see the amazed looks he was throwing at her. This was one of the kimono given to her by her father, but the *obi* had come from her mother, really one of her mother's, passed along to her, and she had thought long and hard about making or not wearing this combination on this occasion. She thought the significance of the mixture might not escape her father — she was the daughter of *both*, still she was independent — but she wasn't too hopeful on that, or that he would accept the reading, even though comprehended. The kimono was black with motifs of long-stemmed irises and the *obi* was dark red. The irises were no mistake either. She knew her father liked to mention the empress Shoken being fond of them and having had several planted in places where she liked to fish.

They would wait for half an hour. Hiroko kept looking every other minute at the clock, and felt her face getting hot with embarrassment each time she looked at Simon.

"Calm down, he must come soon," he kept saying. Now and then, he touched her arm or shoulder to appease her.

They had ordered a course of lobster hors d'oeuvre and orange juice. "Well, at least the food is good in this place," she was telling Simon right at the time when one of the sliding doors, this one on a side that Hiroko had thought was permanently closed, was pushed open by the owner of the tea-house to let in her father, dressed in one of his most ceremonial dark gray kimono with black motifs.

Both Hiroko and Simon, he still wiping his mouth with a napkin, stood up. She bowed first, Simon followed to the same angle, a bit awkwardly, buttoning his suit, and her father replied in kind with a smaller bow, with a stony face. By now, it seemed his mood had turned sour.

Perhaps it's just the day. She suddenly realized her father was ten centimeters or so shorter than Simon; the kimono was brimming with his muscles though.

"Glad to see you, father. Hope you're well," she said in Japanese.

"Glad to see you, Hiroko," he replied, stiffly. "I'm fine."

She rolled out in Japanese the equivalent of "Allow me to introduce to you my friend, Simon Fraser-San," and followed it in English. Simon bowed again after the English fashion, and Kazuhiro Yuasa reissued his cold, well-controlled bow. She thought her father terribly impressive in his kimono and was afraid Simon might not be up to the task of being on the same level with him, but she could see Simon's face was only a touch darker than normal in the spots where his freckles were, his regard open and direct. *Blue waters, how I do like you.*

"Well, let us make ourselves comfortable," her father said in Japanese and sat down on the *tatami* on the opposite side of the low table than the one occupied by Hiroko and Simon. Simon pulled his suit trousers up a little and sat down in the same traditional Japanese male stance, while Hiroko sat on her knees in *seiza*, ready to serve both of them.

"A Campari, father?" she asked.

"No, just sake for me, please." Simon made a sign he would take the same, so she filled a round of three small lacquered wooden glasses with sake. There was no clinking of glasses, slight bows were exchanged and they all raised their glasses to Hiroko's *Kampai.*

Her ears on guard, Hiroko wondered with some trepidation and unease if her father's bodyguards were in the hallway, right behind the sliding door, or downstairs, at the entrance to the tea-house, or in the parking spot, in the car. From her previous meetings with her father, they were probably downstairs. However, he usually made sure to arrive the last and to leave the first, thus she couldn't be sure. With her father around, she could never escape such thoughts, even with Simon now just one step from her.

Without moving too much his lips under his strong nose, nor other facial features around it, her father asked, "*Mistuh Fureza*, which city in the US is he coming from?"

She translated the question to Simon, and replied for him: "New York City, most recently."

"New York City, great place. Visited it. But what does this mean, most recently? How recent is that? Can't they speak straight, these *Amerika-jin?"* The sides of the flattened nose wrinkled in dissatisfaction.

Simon was offered a seriously blunted version of the question. "Well, I'm here for eight months. One year before that spent around the States after graduation. Four years at Columbia. Most of the time before that in Connecticut, with my parents, until the end of high-school, a lot of home schooling," he replied, smiling to Hiroko. "This is it, I guess." Then, smiling thinly at her, "Perhaps we should make sure your father doesn't get hungry. He might launch even more trial balloons, and then I'm gonna be in over my head — but don't translate that, Hiroko."

She translated the first part, then asked her father, "Shouldn't we order something, father? We might get hungry. We had something before you came."

"But he said something about a *baronoo*, a baron, whatever, and you didn't translate that. Is your friend here something the English call blueblood and we don't know?" asked her father, still on edge. "And yes, let's get some food, good idea, all this *gaijin* talk makes me hungry," he added, calling the waitress who rushed in with the menus.

Simon was barely able to control himself from laughing when offered the translation. "Nah, my parents may think of themselves as aristocrats, but we weren't even on the *Mayflower.* We're a more recent sort. Call it *nouveau riche*. We haven't really had any barons in America, not lately. This you may translate, no probs."

By this time, her father was already heavily studying the menu, not offering too much of attention to the continuation. He asked, "What would you young fellows like to eat?"

"My friend eats anything but *fugu*," Hiroko lilted and tinkled in her best Japanese-daughter impersonation, knowing that might just soften her old man. "We'll trust you with the choice, father," she continued. *And with the bill, naturally.*

"Ah, he knows about *that* fish. What a remarkable man we have here. But don't translate this!" was her father's comment and request, uttered still with a stony mask, to which she went ahead and told it all to Simon, under her breath, keeping a cup with tea in front of her mouth.

"All right then, let's have this nine-dish *kaiseki ryōri*, it's good for the body and you young guys might be too economical or modern to have tried it," her father said, and only the "modern" part got into English.

They were somewhere in the middle of the fourth course, when the old man started to have historical musings. "You know, us Japanese and you Americans don't have a long history together; it's basically just since Commodore Perry, stationed in front of Edo on those Black Ships of his, forced us to open our harbors to your wares. Not a nice act, if you ask me: we were small and quiet in our island world." Hiroko conveyed everything.

"Well, yes, I wondered myself several times who and what might have pushed Perry to such a move. Perhaps our whalers," Simon said. "We had our own mind bogglers, none bigger than those leading to the Civil War, several years away only."

"Well, short history, yes," continued Kazuhiro Yuasa, after being offered the translation, "but so damn full of blood on both sides." He looked at Hiroko, as though hesitating on whether to continue, and setting his jaw, he said, "Even my own father, and Hiroko's grandfather, died a hero fighting your ships in the last war. A *Kamikaze*. I doubt Hiroko told you about *that.*"

"No, I didn't, father, and I'm not sorry," she said, but passed this volley to Simon.

"Fighting our ships?" asked Simon, and Hiroko could see his nostrils swell, his eyes flash with that urge to fight, that glint she had come to know in all men of all races. He mastered that outward sign, and continued with some irony, "This story becomes most interesting as, if my memory serves, my father told me my own grandfather died in a *Kamikaze* attack on *Columbia*, his ship."

Hiroko was shocked to see her father shudder on hearing the name of the ship. "Would you have the date?" Kazuhiro Yuasa asked immediately upon the translation having become available, almost wolfishly hunting for that information.

"No, I don't have it, sir, but just a phone to my father could settle that. He lives and breathes history," said Simon, half-apologizing. "We, the others in the family, can't do anything about it."

"Tell him not to insult his father in my presence, because I'm one of the same identical mold," the old man coolly as ice prompted.

Simon had considerably calmed down from the initial reaction he had about the *Kamikaze*, and added, "Well, sir, if I may say so, and I know Hiroko believes the same, even though I wouldn't like to put words in her mouth, I, for one, I'd say let bygones be bygones. World War II has been over for quite a while now."

Kazuhiro replied quite hotly after the translation, "Well, I for one can't forget what we had to sign in front of MacArthur on *Missouri*. This was only a continuation from Commodore Perry, but much worse for us, even more so coming after the atomic bombs. And about my father: I can't forget my own father, of course, though I never met him. I might show him to you once, *Misuta Fureza.*"

The Date is On

Within a week, Kazuhiro Yuasa had it nailed-down by Simon Fraser through Hiroko that Simon's grandfather had been vaporized on the 29th of January 1945 in the explosion of USS *Columbia's* turret produced by a Japanese *Kamikaze* pilot steering his plane in flames at the ship. As far as Kazuhiro figgered, it had taken Simon Fraser's calling his father in the States to get this scoop, as something this detailed this harvest of Americans didn't seem to be prepped to deal with, neither in memory span nor in depth of concern.

He sat now in his office, the only noise in this subterranean hollow the small crackling of old-fashioned filament lamps — for he had never truly gotten used to the fluorescent buzzing. Had the choice of lighting been his, he would have preferred candles, especially for his adjacent museum. Things being as they were, he had decided to use lamps as a reasonable compromise against being labeled a loony by his very underlings.

He had switched off the TV set and was moonily doodling infinite loops with a ballpoint-pen on the huge piece of white paper in front of him, his eyes fixated on it. The sheet of paper was meant for historical Japanese calligraphy lessons. He liked it for the simple, but material reminder of history being there for his attention. He took pride in the fact that while others were made sleepy by it, the hairs on his back went up whenever slivers of history were mentioned, and his mind went churning time's flour. He knew he would always have a tough time accepting being weaned off the past.

His drawing outlined two main clouds — a small, delicate, whitish one, barely contoured, and a darker one, heavily cross-hatched — and his iterations attempted to place them further and further apart, until the viewer could safely assume the large space between them was an ocean now. "They're already too close for my comfort," he was saying. "Keeping these two separated would but help. I could smell it in the air: only because of my being on the spot did he keep his hands off her at the party. I'd better do something before they move something rash to paper, zinging untold hours of *shodo* and *otemae* spent on her betterment. To then undo such rash moves could take years of my life, and once the lawyers get their tails in the affair could be well nigh impossible.

"But whatever is done, it must be done on both sides of the Pond, to have it cast in concrete. I'm sure *they,* the other family, wouldn't like it any more than I do. I, for one, would rather have the young, fresh ones clipped than flying in the face of those who, just three spawnings ago, were the murdered and those who were the murderees. Or, vice versa, for that's how it was in war — you kill me, I kill you. I need to get the story over to the other side in as gory blow-by-blow as it was in darn true life. No ifs and buts about this: they wouldn't like to hack Japanese in *their* family any more than I'd like to hack Yanks on my side."

***

She was in his arms at Simon's place and would not have wished to be anywhere else. This was her *sakura* forever.

"How did you feel about my father?" Hiroko asked Simon with a worried trill.

"He's all right. He's healthy and strong, that was good to see, not the least as a peek into your genes. I'm always curious about you," he said, smiling and going on.

"He loves tradition too. I mean, that kimono of his was something else; I thought old samurai were coming upon us flown from the sky. Loves his food and drink." Simon had been calm in saying all this, but she could sense something coming up in his voice, and it was next there, already froth rippling on words now.

"However, I'm not so sure his vibes about you and I being together are too good. And it didn't play well with me, all his asking scores of times about a day back in '45. It made me fear there's something hidden in there, in all that history, that could spell trouble for the two of us, or for all of us, for that matter," he continued, and she could see shadows sailing over his forehead.

"Well," Hiroko streamed in quickly, as though to cover a breach in a dam, "he talks too much about death, history, and we still have lives to live."

Simon shook his head: there was, it seemed, more to it, and he wanted it out, even though the words came out with obvious trepidation in his voice, in his whole being.

"You see, I'm no philosopher, so I'm of necessity cutting frills here, and grossly, but I think death feels quite at home in history. Human history itself it just a long string of deaths," he said.

Sarcasm and sadness, the venom of one's own perceived mortality, all trickling in his words, she thought, and wanted to hug him with all her power.

"But I prefer," Simon continued, "as a still young, living and breathing individual, to look in time positive — sorry, Einstein — to the future, and not in time negative, to the past. Worst case, I prefer to look *toward* my own or my contemporaries' deaths. I'd rather have that to bring out the pain in me, not the one of past fellows or generations, as worthy as they could have been, or as close to me as blood relatives."

Hiroko, listening to him, thought herself lucky that they were on the same wavelength on this, and a primal swell and flow of love and well-being rose in her from her toes to her neck. Truly, the only man to whom she had talked for any reasonable length of time in her life was her father, and most of the time they didn't agree, or if they agreed they weren't in the same mood at that moment, and so the necessary ping-pong of conversation stalled, and one of them or both left it, feeling dry. Her former boyfriend had been a silent, shy fellow who was the last to tell her his views on a subject, even though she knew he was opinionated. Now, with Simon, they both agreed, the first impulse toward each other had been a matter of eye-and-body attraction — like two sides of a sandwich, she sometimes said, laughing — especially with their limited ability in each other's language. Things being this way, yes, she thought she was lucky to have Simon in step with her on a matter of thought, but also on a keen, instinctive turning under the sun for the direction of life, just like the sunflower does.

"OK, I know I started it, but we won't talk about my father anymore tonight, right?" Hiroko asked.

"I think we can reach an understanding on the matter, yes, Hiroko-chan," he said, smiling, and she felt his right arm sneaking between her back and the bed, to lift her closer to him, to his lips having now the full run of her face, of her naked torso.

"Umm, the pajamas," she murmured, eyes closed.

"No compromises, eh?" he said, but she knew he had gotten the message when she felt him squiggling out of his pajamas pants and shirt and heard the rustling of the cotton. She liked this too: he wasn't one to keep her on tenterhooks. But today, it was she who wanted more of a passage to the fruit, so she pushed his hips gently away, allowing in the bargain full play for his mouth, which started a slow, intricate and wetpointed journey over her inner thighs.

***

"Do you know what idea Father has come up with?" Hiroko asked Simon on another night, while bopping together on Mexican beer to a reggae tune in a Roppongi disco and bar. The place was loud, so she had to speak close into his ear.

"Don't make me too curious: I just might ask the question," he said, and laughed. He then quickly added "What idea?" when he saw she hadn't quite got the irony.

"You should go to work with him for several days, weeks even."

Simon put his arms on her shoulders, stopping her from dancing, looked with utter disbelief at her, and started to laugh, so she felt prodded to provide a reinforcement. "And the big surprise: also, you should ask your parents to invite *me* to stay with them during that time."

He took a double-take at her, and led her, shaking his head, through the large crowd to a table in a corner, as though feeling the need to sit down. Only now he released his answer to her latest. "Wouldn't all that be beautiful! Paradise! What for, all this theater? He doesn't seem to stomach me, to put it mildly, and my parents might be not too far in their treatment of you. Sorry, but that's just it — the kind of parents we are blessed with."

She signalled the waiter for two beers, then turned back to Simon, shrugged and sighed in replying to him. "He says different generations should know each other better, before decisions are taken."

"And what are *you* saying?" he asked hotly, two prominent veins on his forehead asking for attention. "Are you buying into this notion?"

"No, and I find it even risky for you," she said.

"As though my parents are soft as suede," he laughed. "Don't bet on that, I'm warning you."

"But we don't have many other choices. Either play with them, or run from them forever," she argued. "Would you like that?"

"You mean, the running? Certainly not. As well, I like challenges, and I feel your father has laid one at my door, to my very maleness. It says go and challenge him or forget about each other."

"Perhaps not," she said, but her eyes were deep into his, following any motion of theirs, any flicker.

"Perhaps not? Then I don't know anymore what a challenge is and I need a refresher."

"Perhaps he tries to understand you, and us," she issued, barely breathing it.

"Trouble is, to do that — I mean to understand — he would have to forget about the war, and that, I feel, is pretty remote. But perhaps you might know more impersonations, I mean versions, of your father, than I will ever get to know."

"But you know I haven't lived much with him; it has been mostly with my mother," Hiroko said.

"Finished your beer? Then let's go back dancing, and let's not talk heavy stuff anymore tonight," Simon said, and pulled her up from her chair by her arm, smiling. And she loved dancing with him, so she jumped up on her high heels and followed him onto the dance-floor. They had a terrible time to sneak back in through the dense, sweaty crowd, illuminated by the strobed, kaleidoscopic light, but finally they got to the center, where it seemed there was only music and the swaying born from it. That music, the vibes of the place, him swinging in front of her, she knew, were all a lead-up to charmed happenings between Simon and herself during the night — and she was patient.

***

Mr. Fraser,

I am disappointed you have to learn about me through this short message. I would certainly have preferred to meet you face to face, preferably the way our two fathers did, on the 29th of January, 1945, when they succeeded in sending each other to the glory of our respective forefathers. Time is of essence, though.

Fate has decided to continue to test us. My daughter Hiroko and your son Simon are together, here in Tokyo, much more than I would feel comfortable with. They might sign anytime a formal document sealing their rapprochement, even going against the wishes of their families, wishes which I can assure you of on my side.

Consequently, I have decided to apprentice Simon by me for several weeks for an initiation in what life and undying hate might hold in reserve for them, and to send Hiroko to your family in the United States during that time, for a similar treatment. I would prefer to see my daughter leaving this world altogether than for me to be forced to witness another capitulation [to your nation]. I can only trust you respect tradition just as much as I do and, therefore, that you'll proceed accordingly in keeping them at all cost at a healthy distance from each other.

Keeping the contents of this communication from your son and my daughter would be most appreciated.

I am sure I should feel embarrassed by the quality of the English in the present. This is all money can buy this day in Tokyo, Japan, fifty years after the war.

Faithfully in odium forever,
Kazuhiro Yuasa

He was still of two minds on the bracketed words in "*another capitulation [to your nation]*". He didn't want it all to be humiliatingly explicit. And this was his decision, not the translator's. Not a matter of style, but of substance, this, so he needed to ponder.

Leaving from Narita

Simon felt he couldn't tell Hiroko about that dream, not on her trip to Narita, even though hiding it from her caused him a splitting headache, just as he had when he had woken up the morning after it, four days ago. It would have been tantamount to spoiling her whole trip to the States by some ugly, confusing dream he had had, perhaps after having ingested some rotten food at dinner.

Maybe that sushi. Maybe the combination of beer with sake. Still, why then did he feel as that prophetess in old Greece making herself sick by inhaling fumes for the power of getting a peek into the future? Was he becoming an old, sick broad, and no one was breaking to him the truth about it? By the way, was the old broad a virgin? He didn't remember and didn't even care. (Strange games the mind can play with you.) He couldn't tell either why this stupid preoccupation with that very thought had come upon his pained being.

For he felt sickened to his core by her leaving for the States, for his very family. The dream had culminated in her, well, a silhouette of her, going, sliding into something that now, with the awareness of the waking hours, he could see it looked just as a black-hole, as shown in those science-fiction movies. A drop in emptiness that never ended, him never having being able to stretch a helping hand to her, the increasing awful distance between them having become itself a source of ever more acute, organic pain. It had taken him a long shower on the morning following the dream to become functional at all.

They shared a corner bench on the train to Narita and no one was sitting in front of them, so they felt free to speak.

At times, she laughed and pecked his cheek. He was a little embarrassed by this gesture in a crowded Japanese train, where people weren't given to anything warm or demonstrative, but was proud at the same time, and looked around to see if anyone had remarked on it. No sign of that, and he was not surprised, discretion being another Japanese behavior rule that you could count on being self-enforced by most of the locals in such public settings.

***

"My father and your father must be very similar people. I'd expect, say in a risky gambling situation, for them to behave pretty much identically," he had been telling Hiroko in his bed, only two days before her leaving. This was supposed to be a planning session. Mainly strategy, rough lines: they didn't have time for anything more.

"Why gambling?" she had asked, dark, sharp eyes widened in surprise, a fluffy light-blue pajama-set on her.

"Money is the first thing that seems to come to my mind when thinking about my father. All his idiosyncrasies aside, your father seems to be, first and foremost, of the same bent. Am I wrong?"

"No, I don't think you are, but there's one thing that doesn't have a price for my father, and that is history. Especially family history. He simply refuses to compromise on such things," she said.

"No, both of them won't deal on such stuff, indeed," he agreed. After a short moment of reflection, he continued, "You know, this seems to simplify our approach."

"What's your plan then?" she asked. She looked anxious, eyebrows raised at their outer extremities.

"Well, you may laugh or cry, your choice, Little Miss Planning, but I'm flying on the seat of my pants here." He laughed, embarrassed, treading waters. "I'm working on it as we go, if you can believe that."

"So, is first idea to deal with them the same way, even though one is American and the other Japanese?" she asked, and he knew she was trying to have something out by 'n by.

"Right on. The second: money and history are the most important things for them. They might negotiate on the first, never on the second," he continued, chin more set by the instant, face firmer, as though aware of and already confronting the opposition to come.

"This is why I love you: clarity." She giggled.

He flashed a smile, then recovered adeptly the seriousness that had been creasing his forehead. "The third idea is it, I'd say. We should apprise them again and again, even though this should be crystal-clear to them after twenty years of family life on both sides: we two are of a different generation and of a different mold. Even though in the molding they had a first impact — should we call it that? — and we're carrying part of their genes," he laid it out, laughing at the end.

"So, that our values are different?" she asked.

"That sounds kind of sonorous and big, but yes, and I'll be very crude: we must absolutely hammer it into their — pardon me my lady — thick heads, in facts and words, one at a time, if need be. Due respect, but we're not stuck on their priorities as much as they are, on the contrary, we have different ones, such as … " He hesitated, but help came immediately.

"Us? Each other?" she issued quietly, coming close to his ear, love and hope, desperation too, pouring unmistakably out of anxious eyes, out of her entire face, when she sat back against the cushions.

He just nodded and kissed her, and they both went silent, holding hands, sliding then into hugging tightly for minutes, limbs entwined upon each other's. For the future didn't seem a lake in repose anymore.

***

"Do you young people know what you're doing?"

Her mother never said "you and Simon," even though she had met Simon on several occasions when he came in to pick Hiroko up for going out somewhere. This bothered Hiroko, but this wasn't the best of times to complain.

"Like what, mother?"

Her mother was pacing through their kitchen in her long, dark blue house robe. "Well, like going to live with each other's family. You seem to have the zeal of missionaries, and what is worse, some of their blindness too. What mission is that? One thing I know, and I don't pretend to be knowing much about them: missionaries have a holy book and stick to it, right or wrong; it gives them purpose."

It was the first time that Hiroko had seen several creases on her mother's neck, as well as thin lines of white in her hair, as though the care in her eyes had gone and taken mastery of other parts of her body. Luckily, even though on the plump side, she was still full of energy.

"We have a purpose, Mother. We're just trying to tell others in the families we exist."

"Well, I gather you want to tell them you'd like to exist ... as a couple. Thing is, as far as I know, you're not a couple. Fix me on that, if I'm wrong." Her mother had stopped and looked this time straight at Hiroko, who was still seated at the kitchen table, the tidbits of the end of the meal arrayed in plates, cups and bowls that had lost their initial spatial order.

"Well, which comes first, Mother, the egg or the chicken? The announcement from the children, or the approval and benediction of the parents? We would like to put our cards on the table when 'people,' as you're saying, are able to deal with it. Seems reasonable and polite to me."

"Reasonable and polite that might be, but how realistic is it? On both parts, on the children's part, and on the parents' part," Makoto Asaye inquired, sitting down at the table and putting a hand on her daughter's right forearm. "Do we have an engagement in the works, which I know nothing about, perhaps?"

Hiroko, fiddling with a napkin, felt she had to play it straight, even though she sensed the sudden redness in her face and heat going to the roots of her hair. "No, Mother, if that's the question, Simon has not yet formally proposed."

"Formally? Are there any other ways of proposing that should be considered by a serious girl these days? I beg to be updated on the current fashion, for I might have lost a step or two with this world," her mother said. She looked towards the kitchen window, the street empty in the early afternoon. "Mind you, I was crazy enough in my own time to bring to the world two girls without any proposal, but I wouldn't encourage anyone on that path, which as far as I know, it's considered sinful, especially by the Christians. And Simon is a Christian — you should never forget that. You never know when the conscience of a man, Christian or otherwise, turns up, and he himself turns against the woman he has committed the sin with."

"I don't think Simon will ever turn against me, Mother."

"Words of a young inexperienced woman. You don't know men. Men don't like to change, and especially don't like to have their arms twisted, even by what they themselves would grant is nothing but good will. Beware a stubborn man.

"Also, you're facing here two old men, one of which I know for a fact is nothing but very, very stubborn. What do you know? To pour sake for them, perhaps dance for them, perhaps to politely listen to their stories? This is not a geisha story, Hiroko-chan."

Hiroko bristled in her mind, but tried hard not to show it. "Let me bring some rice cakes, Mother." She wanted to escape the pressure of her mother's hand on her arm, her mother's bad feelings about men.

"Perhaps they are not just old dry shells, these two men, Mother. Perhaps we can move them," she said, while coming back to the table with the pastries and the tea pot.

"And what you gamble in exchange, Hiroko-chan, is nothing but your life. Just like I did, trying to change men," her mother said, shaking her head, and started to drink her tea with rice cakes. For her, the matter was closed, she had tried her best.

But Hiroko knew one thing her mother would do with her, go to the neighborhood shrine later in the afternoon, to pray together for what each of them had in mind before this trip of hers started, and clap their hands in unison for godly attention.

***

Simon told her, "My father told me the limousine is going to wait for you at JFK, at the passengers' exit gate after Immigration and luggage pick up. The driver will have a large sign for you, with your name. Please watch for it. I gave you my parents' address in Connecticut, give it to Immigration, I'm sure they'll ask for your address while in the States. Just say 'visiting friends and the country.' Same address for the driver, except if you want to visit in New York City and stay at a hotel. I'll leave that to your inspiration on the day. Sorry, my old student digs are occupied by other students. My parents apologize for not being present in person at JFK to welcome you, they seem to be busy on that day." He shrugged — she could see his embarrassment on his face — and said, "And I apologize for them."

He kissed her on her mouth and told her, "You're gonna do it. *We're* gonna do it." She pressed the small of his back as much as she could with her hand.

Simon goes deep I

Pale light clouded the whole of Kazuhiro Yuasa's subterranean properties, entered each cave and room, sneaked into each nook and cranny. There might have been stone dust too, left over from blasts and excavations used to break open decades ago this space as huge in places as underground tunnels, tens of meters underneath Tokyo, a dust suspended thinly in the air. At times, Simon felt himself moving through something denser and heavier to breathe than natural air. But it could be all this was just worries about Hiroko, about seeing her again, which affected sight and mind, keeping him in check.

Kazuhiro Yuasa hadn't given him any blueprint for his stay there. Still, he had said that if he wanted to do it seriously, "to have any luck," he had to stay in his, Kazuhiro Yuasa's, space for the duration. "Not other Tokyo for you, just my Tokyo," he had told him through Yukio Imashita, acting as translator. "To learn us and our ways."

And Simon's reading of "to have any luck" was all related to his own and Hiroko's fate together, as seen by Kazuhiro Yuasa. Simon didn't know for how long he would agree to go along with the non-existing blueprint, but was willing for the time being to give the whole enterprise a good shot. *There's a chance for peace between the generations. A sliver of a chance, perhaps, but Hiroko and I have agreed to go for it.* He certainly intended to go along only with the first part of "To learn us and our ways," in order to keep his balance with himself, but he knew that in order to travel that first path he might have to do some inroads, some baby steps, throw some peeks, in parts of the second. *Tricky, that. Tricky. Never took Father on his like offer. So then, why should I move here? Only for (staying with) Hiroko, methinks.*

***

Today, he was supposed to go to an "A" party. That meant a night club in Shinjuku, in the Kabukicho area, which had its name starting with the letter "A." For reasons unknown, Kazuhiro had decreed that the subscribers be bussed around bars — well, in limousines, naturally — bars carrying country names, and this night it was "Algeria" for his small group, which included Imashita and a bodyguard rumored to have come from a sumo stable, wide as a door. Imashita was to be in charge with the translation, the bodyguard with the security, which Simon thought meant to a large extent his not escaping "the system."

"That's what we do, entertainment," Kazuhiro Yuasa had told Simon. "And we do it well."

"Did Hiroko ever go to those bars?" Simon asked, just to ping off Kazuhiro, just to see how thick his crocodile crust was.

"You crazy Americans! Of course not. She's legally allowed in such places only for two years," promptly the translation was lobbed back, accompanied by a scowl. "Also, businessmen don't take wives or sisters to such places, not in my system. We look after families, we don't just play loose, what'd ya think?"

"Fair enough, *wakarimasu,*" Simon said, not willing to create waves this early.

Their arrival was expected. An agitated, heavily rouged Japanese woman, her blood all in her temples, seemingly the matron of the establishment, was out in full regalia on the small porch at the entrance of the club, the building walls stuccoed white, the porch floor in ceramic tiles portraying a seraglio scene. She was accompanied by what could only be two of the navel dancers, no doubt two Middle-Eastern girls in their early twenties, thin transparent scarves covering their shoulders and midriffs. The door was left intentionally open, for the languishing music of the Middle East to sneak out, enough to give suggestion to the dancers' swayings.

The taller, more beautiful, and willowy girl was apparently assigned to Simon, for with familiarity she sneaked her hand under his arm and pulled him inside through the entry door covered in Arabian patterns of sparkling green vines, flowers at their full bloom, fruits at their most colorful ripeness, all twisted together in inlay in an "eight" pattern laid out on the white, ivory-like surface.

No, he didn't want to go there, even though he had been told everything on this weeks-long perambulation was covered by Kazuhiro Yuasa himself. The bar was circular, set as an island in the center of the room, serviced by two barmaids, a Japanese and an Arab, both dressed in Arabian costumes with flowing silk harem pants, less sheer than the dancers'. The room itself was circular too, and had on its wall large photographic glimpses of the North African country: the rolling desert, its dunes, camels and bedouins looking into the camera or filing toward the horizon, the Mediterranean shore, the Atlas mountains, flowing one into another. Azure, the ceiling was a hemispherical cupola sprayed with stars, really as seen from that side of the world, as he was to be told. Around the room there were ten or so circular black tables, and the news trickling to Simon from Imashita was that on the second floor there were separate *tatami*-floored chambers.

On their entrance, there was a hush, and looking around Simon got the reason for it: he was the only Caucasian customer in the room, all the others seemed to be Japanese businessmen or thereabouts, all of them in suits and ties, save two or three in black leather jackets and polo-neck sweaters.

Even though the dancer was trying to pull him to one of the separate tables, Simon stepped towards the bar and she willy-nilly gave up on her initial idea, settling herself beside him on another of the tall bar stools with bright nickel-plated legs. Yukio with the bodyguard went accompanied by the other belly dancer to a table in one of the corners, making sure he was in direct view of them.

The Japanese barmaid came over and asked them what they would like to drink. Simon settled for sake and the dancer did the same, but Simon would later observe it was mixed heavily with water by the server for her. Matter of being able to still dance after hours and hours, he thought.

They clinked the glasses with *Kampai!* Not a place where they serve it in square glasses of wood, this, he thought.

The dancer sidled to him and asked, "Are you from America?" She murdered the pronunciation, but otherwise Simon felt her English was passable.

"This is something I can answer honestly," Simon replied, jokingly. "Yes."

"And you come a lot Kabukicho?"

"No, but I pass a lot through Shinjuku. Both for business and shopping. Let's say I took a leave from my work." Which was more or less true: the Company had granted him a leave of absence of one month with no problems, "to visit Japan." In fact, Dr. Sugie had been delighted by his curiosity about the country.

"My name Zarya," she said.

"My real name is Simon." He laughed.

"Ah, you know we not using our real names in bars? Good for you," said the Arab girl, flashing a smart smile to his face. But she would never during that night offer more than that on the issue.

He felt really down for a moment. *Where are you now? New York City or Connecticut?*

He sent a hand wave to Yukio, to keep him at a distance. A-OK here.

"So, what do you do in Tokyo?" the girl asked.

"You mean, for work?" At her nodding, he added, "Professional Photographer." He had learned a long time ago that dropping around the "Professional" part gave him some weight in dealing with others. Otherwise, everybody was making pictures those days, one figured.

"Ah, can you do pictures for my portfolio?" she asked. "I'm a model."

Ah, a model too. Man, oh man. "Not sure, I'm quite busy, and expensive, you know."

"Well, perhaps we can change," she trilled, her hips changed position in space, slightly waving from the vertical, and he understood instantly the 'exchange,' and her part of the deal. And she wasn't a negligible quantity.

"Not for now. I'm sorry."

"OK." She didn't fuss about it. Coming from the Middle East to Japan couldn't have been the most spoiling of experiences. "Would you like see me dance?" she asked.

"Ah, of course."

She went to the audio system, looked through the tunes available on cassettes, and soon found something to her liking. She must have done that dance many times. But it seemed to be something not in her everyday repertory, for the men in the room instantly turned to see her when the song commenced languorously and she went into the small dancing area and started to move by herself.

The music seemed to have a special effect on her body, and Simon soon recognized she was exquisite at her art, so undulating those hips moved, so well-punctuated her navel and her bottom thrusts were, so the eyes looked from under the lashes in a tempting, hot-filtered manner, in sync with those sinuous thrusts.

Her eyes were focused on Simon, and at the end, when after the applause she came to him and put her hand on his shoulder, standing to the side, and had a refreshing drink, he thought all that could earn him some jealousy in those thereabouts.

And that came next, as one of the businessmen, sitting on another of the bar stools, at about ninety degrees from Simon on that circular bar, threw him a daring look and asked with the tone of a vague challenge, in English:

"American, eh, you?"

"Yes, I am American." Simon had a quick look at him and realized the shoulder muscles under the other's suit jacket had tensed, as a bodybuilder's anxious to challenge his competition on a scene. The eyes were mean, troubled by liquor.

"You come here take our fun, eh, *America-jin*?"

Simon waved to him a half-sign of peace and quiet. He thought nothing too demonstrative could silence such a guy, and Simon didn't want to engage him, mostly for not spoiling his own mood. Just ten minutes ago he had thought of Hiroko, now this.

The guy jumped down from his stool. He wasn't too tall, but seemed quite strong. It seemed for all intents and purposes he wanted to come over to Simon, but it was too late. The bouncer of the place as well as the bodyguard with Simon were already by him, barking in Japanese something Simon took to be to the effect he himself was Kazuhiro Yuasa-San's guest. Whatever it was, it had the guy bowing to Simon and to the dancer several times, as well as apologizing in Japanese, then rushing to his seat to pick up his rectangular leather handbag and leaving the place, his huff having been replaced by a sweaty worried forehead.

Next thing Simon knew, the Arab girl had disappeared from just beside him and was presently talking heatedly with the other belly dancer, who nodded a refusal to do whatever the first one had asked.

He moved towards the Japanese barmaid, and having made a screen of his hand in the direction of Yukio and the bodyguards — who were now together back at their table — as for feeling a painful tooth in his jaw, asked her:

"Why did the dancer leave?"

"*Chotto muzukashii.* You trouble," she murmured under her breath, without looking at him, acting as if she were pouring him another glass.

"I'm trouble for others or I'm in trouble myself?" Simon quickly shot back.

The woman made another tour of duty around the bar, gathering emptied glasses, pouring here and there some refills, and when she was back in front of him, passed quickly to him:

"Both."

So a man who had wanted to challenge him hadn't, in the end, but had cleared the spot with the tail between his legs, and a woman who just minutes ago had reasons to keep talking to him, if she wanted that portfolio, was shunning him now. *Being Kazuhiro Yuasa's guest makes some people gag around me. So, being his guest, does it make me a leper or too powerful?* For the time being, the message seemed double-edged. Keep observing, this was the best advice he could offer to himself.

One hour later, after several more dances done at the request of the other patrons, the two dancers were sitting alone at their own table, taking a break, and Simon thought the opportunity presented itself to again get closer to them. Having observed they were close to the men's, he took a detour there, and upon his exit, passed their table and dropped himself upon one of the free chairs. The women were flabbergasted.

“What happened to you? You left me out there in doldrums, or should we say in the Sahara,” he said joking to the one that had been flirting with him at the beginning, the more beautiful one.

Watching him intently, her face remained blank, witness of several years in the business. “I’m sorry, I need refresh myself,” she said after a moment, and took off for the ladies’. Simon thought it had been mostly deer under headlights what he had been able to read behind that façade.

“What d’you want with Zarya?” the other asked, irritated.

“Why did she so suddenly leave me? Something wrong? Am I carrying something like herpes and I don’t know?”

The girl checked to see if anyone at Yukio’s table was looking in their direction. Seemingly satisfied, she continued, hands over her face, as though supporting it for reflection, “Sure there’s something wrong. Last guy who came here, Yuasa-San’s guest, never seen. Two years ago. We newcomers here then. What business are you with him?”

“No business. I’m a friend of his daughter.”

“Her boyfriend?”

“I find that somewhat indiscrete,” he demurred. He had never used the ‘boyfriend’ word with anyone when talking about Hiroko and himself.

“Fine. So I don’t have time. Just wanna tell you Yuasa-San protects very tough what’s his. Like what happened years ago; perhaps twenty. His ex’s lover, perhaps. One *katana* strike enough. Nothing for sure, and I’m not saying. Just watch for yourself.”

“Thanks a lot,” he murmured, and returned to the bar, shuffling, a heavy feeling, not so much about himself, but about the irreparable past. This rhymed with what he knew from Hiroko about her mother’s lover. Shuji Miyamoto and her mother had been engaged to marry back then, she already having had the two girls with Kazuhiro Yuasa, and being separated from him.

Three hours later, Simon took the elevator down to the underground site with Yukio. He was sleeping there, as they had agreed, just several rooms away from Kazuhiro Yuasa’s office and suite. At least he didn’t have to sleep in the same room with Yukio — he didn’t trust him at all. The owner of the place wasn’t home yet: there was just a minimum of light in boss' area, just enough so one wouldn't stumble on the long, cavernous corridor.

Hiroko must be in Connecticut by this time. Perhaps even in his old bed, if his mother caught how tightly knit he and Hiroko were. Not that his mother was on the wavelength of the girls he really liked.

His quarters here were more than spare. A military-style metal cot, a hard mattress, a hard pillow, hard, starched sheets. No windows at all. Again, the pale, dusty air. But he didn't complain, for he thought most probably Kazuhiro Yuasa's place itself couldn't be much more luxurious. Hadn't been invited there yet, and the dog growling — with the noise of a large steam engine ready to explode from behind his master's door — had to have been bred, or wired, in hell.

He was recapping his talks with Kazuhiro Yuasa and thought there was a thing they, Hiroko and he, shouldn't have agreed to: accepting Hiroko's father's suggestion of not communicating with each other by any means during this trip of Hiroko's to the States.

Kazuhiro told him through Hiroko's translation at the time. "You young people think you know everything, that you've lived everything. Let's see how you can live just *in spirit* with each other, across the ocean and continents, without being on the phone every day with each other. Let's see if there's a mood or a pool of will or something out there in the fate, big enough to take in both of you and to make you feel together without all this small talk and pieces of paper, without the stuff, the matter. Only then you might pretend there's some power in you two together." Mind, he had never mentioned "couple." Most probably, to avoid giving them hopes that he's accepting "their thing."

A dangerous trap, he'd felt at the time. However, Hiroko seemed to want to rise to the challenge of her father. Most of the time, this is what children do, but on this item Simon thought she might have chewed on more than she could deal with, and have taken him out on that limb too, as he couldn't have contradicted her in front of her father; not if he wanted to emphasize the strength of their relationship — and this was the whole idea of all this test of will and nerves with Kazuhiro Yuasa — for Simon took it for what it was.

Hiroko! On their last night together before her leaving for the States, at his place, she had spent half an hour kissing all of his naked body with some desperate attention, after their lovemaking.

He had thought she would be worried, but not to this extent. She told him, "All moments, I didn't take advantage of you this close to me."

He didn't want to show her his own worries. She felt that as coldness and cried, her back turned on him.

Hiroko over in NYC

Well, if these New Yorkers don't have the best ice cream anywhere. Having bought a square package in silvery metallic paper from a street vendor, Hiroko licked at it in front of Rockefeller Center, sitting on some rails close to the ice skating rink and the statue of Prometheus. It was so rich, this ice cream; she thought all the Japanese back home would have considered it a crime against their bodies. In size and in richness. These Americans did too, but they just went ahead and enjoyed it. Much bigger, the Americans. She hadn't been prepared for it, in Tokyo she had met mainly young ones, which kept themselves in better shape, many of them having gone vegan or liking anyway the Japanese food — part of their reasons for staying in Japan. Many others, according to Simon, not having the funds to really enjoy lots of food in expensive Tokyo.

Simon. She would have loved to have him as a guide in her first visit in North America. She felt kind of lost this way, just with *Fodor's* and a map of New York City, bought back home at an international library in Shinjuku. They had been together on that day. Together — the word rippled so deeply within her. Haiku.

She — a violin,
And a string pinged on its mouth.

***

She had called Simon's parents' home in Connecticut yesterday, from her hotel room around 50th Street in Manhattan. Looking back at it now, it might have been better not to have called at all.

The ring at the other end of the line seemed to be custom-made, very sonorous, warbling. She had never heard anything similar. But then, she had not called many homes in America either; this had been her first.

"Fraser residence. Whom would you like to speak to?" a baritone, British-accented voice had asked. The part on the accent she would realize only later, when replaying this conversation over and over.

"I would like to speak to Mrs. Fraser, please." She had forced herself to speak clearly and slowly, as Simon himself had taught her.

"May we know who's calling?" Hiroko was surprised for a moment by the plural, not recalling it having been used in any of her lessons with him.

"I am Yuasa Hiroko. I'm sorry, I'm Hiroko Yuasa," she babbled.

"And on whose behalf would you be calling?"

"Er … on mine. I'm from Japan. I'm friends with Simon." She always had problems with the word "behalf." It seemed so indirect.

The voice at the other end hung in the ether for a moment, then came back.

"Ah, you mean, you are friends with the young master? What can we do for you?"

She felt obfuscated by this peremptory voice, demanding so much information, and calling Simon an old name, "master," which she had heard only in imported historical movies, but she remembered their decision, hers and Simon's, to be patient in all this, on both sides, irrespective of what they would be facing, so she continued as though all this was just natural to her. "Simon Fraser told me to call Mrs. Fraser once I am in the States. I am now in New York City."

"Fine, then," the imperious voice concluded, "We'll see whether Mrs. Fraser is at home and available. Please remain on the line."

Which was all she could do. It was just as well she was seated on her hotel bed, for it took the whole of four or five minutes.

Finally the severe voice came back on the line and said, "Mrs. Fraser will speak to you now."

"Hello. This is Mrs. Fraser speaking. How can I help you?" This voice finally coming on the line was moderate in volume, singing or perhaps clinking, but cold; there really wasn't any perceivable curiosity in it.

Hiroko thought she had to start the whole thing all over again and felt ridiculous all the way through in doing it.

"I am Hiroko Yuasa. I am from Tokyo, Japan. I am friends with your son, Simon. He told me I should call you when I am in America."

There was first a long delay, as though huge stores of memories had to be combed through. "Yes," the answer finally came in a flat, equal voice, "Now I remember. Simon told me something about someone coming from Japan. I'm not sure if he said 'friends,' but no doubt I can take your word about that. And where would you be at this time?"

"I am in New York."

"Visiting, I suppose?"

"Yes. I like it very much," Hiroko said, only one moment later realizing no one had expressed any interest in her current state of mind.

"Ah, yes? Interesting. Now, this being said, what can we do for you?" The voice clinked with lack of interest.

Hiroko felt her cheeks purple with embarrassment. "Simon suggested … "

"Yes?" — The voice continued to pull teeth, yet obviously expecting no information — "What did he suggest?"

"Well, Simon said he had talked to you. That you said I could come and visit you. I mean, his family." Hiroko clipped everything, in the hope of achieving some clarity.

"He might have said that. I'll trust you *on that*. And when would you like to come and visit us?"

Hiroko's take on what had been just meant was that Simon might be that young man who flings such statements into the wind with not a care in the world.

With half a hope after "when would you like" had been uttered, she replied, "I plan to spend three or four more days in New York City. Perhaps after that?"

"Yes, perhaps after that it could be a good time. Should you still want to visit us then, please call us one day in advance and leave the message with Brandon here, our butler."

"Thank you very much. I will do so."

"Good day, then." The line clicked, went dead.

Hiroko kept the receiver at her ear for one long minute, before putting it very slowly down. She went to the bathroom, washed her face with cold water, yet it refused to change its deep paleness.

She had realized right at the time of speaking that "invitation" and "stay" had not been mentioned by either party. She was to continue to have festering doubts all through her stay in NYC about the point of going to visit the Connecticut Frasers at all.

***

Hiroko wanted to go to the Metropolitan Museum on her third day in Manhattan. Simon had talked to her too much about it back in Japan for her to ever consider passing through New York and not visiting it. He was in love with their Costume Institute but had mentioned to her the Asian Art department and that's where she wanted to go. She wanted to see for herself how the Japanese art was shown — and what parts of it — on this side of the Pacific. Well, in the world.

During her second day, she had gone to the Museum of Modern Art and spent one full hour in front of the water lilies by Monet, taking them in from all sides. In Tokyo, the National Museum of Western Art housed one of Monet's *Water Lilies*, but the collection here was something mind-blowing (Simon had taught her to love this adjective, and always accompanied it by animated gesticulation). Walls upon walls just for one painting, the *Reflection of Clouds on the Water-Lily Pond.* It was worth dying to be able to paint something like this, even though, she believed to remember, Monet had lived a long life. This had been such an absorbing immersion in European painting, that she wanted for today something, so the idea with the Japanese collection at the Met.

It was there, that she met Richard Selznikow, the young curator. He was making some final arrangements on a temporary exhibition to start the next day and she got to discuss with him the finer design points of one of the kimono to be shown there.

"Very beautiful, isn't it?" he asked her.

"Indeed. I recognize style: something like seventy years ago. Kyoto, I think."

"Oh, I fell upon an expert here!" he said, beaming. "Yes, it was made for one of the *o-maiko* there, between the two wars. Too bad we can't show it in a dance, it would be much better for the live event of the opening. We might get TV coverage, some of the major networks seem to want to show something on the morning shows the next day. Nothing too long, but it could bring in sponsors, you know." He murmured, mostly for himself and the other colleagues around him, "Nothing to be sneezed at, mind you."

"Perhaps I can help." She smiled at him.

"What? Don't tell me you're a Japanese traditional dancer!" He looked again, guardedly this time, at her. "Sorry, but we would need a professional. Otherwise, there are so many Japanese dancing clubs in New York, but we haven't been able to quite come up with someone very good in dances on music of that specific period, or thereabouts. For this is *Interwar Japan*, our show, you know."

"I can dance both traditional and modern Japanese styles. I'm professional dancer, not *geisha* or *maiko*, yet based in Tokyo. But—" she hesitated, smiling "—I don't have kimono with me in the States. By the way, I am Yuasa Hiroko." She felt, listening to herself, that for a moment all the English learned with Simon had gone down the drain. *How awkward I am.*

"Look, Miss Yuasa," he said, and his face became very serious, "let's have a short test right now with one of our other, more modest kimono, and if we find a *match*" — he coughed with slight embarrassment — "I think we can pull enough strings for you to get to dance live with this very one, even though we would need to pair it with an appropriate *obi* and organize the small set of small accessories on them, the *obi jime*, the *obi* cord, the *obi makura*, the *obi* pad, and so forth, in order for them to fit you well."

It took three ladies working in the Asian Art department two hours to dress up Hiroko in some makeshift form: they lacked the appropriate pins, they lacked strings positioned in critical places. Also, she could see they were none too experienced at it, even though two of them were Japanese Americans. Being a dresser is quite a demanding job, she thought, in any *geisha* house back in the home country. They even gave her an appropriate pair of shoes from the collection, as well as *tabi*, and a Japanese parasol. An audio system was rushed in in one of the halls that had been cordoned off for the exhibition, cassettes with dance music for the period were found, and everybody still around at that hour of the evening, something like ten people, flopped themselves, tired, on plastic chairs or right on the floor, and prepared to watch her dance.

She didn't know the first song, but she was very familiar with the themes, the tempo and the required steps.

It was the young *maiko* learning *ikebana*, the floral arrangement, while her thoughts run to her family left behind when she entered the *geisha* house. The tune came out plangent and a bit screechy, most likely the original recording having been an old LP.

She walked three small steps down the center as though to get to her worktable, which was located near where the stage was supposed to be, then stopped, head tilted to a side, contemplating the tough work of cutting flowers to the required size, shortening their lives, then their bodies, for the passing beauty of a floral arrangement. Her hands thereafter went slowly away, from being clasped together on her chest, one to the right to pick the first imaginary flower for the sacrifice, the other, just one moment later, to take the deadly implement, the knife, from the left of the table.

She held the flower and the knife together for a moment. Then, as though confronted with the enormity of the crime she was to commit against nature, she went away from the table in a quick succession of small steps along a half-circle, and came back following with the same path, pain marking her face. Through all this, her back was straight and tilted backwards for just a tiny angle.

She felt she had done very well the rapid, precise firing of the feet and the play of the hands with the wide sleeves of the kimono, and she could hear already small applause from several corners of the room.

Back at the table, she proceeded to cut one by one the imaginary flowers and to set them down in the base of the arrangement, after each taking a small respite to admire the new shape, walking a short arc around the vase containing them, to view them from another angle, and to readjust them. Her hands sniping, placing, re-doing it for a better effect, her eyes assessing the results, her head swaying from a side to another, the better to see the whole, nodding in ayes, dismissing in nays with horror of a second.

She knew the difficulty of it all was in timing it with the pace of the music, yet she felt so confident, at times having her movement anticipate the turn in the tune by a blink of an eye, instead of following it. She felt as though no surprises could lie in store, and that at first hearing the piece.

Three dances and twenty five minutes later, everybody stood to applaud and congratulate her. Richard, the curator, was flabbergasted.

"Great dancing. I can't call this but plain luck, to have found an artist like you at such an opportune moment. We're very grateful.

"Now, would you be available and willing to help us during the big show?" he inquired, and Hiroko could sense the anxiety in his voice.

"Yes. My pleasure, of course," she answered.

"Great! Could you then come by to be with us tomorrow morning at eight o'clock, so as to enable us to prepare you in our best regalia for the inauguration of the exhibition at eleven? Yes? Fine. I know, short notice. Always like that, here. But I assume Tokyo is no less demanding." He shrugged and smiled at her.

Her head was buzzing. *This is New York! I cannot believe it, Simon. Please be tomorrow with me again. Love you.*

***

George Julian Fraser II's phone was ringing off the hook in his office on the Street.

"What is it, Mary?" he asked his secretary.

"Sir, Mrs. Fraser is on the line. Something urgent, it seems," Mary Ackroyd replied.

"OK, put her through. Otherwise both you and I know we won't have peace for two more hours." He pounded his desk. His wife and he had this agreement whereby she shouldn't call during business hours, except in extraordinary circumstances.

"Georgie, this is amazing." At this end of the line, it sounded as though she was trying to catch up with her breathing.

"Come to the point, Selma dear. I've got some huge action going on, can't miss it." He hated being called Georgie, but Selma was past the point of no return for over thirty years now. The name made him feel kindergarten age. "And I'm not yet in Alzheimer's, Selma," he usually told her in such circumstances.

"It's Simon's Japanese girl, Georgie. Can't still believe it: she got an interview on the *Tonight* show before you and me."

"Which Japanese girl, Selma? The one who showed up in New York several days ago and had that friendly conversation with Brandon and yourself?" Selma had been proud of having appropriately dealt "with that Asian girl that Simon tries to shove down our throats." Still, George didn't see any reasons for the *Tonight* show to interview Selma. Johnny Carson certainly must have had better offers.

"Exactly, Georgie. Imagine, she's a dancer." Mrs. Fraser said it in the tone of splashing some huge news.

"Simon must have told us that in one of his letters," he said in one phone. "Karl, hold that transaction for five more mins," he said in another.

"But you don't read any of them," she said.

"And if you do, you don't have any memory of them. Why would that be? I'm the who's supposed to get the first Alzheimer train."

"Come on, Georgie, you know my philanthropic work doesn't allow me to focus on narrow-minded family matters."

"Now then, let's go back to the girl now. Why did she make Carson's show?"

"For — imagine that — having caused raves with her Japanese style dancing at the Met. She's getting famous."

"She's just getting *notorious*, New York style. That's all it is. Still, I'll grant you it's going to be even more heavy sledding to keep her away from Simon. We'll have to talk about this. But tonight; I'm leaving you now. Need to earn some folding green, Selma. I'm the only one doing it in this family."

I'm bad. Selma brought at least fringes and shadows of that Vanderbilt fame into the family. Just a loser branch wiped out during the Depression, though.

Simon goes deep II

Tanaguchi-San seemed to be one of the people, men mainly, in charge of the crowds in these urban caves of Tokyo. Yukio had told Simon to stick with him, for he knew a lot about the "high scheme," as Yukio had called it. Simon had to do it for no other reason than Yukio himself being stationed in that neighborhood, and his own need for translation. Not that he trusted Yukio being able to put across in reasonable English the quite abstruse mumbo-jumbo that Tanaguchi obviously delivered with some authority and cursive quality, for it seemed that many of the Japanese around him looked up to him on spiritual matters.

Simon had been introduced to the concept of the lotus flower and found it beautiful per se but, more than the high scheme, he wanted to see the details of the human maze and power scheme it projected or reduced to down here. The world seen as huge water, ocean, lake, whatever it was, also the huge elephants supporting it, looked to Simon as beautiful, high-flown poetry, though old-fashioned in some of its details. Nevertheless, what the people did among them with such images, for what worldly possessions they transacted them, and what they did to each other in and as a result of doing all this, was something else. He felt his father's pinch and pitch in thinking this way, for his father never wanted to look further than how the moneys exchanged hands and the channels thereof. Simon wanted to escape this pinch by being broader minded, but he couldn't run from the remote reality of New York staying and working on him on some intangible level.

Over several weeks, he had learned that Tanaguchi was extremely fussy about who was to get to talk to him on a given day and that as a result the people around him screened the potential interlocutors assiduously, dropping the boom on someone for the most unexpected of reasons.

The way things worked out, Tanaguchi seemed to count on anything from fifteen to twenty-five people among his underlings at any time. They came to him one by one, patiently and almost with reverence waiting for the previous one to leave. Sometimes Tanaguchi and a supplicant left to pray together at the shrine in the underground location. Only very rarely, did Tanaguchi take people to shrines in the above-ground Tokyo. On those occasions, both Tanaguchi and the person accompanying him dressed in gray, modest suits, black ties, white shirts, as if ashamed to appear among the wider public of the capital city in the older-styled, semi-ceremonial robes they wore on the day-to-day basis. Simon wasn't yet able to tell the difference between the prayers above ground and those underground. It might have been that for really complicated cases, Tanaguchi appealed to real Shinto or Buddhist priests or monks. Going civilian on those days might have been related to showing humility by not wearing clothes too close in shape or cut to those of the real priests.

Or, just perhaps, Simon thought, they did not go to some outside shrines, but it was something else, something related to the business of the sect or of the sects underground.

The business of the sect. Indeed. Simon thought about it many times. The basic question was: how did they survive? Most of their time, each of them seemed to spend it underground. For those he knew, in Tanaguchi's group, he saw being there with no breaks.

I see the mill of words all around me in chit chat and murmuring. I just wonder where the mill of money is, for there is none — there is no money-bringing rain.

Could it be the government sponsored them, say on some social programs, handouts just like for the unemployed?

Or some religious-based organization above ground? Praying to the same gods, sharing their moneys, that kind of thing.

Could it be the Kazuhiro Yuasa's organization, his *gumi*, the very Yakuza branch? It had transpired through Yukio that Kazuhiro Yuasa seemed to have sold or given the sect a lot of this underground space for using. The whys and wherefores of this move were still in haze for Simon.

***

Hiroshige Tanaguchi had arrived in the Sendagaya area by subway. It was quite late at night, past ten o'clock. The only walking traffic around the station were *sararimen* sneaking to the local love hotel — *rabu hoteru* — and to the bars, under the ready-for-complicity dim lights of the street. He had been here many times, so he quickly found the elevator going to the local underground site, right behind a tall old building. There was a special key to its door, thus local wanderers couldn't intrude. One could easily believe the elevator only served one or two stories down, no deeper than the building's underground. In fact, it went several tens of meters lower, to reach the sect's local cave.

Out of the elevator, he passed the guards and the helpers and went straight to the local honcho, sitting on a *tatami* mat. He was surrounded by helpers and they were all deep into prayer, reciting a sutra. Tanaguchi-San waited patiently until the prayer was finished, then closed in to the boss, sashaying among the others, all sitting down on mats.

"I was told I should come and see you," he told Takashi Tanaka.

"So it is," Tanaka answered. "People," he told the others, "thank you for assisting me in prayer. See you later." They saw Tanaguchi, they understood, and left the area.

The large hall, the ceiling of it ten meters above them, was full of *tatami* mats. They all slept there. The baths and the washrooms were down the hall. The meagre properties they had they kept in bags. The rest they had forfeited to the well being of the community, by selling them and making deposits in the support fund.

The local boss took Tanaguchi to a side and they sat face to face, so that a breeze would not pass in between them. "Tanaguchi-San," he said with a low voice, in whisper rather, "I'm keen to pass on to you the latest request from the Lotus Flower — all according to the Plan. In medicine, if you know in which state the organs of a body are, you can plan then how to regulate the blood flowing through them, so that its stream heeds you and the patient is ready to acquiesce to the upper harmony. The Lotus Flower has read the godly tantras and by them Tokyo and Japan are our patients, in great need of healing from the oppression of the so-called government of the dictatorship. In this instance, the traffic is as good as the blood stream. We need to map the main subway and train stations about Tokyo. You are to use only your most trusted men on this, though, those you would trust with your health and life on your worst days, for we should not allow the enemy to litter our path to freedom and enlightenment with hurdles. Let them sleep the fool's sleep for as long as possible, and then Judgment Day will come and the righteous will prevail. If someone asks, they're just preparing a guide about moving around Tokyo reasonably for our followers and followers to be, those come from the country side."

***

Simon had been designated the official photographer of the Tanaguchi group and he didn't quite know why. There were so many photographers in Japan, there must be someone down there in those caves able to take perfectly good shots.

Yukio, his forehead frowned, still with eyes flickering from his habitual shrewdness, had caught up with him three days after Simon had been introduced to Tanaguchi's group.

"Do you think you can help us, Fraser-San?" He said Simon's last name the way of the *katakana* reduction: *Foo-ray-zuh.*

"Help? Whom exactly? And how?" Simon was on his figurative toes, for sometimes Yukio came up with ridiculous ideas, the simple consequence of mulling only over his own interests. Yet, with nothing much to do since coming into the underground, Simon didn't think it necessary to be more reserved than that. He wasn't doing anything but sleep, talk — or mostly listen — and walk from one location to another — the mass migration, as he called it in his mind.

"Well, to help all of us down here with some technical photographs. I understand in the USA you are a top building photographer."

'Architectural' seems too much for him.

He had accepted though.

Then Simon realized: the cause for his promotion was the same as the one that had saved him from being at least punched in that bar weeks ago. Being Kazuhiro Yuasa's guest seemed to count for a lot here too. Even though he had learned that one of the top principles of the sect was to go against anything American. Yukio had told him one of their main running slogans was "America is the seat of corruption."

"This sounds taken from one of those red books by Mao," he told Yukio at the time, only to realize in a moment from the furrows on the other's forehead that he didn't appreciate it. *Long history, the Chinese and the Japanese have, and WWII hasn't helped this particular case one iota.*

But who knew about his photographic talents? Who recommended him first for the job? Certainly not Yukio, he hadn't known anything about his talents, not at that time.

Recoiling at the thought, he realized it had to be Kazuhiro Yuasa himself. And earlier, at the origin of it, it must have been Hiroko telling her father about his skills, about his pictures of herself, the exhibitions and so on.

Somehow, it didn't feel comfortable to be protected by Kazuhiro Yuasa. A very long arm he seemed to have, Yuasa-san. It felt good to know that at least Hiroko wasn't close by, for her to see what he was forced to do now. For he was forced to do it, wasn't he? Otherwise, he might never really get a chance to marry Hiroko. And he had started to think a lot about tying the knot; enough for it to make him sleep badly on his mat in the underground common hall; enough to make him have dreams about her and daytime visions of her.

Why, indeed, did *they* want the pictures? It was, for the stations he covered, every nook and crane, every entrance, turnstile, passageway from one station to another, every platform, every staircase and escalator, every tunnel entry. He felt sick at the level of detail. All black and white though.

For the time being, he was doing all this just for the stations near the sect's underground sites. But they told him there was much more work. That, to him, couldn't matter much, especially as they didn't pay a sen. Once Hiroko returned from the States, he would go back to work at the Company, which had allowed him a leave of absence of undefined length, probably at the behest of Dr. Sugie who knew he was for all intents and purposes a prisoner until she came back. A guarantee against the evil-doings of the Americans, as Kazuhiro Yuasa put it, conveniently forgetting it had been himself who had first suggested this visit — the-other's-family thing.

He had been told to avoid the rush hours, at which time even walking through those places might have been difficult. Also, to avoid being too conspicuous and to take pictures when policemen or train and subway personnel were at hand. At the time of getting the latter instruction, he had realized something wasn't kosher in the whole affair. Why so much secret, if this was a public service for the other members of the sect? Well, Tanaguchi patiently explained to him through Yukio, just because the government, their dictatorship, didn't like their organization, their company of the heavens. *Funny describing themselves as a company of whatever.*

Thing was, when all this was taken into account, it never seemed appropriate to use tripods; in this way, he shot everything from hand, from a very professional camera provided by them. *Man, these people are well equipped.*

He was now in Shibuya around three on a Monday afternoon, capturing the entrance of a passage tunnel housing an escalator and a staircase, together with the labeling and instructions on the walls. Yukio was several meters away, not in the typical garb of the sect.

Simon thought himself being chosen was also a good thing, as *they* saw it, seeing that he was a *gaijin* and thus less conspicuous, as any tourist in the free and capricious exercise of his curiosity.

***

I think about Hiroko's skin. How marble-pink white it is, how smooth it is to the touch, how reliable in ever conveying it is her underneath it. It could be warmth, temperature, it could be firmness and shape from the muscles underneath, it could be silkiness from itself and the pores in it and the blood feeding it, giving it also freshness. But I'd always recognize it to the touch.

In my hands, it always shivers at the first touch, which in turn makes me shiver. She tells me "Don't worry, this is just me liking your hands on me!" and I have to trust her saying it.

I go in that space we have, passing through the wall of the cave. Since we discovered it back in Japan, she has always called it *our Sakura*. I'm looking around for many hours, trying to find her. Finally, I see her at a distance, but I can't get any closer. I realize she's confined. She doesn't seem to see me. On her face, the reflection of terror; and this sinks me. I haven't learned or known until today that anything bad might be happening to her over there in America. But I feel the vibrations of her soul, and it is looking for mine. Her soul is frightened about herself and about me. She very much wants to leave the place she's in, which I don't see clearly, and to come over to help me, to be with me. Help me, why? Have I grown into a help-deserving man? Am I in any danger and I don't know it?

Hiroko in Connecticut I

On a late morning of a clear Saturday, feeling in a huff, Selma Fraser called their butler on the internal house phone.

"Brandon, how about Mr. Fraser's bath? We only have one hour until that Japanese girl comes over, if that taxi driver is any good."

"Mrs. Fraser, if I may say so, everything is under control. Mr. Fraser has just been provided with fresh towels and the French salts for his final washing. I've personally attended to the matter. In a quarter of an hour, he should be able to start dressing." Brandon was, as usual, the definition of cool and collected.

"Well, let's pray that, for once, he's not later for an event than I am. Not that this particular event would be anything major. Casual's the word. Nothing fancy for him. Just a tie and a dark, but not black, suit. White shirt, no cuff links. Black slip-on loafers and socks. And no exotic flowers, god forbid, only American ones. One exotic visitor is just enough for us today."

"Yes, ma'am. Now, if you'll excuse me, I need to go back to my attending Mr. Fraser's completion of his ablutions."

"OK, Brandon. Just make sure his side is on time," Selma Fraser said, turning her head back to the care of their personal maid, who continued combing and re-arranging the multi-tier towery construction that was her coif on that day. The latter had been initially set up by her hairdresser one day before in the lustrous blonde hair that made her pride for over fifty years — not that anyone would be told her real age. She was happy that her husband would not upstage her on this occasion. Wasn't this part of the fun of planning life just a wee in advance?

***

Hiroko had taken a taxi from New York City to Connecticut. Thanks to her having performed her dancing at the Met for close to a week, and having been paid well for it, she could afford the taxi, and she needed it as well, as she was wearing a kimono.

No, it wasn't a kimono from the Met, say the one used in her dancing there: that would've been too much to ask to borrow, even short term. Regulations, she was quickly made to understand when she delicately tested the waters. However, upon learning of her having finally decided to show up in Connecticut in a kimono, Richard Selznikow, the young Met curator, had suggested instead she borrow one of those in his modest personal collection. He even had wanted to offer to drive her the whole way to Simon's parents', but Hiroko thought that too much. *Nice man, Richard. Let's not confuse people, and let us not allow them to confuse us, though. Who said that?*

But she insisted Richard take the Frasers' address and phone from her, for him to have at least the whereabouts of his kimono.

"I'm not really sure for how long I'll be there," she had told him. "You better know where it is in case I have to rush back to Japan and you need to recover it. Apologies in advance, if that happens."

Richard had seemed perplexed at her arrangements in the US, but remained silent.

The kimono she had borrowed from him showed tall, thin, white cranes busying themselves among rushes, on a light green background. The *obi* was dark green. Quite tasteful, the whole of it, she thought.

She was happy to find that this cab, just as other American cabs, was spacious, that she didn't have to sit crammed in its back. *There is more space in America than in Japan, and that is everywhere. The Americans must be very grateful for it.*

***

After the introductions, everyone sat at a long, rectangular table, Hiroko on one of the longer sides, the hosts one each at either end, the butler navigating stately among them. Hiroko realized that, like the white birds on her kimono, she would have to crane her neck a lot from one side to another in order to give equal attention to the two Frasers. A small island, two distant shores.

"If I may, Mr. and Mrs. Fraser," — she turned her head in turn to each and made a long enough pause to draw attention — "I would like to present the gifts I have brought from Japan for you."

"Ah, that is very nice of you," Mrs. Fraser said in her voice that clinked just as it had during their initial phone conversation. Hiroko saw a slight inclination of the head, but no discernible smile.

"Simon and I bought these presents together."

"Thank you very much for telling us this detail, Miss … Yuasa," Mr. Fraser said.

Hiroko had seen with a corner of her eyes a flash of Mrs. Fraser mouthing to her husband her name. *Was there a bit of irony in what he said? I wonder.*

"We're grateful to have news from our son, and to see he has not totally forgotten us," George Julian Fraser II continued, "for the beauties of Japan." Hiroko thought to perceive a discrete curlicue of a smile in the left corner of his mouth.

Hiroko stood. She went first to the end of the table where the master of the house sat. From their regards, she was aware that her manner of walk in the kimono and *zori*, with minuscule steps, was at the center of their attention more than her own face, but she kept her back and her head straight, and was glad to be imparting that traditional view of glossing over waves.

"May I present this gift to you, Mr. Fraser," she said and bowed quite deeply. She waited for him to open the box. It was a small pipe with nice filigree. Nothing too expensive; she and Simon couldn't have afforded anything of the kind.

"Ah, from Mitsukoshi," Mr. Fraser said, after having read the label on the bottom of the box. "Nice store. We, my wife and I, visited it when Simon was ten. He stayed behind at some camp here then, though. Thank you very much. Very nice pipe indeed." Hiroko couldn't tell if he had really warmed to it.

Turning slowly, she walked to Mrs. Fraser's end. Their eyes were still fully on her walk. The mistress of the house had on a yellow silk dress with three-quarter-length sleeves, in a V-neck cut with no collar, which showed to good advantage her long neck and well-shaped forearms and hands that here and there were dappled by the freckles that no doubt Simon had inherited. However, his large blue-green eyes could not have come but from his father, as Mrs. Fraser owned dark brown ones.

"And may I present this gift to you, Mrs. Fraser," Hiroko said, and by extending both her arms slowly, deposited with care on the table something that showed to be a small lacquered wooden box for storing cosmetics and other small items. She bowed. Simon had taken lots of care in selecting it. It featured painted, long, tall irises on all sides.

Mrs. Fraser clinked while bowing slightly, without standing though, "We appreciate your gifts very much."

Hiroko was satisfied for having returned to her place at the table: with her sitting now, her hosts would have to be focused more on herself and less on her walk, her stance or her kimono. Yet, she was grateful for having had the idea of using the kimono. It may have deflected some of the initial attention from herself — and she felt in fact more relaxed presently than upon her arrival — at the same time showing her unmistakably a Japanese. She didn't want to be anything else in elder Frasers' sights, whether they liked it or not: this was one of her hard, diamantine truths.

"Hopefully, you won't be surprised if we would like this early in this conversation to learn how our son, Simon, is doing," Mrs. Fraser asked.

"Oh, not at all, Mrs. Fraser. I think he's very well, also doing great in Japan in his profession. He has just had very successful exhibition with pictures of the Shugaku-in imperial villa in Kyoto."

Hiroko made only a short eye contact with Selma Fraser, right at the beginning of this statement, after which, careful not to slight any of them she turned a little and shifted her gaze to Mr. Fraser, who nodded with dignified satisfaction upon the receipt of the news. His face continued to be cast in stone, ready for poker; just his eyes flickered shortly. Hiroko wasn't sure how to act around him. Even though sitting, she felt kept on her toes.

The butler was serving the soup from a huge tureen.

"Yes," Mr. Fraser said, taking up the conversation in an indolent tone, "we learned about the exhibition at … what was it? Ah, yes, one of your national museums, I guess."

"Indeed, our Tokyo National Museum, *Tokyo Kokuritsu Hakubutsukan*," Hiroko rushed to confirm.

"Yes, I learned about it in *The Japan Times*. We're getting it at work for business purposes, of course," he continued his steady course on words, as though munching them from existence. "This is where I find information these days on our son's whereabouts. He's not writing or calling too much. I guess he's too busy with sightseeing. Or should I say the locals?" On the last words, he had raised his sight from attending to his soup to her and kept it there. Hiroko held his sight for a moment, then moved it to his ear, or was it his shoulder, she wouldn't know, her feeling lost for a moment.

"Well, he calls," Simon's mother said. There was a sniff from her long nose, perhaps trying to smell the soup. Her tall, straight forehead was just a touch worried.

"Not enough," Mr. Fraser mumbled under his breath. "Not enough. And it's like he never talks to me."

"But you're never home, George," his wife uttered. "My husband works very hard," she explained to Hiroko. "The Stock Exchange, you know." Mrs. Fraser's face was less concerned now, perhaps years of life together had taught her something about his present mood.

"Well, enough about Simon, let's take care of our guest, Selma," Mr. Fraser said.

The plates were being changed for the second course.

The butler came beside Hiroko and asked her in a low voice, "Chicken or steak?"

"Chicken, please."

"Would that be rice or potatoes and vegetables on the side?"

"Potatoes, please."

"We have *teriyaki* sauce, if you would like it. Chicken tastes great with it," the butler recommended.

"Yes, please."

"Come on, Brandon. Miss Yuasa must be quite familiar with *teriyaki* sauce. It's the Japanese who invented it, last I've heard." Mrs. Fraser laughed lightly, as though skipping over the surface of words.

"I believe that too," Mr. Fraser said, his face still not committed to expressing anything.

The *teriyaki* sauce was served to her in a small dish.

"As my husband said, perhaps you wouldn't mind telling us more about our visitor today?" Mrs. Fraser showed a reserved smile, looking with a bit of insistence to Hiroko. Perhaps she was suggesting George Julian would get that information out of Hiroko anyway, sooner or later. Thus, Hiroko decided to commence speaking to him, which demanded not a small effort on her behalf, as he didn't seem to react in any way to her words. At least, his face didn't register any changes. His eyes flickered here and there, so short though that she wasn't able to gauge the temperature of the feeling.

"I am professional dancer," she started. She might have seen with the corner of her eyes Mrs. Fraser nodding slightly, but she continued to face Mr. Fraser, who after a break suddenly uttered:

"So Johnny Carson seems to have told us, I mean the entire United States." However, Hiroko couldn't detect any enthusiasm in it.

"But of course, George, I saw Miss Yuasa myself on Carson. You were sleeping then," Mrs. Fraser interjected, to which Mr. Fraser looked miffed at her, as though resenting having revealed deep family secrets to a newcomer.

"And when did you start the preparation for this career, Miss Yuasa? You certainly look very young, if you don't mind me saying so," the man of the house continued.

"Ah, I started learning traditional Japanese dance and music when I was four, little by little," Hiroko said. "Later on, more intense, during my high-school."

"Not much money in that business, is there, or am I wrong?" he asked.

Feeling her own face reddening in a burst of fire, Hiroko looked embarrassed at Mrs. Fraser first, who didn't react, then to him, and murmured, "I think not, unfortunately."

"Was the Met nice toward you? We understand you did some dancing gigs for them, didn't you," Mr. Fraser asked.

"Come on, George," Mrs. Fraser said.

Hiroko had re-established the normal pale-pink color of her cheeks. "They very nice indeed. They paid taxi to and from my hotel and all the hours with them, dressing too. Better rates than in

Japan," she said, lowering her eyes in her plate, a signal to whomever was looking that she wasn't comfortable with sharing more details on that item.

"Well, I'm glad to learn from a Japanese young lady us Americans were fair this once. Not that I'd say we were not in other instances," he continued to bulldoze his way through the conversation. "Like when we had to end the war the way we had to. Not that we hadn't tried other ways before that."

Hiroko sensed the reference to Hiroshima and Nagasaki and a freezing shiver went through her, but didn't say anything, raising her sights slowly to look at him though.

"Come on, George." Mrs. Fraser seemed to have felt the need to intervene. "Tell us, Miss Yuasa," she said focusing on Hiroko, "the piece you danced on Carson, was it the same thing as at the Met?"

"No. As a matter of fact, Mr. Carson didn't want traditional, wanted something more modern, thus I danced in the *butoh* style."

"Ah, I knew that wasn't quite traditional," Selma Fraser said satisfied.

"You're right, *butoh* more jumpy and jerky. Not like the old beauty. Perhaps, another kind," Hiroko said, reserved, not really sure whether Mrs. Fraser had liked it.

"Tell us, please," Mr. Fraser intervened, "did Simon shoot many photographs of you?"

"I think many," Hiroko answered, feeling again heat rising to her face and neck. "But perhaps not." She didn't want to appear overconfident.

"This means perhaps he appreciates you."

"Oh, George," Mrs. Fraser intervened in embarrassment.

"Oh, Selma, for heaven's, am I allowed to finish what I meant?" her husband continued measuredly.

There was an eye-to-eye confrontation between the hosts, and Hiroko didn't wish to be of the place for a moment.

"Only thing I wanted to ask Miss Yuasa is what plans she may have for this trip."

"I wish go to Philadelphia or Boston. Simon felt they are great cities for a tourist," Hiroko answered.

"Would you happen to have all your luggage with you?" he asked.

Hiroko felt cornered. "Yes, I do."

"If that's so," he continued, "would you have the time and pleasure to spend several days in Connecticut? I mean, in this home, of course."

Hiroko noticed his indirect way of making the invitation. She and Simon had discussed this possibility several times back in Tokyo, but she had been adamant that he should not make a request for an invitation to his parents, that it should be issued naturally by them, with no interference on his part. Having seen the way the phone conversations and this very meal had evolved, she had put this alternative on a very remote back-burner. Now, this. She was flabbergasted.

She turned toward Mrs. Fraser, whose huge eyes said she was just as amazed as Hiroko by the turn of events. However, this didn't bring any change in the countenance of her husband, who came back first in the conversation only to confirm, "Of course, we have several guestrooms."

Hiroko knew it was all true now, also that she had only several moments to answer before her silence would be considered impolite. She babbled, surprised herself at the speed her words came out:

"Thank you very much, Mr. and Mrs. Fraser, for kind invitation. Very nice indeed to spend several days at your home." She bowed to each of them from her hips, but she decided to remain sitting.

"I'm sure you'll enjoy the Connecticut countryside, Miss Yuasa," Mr. Fraser continued. "We may have time for deer or fowl hunting, if that's of any interest to you."

Hiroko had never considered hunting in Japan, but she decided to take any offer coming her way. "Yes, of course, I'd like to see wild life here."

***

"Now, what was this all about?" Mrs. Fraser asked her husband after Brandon had taken Hiroko to one of the guest rooms upstairs. "You've never told me about this Japanese girl staying overnight."

"No, Selma, but this was one of those great ideas waiting for their time, just as on the exchange: the longer this girl stays with us or in

America, the less she is with Simon, and the less chance there is for us having to cope with much more. Just think about it.

"And thank you for not having the idea of showing her Simon's room tonight.

"Father must be laughing from his grave, for he must have been quite worried lately."

Her grandfather too.

Simon goes deep III

This was past the restaurant at seven o'clock with its *kaiseki ryori* and its nine courses, past its French wines, past hopping to the bar at eleven, with beer sipped from wooden square cups with salt on the border to burn the lips and sharpen the taste, past the dry Scotch whiskey and the flaming hot Serbian šljivovica.

It was only Simon and the women now, and the two of them seemed to be on a mission. They had him captured in a private room at the back of the bar, no one to bother them. The other men, Yukio, the bodyguard, the businessmen dropping in this night, had to be somewhere private too. It had taken the girls lots of wheedling and pushing with expert fingers, a lot of pulling on his shirt and belt, but here they were: the music and the lights low, a king-size bed but no waterbed to bother you with squishing and sloshing when doing a roll or a press. And, most of all, no Karaoke, the bane of anything requiring attention.

They had him sandwiched, all three of them sitting on the edge of the pink-sheeted bed: the tall, svelte, bosomy Polish girl, Marusja, on one side, the compact — yet flushed everywhere in sweet, round details — Japanese girl, Kimiko, on the other. The long blonde hair up in a chignon at the back, the long black hair let down in flushsmooth, heavy waves to the hips.

Half-empty glasses and bottles lay in front of them on a low, wide table with a glazed ceramic top divided by a patient designer in regular square tiles.

Kimiko pressed him on the small of his back, right on the spine. "I wanna change music, OK?" she asked.

"Be my guest, it's the club's equipment, not mine; you can do to it whatever you want, and worse." He laughed. "It's not coming out of my pocket."

Barefooted, skipping on her toes, only in her panties and a thin silk chemise, she trotted happily to the all-black audio chain in a corner of the room. "Whatever I feel like? Sex with it? No? Better: I'm gonna give you Neil Diamond," she threatened jokingly.

He threw his hands up. "We are gonna listen to him, aren't we, Marusja?"

With most of her clothes spread all over the room, in the same degree of *deshabillée* as her rival to his attention and companion, she left all the words to the dogs as she of a sudden grabbed at this neck with two hands, throttling him jokingly. Yet with sudden power and intent she pushed him back onto the bed, sandwitching him under the fully addressed heaviness of her chest, and started biting at his neck. Simon could feel she meant to make good use of the temporary lapse in the Japanese's immediate presence, having no qualms about it either.

How did I get here? Fell into the trap. I wouldn't be surprised if there were some cameras around for solid evidence. What now?

Kimiko, coming back to recover temporarily lost ground, plunged long red fingernails into his belt, between Marusja and him, fought with his scurrying-to-many-places hands and unfastened it, then backed off from the bed, straining to pull off his pants. Going down, these caught his Jockeys that were left around his knees by the time the longer apparel had left his body.

"Well, well, wild boy up already!" Kimiko tweeted, followed by Marusja instantly changing the focus of her right hand; soon enough, Kimiko's lips had joined in wet promenade.

Waves of heat appeared out of nowhere promising to send him afloat, his skin barely able to contain them. Soon, he would be a balloon, a Zeppelin of desire, ready to crash in flames. His hands were massaging, carressing, massaging again, sharing bodies.

All of a sudden, above him of all places, things came to a boil: with him crucified to the bed, the two girls started to deepkiss each other and to dispense of whatever articles of dress still on each other's body.

Wow, this isn't for me, ladies, sorry.

He slowly eased out from under their arc, dressed up in a rush and left for the hallway, the moanings continuing behind him unabated save for just a moment of surprise and unarticulated disappointment. Yukio was there already. "So soon, boss? No saaa-tis-faaction?" he bleated. Nodding towards the private rooms, he said, "These here: the best."

"Moving off, are we ever? Let's get a taxi," Simon demanded.

***

Kazuhiro Yuasa had asked him to come to his office in Shinjuku. Even though Yukio Imashita was around at the time at the Ueno underground site where Simon had lately migrated with Hiroshige Tanaguchi's group, the message had been passed by the latter himself. By the commotion in the group, Simon understood that was an unusual honor.

"Fraser-San, Yuasa-san would like to talk to you at his office." Where Tanaguchi had suddenly unearthed his English "would"s was a mystery for Simon, but he thought he would get nowhere by asking about it.

Tora-Tora was at Kazuhiro Yuasa's side this time too, and from his awesome growlings Simon guessed the huge dog would have enjoyed snapping a very large piece of him, but mostly just finding a place for those worrisome fangs of his anywhere on his body would have been totally acceptable to him. But his master had provided him with a leash and had tied it to one of the huge legs of his desk.

"I can tell you don't enjoy the company of my dog," the older man said through Yukio's translation.

"Not this close, no. But I'd say he feels much worse about me, so we're most probably quits." Simon laughed, but there was no denying the dog made him uncomfortable. "Where did you get him from?"

"From a dog expert in Germany."

"Do you really need him?" Simon asked.

"There are many people who would like to kill me in order to get a piece of my business. At least with him around they are wary of getting too close to me," came Yukio's translation.

There is little chance of ever being told the nature of the business. Not even Hiroko was afforded this favor, if I remember well. Not that she would enjoy knowing about it from her father's mouth.

"It's time I showed you a piece of Japanese history," Kazuhiro said.

Why do I feel he means personal history? "Yes, of course, please do. I'd be most interested in seeing it."

"Let's leave the dog here, for in the place we go, we need silence," Yukio said translating Kazuhiro, and Simon realized they would go where the wind of time wanted hush.

Hiroko had told him about her father's personal museum, but had never described it. In low light, they followed a long hallway, then entered a spacious hall with walls covered in white silk, Kazuhiro in front of them in one of his formal, gray kimono spreading his shoulders as the wings of a prey bird.

Then Simon saw them, the lost warriors frowning or smiling at him from behind the divide of no return, with their bandannas or caps, marching towards them as they advanced past, but remaining in the distance of their portraits. He knew he might well be the only enemy to have walked in front of them in over forty years, even as he knew that most of them would not have known any people of his nation up this close at any time.

Wave upon wave came they, from the carriers, on wings of planes, in torpedoes, to the beat of a distant *taiko* drum that would never stop for them. Their eyes would not blink; their faces would not budge a lineament.

In the corner, they reached the alcove, and closing in, Simon saw more and more of Kazuhiro Yuasa's features in the larger portrait.

He halted, remained standing at a distance of several steps, let the older man advance to the very shrine, and Kazuhiro Yuasa never turned to motion him to advance beside him on the stairs where he had genuflected in prayer under the portrait that so much contained himself. Yukio had stopped at a distance also.

When they left, on the way back, the old man stopped for a moment, motioning to Yukio Imashita to close in for a translation and, looking straight and stone-faced at him, he had only several words for Simon:

"My father. Your grandfather. 29th of January 1945. Forever. ... And never."

Then he turned abruptly and walked away alone to his office.

Simon returned with Yukio Imashita in deep silence to the Ueno site of the sect. It's as though both of them had understood that this had been Kazuhiro Yuasa's final stance, something that, as long he would live, he would not modify, just like a message scraped in flint thousands of years ago by shadowy hunters is meant to survive rivers of water, lightning, and the man, losing just a bit its definition, but nothing of the essence immutable, the form of the prey, cut into it.

Trying to sleep on his *tatami*, he recalled telling Hiroko's father about his own grandfather having died on *Columbia* in a *Kamikaze* attack. Try as he might to avoid facing the truth, tonight he had been told in no uncertain terms that the *Kamikaze* pilot had been Hiroko's grandfather. And the "never" could well mark in flint what the old man had in mind about the young ones' relationship.

Hiroko in Connecticut II: Hunting

Hiroko felt tight in the khaki velcroed hunting overalls she had on for the occasion. It was not their size — that was *Small*, as the label on the unisex outfit proclaimed. No worries, as Simon liked to say, she was thin by any American size. No, it had to be that strange constriction she had felt first in her chest and neck when, just two days into her stay with the Frasers, she had agreed to go with George Julian Fraser II on a deer hunting trip in that corner of Connecticut that Fairfield County represents.

***

Mr. Fraser had told her then, "Don't worry, Miss Yuasa, there is no shame in killing deer in that county. We are, in fact, encouraged to do so by the state. Their numbers are beyond any reason these days. They've become a public nuisance. And getting a trophy buck is a memory for your whole life, I guarantee you." He sneered, "You'll still be able to put on your kimono and feel great about life and yourself."

Her mind was rushed by those frail-looking deer coming, in Nara, the former old capital of Japan, on the alleys in front of the Todai-ji temple, to nudge you with their nuzzles into feeding them. The memory had made her cringe — as she saw herself as a would-be criminal against nature already, to be hung in effigy. That deer had been unabashed, as she remembered them, might have swung the balance when she thought of their wet eyes. *They might be too much into our territory. Trespassing. As we are all trespassing all the time into their domain.*

Mr. Fraser continued, "And you can be a hunter yourself, not just watch us guys at it. Just put to practice those martial arts skills you told us you have from Japan, like archery and kendo. Only archery this time, of course. But you'll need to train several days with our bows. They might be different from what you used in Japan, as these are compound bows. I'll take out from storage that old compound of Simon's, he never practiced too much with it; it should work out for you, with your training."

He squinted, saying, "He much preferred to come with us on hunting trips to shoot pictures of us, than shoot his bow, old Simon."

Hiroko's felt a rush of gratitude for this report, yet decided to keep it for herself.

***

She started to train on the edge of their property, shooting at a target propped against a rundown wall.

"You can shoot here at will with no fear to needle someone by mistake," Mr. Fraser quipped, face busy, absorbed by something. "The Walkers, the neighbors, are off for the summer to Alaska. Your arrows won't fly long enough to get them over there. Not that I'd mind that. Troublemakers, that's all they are. Never agreed to repair that wall, for one thing."

Hiroko didn't know these older Americans, but she could tell Mr. Fraser was steadily irked by something. He would look at her for a moment, would say several words, more like sniping or munching them, then he'd break away, as though staying with her long in a conversation was tough on him. But she couldn't tell for sure, for she had never seen him talk to others except Mrs. Fraser or Brandon. She could not imagine him working the Exchange, so absent-minded he sometimes seemed. She thought sharp people, on their toes, were needed there.

And she thought he never stayed for long in eye contact with her. But she couldn't tell for sure, as she herself would not easily go into or hold such exchanges. To confront an elder this way was against the grain in Japan, for a woman.

***

"May I know what is going on, Georgie?" Mrs. Fraser asked her husband.

"What are you talking about, Selma?"

Mrs. Fraser went, tapping with stress her high heels into the parquet, to a bedroom window looking into their flower garden, pulled the curtain and looked out. "Nothing but this sudden attention you're showering on this Japanese girl. Before she showed up, you barely mentioned her. You didn't look for a moment at her dancing on Carson. Now, after just one talk during lunch, you've presented her with an open-ended invitation to stay here *and* to go hunting with you boys. I don't remember any woman ever having gone with your gang on those outings. Have you caught, by some special influence from our son, a passion for her? Then, I demand to be told. Perhaps it's time for me to put on a kimono and take dancing lessons."

Already in bed, he didn't even turn toward her from reading *the Wall Street Journal* editorial. "You cannot be serious, dear. You cannot be serious."

"So, now you're using on me lines by that spoiled brat, McEnroe?"

"No, I'm just telling you you're way off the mark. You don't realize what a menace this girl is. Do you think I'm going to just contemplate with crossed arms my hard-earned moneys disappear into a black hole called Japan though the splendid mechanisms of marriage and inheritance, when my own father was killed by the Japanese?

"She has all the assets to grab Simon, and she's just done that to a pretty good extent. The longer we keep her away from him, the better," Mr. Fraser said.

"Well, tell me about those assets, perhaps I'm blind," his wife interjected.

"What for? Just so you can become more jealous? Why don't you ask Simon, if you want a listing on the matter?"

"Simon's disappeared from his home in Tokyo. For days, I haven't found him there to talk to him."

"Right now, with her here, the farther he is from us, the farther he is from her too. This knowledge creates a nice situation for me," he said, sneering.

***

The hideout is a wooden structure with two stories, on stakes hammered into the earth. The ground level allows shooting from the standing position, and that's what they're going to use with the bows. The shooting stand is camouflaged with branches full of the changing leaves of autumn, some of the branches old, some freshly cut by Mr. Fraser with an axe from the maple leafs and the oaks nearby.

He said, "These deer are clever. One needs to be well out of sight. We'll also have to wait until the wind favors us. Otherwise, they might disappear in a whiff. Right before the sunset might be a good time to take a poke at them. They might be tired then, slowed down from a day of roaming around, and hopefully full."

Hiroko asked, "What is a good distance?"

"Well, the shooting distance is just about where I've put your target practice, about thirty yards. You seem to be mighty reliable from it when using Simon's bow. Better than yours truly. But we'll have to wait until they come into that range, and that's a matter of luck. And patience, lots of patience."

"Do we really need to hide? It seems coward to me," she chided him.

"Well, Miss Yuasa, to expect to get out in the open and to take a shot at a deer, I mean like challenging it, it's only for dummies, honestly. They'd run before you take a step out of the stand. It would only spoil hours of patient waiting, and for many hours to come too. Once their radar tells them there's something strange in an area, their memory is long enough and they're clever enough to avoid it for the night."

***

The deer is to the right of the tree-stand, perhaps at fifty feet. After two bad days, Mr. Fraser has decided to separate himself from her and Mr. Johansson, a tall, burly man, with a large, old-fashioned beard and cold eyes that ignite at times when looking at her — "One of my regular partners, here," Mr. Fraser told her during their introduction — and to take a more advanced location on ground, something like twenty feet now from this animal. He has a full-face mask on him, which reduces the chance of detection by breathing.

Noiselessly, he has pulled the bow to full draw. The broadhead arrow is released in a flash and catches the deer in her neck. She hobbles for five or six steps, then crumbles to the ground, flooded in her own blood. Mr. Fraser goes to her. It seems she's finished. He comes to the stand, takes a tarp they have for such occasions, wraps the animal in it and brings it over to the stand, helped by Mr. Johansson. Hiroko is amazed by the smoothness of the deer's pelt, by the fixity in its eyes. *How young. Guileless and guiltless.*

They're waiting again. Mr. Johansson tells her, "Be back," and leaves her alone in the stand, with Mr. Fraser still in front of it, but this time on the left side, behind a large bush. She stands, bow at the ready, but not drawn, on the ground level of the hideout, peering intently through one of the openings in the branches and the leaves covering it. It's dark outside, a violet-black whole in which they are dropped and immersed. She barely distinguishes Mr. Fraser, and likewise he shouldn't be able to see any incoming deers except from close range. All of a sudden, he disappears too. It's perhaps just the dark.

Padded steps rush behind her, and by the time they register with her, from dark the dark drops on her. A curtain suddenly falls around her head, obscures her face before she's able to move, while her elbows are imobilized in the thickness of it and caught tightly behind her as if in a vise. The curtain feels now like a dark bag and she's in the center of it. Self-defense reflexes flash to awareness, and she hits with one of her heels repeatedly behind her until it encounters what it must be an ankle and both she and aggressor are falling to the ground, but she is captive underneath. She puts all her strength in a reverse head butt; the back of her head meets the protruding hard bone of the other, a jaw, maybe. There's a hoarse curse under someone's breath, but one hit to the back of her neck dazes her and she doesn't get the rest.

Hiroko: Distance in the West I

When she wakes up, there's this confined, dull rattling around her that sounds like the inside of a van. From the vibrations and the whooshing of the wind, it seems to be moving fast on a highway.

With tied eyes, hands and legs, she is still in something like a bag. The mouth is freed from time to time to spoon-feed her with liquids: cold concentrated soup, orange juice, water. There are two women at this, speaking few words, in English, just telling her when to open her mouth, murmuring between them.

In certain parts of the journey, her mouth is taped, over and round the bag, on again, off again. The women have told her not to shout, if she wants to be fed and not taped all the time. When the car turns off sharply from the highway, perhaps for gas, they press something that feels like a towel on her mouth, through the sack and all.

A cold fear has replaced her skin, and there is this emptiness in front of her unseeing eyes.

Where are you right now, Simon?

***

She is now in a house built wholly from reddish wood, in a high-ceilinged room. The air is piney. It's colder at night. They might be in the mountains. Her ankles are fettered together through a flexible metal cable to one of the pillars supporting the ceiling. Her hands are free, and she can eat by herself at the stark wooden table that has no tablecloth. The two women come now and then with the food, to remove the plates, or the chamber pot. They must be both around forty. Their hair is streaked by white, pulled back and caught behind the neck in a simple clasp.

She has asked and cried out loudly many times, “Why am I kidnapped? Where I am? Kidnappers! Kidnappers!” glad she has found the English word, but feeling an idiot, as she knows what kind of people these might be, for the only answer from them has been a cool, collected, “You be in the way of God now,” accompanied at times by “Hush now, and ready yourself for the better way,” and light touches on her arm or shoulder, which she takes as attempts at appeasement. They move about her room through her crying. No one seems to be concerned about her being heard now — they might as well be in the middle of nowhere.

On the hallways outside the door of this room, she hears other voices, men’s and women’s, but only the two women have entered. Sometimes, she has the feeling that they stop in front of the door and convene, those people, that they talk about her perhaps, but she can’t understand anything. She wishes she were able to get to the door, that she were able to face them, but her tether allows her space only to move to the bed and to sit on a chair at the table.

***

Today, they’ve come for her, the two women. They tell her, “We must to the river.”

What could this mean? Drowning me?

She lets them unshackle the metal cable from her ankles, then crouches and in flashes delivers to each of them a kick to the ribs that leaves them sprawled on the floor, heavily panting and holding their sides.

She runs for the door, but is met by the huge figure of Mr. Johansson, the bearded man on the deer hunting party back in Connecticut.

“You! The kidnapper!” she shouts, and wants to get at him with all she has, but her arms have been already gripped by hands much more powerful than hers, and she’s taken to the ground.

The man immobilizes her through her thrashing, the weight of his body and the strength of his hands impossible to displace and conquer. The two women come carefully and undress her naked, then bring a long white, plain robe to pull on her. From the long days of near-fasting, she feels the lack of energy and purpose sapping at her opposition. Also, she prefers to be in that robe than naked in front of that horrible man with dark, intent eyes that gore into her from underneath bushy eyebrows. Still, she wrestles and finally manages to be on a side under him, not frontally exposed.

He hasn't spoken to her since the time they were in Connecticut. She hears now and then his words to the two women. The words come in spurts and low, and she can't quite make sense of them with her English, but they surely are clear enough for the women, as they move with purpose and precision to attend to his commands. When they look at her, there's a dullness, a distance — she can't quite tell what that is — that overcomes whatever fear they might have had of her, something that tells her she can't really get them to react to her, or feel for her. They both wear now white bonnets tied under their chins with ribbons and white dresses, something out of this time, something — the thought flashes — she might have seen in old Western movies.

When she's dressed, the women hoist her from the ground, grasp each of her elbows in their arms, clamping her between their bodies, and take her to a pair of sabots.

When she's put them on, they all advance as a block in front of a man along an empty long corridor that opens into several rooms, perhaps a dozen of them.

The sun is close to setting down, and the sky is tinted violet and grey. After walking for five minutes they get to the river and that's where the others are waiting for them, ten or so men and many more women. That they are only to their midsections in water makes her believe this is not such a dangerous place, in the end.

"Welcome to your baptism, young sister," she hears from some of them, and right now she can't see any meanness to them. The way they all look behind her towards the man tells her he is the one in charge of this group, of this place.

The water flows slowly, this is in fact a pool with rushes on the margins. She feels the bed of this river under her feet now and it is rocky, there is no sand to it. The place must be high for all around them are they — huge mountains bare of any vegetation, red rock upon red rock, getting blacker by the minute with the sun setting, stealing to find refuge behind them.

She is brought in the middle. She looks at several of them and shouts to their faces:

"I was *kid-na-pped*! Call the police! I am not free!"
thrashing the water with her feet, beating into the hard floor of the river until the soles of her feet feel numb and she thinks she might have hurt herself.

But none of them, man or woman, changes the expression of indifference to her plight; no one utters a word of response or concern, a question. They have something else, infinitely more important, on their minds, and they all seem to want to proceed to it.

The one who is the chief, and had been introduced to her as Mr. Johansson down in Connecticut, replaces one of the women at her side, grasping Hiroko's arm, and chants with a firm, resonant voice, as if meant to be heard by all present:

"Brothers and sisters, we are assembled together here at this river of God to pass the rite of baptism over this woman, for her to be one of us in spirit first, before she is of one body with us.

"We'll baptize her as Sister Pauline in the name of the Father, of the Son, and of the Holy Spirit!"

At this, he puts his large palm over Hiroko's head and presses down on it, and the woman remaining by her pulls down on her arm, and she doesn't oppose them, for she feels she might die next, and death would be just an escape from a horrifying dream.

But one instant into the dip they bring her back to the surface and she thinks that even death is being denied to her.

Then they all climb out of the river and up the river bank, and return to the big house surrounded by large pines. It's night now, and she and the two women that have been from the beginning with her go into her room. She is told they will have supper together and that she should remain in her room, that she should not try to escape, as this is God's will for her, as shown by this baptism.

Now that she has seen the surroundings, Hiroko realizes any escape would be fraught with huge danger. Who knows what the distance might be to the next place where anyone lives, perhaps tens or even hundreds of miles. She decides to stay in and to accumulate more information before anything else.

"Where are we here?" she asks the women.

They look at her, and one of them, the older one, says, nodding disapprovingly, "Sister, we're not at a liberty to tell you that. However, be sure this is a place of God and He watches over us in His almighty goodness. Let's pray and eat."

They bring food from outside the room, cheese, bread, and boiled eggs, only one going out of the room at a time. She figures this must be their way of guarding over her. The light seems to quiver in the lamps affixed to the walls, during this, her first time hearing a Christian pray. It might be just her having become weak from fasting and stress. She decides to eat, to keep her wits and strength about her. She keeps her head down while the women recite the sermon; perhaps this will reduce their vigilance and she might make a move.

The younger woman sets the cutlery on the table; then the older one places the food on platters and passes it to the other two.

They eat quietly. There's only cold water to drink, but Hiroko recognizes this is good spring water; another sign they are deep in the mountains here.

At the end, the older woman gives a black book to Hiroko. She tells her:

"This is from the Shepherd. He wants you to study the Holy Bible, Sister Pauline."

Hiroko is wide-eyed. "But we have other religions in Japan. Shinto and Buddhism. Don't you know that?"

"Japan is of no account now. Your future life is all here."

Hiroko is furious. Words escape her control. "Why should I stay here? You've kidnapped me."

"We've brought you to the best place in the world for you to be the Shepherd's wife, just like us," the young one says.

His wife. Simon! Simon!

Only now does Hiroko have an inkling of their purpose, but it only makes her more adamant. "You can kill me: I will not do that. I will only marry someone I want."

"No, dear," the older one says, soothing, "we must all submit to the Rule. We are all part of the Shepherd's flock."

"I will run away," Hiroko says, leaving care to the wind. She doesn't want them to be comfortable: frazzled nerves may lead to mistakes. Yet, she is aware this could make any escape more difficult, with them on guard.

"Where? To Japan?" the older woman asks with a cold voice. She does not sneer, nor does she laugh. She does not seem to be able to tread those waters any more, as there are facts she has down pat. "We're two hundred miles from the closest village. And this is the best place for anyone. You'll just see it in time. We're under God's care here, straight under his hand and heavens. The rest of the world is a terrible place of loss and sin."

So they *know about Japan. Therefore they might be not so broken from the world as they pretend to be. Perhaps they can't dismiss it, the world, in the end.*

***

It's deep in the night, one or two hours after midnight. She tiptoes out of her room in pajamas and housecoat, watches left and right. The hallways of the house are empty, there is no light in the windows at the top of some of the doors, and they are closed, perhaps on account of the cold. There don't seem to be any guards around.

Outdoors, in the courtyard, the air is crystal and ice, clear and cold. She feels November to her bones, as she doesn't have on any heavy clothing.

She sneaks as a shadow against the house, crouching in front of each window to pass, with the aim of getting to the dark around the tall pines she has seen when coming back from the river. There are three lamps in front of the house, and none at the back, where the pines are.

Simon goes deep IV

Takao Shimizu, a trusted Level Three Shrine Servant, knew what he had done was not enough. He had the emplacements for the explosive charges mapped, but not those for the gas. On Omega day, the explosive boxes had to be carried into the tunnels, to wreck the tracks and paralyze the traffic. The deeper in a tunnel a train was stopped, the better — less chance of a fast recovery. The gas had to be left in canisters in niches on the platforms, to strike to the quick the mobs heeding the dictatorship. To avoid early detection, the niches had to be spacious enough to hide from view the canisters for several hours. The pictures he had didn't cover in enough detail all the required areas of the Ueno station. He had to lose too much time in the field and, many times, he felt those decisions should have been made for him, at least pointers given, by his betters.

Shimizu reported to Hiroshige Tanaguchi, who was Level Two in the hierarchy of the sect, and within two hours the latter had Simon in front of him.

"Fraser-San, haven't we made clear to you that all the platforms and tunnel entrances of the Ueno station are to be photographically documented?"

"Tanaguchi-San," Simon said, feeling close to the boiling point, "at the time on last Wednesday I went to Ueno with my personal guard, for I can't give another name to those people in your group — and that includes Yukio — that tail me all the time, it was pretty much the afternoon rush hour already and our freedom to go everywhere was seriously curtailed by the physical presence of many people. To say nothing that we had become obvious enough for some of them to be looking strangely at me. Were you not in such a rush, I could go to Ueno station again at a more appropriate time, say a late evening, and attempt to complete the job."

"Fraser-San," Tanaguchi said, "what it is, our timelines have changed. We need to deliver those guides much earlier to the community."

Simon knew that in Tanaguchi's parlance "the community" was the sect. *And why would you need each and every nook and cranny photographed? A guide? You don't say. This is so fishy.*

"So, what would you suggest?" Simon asked. He didn't want to raise any alarms, cramping his access to more information. He was suspicious enough already to them, as a *gaijin* and a young one at that.

"Well, if you could, please go tomorrow again at Ueno station, at your convenience. This station is so important for the orientation of our members. As to the other stations, just follow our instructions: get the required detail," Tanaguchi said.

***

I can't reach with my hand and touch Hiroko. That, I can't do at present. But right now I've got myself in something like a telephone call in which I see her at the other end of the line, only I can't hear her. It's as though we were in a penitentiary meeting room, and the guards had intentionally disconnected the signal. There are no devices as such, headphones or microphones, but she speaks to me as from behind the glass wall in a prison.

Her face is as troubled as I've ever seen it. The eyes are ringed with what only be but bad sleep and worry. And we never bargained for something like this when we agreed to her trip.

In this contact, she seems to be outdoors. The lay of the land behind and around her is nothing like Connecticut, not like anywhere I've been, at least. I see huge boulders, vertical walls with cracks, evergreen pines; just glimpses of them all, as there's a camera with a limited view angle at the other end.

We mouth words to each other, both of us aware by the minute that they won't pass through this huge distance and whatever other barriers are between us.

The only word I think I can decipher on her lips is 'love.' However, each time it comes through there is, right in the middle of it being spoken by her, an awesome tremble in the image as though what we have in front of us were huge TV screens and a giant — and I see with the eyes of the mind Polyphemus — took them and shook them at the most inopportune of times. So, even though I expect the continuation — 'you' — it never comes about.

***

The Lotus Flower sweeps and weighs the alphabet of faith, and wonders if the Upper Levels have gone through all the letters with the people. If the people won't be surprised when any one of the keys is punched and the consequence asked to be delivered. He means *any*.

Take for example G. Gas. Deadly. Killing within instants after the paralysis of the central nervous system. Military grade. Only few know how difficult it has been to get it from Russia of all places. Our rival for ever.

The people, the lower layers, know the reason for the delivery. Hacking at the roots of the dictatorship by hacking at the obedience, at the spirit of the mob being a subservient one. But understanding and execution aren't the same when you strike others that apparently are just like you, only they aren't, for they aren't in agreement with the final thing, the coming back of the Great Swan on the Day of Judgment, in spirit and flesh, to save us, before we're swept for eternity by the flood of sins accumulated for centuries.

***

Simon went again to the Ueno station, as requested. That evening, around 9 p.m., the rush had petered off, the clusters of people on the platforms vanished as waved off by a magic wand with each train; no pushing and shoving. Still, parties of late, owl-eyed returners from work continuously popped in from the nearby restaurants and bars, humming with the day's jokes, backslapping each other, in pockets of two or three. What was out at this time of the night was mostly a male population, the females having absconded earlier from the reveling parties, bowing their excuses — family waiting at home.

Unfortunately, his previous impression held: the fluorescent light on some of the platforms wasn't quite enough. The light exposure meter confirmed it. He reached into his equipment bag for his largest flash and snapped it to his camera. Thinking for one moment about the tripod, he finally decided against using it: it all became too much of a show and attracted attention. That much he had been told, to avoid authorities. Encounters with them may become unpleasant, had been the warning.

With the fifth series of shots for the day still to come, he found himself bored. Nothing interesting for himself, just drudgery. Baseball capped, blue-jeansed, sneakered, equipment bag on his right shoulder, camera in his left hand, he shuffled to the end of the platform, towards the opening of the tunnel.

"Are you American?" He would have whorled on his heels, prized in surprise, but for the equipment hanging from him. The words had to have come from a spectacular, tall, blonde Amazoness who seemed to have trailed him, so close she popped right behind him. Trouble was, such sights capture attention in Tokyo, Japan, and two uniformed policemen closed in. He was in the wrong corner, marked by isolation — to boot, a *gaijin* — flagged to everyone in sight by this fetching apparition.

"Yes, I am, but I'm busy. Sorry," he said, and he avoided establishing eye contact. *Bloody you, this isn't Hollywood. How about making yourself invisible.* Now he knew he had to wait, perhaps the police would find other attractions to look at.

But no, the woman hadn't left, she just took herself several meters away from him, crossed arms. From under his brows he saw her sneering. At him, or at the whole situation? For the two policemen continued to come in, and they went straight for Simon, passing with just a flutter of hesitation in their looks by the blonde hook that just happened to be set in their path.

"*Anata,* Mistuh, why photograph here?" one of the policemen asked in English.

"I'm working for a guide of Tokyo."

"Come with us, please, *koban de.* To explain," the same policemen clipped on his English.

With no protest, but weary at the end of the long day, he lugged himself and the equipment out of the underground, to the police station located on the edge of the plaza outside. *Why do I have the impression she's following us from the distance?* He didn't want to turn to check where the woman really was, but his antennae told him she was just floating around.

As usual with them, Yukio Imashita and the bodyguard had kept their distance during the scene in the subway station, and didn't enter with him in the *koban* either. Not at the beginning, that is, he found out.

"Mistuh Freizuh, your work where?" he was asked by the young policeman in the presence of a sergeant, in a separate office, cut by walls with large windows from the common area where seven or eight seats were free at that time of the night. The constables were probably making their rounds.

He mentioned the Company. The two Japanese policemen looked at each other, with respect, mumbling, "Aah."

"This work, Tokyo underground, for the Company?" the junior guy asked, more respectful by the minute.

"No, I'm on a temporary leave from the Company. I'm doing some work for a charitable organization, *The Gamma*." That was the name of the sect, used in any PR connection; this he had learned, so he used it.

The two looked at each other, seemingly avoiding saying anything in his presence, but went out the closed cubicle and conferred hotly — Simon could tell it from the veins in their necks and their gesticulation, seen through the glass encasing the cubicle — standing in the common area, for two minutes. After that, the junior guy came back in and sat in a chair, suddenly morose, looking somehow concerned or fearful, without speaking to Simon. During this time, the senior guy had gone across the room in another glass-enclosed cubicle where another older, senior officer was talking to, of all people, Simon now realized, to Yukio, seemingly come into the *koban* without the bodyguard. Yukio was bowing all the time, but the expression on his face was closer to menacing anger than to anything else.

Yukio pointed to the phone, as though suggesting they call someone. The senior policemen who had been originally in the other room made a sour face at Yukio as though in reply to his imprecations — whatever they were — but lifted a phone and dialed slowly a number. Simon was surprised at this, as it can't have been a police phone at the headquarters or such he was calling, for they wouldn't have called in Yukio's presence or at his behest.

It can't be but Kazuhiro Yuasa's phone. Yukio must have just asked the police to call his boss for a confirmation of something.

The senior policeman spoke briefly into the phone, then waited, shooting a glance toward the room where Simon was. Then he spoke again for several moments, apparently waiting for an answer. That seemed to come soon enough, for he lifted the outer ends of his brows, as though upset. However, he didn't linger in the conversation, but plunked the receiver back in the cradle. He spoke briefly to Yukio, whose face relaxed now. Looking straight ahead as a blinkered horse, Yukio Imashita left that other room, crossed the large one and went down the stairs, apparently toward the entrance in the *koban*.

The senior officer returned and called the junior guy out in the common room and they spoke for several minutes. The junior officer seemed dumbfounded, and kept that expression while they both came in and sat close to each other in front of Simon at the round conference table.

"Mistuh Freizuh, you're free to go," the younger policeman said.

"Excuse me, what was this all about?" Simon asked.

"Oh, just a confusion, we think now," the officer said. "You know, we have responsibility on the security of the Tokyo underground." Then, suddenly, the elder officer bent and whispered something to the other.

The junior added in what to Simon appeared strangely to be a lower voice, "However, if during your work with *The Gamma* organization you find anything strange, come inform us here, please. Your discretion will, of course, be appreciated."

If you knew how difficult it is to get rid of Yukio's or Tanaguchi's group's company. Day and night.

He just bowed, picked up his equipment bag and left.

Yukio and the bodyguard were waiting at the exit.

However, before reaching their car, a shadow interposed and someone tapped him gently on his arm. "Glad to see you out," the

Amazon said when he halted and turned. She must have waited there for over one hour, pretty incredible. "I was concerned." She looked serious, not just posh, this time. "You look like you need to go," she added, "here's my phone number, in case you need friends."

There were no names on that piece of paper.

Her taxi had left by the time their car pulled out.

What's her play? For people just don't pop in to help others.

Hiroko: Distance in the West II

The dogs, black and huge, were there, at the back of the house, baring fangs.

Hiroko had sensed them even before turning the corner: a rumbling growl sneaking through the silence freezing the night in place. Yet, she had advanced, for what could be worse than what was waiting for her in this place? Death, perhaps.

She wanted to see what there was out there besides the huge distance from any other habitation, the feeling of which had imbued her as a bad poison, for she had believed that information. *They* had seemed too confident and outspoken about it for it to be just a bare lie. And the lay of the ground seemed to fully bear it out.

Hiroko raised her right arm high up, snapped the fingers of her left hand twice, very sharply, and looked into the eyes of the dogs. The Ninja trick worked again: they all sat. With them as though fixated in cement, she went past.

She reached the meadow where the closest pines were. Past them, she recalled, the ground went down abruptly to the river snaking through the stony hills. It being so dark now, she had to watch her step, to avoid tumbling down the face of the bare, steep slope.

Hiroko stood in the shadow of a pine for several minutes, looking around, trying to get a grasp of the space around the big house, the sinister building that from here just loomed large, without any of its contours clear.

She decided she needed to know more, if she wanted to try any escape. At least the points of the compass and where that closest inhabited place was located. She came back to the house on the same path. The dogs cowered away, seeing her come.

The large wooden door squeaked behind her. *Bad luck again.*

And indeed, one of the doors toward the end of the hallway opened and the large figure of the Pastor stepped out of a room, in a long nightshirt.

"Can't sleep, Sister … Pauline? Perhaps you need company," his voice boomed sneering, indifferent at waking or disturbing the others. From inside that remote place, women's voices giggled.

Hiroko rushed inside her own room, with shaky fingers tried to find the bolt to lock the door, but no such implements were present. At a loss, she ran to the bed and rushed under the covers the way she was, half-dressed, shivering as a leaf under autumn winds.

She stayed up for two more hours, guarding the door with her eyes. No one came. Stone-weary, she fell asleep not far from dawn.

***

She was woken by the older of the two women who had accompanied her on the way over during the kidnapping.

"It's time for breakfast, Sister Pauline. Here, we do it around seven." The name was still enough to make Hiroko shake, reminding her, as though by hammering a nail in her palm, of how far she was from Simon, from her home. The other continued, "This time, it's the common room for you too. Can't eat in this place. Pastor's orders."

The woman stayed with her through her dressing, intently watching Hiroko first getting naked from the night clothes, at which point she found glee in saying, "Very nice body you have. You'll beget lots of healthy children to the Pastor, no doubt."

Horrified, Hiroko had the presence of mind to use the moment for a confidence:

"How many children do you have?"

"I'm one of the better ones," the woman replied, opening her family's books with no apparent hesitation, "I have four with the Pastor, and two with other men of ours."

She needed to learn more, thus Hiroko asked another question. "Were you married to any of them?" She didn't let on that her stomach turned upside down.

"No. I could have been married, but perhaps not with the Pastor. To marry him, you need him to ask that first, and I'm not so fussy as that."

"And how do you know the father?"

The woman blushed just a tad. "To be honest, I could say that only for four of them: Pastor's are all bigger and darker haired than the rest."

Hesitating, Hiroko pushed the envelope. "Doesn't just counting help? Nine months?"

The woman smiled mischievously, pushing her hair under the bonnet. "You mean, counting *back* nine months from time of birth? Not for me. I might have enjoyed two men at about the same time. I mean, here too, not only on the outside. That doesn't work if you're married to the Pastor, he's very keen on being the only one then. Sez the marriage's sacred. But if you're not married to him, he doesn't bother about it." Her eyes went to the wall clock in the room. "We'd better rush to get to the breakfast now. People eye you if you're late, and that may breed ill will both ways. By the way, I'm Sister Sarah, Sister Pauline."

She extended her hand, but Hiroko pretended not to have seen the gesture, and went to wash her hands at the washing sink.

***

I am alone in my room after dinner. Perhaps *they* will leave me alone tonight. I'm tired by them being around me all the time, in the dining room, in the stern chapel at the end of the building, in the kitchen, in the workroom, as though a dark cloud shadowed and hounded me from the sky. This is perhaps the first time since this morning that I'm left alone with my thoughts.

I am lying down on my back in my bed, fully dressed, eyes closed.

Being there, I know and I feel when I stand and I enter my space of cherry blossoms, *Sakura*, by stepping through a sidewall of the room, penetrating it as it were water that doesn't wet me.

Somewhere in there, if not today some time in this future, will be Simon. I'll just have to look for him; I just have to hope he comes in at the same time; for I know once in, he will look around for me.

I know we will pardon each other the sins to which the world and its people dragged us into; and the worst is this neglect, this not being in the sight and the feel of the other, in each other's touch.

But today, after roaming through many rooms, many buildings, many alleys, there is at some remote end a wall, and this is a wall of evil, stoneimpenetrable, and I understand I can't pass through it today. Without even touching the wall, without being repelled, I sense I need more power.

And I return to my real room, not knowing how I will go about gathering that kind of power.

***

The men came back from their hunting with many deer, carrying both guns and bows on the beds of their trucks, and Hiroko, looking out to them from the work room, wondered if they were poaching. She didn't have any idea about the hunting season in the area, nor did she know how far they went. Far enough for the Pastor to have kidnapped her from Connecticut, for one thing. However, they didn't seem to stay out overnight on most days, thus Connecticut might have been a one-off trip.

Two women were teaching her tailoring: basic cutting and sewing; just with cotton that day. Most of the clothes for children and women were made in house, except for the coats. The men, going out more frequently, seemed to have more opportunities to buy their stuff from outside. Thus, there was this mismatch between the styles of the men and those of the women.

She was now for about a week in the compound, and there hadn't been any trips outside for her since the baptism at the river. Now and then, she saw women leaving in wagons or two-wheel buggies, always accompanied by their men. Only the men seemed to be allowed to ride, and the riding horses were only few and far between, most of them being team horses.

The men also logged. A lot of the fell wood went for providing fuel for the compound, kitchen or storage for winter heating, but some seemed to be taken out for resale. Where, she didn't know. Perhaps some of it was rafted on the river. No gas nor heating oil was used, from what she could tell.

In the workroom, the women's words still didn't reach her fully, as though she was in a mental mist. She moved the scissors absent-mindedly through the cotton cloth. She couldn't be or become of that world.

The river could be the best way to escape. A car is no go, as I don't know the roads around and I might just get lost. At least a river can take you only to a lower level, to the plains, sooner or later. I would need some kind of raft and paddles, or a boat. Or even just a log, me hanging onto it, but the water might be freezing-cold at night. It might take me very far from there, but there could also be falls. And I have to do it before the winter comes, for the river might freeze over and nothing would move on it. And they might force me to "marry" someone very soon. I fear it's the Pastor. He wouldn't have gone to such lengths to Connecticut for others. But perhaps he had an obligation there, and he had been reminded about it.

***

She went again past the dogs tonight, and sneaked alone down to the river for the first time. Her memory of the lay of the land from the day of her baptism was right. Before reaching the bed of the river, there were two flat platforms on the face of the low mountain upon which the large house was located. Once her feet were on the second of them, they took her straight to the river —*my dancer's feet, they know any ground they stepped upon beforehand. Automatic pilot, would say the Americans.*

The river, dark silver licked by the crescent moon, meandered among red boulders, black at night. She crouched and lay one with the ground and observed the course of water. The central part was speedy, as she could tell from its febrile tremble. Whatever implement she might have, raft or log, she would have to lug it to that part through low waters, and she foresaw it bumping against the boulders half-submerged, she pulling at it desperately. Not an easy job at all.

First though, she needed to decide on the floating device. It was obvious that the loggers didn't come here to launch their cut trees into the water. The distance from the shore and the small depth of the water wouldn't allow that. A more abrupt slope was required. Even more, around her the trees were sparse, pointing that the serious local logging was a sign of the past.

Most probably, it was lower down the course of the river that they logged and pulled their trees down into the water. But she could not walk there: it might be too far. She would have to float or swim to that area, and swimming might be too exhausting in the cold waters of the season. Then, in the second area, she would have to piggyback on a bigger log, one able to take her through the falls. She remembered *The Mission*, seen on screen in Japan just one or two years before.

Pray for me, Simon, if it gets to that.

She looked around, and found that between boulders there were logs or stumps snagged from the current. The water wasn't deep, just to her middle section at the most, but already quite cold — November. She waded into it and gave tentative pushes to some of the stumps. Some seemed solidly caught in place and didn't offer any hope, but others seemed to need only a slight push to tumble from their traps into the water rushing by.

All of a sudden, she froze. Two trucks had come up on the flats surrounding the river, the thrum of their engines sneaked to her on the water, and flashlights placed on their roofs sliced through the darkness, searching. Somebody must have found she was missing from the compound. She ducked, crouched and hid behind the stump closest to her. The light swept around as a scalpel, rooting here and there, skimming over the water and the stony shores.

They didn't find her and they left soon, the lights peeking further down the river. A good sign, which told her they really didn't know where she was. She stayed in the shallow water for another half an hour, then went back shivering to the compound, and waited for a break in all the shouting on the corridors to sneak to her room and disrobe. They must have searched for her in her normal thereabouts much earlier, thus that area was now free from surveillance. The shivers stayed with her in the bed for another half hour. She couldn't tell how much of them were coldness and how much plain fear.

She didn't know how late it was when someone woke her by entering the room. She didn't know who it was either, for they hadn't switched the lights on. But soon enough he recognized Pastor's gruff voice, coming to her from the edge of her bed, which had lowered itself under his weight.

"So, we're playing games of hide-and-seek, aren't we here? Keeping everyone on their toes, eh?"

Under her covers, she pulled away and turned away from him, but she was a prisoner between him and the wall. And he knew that, inching towards her.

His voice rasped on, hard as a file.

"Well, they say there's two that can play at it. Let me show you part of that, the sweet and no doubt the saintly part of it."

Maddeningly, she felt his rough, big, hairy hand sneaking under covers, entering from down low under her long nightshirt, trying to get between her legs from behind, all the while his body pressing her toward the wall and starting to lay on her with all his weight and might.

She thrashed and punched at his body, his head coming closer, but his hand had arrived where he wanted. She felt his fingers going through her hairs down there, starting to play with her, her finger penetrating now and roughing inner walls, the other hand keeping the legs parted. She pushed and stepped back quickly into her soles, entered an awkward judo bridge between them and the back of her head on the bed, and with all her now mad energy and might put into it, threw her legs over her head, the legs falling to a side over him, starting to deliver heavy heels to his ribs. She could feel him retreat from the bed, breath heaving heavily.

"I'll show you, you slant-eyed Jap bitch! Don't you think I wasn't told about your sneaky ways. Just wait. I'm gonna grind you through all the men here! *Shared*'s the word. And not soon enough. You'll have twins, guaranteed. Only they're gonna be all different. Bitch." He crashed the door shut behind himself.

She waited for all the sounds to die down on the hallway, and then went to the shower nearby and washed from a washbowl, rubbing heavily. She would not have the courage to take a full shower until right before dawn, when everybody was presumably asleep. But she had to take one; this much was as clear as death.

Simon goes deep V

Simon didn't need long to realize Hiroshige Tanaguchi's interrogation was to be an altogether different kettle of fish than the one by the police.

"Fraser-San, what did the police want from you?" Tanaguchi asked first, after taking him aside to a corner of the underground site. They both sat on *tatami* mats bare of any covering. There was no tea nor anything else served. After being with people for weeks, Simon remained shocked at the starkness of the place.

"Well, first they wanted to know who my employer was," Simon said.

"And what was your answer?"

"Well, of course, the Company."

"And what did they then ask?"

"Whether the work carried out by me in the underground system was for the Company. I said it wasn't, that it was for *The Gamma*, I mean your organization. I also mentioned I was on leave from the Company."

"Hmm," Tanaguchi, furrows developing on his forehead, said, "perhaps we should have given you a better answer. I am sorry for having neglected this aspect."

"But isn't this the truth?" Simon asked.

"The truth, Fraser-San," Tanaguchi said, while fidgeting in his seat, "is like an onion with several skins. You can peel and peel, and find something new and surprising for quite a while. But while you're peeling, you shouldn't tell others what exactly you're doing. For one thing, the state and the government only want to control everybody's lives. The less they know about us, the better we will be. We should be like storks: no one else should know how much fish we already have in our gullets."

"So what should I tell them?"

"That, say, you're working for a guide that hasn't yet customers and funding," said Tanaguchi.

"But I've already mentioned your organization as being the customer of this guide." Simon squirmed.

"Well, it might be that next time you'll be asked questions by police from another district or another *koban.* You would be surprised how badly the information passes from one side of the police brain, so to say, to another."

Simon frowned. "But, sooner or later, they might get to the original files from Ueno and accuse me of perjury."

"Next time, please call this number from the police station. It's for one of our lawyers, who will be informed on your case and come over immediately to the *koban* to assist you. Please don't talk directly to the police."

Simon went through his recollection of the police interrogatory and tested the waters after a moment, "Well, I guess something similar happened this time too, as Yukio Imashita-San arranged for the police to call some number and I was freed."

"Yes, but that wasn't us and we prefer it to be us, while you're working for us."

As Yukio had refused to shed any light on the issue, Simon tried his luck again.

"But could you tell me to whom do I owe my freedom?"

Tanaguchi bucked. "Even if we knew it, it is not our custom to talk about others, Fraser-San, especially when those may be friends. However, please remember next time, if it happens: we prefer such matters be dealt with us directly, for we know better how they might affect us, our aims, and our people."

Why do I get the impression that whoever Yukio arranged to be called — and that can't be but Kazuhiro Yuasa — and The Gamma *aren't fully aligned? They might not see eye to eye on some issues. I need to watch things around here.*

***

There were just three phones in the current site, all of them old, wall-mounted, rough units with cracked or worn out paint. No cabins, thus he felt he needed to be careful, even though he spoke in English, as the people waiting were just steps away, milling around or just standing still. Long lineups at each of them, which he found odd having discovered that many of the members had practically severed all ties with their families or the outside society.

He had waited and waited to call the blonde lady he had met at Ueno station, but he more and more realized he needed to get through to someone on the outside: he was becoming too much of an island. And he had absolutely no news from Hiroko, nor from his family. As his home phone was their only contact to him, he was not surprised.

"Veronica Johnson speaking. May I help you?" Her prompt came faster than his being able to feed in any greeting formula. He thought for a moment that only in Japan someone would come up with their names upfront. In the States, plainly speaking for personal security reasons, one would temporize, trying to find who the caller was, and so on and so forth.

"Yes, er … Hello, this is Simon Fraser speaking. I think we met at Ueno."

"Ah, Mr. Fraser, yes, certainly I remember. If memory serves, I still have to apologize for barging into your work there," she said.

"Ah, no, if it's to apologize, I — "

He was interrupted by her laugh, deep, powerful, unrestrained.

"Mr. Fraser, I think we both have better things to do than trying to apologize to each other. I, for one, need to convey to you an urgent message from your father. Are you using a secure line? This is confidential."

"Well, no. In fact, I'm in the middle of a crowd waiting to make calls. Thus I can't speak freely, but I can listen, I hope, to anything. Try to make it short, please." Simon thought this was one of those long messages from his mother, reporting on sundry events in the family until the patience of her listener was brimming over.

"You're sure we can't meet somewhere in Tokyo?" she asked, and the tone was businesslike, and not catty, coquettish.

"Not for the time being, no."

"Well, then, I guess I have asked all the requisite questions to try to make this a safe communication," she said with a light touch to her voice, which switched to a serious tone as on a dime, "and I have to convey what I am mandated by your family, in fact by your father. Your Japanese friend … I guess her first name is Hiroko, right?"

He streamed his answer. "Yes. What about her?" His soul dropped already saying this to a sinking feeling of being on the edge of a colossal face of a mountain, ready to tumble into the unknown.

"She has disappeared."

"What? Hiroko? Could you tell me what has happened?"

"Well, she visited New York City, extended her stay there in fact, dancing in a show at the Met. Then, she visited your family in Connecticut for several days," Veronica Johnson was saying when he interrupted.

"Do you mean she disappeared in Connecticut, while visiting my parents?"

"Well, not quite."

"For heavens' sake, Miss, would you please tell me what exactly has happened to her."

"Truth is, your parents really don't know. She and your father went together on a hunting trip in some deer hunting reserves. On the third night, while on site waiting for a buck to show up, she vanished."

"Wasn't my father with her?"

"No, they'd just separated to follow separate trails and angles."

"Sounds like a kidnapping to me."

"Your family has the same assumptions. However, no ransom notes have been received since."

"Since when?"

"The trip was three weeks ago. By the way, they did inform the police — the FBI is onto it too — and the Japanese consulate. No news yet whatsoever."

"OK, Miss Johnson," Simon said, in a rush of feelings, "I need to leave this phone now. There are people waiting out here. I need to think about it all. Thank you very much. Good bye." He cut the call without waiting for her reply.

For over half an hour, he wasn't able to recover his senses, wandering in the huge underground space, deeply ruing now

Hiroko's and his decision of going to the parents of each other, on Kazuhiro Yuasa's suggestion. What had been an attempt at rapprochement, of proving themselves into the eyes of each other's family, had turned into a big snake of a distancer, snatching everything between them, snatching Hiroko now.

***

"If want to tell Kazuhiro Yuasa-San that his daughter kidnapped in America, he knows," Yukio Imashita told Simon when he approached him with a request for an audience, the next day. "For fact, he told me he doesn't want see you until his daughter is safely back in Japan. However," and here the tone changed to ominous, "until that happens, you be held safe place *The Gamma* community."

"But I wanted to leave for the States immediately, to help out in finding Hiroko," said Simon. "This doesn't make sense, keeping me a de facto prisoner here, until some impersonal organization back in the US, the police or the FBI, get to find her. I care deeply for Hiroko-San, those guys don't know her. "

"Yuasa-San can't agree anything like that. He feels it's fair. You physical guarantee that his daughter back here. Please continue work for *The Gamma.*"

"And by the way, Imashita-San," Simon asked, "*what* did you tell police to get me out of there two days ago?" They hadn't had time to discuss the *koban* matter yet.

"Not us. Anyway, police and Yuasa-San — professional secret." Yukio sneered and shut down the conversation as a clam.

Simon realized there wasn't any point in pursuing the matter. "OK. Thanks, anyway." *They don't even want to recognize it was them at the police station. OK, good for them. At least they showed up in time then. Guess someone needs me still in Japan, and not for Hiroko's sake.*

He tried to ascertain if there was a point in trying to escape and fly back to the States. Somehow, he recognized the old man Yuasa had a point in holding him as a bargaining chip for whoever was on the US side. Not that he himself would be terribly precious. It was also plain that Kazuhiro Yuasa still saw this first as a family-versus-family war, only then as a nation-versus-nation one.

For the old man, it's still the Capulets against the Montagues. And pray that your young heads will not roll here too. But pray first that Hiroko is alive. There are crackpots enough back at home.

He knew that international calls couldn't be done from the underground compounds, as he'd already tried that way before he knew about Hiroko's disappearance. And even had he been able to do it, what for? His family didn't seem to know anything and he didn't need another confrontation — in the end, they were responsible for not having provided enough security for her. He imagined traffickers in human cargo at work, perhaps prostitution rings. He hoped Hiroko was in a place where contacting authorities was possible without risking limb and life.

Soon enough, he found the decision whether to go or not to the States had been made for him.

Hiroko: Distance in the West III

When in the morning Hiroko saw the men leaving with their logging kits, the Pastor among them, she knew this was the day to act. Who knew what was planned for her when they would be back?

She wanted two items: a thick rope and a hard hat. One hard push on the door of the tool storage barn at the back of the house and she was in: a weak bolt. She put the items into a bag and placed it right after the corner of the house. Sister Sarah was all eyes during lunch, but Hiroko excused herself to go to the restroom, then turned sharp toward the back of the house to pick up the bag. Watching for any bad signs behind her, she ran toward the river, from the shadow of one pine to another. It seemed no one in the mess hall had caught drift of her move.

She was happy about the day being hot, this would help her stay longer in the water. Wading into the river, she found one of the large stumps tested the night before. Indeed, she was able to make it wobble again easily enough on the boulders underneath. She tied one end of the rope around a short stump of a branch issuing from it. Then, she put the hard hat on her head and tied the strap tight under her chin. Crashing her head on some rocks was just one of the concerns. Part of the remaining length of rope she rolled around one forearm. The idea was the stump to act as a tug boat taking her fast down the river without her doing too much work. Just floating, supported partly by the large piece of wood and carried along by it. Swimming all the time would be a recipe for exhaustion and drowning.

Looking around, she saw no one. Half in the water already, she pushed the tree stump into the deeper water. She was instantly dragged under by the current. Luckily she had the rope around her arm and swam to the surface, gripped a snag on the stump with the free arm, and was taken by the swift current into the middle of the river.

The scheme seemed to work for the time being, the size of the stump being just enough for it not to be submerged significantly by her hanging onto it. The water was rushing them along under the bright, calm sun of the afternoon. They moved fast. She kept moving her legs, mostly in order to keep herself warm, the November water being chilly. That her yellow hard hat might not help in terms of hiding was one of her concerns, but she couldn't risk not having it.

The river widened gradually. Her leg-paddling work was now mainly pointed at keeping the stump in the center of the flow, where the speed would be greatest.

Abrupt walls of stone and sparse clumps of pines standing precariously on meager ledges and platforms was all that at times she caught a glimpse of for now. But her focus was in front of her. She was aware that sooner or later there had to be a wider area, where the men from which she was running away might bring to the water their logged trees, to carry them down the river to be sold.

Simon, pray for them to be somewhere else, perhaps in the woods, not to see me, not on the shores.

Something was rushing towards her, hanging right above the water. Blinded by the reflections of the sun, she recognized, just twenty meters or so away from it, a frail bridge, made of short planks suspended from two cables crossing the river in a narrower area. This must be the sign of habitation, perhaps the logging camp.

Indeed, soon after the bridge, the river was tapering into its widest incarnation until now. She saw tree trunks, floating in the water against the shore, tied together into rafts of four or five, probably the largest grouping together allowed by the size of the river, or the trickiness of its current or its curves down this point. None of them was moving down the river; they seemed all anchored in wait of launch. Nor did she glimpse any men yet. Was she that lucky? Her mouth was hugging the surface, behind the stump. Any more and she could be observed. And here the river was much slower. Should they see her, here it would be easier for them to get at her by boat or by shooting.

But no, she swore they wouldn't get a chance to see her, these evil people, not for anything. She deeply inhaled three times, then ducked underwater behind the stump, still connected to it via the rope. She hoped her air intake and the speed of the river would be enough at least to pass most of the area given to logging.

The water was cold, but her swimming and paddling all the time surely helped her stand that. Also, the water was clean, so she could still see the sunlight coming in at that depth. She saw through water now the rough bottom of the stump, several old branches cut very short pushing out their noses, large deposits of moss feeling velvety under her hand when touched.

When the latest air intake had been burned in her lungs, she very slowly raised her face to the surface, on a side, so she would have barely one eye aiming at the shoreline and the mouth and the nose out of the water. It was not over. Cabins and, left deep into the ground, tracks of trees coming into the water from the shore, barely perceived half through the water, told her she was still in the danger area. So she plunged once more, at the same time pushing the stump and letting herself be carried by it, feeling more like a prisoner through that rope than an active agent of her own escape.

Flanked by abrupt walls again, the riverbed was suddenly narrower and the current much swifter. The shadows projected by the pines on the shores arched from one side to the other. Underwater, she wasn't able to distinguish the bottom of the stump anymore.

Falls might be coming up. Come in, Simon!

She lifted her head again to the surface.

Twack!

Something had come at a high speed, bumped into her head gear, yanking it to a side, and ricocheted into the stump. Seconds later, before being able to react, a second projectile — for now she realized it couldn't have been anything else — hit the stump, dislodging a splinter of wood. She immediately went underwater again.

It seems to have come from the side. Still, are they in the water behind me or on shore? Someone must have phoned from the house to the logging area.

The water was pushing her to the side. She felt as though a curve in the river was doing this. When she took another gulp of air to a side of her head, there were no cabins on the shores anymore. Several more gulps and several other minutes later, it seemed there was no shooting at her anymore. She looked quickly behind, and no one was there either. They must have been located on the shore when shooting. Through the air, there was a heavy thrumming sound down the river.

Ten or so minutes later, the sound was more intense, booming and rapping.

She could see just that the river continued to be in her view for a short distance — flanked by stones only now, no pines nor mountain grass — then disappeared as though screened by some miracle curtain.

She knew the falls were coming, but she couldn't do anything.

At what had to be the edge of the falls, she felt suddenly yanked down through the air by the big stump through her rope connected to it, the big rushes the water somewhere behind her in the air falling down too with a huge crashing noise. When she fell atop the stump at the base of the falls, water, air, light — everything — was lost from her mind and senses.

Simon goes deep VI

The "entertainment" junkets to Kabukicho and other *mizushobai* places in Tokyo had disappeared in a flash for Simon, and Yukio Imashita had told him as much he now was a guarantor, by his presence, for Hiroko being returned to Japan from wherever she was in the States — or in the world, for that matter. Also, as though overnight, the sect seemed to declare itself satisfied, through the earnest voice of Hiroshige Tanaguchi, with what he had already photographed on the Tokyo underground and train system, which meant another reason for temporarily leaving the site had vanished. He started to feel as though the underground site of *The Gamma* had turned into a de-facto prison for him.

Hiroshige Tanaguchi had told him that "the guide is about to be delivered to the community and it will be a mightily surprising one for great many." Simon had detected an unsaid threat to those words, and still wondered what they really meant.

After hearing the news about Hiroko from Veronica Johnson, he had been in a daze for days, slamming as though unseeing or blinkered into people at the site, absent to sound and light.

During his better patches, he wondered who really this Ms. Johnson, bringing such fateful news, was. Was she the better-looking version of a PI, hired and sent by his father on his tracks? Not necessarily, perhaps, to save him from the claws of a Japanese girl, but to assess and if possible to minimize the collateral damage. Had she been in contact with Kazuhiro Yuasa's outfit? For her popping up was too coincidental with the time when Kazuhiro Yuasa seemed to have learned about Hiroko's disappearance.

Reduced to inactivity by being banned from photography, he had lots of time on his hands. He took to roaming around the interconnected caves at the site and what he saw reminded him of the Japanese police request to open his eyes. People in bunches and bunches, being lectured. Listening and nodding. Nodding and listening. Chanting in low-voices. *The only thing they seem to lack is the Bible or Mao's little book, but they might have the mantras in their heads just as well.* And now he realized that lately he had had a feeling that some of the senior sect people buzzed with something that he couldn't put a finger on. A certain focus under their furrowed brows, a certain watchfulness, sneaked peeks about themselves, and suspicion oozing.

On this particular night when he saw what he now knew he shouldn't have, the day had passed unremarkably.

In a corner, there was this group, unusually quiet, not nodding, not saying anything, attending to two people who seemed to have fallen sick, lying down on a *tatami* mat, covered with white, dusty sheets except for their faces, pale under the lights of the electrical lamps. When closing in, he distinguished the *rigor mortis.* They must have died recently, for no one in the rest of the large hall moved in their direction in alarm. When he got really close, one of the members of the group pulled the sheets so they would cover their faces too, and gave him a bad look, so Simon removed himself from the area. By this time, he had realized what was strange in those deaths: both people seemed adults, but young, and carried no apparent signs of any long-terms illnesses that would have gradually, insidiously, sucked all their strength. No, their faces showed the vigor and fullness of youth, harrowed though by the apparent lack of air.

Minutes later, from the distance, he saw that group bringing stretchers and carrying the bodies from the cave, all of them leaving together. Yukio Imashita and Simon's bodyguard were not to be seen, perhaps up above ground in Tokyo for a beer. He casually weaved his way through the other groups, some on *tatami*s, some standing, some walking around, and had a look at the stuff left temporarily behind on the *tatami* mats. Lots of booklets among them, in Japanese, English, German, French. The third he took in his hands was in English. It read, *The Gas as Weapon of Mass Destruction.* He leafed through it: a lot of it dedicated to WWI. Then there was a section on "Agents" and in it one of them had been underlined: Sarin. He put everything back and continued his walk, watching again if there was a tail on him. Everything seemed nice and dandy for the time being.

The police hadn't left any phone numbers with him. They might have assumed he would just drop in at the *koban* and chirrup his story. But he had tried once already to leave the compound and the guards at the elevator shaft had turned him back, even though Yukio was not around. They seemed to have their instructions about him.

He called Veronica Johnson's for three days. She might have left for the States, for there was no answer. He was ready to give up, but on the fourth day he recognized her voice.

"Do you have contacts at the police here?" he asked her.

Her laugh warbled through the line. "I've got contacts everywhere."

"Could you go to the local *koban* here, the people who arrested me?"

"I might find a way to recall them, yes," she said. More ringing on the line.

"OK, then. They asked me to tell them if I saw anything suspicious where I am."

"And where are you?" she wondered.

"I thought you'd know by now. The underground site of *The Gamma*, a sect." He rushed his delivery, as other people came closer to use the phone where he was. "Tell them I found a book on nasty gases, one of them the sarin. Underlined."

There was a pause, then her voice sounded serious. "There might be some crackpots with you there."

"Perhaps, but two of that group seem to have fished a nasty death. Sorry, I need to terminate the call *now*." The people in the lineup around the phone had come too close for comfort.

***

He was still sleeping — probably dropping like a log towards the morning, when his sleep was at its most profound — when they must have wrapped him in the sheets on the *tatami* and, while he was still trying to realize where he was, thrashing about, they carried him to this place that was to the side of the cave and was for all intents and purposes a cell. It was like an alcove or a niche in the larger wall of the underground hole. There was no light from the outside — which was only natural for the depth where they had to be located — nor from inside, for a wooden wall had been built there from planks, to surround the space that couldn't have been any larger than six by six feet in terms of floor area, and eight or nine feet tall, but quite irregular in shape, not rectangular.

As this was not at any police station, he conjectured quickly the people putting him under this kind of isolation or arrest must have been from the sect or from Kazuhiro Yuasa's outfit. He hadn't seen their faces, for he had been dropped on the *tatami* in the corner of this cell like a stone and left alone, with only a night pot for company.

It must have been his talking to Veronica Johnson — reported somehow — that had moved his captors to proceed this way. Someone hadn't liked what he had meant to report to the police. Rotten police members sold out to the sect or to the Yakuza, or Veronica Johnson herself. He didn't know anything about her, except what she had told him. Someone had ratted on him and someone had reacted and ordered things.

There was no judge no jury, but surely a sentence had been passed by someone and his first concern was of which length. For, whether this was a legal or illegal process, those who had so captured him, had it in their power to keep him there until hell and high water. This might also be the end of his life. He felt a dropping feeling to his stomach. *Hiroko ...*

***

The chipped porcelain bowl of fish and rice was set on a white-painted stool in front of him twice a day. He had banged for hours on the wooden door of his cell, but it seemed it was isolated enough not to bother anyone outside. Finally, after doing it at the time the food was brought in, the attendant, a worried, modest, small woman who didn't speak any English, asked wide-eyed:

"Sumimasen, nan desu ka?"

"Tanaguchi-San! Doomo arigato," he answered.

After going at it in the same way for three days, the slim, severe figure of Hiroshige Tanaguchi presented itself in front of the open door of his cell.

"Why I am detained here, Tanaguchi-San?" Simon asked.

Tanaguchi looked him over as though he were a child asking a question with a self-evident answer:

"Higher orders. Better for your security and for our security, both."

"My security? Am I somehow not old enough to know what is better for myself? " Then, sarcastically, Simon continued, "And what security risk do I represent for the community, may I ask?" He was weak and felt ridiculously feeble minded, but took care not to mentioned the word "sect," which was very irritating to community senior members.

"I was good enough to travel all over Tokyo to make those pictures for your guide. Now, I seem to be good enough only for this prison cell, or whatever it is. I am going to make a formal complaint to the authorities for kidnapping and illegal confinement."

He could see that mentioning the authorities was only making Hiroshige Tanaguchi boil — he started to pace back and front in front of the doorway — but this was no time for fudging the issue.

"Fraser-San, you know quite well there are other reasons for keeping you here underground. These have been mentioned by others to you and I would not repeat them."

Simon thought about Hiroko but didn't want to mention her name. This was the least he could do for her. "Ah, you mean Kazuhiro Yuasa-San's concerns?"

Tanaguchi didn't reply, just looked back at him, scrutinizing him, as though measuring him.

Simon continued. "And for that and for your community reasons, isn't keeping me in the underground good enough? Does someone insist on my being kept in a cell? Am I a threat to someone and I don't know?"

"I can tell you only that this has been a common decision and it's for both your and others' best interests, as I mentioned," said Tanaguchi.

"And for how long, if you don't mind?" asked Simon.

"Weeks, months, perhaps. As long as required by those security concerns," said Tanaguchi, adding, "Now I have to leave you, I am very busy, sorry." Two of his guards closed Simon's path and shut the door of the improvised cell in his face.

"This is highly illegal and I protest against it! I will take you to both Japanese and American courts!!" shouted Simon through the wooden door, punching it with his fists, but the steps he heard were going away. He stopped beating on the door, but he felt his knuckles, already bloodied.

He was truly in a hole, with no idea how to escape and no friends to help.

I just hope Hiroko is in better shape than I am. Lying down crouched on the *tatami*, on a side, eyes closed, he started to pray, something he hadn't done in years, for her well-being and freedom.

Simon goes deep VII

"She seems to be waking up from the tranquillizers. Sheriff, I'll leave her to you. Do us all a favor and don't ask more than five questions for now."

"OK, doc. Ma'am, Sheriff Gilchrist here. Could you tell us your name, Ma'am?"

"Hiro — ko Yu — asa." She wasn't sure how badly mangled her sounds issued: she had something across the head. There was also a buzzing around. She couldn't tell whether it was located in her head, in which there was also ample place for a splitting headache, or it was just from the blinding fluorescent lamps that she'd seen hanging from the ceiling.

"OK, I take that to be Hiroko Yuasa, right?"

She was glad to find she was able to nod, but she felt a sharp stitch in her neck.

"Where are you from, Ma'am? Which state?"

"Tokyo, Japan."

"Japan? Oh. Glad you understand English then. Thought you may be Japanese-American; er, Asian-American. Sorry for that. Why did you have to swim down that river, especially across the falls, Ma'am? Looks like a daredevil's feat or worse to me. If we were at Niagara Falls, we would have to arrest you. Here, in Oregon, we'll just have to ask you to pay a fine."

The mustached sheriff, beaming his smile on her, seemed to have a light moment.

She didn't feel like sharing in it and breathed out her answer, "Kidnapping."

Somehow, the sheriff slid closer and looked much sharper at her. "You mean, you had been kidnapped and you escaped?"

She felt the pinch again in her neck, nodding.

"OK, doctor's orders: last question. Would you know those people who kidnapped you?"

"No. Very … religious. I think. Kidnapped … in Connecticut."

The man in white, suddenly a big slice of her field of view, advanced from the corner of the room.

The sheriff muzzled, then bit his moustache, but said, "Yes, doc, we'll leave it at that. We'll contact ASAP one of your consulates in the States, Ma'am, to arrange for the medical coverage here and your safe return home, for we know you don't have any documents with you. Talk to you tomorrow. Speedy recovery!"

I need to talk to Simon or Mother. But where is Simon? I was never able to talk to him from America, not at his home, nor at work. Father might know, but would he tell me? Let me do all this tomorrow, when this man, who seems kind, comes back.

***

Hiroko is presently aboard this Japan Airlines Boeing 747 heading from JFK to Narita. In front of her, a five-day-old edition of the "New York Times" offers on its 17th page, on a side column:

> *Japanese Dancer escapes Captivity by Oregon Polygamous Sect*
>
> Little did Hiroko Yuasa, a 20-year-old Japanese Traditional Dancer from Tokyo, know that America is so fraught with peril these days.
>
> Having come to the States in the hope of meeting her prospective in-laws, and after dazzling audiences at the Metropolitan Museum for several days with her dancing, she was kidnapped in Connecticut, while a member of a hunting party, and taken to Oregon by members of a polygamous sect.
>
> Their apparent intent was to make her into one of the wives or concubines of the sect leader, one Joseph Applecider, who is presently held under federal charges of kidnapping, unlawful confinement, life endangerment, and attempted rape.

Also held under charges of aiding and abetting an act of kidnapping are Mary Jo Sussa and Jennifer Johnson.

After being baptized in a river passing the sect's mountain site, Ms. Yuasa managed to escape her captors, and navigated attached to a tree stump the dangerous waters of the river Nahmsiwake for over ten miles, until she reached the 45-feet high Wall Falls.

She further survived the drop through the falls, but lost consciousness on impact. Fortunately, she was observed and rescued by a couple of quick-acting tourists, at the time fishing on boats downstream of the falls. Air-lifted by ranger helicopter to the nearest hospital, she was treated for a fractured forearm and multiple bruises and lacerations.

She has been released into the care of the Japanese Consulate General in New York City, which is busy arranging her speedy repatriation.

Mike Stepanieff reporting

She looks at the article with the terrific feeling of a survivor.

The tea brought by the steward doesn't make her more comfortable recalling that no one from the Fraser family in Connecticut contacted her in the hospital or thereafter, even though the police and the Consulate tipped them off on her story and whereabouts. They seem to be talking only through lawyers' mouths these days, these Frasers, the sheriff in Oregon told her, still munching on his mustache. She doesn't have a good feeling going about it this way, but has decided not to trouble their waters under those circumstances.

Over a patchy transoceanic connection, through which operators on both sides seemed to bump in and leave at their pleasure, her mother told her that her father couldn't be found at any of the phone numbers in her possession, not that those numbers had been recently used and checked. She added there were no answers at all hours at Simon's home; also that the Company didn't know what had happened to him for close to two months now. He was on an indefinite leave at *his* request, that's how they called it. It seems to me, went on her mother in her dry, matter-of-fact way, they're washing their hands of him: he asked for it, the leave or whatever that was, and that's that.

She extended herself in the first-class seat, all paid for by the Japanese General Consulate. *Now it's time to go in our* Sakura *space, Simon, to look for you, I know. I have had bad vibes from your side of it, wherever you might be, and I wish this plane would take me faster to Tokyo, to you. We would at least be together, whatever happens.*

***

Hiroshige Tanaguchi hears Tora-Tora growling on the other side of the massive door to Kazuhiro Yuasa's office. Nervously, he fingers into the special pocket sewn on the inside of his gray everyday robe. Just before leaving, he thought of putting on the ceremonial golden robe, in order to look more imposing in this parley with Yuasa-San. In the end, though, he decided that carrying the word of the Lotus Flower should be enough in these circumstances, and castigated himself for entertaining such empty thoughts. This was power against power, and he knew on which side the balance leaned.

Yukio Imashita pulls open the heavy door from the outside and lets the messenger in.

Tanaguchi makes sure that Tora-Tora has been called to a corner by his boss, that it is under leash. A devil of a dog, huge as a house, and he has to deliver an unpleasant message. He shuffles in with small steps and approaches Kazuhiro Yuasa's huge desk.

"Yuasa-San," he says. He puts together his hands in front of his chest, and bows, noticing that Kazuhiro has not even faked to stand, just nods and makes a vague sign to sit. Tanaguchi swallows deep, in controlled anger. Only a Yakuza *oyabun* would behave with such want of respect to the entry of a messenger from the Lotus Flower. He puts down his simple, cotton-made traveling bag on the floor of the office, close to Kazuhiro's desk. Kazuhiro Yuasa waves off Imashita with a hand move. This is not surprising to Tanaguchi: it was his side that had requested a confidential audience with the boss.

"What is this whole whiff of rush I am getting, Tanaguchi-San? The call this morning from your headquarters was most unexpected, for that time."

"I deeply apologize for the circumstances, *oyabun*." He will never apologize on behalf of the Lotus Flower, even though this could mightily upset his counterpart today.

"Well, let's get to the brass tacks then."

"Well, there's first this disturbance with the *gaijin*, with *Fureza-San*."

"Last I checked, you had him under lock and key. And I don't remember complaining about it, or did I?"

"No, *oyabun*. But he nosed around too much and I guess he was able to pass some of it to the police," said Tanaguchi. "About us, about you too."

"Not that you don't have that angle covered. I thought you and the police were hand-in-hand, at least on some of the things."

"*Some* is a good word here, *oyabun*. And if he ever gets out, he might wrangle further damage."

"So, what's your take on him then?"

"We'd like to put him much lower. There where he could do no damage to The Word."

"Sounds to me like putting him out of dear life. Is that what you would like to do?" asks Kazuhiro Yuasa. "If so, why do you come to me for it?"

Tanaguchi avoids answering the first question. "For we don't like treading on any toes, not the toes of those allied with us. Also, because we don't want any old spirits to be roiled up and brought into it because of your dissatisfaction. In any shrine."

"Let's go on to the second item."

Tanaguchi knows this is as clear a decision on the first one as he is ever going to get from the boss. Kazuhiro Yuasa-San pays too many lawyers not to have picked up lots of crumbs of lawyering from them.

"The second is about space, *oyabun.*"

"Didn't I rent everything I own out to you people? Except this place here. Five tunnels you have."

Tanaguchi can't but agree, not that this is his mission as messenger.

"More and more people are listening to the word of the Lotus Flower, *oyabun*. In Tokyo and all over Japan. Everyone comes here. They want access. They want to live in truth. There is nothing else for them. And when they show so much commitment, we must accommodate them."

"Why don't you buy something above ground?" Kazuhiro Yuasa asks.

"With the price of land being what it is these days in Tokyo, *oyabun*? With the bubble in real-estate, as they call it?"

"No one forces you to stay downtown. Chiba or Tachikawa would be just fine. You don't have to reside smack on Yamanote line. No one does."

"This is where the government is. You know that better than anyone, *oyabun* — we fight them on their own ground, where the people are, where the power spheres are. We can't go to a place where the radiation of power is practically nil."

"You people are going to make me sick in the head. What radiation of power? Pleeze. Don't sell me this. I mean, business is business; I'm not supposed to run to the bank for everything you sell." Kazuhiro Yuasa sneers. "Spare me the ads." Tora-Tora senses his irritation and growls, bass-like.

Hiroshige Tanaguchi feels this room is growing too small to breath, even though he is thoroughly used to the other five caves. No windows, the same pale light, the air stuffed, re-circulated for years. And it's as though Kazuhiro Yuasa knows what his message is before he has even articulated it. He decides to go ahead. He knows a storm is brewing, but he has come prepared for it.

"The Lotus Flower kindly requests your consideration for renting our community this space too. I'm sure you have plenty of space above ground in your organization, a lot of it centrally located too. It can't be too much of an issue for you, *oyabun*."

The boss stands up and walks behind his huge desk. "You people must be crazy. You know I have the War Dead Museum here. You know that my own father is among them, that I revere him."

"Our faith people can help you with a smooth relocation, Yuasa-San, once you tell us where you would like to go. They will pray with you and for you until your soul attains peace on this issue."

"Listen, Tanaguchi-San. Tell the Lotus Flower this is a no go. I'd rather cancel the rental contracts for the other places, then give up using this piece of property. It means too much to me."

"Could we come back to you in several weeks' time for reconsideration?"

"Several weeks? Someone's joking here, and it's not me." His eyebrows still lifted in their outer corners, Kazuhiro Yuasa sits down. The monstrous dog settles on a lower, calmer growl, while his master continues, "Only in many years from now. Same for a straight buyout, just in case you thought about suggesting it."

"Well, honestly speaking, we did think about this alternative too."

"It doesn't exist, Tanaguchi-San. Forget about it." Kazuhiro Yuasa is very firm. In truth, Tanaguchi doesn't remember ever seeing him this decisive — not that he has seen him in many business situations.

Hiroshige Tanaguchi feels humiliated. No one in the community has told him about Yuasa-San being so dug in about this piece of property. The other councilors, the Lotus Flower himself, seem to have taken him for the sacrificial lamb, good to be thrown to the lion in the hopes of appeasing him. But he has prepared himself for it. He knew this could come, and what the Lotus Flower needs Lotus Flower will get. He bows stiffly, bends down to get his bag from the base of *oyabun's* desk, lingers there for a moment, then backs out quickly from the room. The dog barks once loud on his closing the door after him. He rushes to the elevator to get out to the surface.

Again I

When she arrived, late in the afternoon, her mother was not at home. However, the keys were with the neighbors and Hiroko let herself in. She only had a khaki, military-style bag for luggage, half-empty too. All of the things she had had with her when leaving for the US two months before were now lost for ever as in some black-hole, but she didn't regret. Reminders, she didn't need any.

No one had waited for her at the airport. It was eerie that it didn't bother her that Michiko had not come, and she felt for a minute ashamed. She told herself their mother was calm enough about traveling to stay at home and wait for her there.

Only that on the low, brown-lacquered kitchen table there was a short message.

"I'm leaving for the Tokyo Central Hospital with Michiko. Your father is there in a very serious condition, they say."

She threw the traveling bag in a corner, washed her face, and immediately left with a taxi for the hospital. After five minutes, she realized she had taken the keys of the house with her, but she was confident her mother had another set with her, and anyway felt too hot with emotion and rushed to return and leave them to the neighbors. Only now did she recall the worried, or perhaps scared, face Yamaguchi-San had made, putting her right palm to the mouth, when she saw her first, upon opening their door. There was also the flashing recognition the neighbor had avoided to look her in the face.

She started from her thoughts and asked the driver to switch his radio to the local news. For ten minutes, there was only the everyday amalgamation of indifferent items. Suddenly, there was this voice of authority, an anchorman saying:

"We interrupt our regular news broadcast to switch to our correspondent at the Tokyo Central Hospital," which was followed by this agitated female voice:

"Good evening. I am Aniko Kuroda, reporting to you from the Tokyo Central Hospital.

"The well-known Yakuza figure Kazuhiro Yuasa is dead. The doctors here confirm very-toxic-gas poisoning is suspected in the case. His dog was found dead on the premises of his headquarters, which strangely enough for many of you, I am sure, are located in a large underground bunker, bought years ago by Kazuhiro Yuasa from the Japanese Defense Forces."

Feeling sick and overcome by sobs, Hiroko asked the driver, "Please shut off the radio. Please."

While rolling towards the hospital grounds, she asked him, "Please take me to the back entrance, if any is available. A less crowded entrance, anyway."

She was lucky. There were no news crews there. She put a handkerchief over her mouth and nose, found a nurse at a computer terminal, took a pen from the desk and wrote on a piece of paper that she handed to her, without saying anything: "I am Kazuhiro Yuasa's daughter. Could you discreetly take me to him?"

The nurse started up when seeing the name, and then nodded. She typed something in her computer, waited a while, then said, "I know where your … where the room is. Please come with me." They took the service elevator to the fourth floor, to an area that was cordoned off by police. The nurse signaled her to wait behind a pillar, then went inside the perimeter and brought over a policeman to her.

He asked "Are you Yuasa-San? Do you have an ID with you?"

Luckily, Hiroko still had the passport on her, from the immigration control.

"Please come with me," the policeman said and took her to a room where she first saw her mother and sister, looking lost at a bed, with praying hands. On the bed, the terribly colored face of her father issued from under a white sheet.

"Hiroko!" her mother said. They embraced, and Hiroko felt as though her mother embraced in her whatever was not there any more to embrace of her husband. “I am so, so glad you are well,” her mother whispered into her ear, while still clutching at her shoulders.

“Do you know where Simon is, Mother?”

“He has not called to our place after you left.”

“I must find where Father took him. Something tells me he is still in one of those places, under a huge danger himself.” She was shaking, hanging from her mother’s shoulders.

***

It was proving difficult for her to find Yukio Imashita. She called some of the night clubs which her father had owned in Kabukicho. All of them recognized the family name instantly, and spoke in well-acted, humble tones, but most of them didn’t want to say anything about Yukio, or about anything, for that matter — it was so obvious. In the end, it was a pachinko parlor owner who broke the silence and told her Yukio was coming to his place every night about seven and played for about one hour.

The next day, around six-thirty, she went over dressed very modestly, also wearing dark glasses, and occupied a quiet machine that was hidden behind much noisier and bigger ones.

After half an hour, she was dazed by the noise around her, by the jingling and clattering of jumping balls ricocheting all over the face of the machine. She was lucky though, as just five minutes later, Yukio showed up at the entrance, accompanied by a giggling woman, hung on his arm.

Hiroko let him get seated, then made her way to him through the crowded machines and customers jumping with excitement or foundering with disappointment around her. There was no time to lose. *Simon’s life could be at stake.*

“*Konban wa*, Imashita-San!” She bowed curtly.

It was as though he saw a vision, perhaps her father returning from the dead and asking him to account, for he jumped up and stood open-mouthed for a long moment. Only then did he bow low.

“*Konban wa*, Yuasa-San. My condolences.”

“Thank you. I am trying to find Simon Fraser-San. I knew he was supposed to be in the company of my father, but I have no idea where he might be.”

"Well, your father tried for a week or two to make Fraser-San to have fun."

"That means going to hostess bars and places like this in Kabukicho?" She pressed the knife to the bone as he hesitated. "Forget about hiding things. I know my father's preferences, it wouldn't be a surprise at all. And when I am finished with you, I am going to the police, thus you had better speak the truth. I'll find Fraser-San one way or another."

The girl with Yukio seemed to have read quicker the situation on Hiroko's face. She nudged his back with her closed fan.

"Say something, Yukio! Don't just stand there!"

Yukio Imashita's face turned pale, his eyes dilating. Next she knew, he had turned on his heels and was running like a demon.

"Not so fast, Imashita-San!" heard Hiroko among the noise of the machines, and by the time she was at the door of the establishment, she found Imashita sprawled down on his stomach on the pedestrian walk, the apparent result of a kick to his back from the owner of the place, a mountainous man in his forties, who was right above Yukio, with a threatening face and a knee to his spine. "Yuasa-San has had a question for you. Now, don't give up on her as you did on her father or some of us others in the *gumi* will make sure you find great trouble hunting you."

"Last I saw him he was being taken to a cell by Lotus Flower's people. They seemed to be really angry with him," Imashita moaned.

"Which underground site was that?" Hiroko asked.

"Sendagaya."

She hailed a taxi and rushed the driver all the way to there.

***

Simon had been gently knocking into the walls around him for the last two nights — he knew them as nights by the lack of tread and shuffling behind the door of his improvised cell — and there was a difference. Some of the areas issued a dull, short sound; some others, located in an area close to the floor, reverberated empty.

He crouched down, went on all fours, and put his ear again to the ground and to the wall in that area. From time to time, perhaps in just an illusion or echo of his tired system, there was this hissing sound, and some remote rumbling. The wall had to be thinner here — whereas it might be solid rock all around in other areas. *Another cave, perhaps, separated from this one. Maybe just a storage area.*

They had brought him a low, four-legged wooden stool. It took him hours, still he managed to weaken and prize away one of its legs. Its stump a dull chisel and file all in one, he commenced to work away at the wall in the area where the hissing sound made itself audible at times. His ears ached with how carefully he listened for any movements behind his door before starting each digging. He had this feeling that at night they forgot about him in the larger scheme of sleep — they rarely entered his cell.

The next night, he got through the wall. It was just drywall, and only several centimeters thick. His hands all bloodied, he was concerned his guardians would observe it, and worked at widening the hole for his passing through on the same night.

When on the other side, his fingers were confronted — for it was totally dark — with a one-meter wide, sharply-inclined tunnel going up, probably to the surface of Tokyo. He had now the reason for the hissing previouly heard: that must be a ventilation tunnel. The air draught was obvious to his face. Somewhere lower, huge fans must be busy at moving the air from the underground caves. Defense Forces design, no doubt. Shuddering at the thought of sliding down into gullets of rotors, he carefully advanced, most of the time on all fours on the rough inner side of the tunnel, toward a surface expected to hold true several tens of meters above his present location. At two-meter or so intervals, he thought himself again lucky to find, embedded in the concrete of the tunnel walls, metal steps on which he could hang on to recover his breath.

He was close to the surface now. The bit of bother was that above him there was this, no doubt heavy, metallic grille, its crossed bars at least one-inch thick each, and by touching it he hadn't discovered anything that would allow him to believe it could be pushed up from inside — he had tried that already for one hour. He thought one would need to be helped from outside to move it even for just a tiny bit in its seat.

He couldn't hear any steps outside, and it might be the same during daytime. Who knew what remote corner of Sendagaya this opened to. And he had to get out to the surface, for first thing in the morning they would come up after him, upon discovering his empty cell with the gaping hole in the wall.

***

It was late, already ten in the evening, when she reached the *koban* in Sendagaya. The four police on duty didn't know Hiroko, but the one playing the receptionist recognized her last name, and the story of her father flashed immediately on the faces of the others when he repeated the name out loud for their benefit.

"You've got to help me," she said, "to find Simon Fraser-San, my friend."

"Is he an *American-jin*?" the stocky lieutenant seemingly in charge of the *koban* at the time asked her, nonchalantly sitting at his desk.

"Yes, he is American." Standing right in front of him, Hiroko made a pass at arranging her skirt. Having come here in such a rush, she felt something might not be right with the way she looked, and the men are so quick to judge.

"Why are you coming to us in Sendagaya, Yuasa-San?" Lieutenant Uchida — she saw his name on the desk tablet — asked, shifting in his chair. Still not inviting her to sit.

"Because he was last seen being taken to one of the underground caves here in your neighborhood. They belong to my late father, Kazuhiro Yuasa, but are leased to a community, a sect, I don't know what it is, the Lotus Flower people."

"Ah, them." The lieutenant's face twitched, and Hiroko could see his discomfort. He took his time, then proceeded slowly and demurely, his face probably the best stone impression he could make for her. "We know them, but we can't just barge in on them and perform a search, especially with no warrant."

"Even if I tell you that I have information that they may have kidnapped Mr. Fraser, that they keep him under illegal arrest?" She switched from one foot to another; she felt the fear and the anger coming to a boil in her.

"You used the word 'may,' and it has a lot of power," noticed the officer. Still, something had moved him, for he stood and started to pace around the small room, without looking at her, preoccupied.

"My father, Kazuhiro Yuasa, is dead, and he might have been killed by them. Even the press are saying that. I don't want Mr. Fraser to share his fate. I think he's under a very serious threat of death. You have to do something about it."

"The press are saying many things. The results in the investigation on your father's case, unfortunately, have not yet been made available to us. Sendagaya is not that important," he continued with some irony.

"Well, you're forcing me to call my lawyer and to talk to the press about the police not doing something to prevent a murder."

The police officer looked at her, annoyed. But something had changed in the air, for he asked her to sit down while he made some calls. He went to a small room in the corner of the building and closed the door after himself.

Two of the other three men, all in the dark blue, belted uniforms, who hadn't said a word during the conversation, went to the desk of the third, and all now shuffled words under their breath, turning now and then their eyes toward her. It was as though without an order from lieutenant Ushida they would not move an iota, thus she waited for him to come back.

Hiroko felt her eyes were about to close soon. This had been a very tough day, starting with the whole hunt for Imashita, then this matter with the police here not willing to do anything.

But she couldn't let go, for letting go meant perhaps not to ever see Simon again. Simon, toward whom she felt pulled so hard now, when alone without him, without seeing him in over two months.

When he came back, the officer's face was cast in less stone than before.

"Look, Yuasa-San, we will do whatever it takes to find your friend."

"I hope by that you mean *now*."

"It's past ten at night now, and we don't have many people on detail. You can see it yourself." He walked his eyes demonstratively over the other three men in the room. "Perhaps tomorrow morning."

"That's too late. I have a strong premonition that could be too late. Why don't you assign right now two of your people to this case? We could look all over the neighborhood during the night. I'll go and be with them, not matter how long it takes — until we find my friend."

"In our business, we can't follow premonitions. We need facts," the officer said. But it seemed something in the calls he had just made pushed him to change opinion. "But I will assign sergeant Koraira to this case. Very able man. He knows the neighborhood. You can start right now, if you feel like it." One of the three stood up and came over to his boss's desk.

Hiroko focused on him. An indifferent face, but strong shoulders and a a quick step. Perhaps that spoke to something.

She stood. "Let's go, sergeant Koraira, if you don't mind. Let's see some of the places where the Lotus Flower congregates around Sendagaya. You must know them. There can't be too many, but each of them could be very large. I know some of the other ones in Tokyo. My father owns all of them — I mean, owned them."

"Koraira-san, take plenty of flashlights, batteries and rope. Those are deep places, and the elevators might not work at this time of the night," the officer instructed the sergeant, then pointed to several places on a map that he gave him. He looked into his eyes, "Call us in case of any emergencies." Then, he turned to Hiroko. "I hope we'll find your friend, with your help. I don't think there's anything threatening him."

"Lieutenant Uchida, please be prepared to have someone else on the case tomorrow morning, for I will not give up on the case until we find Fraser-San." Uchida's face jerked one of its deep lines.

Again II

Crouched, and perched uncomfortably on one of the last stairs in the inclined tunnel, Simon thought his whole trek in the dark for getting to that ventilation grille right under the asphalt skin of Tokyo could not have taken more than three hours. By that count, the time had to be between midnight and one a.m., and the absence of passers-by, of any noise, except for the street-sweeper machines passing now-and-then, agreed.

The stress of climbing ended, except for his raw hands, he was able to think now about the huge metropolis above that grille. He had the strange feeling that Hiroko must be close by. As though she had come back from the States. Could that be true? Was he in his right mind at all?

All the signs coming to him during the latest weeks pointed to her being under a heavy, perhaps mortal, threat and he couldn't imagine where that could have come from in the States. Such a sweet girl: who could have any bad designs for her? But now the resonance in their space was calmer, quieter, so he had been able to better sleep lately.

The metal grille was solidly clamped in the asphalt and the concrete around it. It refused to move even a millimeter when pushed, so he decided to wait for people to pass by, once the dawn was up, to cry for help. His jailers could at any time discover his disappearance and climb after him in the same tunnel. He hoped that would not happen earlier than seven a.m.

The light coming to him from the outside was black-blue; a slice of moon in it. It was getting cold, so he pulled his jean jacket tight, pushed his hands in its pockets, and tried to remain awake for any passers-by.

***

Sergeant Koraira proved himself to be faster out on the streets of Tokyo than he had appeared to be inside the *koban*. It was past eleven, but he seemed in his element in the late night, passing by the late noisy young partygoers or the older *sararimen* having had a late drink in a small neighborhood bar after a tardy dinner in a restaurant, now supporting each other toward the train and subway stations. He waved and nodded to some of his acquaintances, *pachinko* parlors, shop, restaurant and the odd *rabu hoteru* keeper, standing and watching the passing of time on the gates of their establishments, and to their customers coming to and going from their places of business. All of the grocery stores were closed for the night, and past midnight the street machines would not deliver beer cans.

Hiroko looked most of the time to his back, so fast he was walking and crisscrossing streets and the closed small markets, which she felt to be a good sign that he was putting some real interest and energy into their task.

They went into a small park, and she worried about the darkness in it. In a corner, the sergeant identified an old one-floor all-concrete square building. Its doors seemed to have been closed for the night from the inside, for he knocked, but no one answered.

"What's in here?" Hiroko asked.

"This is the entry to one of the elevators going down into the underground location. You must have seen something like this at some of the other places," the sergeant said, looking a bit strangely at her, as though asking, "Don't you know it, Miss?"

She realized he meant some of the other underground sites of her father. She appreciated his delicacy of not mentioning him. She knew from the absence of any guards that this one had to be totally vacated by the Yakuza.

"Do you think this is still being used by the Lotus Flower community?" she asked.

"Well, I saw some of them in their garb just one week ago around the place. They couldn't have disappeared into the thin air, could they?"

"So, you think they've locked the doors just for the night? That may be, Koraira-San, but we can't wait and see what happens tomorrow morning, whether they reopen or not. We need to get into the facility tonight. I know and I feel that my friend is under great danger."

Koraira had a double take at her, then said, "Well, according to the map we have at the *koban*, this should be the main entry point. The rest are to be used just in emergencies. There are places — tunnels, tubes — for bringing in fresh air down there, also water and electricity, places drilled right at the time of building the caves against the Bomb in the early fifties."

"Do you know what these access places look like?"

"No, they were marked off years ago by policemen, but their location wasn't clearly indicated, they were written down more as those policemen's presumptions than anything. And I for one haven't been in any of the caves either. No reason — this community seems very peaceful. Like monks, if you know what I mean," said Koraira, and seemed convinced about it.

Hiroko shook her head. "Well, look at what happened to my father. By the way, I have been in one of the main caves, the one he used for his office, the only one that he still occupied, I understood. It was very deep. I remember thinking the elevator seemed to go down for something like twenty stories." Hiroko made a break and the thought came over her that they were just talking, not acting. She pressed on, "Could we go immediately to some of the other places, please? Perhaps we could get in there."

"Trouble is, Yuasa-San, those are well-hidden places by design. Look," he said showing her a copy of the map seen at the *koban*, "they are marked as being in some vague areas, these encircled by dotted lines. And they are all up to two street blocks each crosswise — not a small area to plough through."

"How many such areas do you have on your map?"

"That's another trouble: eight. Too much to cover for a night, if I may say so, Yuasa-San."

"You don't know any of those alternate entry spots yourself?"

"Honestly, no. They may look like any sewer cap or grille, ventilation mask or hole. Anything that does not resemble solid ground and could lead deeper could be it."

"You don't have phone numbers for them, for this community?"

"They rarely answer them, and if you tell them you are police, forget about it. They despise government in any shape and form."

"Then let's start working on the area closest to here that might hide an entry point," she said.

"Fine. Let's go to one of them. It's a park two streets from here. Please remember, Yuasa-san, that tomorrow morning at eight, I am out of my duty shift. Not that I have anything against helping you." He shrugged and started off apace to his right.

Where are you, Simon? Tell me, give me an inkling, please.

After several moments of meditation, she ran off after Koraira, who hadn't even waited for her.

"Koraira-San, do you know of any such areas to your left? I have an inkling we might have a better chance this way."

He stopped, looked carefully at her, breathed out, and said, "Yes, I know one, but it's further away, five or six blocks from here."

"Let's go there first, please."

"OK. Somehow, this is your and your friend's time, so why not?" Without changing his stoic expression, he turned around and started in the other direction, just as fast as he did it before. Only this time, Hiroko kept pace with him, even if that required her to run or skip for several steps at times.

***

Simon woke up. It had to be about half past three or four in the morning; the cold had been insidiously and gradually getting to him. No passers-by since he had gotten right under the surface of the street. No one to cry to. There had be a moon out there, if he considered the kind of light it got to him through the grille. Somewhere in the background of the street above him, as far as a block or so, a truck passed by, probably a band of rock musicians clamoring for popular attention and not getting any, by the lack of response to their rumble and din.

The digging and the climbing had gotten to him, for he was spent, kept awake mostly by the lack of food and the reflex of the morning.

The latest awakening, though, had been different in that he had roused to something — the feeling that, somehow, she, Hiroko, was close, that just by extending his arm he could reach her. In this vision, she came running toward him in a white pair of tights and a white thin turtleneck that showed off the buttons of her breasts springing underneath.

He pressed on his ankles; there was pain in them from his cramped perching on the metal stairs.

He thought this exit must be located in a very isolated area, for during half of the night no one really had passed by. Perhaps the back of a warehouse, or of an apartment building, its garbage disposal.

Still night, perhaps five in the morning. There was a rattle somewhere lower in the tunnel. Couldn't be but human voices. He had been found. In a matter of tens of minutes, at the most, they would be upon him.

He started knocking again at the grille, but it was as solid as ever. As though cast in place in the concrete around it. He tried to acquire the most stable perch position he was able to, to enable him to hit out if someone came up at him from below. But he didn't have any weapons except the wooden stool leg brought up with him under his jacket. Good thinking.

Below him, he could now hear boots stepping, clanging, on metal, and they were growing more distinct by the minute. The way they overlapped in sound, he was sure there were several people sent after him in the tunnel, not just one. They didn't seem to speak to each other, and this rattled him more than any shouting: it was as though they didn't have time to lose and were all set upon their task.

A flicker flashed down to him from above the surface through the grille. These had to be the leaves of a tree located above the manhole, for he heard the wind ruffling something, with still no human voices around, above or below him.

***

Hiroko looked at her watch: it was five-thirty a.m. already. Sergeant Koraira and she had dragged and combed three parks and plazas already, two of them at her suggestion. She had seen enough concrete and asphalt to last her for months. Nothing close to an entry to underground spaces, nothing like gates, nothing they could at least hope to use to sneak down to the caves. Nothing with locks on that could signal even just a past use as a passage. She was lucky to have comfortable, low shoes on her. Even so, her toes felt bruised, but she wouldn't look at them now.

She deeply felt she only had one choice: to keep at it, with this sergeant and the one after him and the next one, until she found Simon. She wouldn't have known what to do with herself without him. She didn't want to even think about it.

She heard a noise in the park they had just entered, in another corner. A couple seemed to call for help, crouching down, with no apparent muggers upon them. The dawn was barely upon the capital, and the light pillars were rare over there. This was a change — they hadn't met people for the last two hours in the places where they had been.

"Let's go there," she shrieked to Koraira, starting to run in the direction of the call, fighting with the grip of her shoes on asphalt. He padded heavily following her. Clever guy: his flashlight was on, powerful, illuminating the couple, who seemed now to be on all fours, pulling at something.

While still running, she heard "Help!" in English and instantly knew it was Simon.

"Simon! Is that you?" She barely breathed and thought she wouldn't recognize her own voice, so wild.

"Hiroko! Great God! Yes, it's me!" his reply came as they were upon the grille where only his face flashed at times. The rest was dark and she could hear, muffled, strains of a fight going on underneath the metal.

The couple was pulling away at the grille. Hiroko and the sergeant were trying to help. Huffing and puffing, the sergeant told her, "We need help, a machine, this is too heavy. I'll run to stop a car!" He was calling into his cellular, while he scurried towards the adjacent road. But Hiroko knew there couldn't be too many cars passing by at this hour of the dawn.

"Open this grille! Quick!" Simon's breathing was heavy and he spoke while the hitting noises, punches or kicks, were being heard, heavy, delivered as against a training bag. Only Hiroko knew these were real bodies, and one was Simon's, and each of the echo blows cut her to the quick. She was desperate, feeling helpless and powerless. She looked around for implements that could help in prying out the grille.

***

There had been two of them coming at Simon up the tunnel, both with tights like Ninjas, face masks hanging to a side of their heads, air tubes at the back, expressionless faces. At a distance of just about ten meters below him, as if at a signal from one of them, they both put on their masks. The scene was unreal under the late blue-silver moonlight trickling through the grille, but Simon had all his senses sharpened now, and he focused only on their advancement.

It's gas that they want to do me in with. Focus on those masks!

They started to wave to him with their gloved hands, while still climbing toward him, as if inviting him to come over.

Not me: I won't come down with you. Not now, not ever. He didn't say anything, nor did he wave back to them. He knew enough about the Lotus Flower to last him several lifetimes. There was no point in convincing each other.

He took the stool foot out of his jacket and grasped it hard. His only weapon — it and his body. Then he turned his body to face the center of the tunnel; kind of tricky: he had to stand on his heels. *Never leave your back exposed.* With one hand, he grasped the top step; with the other, the wooden piece, up, ready to strike.

The guy higher in the climb waited now several moments for the other to reach the steps right below him. They sure as hell wanted double the power to attack Simon, but he knew only one of them at a time could pass and push up through the narrow stairs. Also, the stairs were at about three quarters of a meter, quite distant, from each other. And a fall of tens of meters down the very abrupt tunnel had to be the end of anyone.

Simon, forcing himself to overdrive-think, flashed a wonder whether they wanted to *spray* him with the gas agent. He wasn't able to see any spray bottles in their hands. Not yet, that is, as they were not yet right under him. *And they cannot do that, the draft could take the whiff underneath, to* their *crowd. Even with the distance, there was the risk.* The masks seemed to make them breath hard: he was able to see the swollen veins on the neck of the top man, who was not more than five meters away. The dawn, sharper by the minute, launched black-mauve javelins of light through the grille on the walls and into the emptiness of the sheer tunnel.

Their masks had sun-reflecting goggles too, so the eyes weren't visible to Simon. Huge spiders yearning to annihilate and digest him.

Four meters away from Simon or thereabouts, the man at the top raised his hand and, taking a fast swing, threw a metal hook or tomahawk trailed by a string toward Simon, but Simon caught it in the air with the wooden piece and repelled it down the tunnel. Surely pressed for time, the man didn't try to pull up and throw again the hook, but let the string go from his hand, so the weapon fell, tumbling down clanging on the walls and stairs. The second man barely had the time to duck away from it.

The top man continued to advance, step by step. Simon watched the guy's hands so hard his own forehead sweated. The second man stayed back, and Simon knew they would come in waves, as there wasn't space enough for them to pounce on him at the same time.

The gas, where is the gas?

Just a moment later, the top man, now just two meters below, tucked his right hand under his jacket and got it out in one swoop, his fingers now clutching a mask with no tubes on it and no goggles either, with what could be support bands hanging from it.

He was with his hands just one step below Simon, who started to skip from one foot to another on his own base rung, to avoid having his legs caught. Also, Simon readied himself to step on the man's fingers, in case the guy decided to advance.

The man moved up his legs, effectively crouching in a spring, setting up for a vertical lunge at Simon. When that happened, the other threw himself with his hands at Simon's ankles, trying to pull him down. With a side kick, Simon swept the guy's hands away from him, but the attacker managed to grab Simon's bottom step and, in a terrible rush, pushed himself up with all he had, aiming for a strike or a grip at Simon's core. *Whoosh* came the wooden stool leg down over the extended hands.

And this mask is gone!

But the hands falling from their intended target managed to get a grip on Simon's base stair. Losing no time, in one motion, Simon stepped heavily over the gripping fingers, and when the man released his clasp, Simon dropped himself in a flash to a sitting down stance on that step, and then hit him in the head with the piece of wood. The man lost balance, next tumbling through the tunnel. The other man, just three meters down, pistoned out a hand to grab his cohort, but the gravity had made its effect already felt and his catch of the first man's hand was barely a touch. A horrific cry was heard, then just bumps and a final dull sound.

Suddenly, there was sound coming from above the grille, shuffling of steps rasping on asphalt, and Simon cried out, "Help! Help!" with the thought it might deter a while the second attacker. But there was little hope for that: he was already coming on up.

Still, someone — perhaps a couple passing by — seemed to have heard him, for he heard them now just above him talking to each other, and then asking him:

Anata, do shimashita? Anata, nan desu ka? Ii desu ka?

He shouted, "Help! They want to kill me! Killers! Open this thing, please! I want to get out of here," but could not continue, for the second man was closing on him, turned rabid by the death of his fellow sect member, for he literally was jumping from a rung to another.

Then the man was upon him, and Simon instantly knew this was going to be a much tougher fight, for the other fended off with a left karate chop the wood piece coming at his head from Simon's right hand, while with the right hand grabbed Simon's jacket, so now Simon had to hold both of them above the abyss, as it was him who was on the stairs and the other guy straddling him and clutching his legs around Simon's. Yet, Simon was relieved not to see the mask in his hand. But he realized this killer would willingly take him with him down the hole to the end.

Simon lifted again the wood piece with the right hand, grasped even tighter the highest rung with his left, and punched the back of the man's head, which wobbled like a puppet's. The man detached his right hand from Simon's jacket and threw it up. It passed by Simon's left ear and he knew the man had it anchored on the highest rung too. So he had changed ideas and tried to survive by himself this fight.

Simon threw a sweeper with the right leg by swinging it from the hip sideways as hard as he could in order to detach the man's legs from around his. He managed to free himself from the other's left leg, and punched up with his right knee in the next motion, hitting the guy in the groin. But the thug's free left hand went past Simon's wood, and exploded on Simon's right ear. Simon inhaled deeply in pain, lifted his right hand, deflecting the attacker's left and again hit him hard on the back of the head with the piece of wood, and when the man's head waggled forward, Simon knocked him into the face with his forehead.

It was now that Simon heard:

"Simon! Is that you?" and, instantly recognizing Hiroko, he replied.

Yet right at this moment, using the break in Simon's focus, the man cut through his defenses with a karate punch to his right ribs, which burned and hollowed Simon out in his core and dazed him.

Next thing Simon recognized, was something tight being pulled around his face, and he knew it was the mask. With whatever he had, releasing his own hand support from the stairs, he delivered a karate punch with both hands to the chest of the man, who went backwards toward the center of the tunnel, supported only by his legs, clamped around Simon's again as the arms of an octopus around its prey. But by this time, Simon had snapped back his left arm to grap the rung, and had it anchored there, so when the man's full weight tried to snatch him from the wall, he was prepared, stable, and delivered again a leg slide sweep that detached the man from himself. Tumbling back, this hit man went down after the first one, and there was no one there this time to attempt to catch him on his trajectory.

First avoid falling yourself ... then the mask ...

With burning breath, Simon heaved himself on the rungs to have his upper body level with the very last one of them, pushed his right arm to the armpit between the stair and the wall, hanging the arm downwards, leveraging the all of himself on it clamped there.

That ... will ... have to ... hold ... me ...

Now the damn mask ... Hiroko ... Sakura ...

In a daze, he hoisted, terribly slowly, his left arm to tear the mask off his face —

Not alone

The taxi cab rolled back and forth. The metal cable, which, in a moment of good fortune, the driver had found in the trunk, and was now attached to the back bumper of the car, pulled at the grille.

On the third attempt, wheels spinning angrily in place, the heavy, rusty grille jerked open and flopped clanging to the side. The dark mouth of the ventilation shaft exposed Simon hung as Christ on the cross on the last metal rung of the staircase, eyes closed, mouth wide open as though gasping for air, face dirty and blueish, the mask still in his right hand.

"Simon! Simon!" Hiroko cried out. She crouched down, patted and caressed his face, tapped his shoulders and chest. He didn't react at all. An awful feeling caught her in its clasp, and she could not stem the hot tears streaming down her face.

"Help me! Help me get him out of this place!" she cried, turning to sergeant Koraira, to the taxi driver, to the couple that had called them over first.

"I'll go call an ambulance!" Arms flying, the young woman rushed to a phone cabin.

Koraira hunkered down, took Simon by his armpits, but he could not shift his body, so tight had the young man inserted his arm between the wall of the shaft and the metal rung.

The other man didn't speak, but with a determined face stepped into the shaft, finding place for his feet alongside Simon. In seconds he was a human jack in position. Pushing up in sync with Koraira's heavings and Hiroko's pulling at Simon clothes, they managed to get Simon out and on the ground.

"We should help him breathe! Let's give him mouth to mouth!" Hiroko cried out.

Koraira stepped back. "I think that could be dangerous, Yuasa-San. Those people down there are said to have poisons. Perhaps they poisoned him."

"Yes," said the other man, "look at the mask in his hand. They might have forced him to breathe something bad."

Hiroko felt a chill down her spine. Desperate and angry now, she snatched the mask from Simon's arm, bent over him, opened his mouth, pried his teeth apart with her fingers, took a huge breath in, then put her lips to his and tried to force air into his chest. She repeated the maneuver several times, but Simon didn't come up from his lost state.

Sergeant Koraira asked her, "Let me have a go at it."

Simon is my man. Hiroko looked at Koraira with reserve, but pulled back, and the sergeant turned Simon's body to a side on the ground, inserted his own arms under his armpits from his back and clasped them on Simon's chest. Then, he heaved and jerked him up and down several times, in a Heimlich maneuver.

Hiroko couldn't see anything on Simon's face that had changed since they discovered him.

Spinning flashes, the ambulance was there already.

"Quick, please give him oxygen!" she told the two men carrying the stretcher. They rushed back to the minivan and brought a cylinder and a mask, the latter of which they applied to Simon's face. They didn't lose any time, and ferried him inside on the stretcher. Hiroko and Koraira jumped in the back and the vehicle sped through the streets of Tokyo, siren blaring.

The morning was fully there now, violet and strange.

Hiroko kept her hands on Simon's forehead.

We're back again together, Simon.

There was an answer from Simon, but not from the one in front of her.

***

The doctor came to her with the most serious face she had ever seen.

"Fraser-San is unfortunately in a coma. He appears to have been exposed to the poison gas Sarin, which is designed for wars. We have applied the best antidotes available, and we can only hope he will recover. However, his case is very serious."

Her mother tapped her hand. "Let's sit there, Hiroko-chan. You need to eat something. You look very weak."

She felt the push of a *bento* box. Then she lost it from the fore of her consciousness. She started to open it after ten minutes.

She saw Simon and herself playing Frisbee, the plastic disc lackadaisically floating from Simon to her and back to him, the comfort she had felt then, the I-don't-need-anything-else feeling. Then the night at Shinjuku Gyoen opened its wings to her memory, with all the stars above them.

And she hadn't seen Simon for close to a month — the lost time cutting deep as a knife.

***

They called her to his room several hours later.

"Unfortunately, Yuasa-San ... " the doctor said, flapping his hands uselessly.

She looked at Simon and she knew it. There was no movement on the monitor above him, just a flat line.

"Could you leave me alone with him?" she asked, and the doctor and the two nurses, and her mother, all walked out.

She pulled closed the beige curtains around the bed.

She went to Simon, kissed him on his lips, and felt the coldness. She detached the electrodes from his chest, pulling hairs. Then, she put the right side of her face to his chest. Where it had been just over a month ago.

Simon was not there anymore. He had gone to a better place, where people had less reasons to hate, where there was no ambition, no history, not even families.

To our Sakura. *There are no reasons for me to remain in this place. Look what they did to us for trusting in them. I am coming, Simon.*

Full of purpose, she searched into her bag, found the mask, extended the elastic braces, fitted it over her face, and deeply inhaled several times.

Then, she lay down on the bed alongside Simon, and draped herself around him.

Epilogue

Makoto Asaye knows it now.

The ashes of Kazuhiro should rest at the Sengaku-ji shrine, close to the graves of the forty-seven ronin, small dust to the atonement of their everlasting anger against his family. A painful decision, this, for just as well he might have wanted to repose in his underground museum, together with his father and all those lost warriors. But who knows how long that place will last, now that he is gone.

The ashes of Simon and Hiroko shall be together on the holy grounds of Kamakura, the old capital, for there the hydrangeas are building rolling hills in late June, and in March and April there is a great Sakura.

And the distance between the two places should help their spirits in having repose.

Japanese words and phrases

anata - (respectful) you
Anata, do shimashita? Anata, nan desu ka? Ii desu ka? - Sir/You, what happened? Sir, what is it? Are you OK?
bento - Japanese lunch box
Butoh - a kind of more modern Japanese dance
butsudan - altar
-chan - diminutive used for younger people inside a family or for friends
Dai-Nippon Teikoku Kaigun - the Japanese Imperial Navy
desu - (I) am
desu ka? - are you?
Doomo arigato - Thank you very much
gaijin - foreigner
getas - Japanese traditional footwear
goen, gyoen - park
gumi - Yakuza family, sindicate
hai - yes
henna mono - strange thing
Hinomaru - national flag of Japan; during the war;
ikebana - the floral arrangement
Kabuki - traditional Japanese dance-drama
kaisha - company
kaiseki ryori - traditional multi-course Japanese dinner
Kamikaze - "divine wind"
kamikaze tokubetsu kōgeki tai - kamikaze special attack unit
katana - samurai sword
kiremono - schemer
koban - Japanese police box, small precinct

Konban wa - good evening
kurabu kara - (calling) from the club
maiko - young geisha in training
matsuri - folk festival
Matte, kudasai - please wait
mikoshi - portable Shinto shrine
Mizuage - deflowering ceremony
mizu shobai - the water trade, is the traditional euphemism for the night-time entertainment business
Missouri
Mitsukoshi - famous department store
Moshi-moshi, Konichi-wa. Hiroko desu. - Hello, good day, this is Hiroko calling
Nihon buyo(n) - traditional dance style, intended for entertainment on stage
Nihon Komintō - Japanese nationalist right-wing group
obi - sash/belt for kimono
obi jime - the obi cord
obi makura - the obi pad
odori - traditional Japanese dance
onsen - hot spring
ohayoo gozaimasu - good morning
otemae - tea ceremony
oyabun - Godfather, supreme boss (same multiple meaning as in American Mafia)
rabu hoteru - love hotel (for trysts)
ronin - samurai
ryokan - inn
Sakura - Cherry blossom (here figurative, poetical)
sararimen - salaried men
sayonara - good bye
seksii - sexy
seppuku - harakiri
Shinrikyo - cult, "religion of Truth"
shodo - Japanese calligraphy
Shugaku-in - Japanese imperial vila in Kyoto
soredewa mata ashita - see you tomorrow
soba - Japanese noodles

sukiyaki - Japanese dish of meat (usually thinly sliced beef) which is slowly cooked or simmered at the table
Sumimasen - (I am) sorry
Sumimasen, nan desu ka? - I am sorry, what is it?
tabi - traditional Japanese socks
taiko - large Japanese drum
udon - Japanese noodles
usunoro - megadork
zori - Japanese sandals

Acknowledgments

I would like to warmly acknowledge the following individuals and groups:

- Eva Fingermann, Traian Mos and Dan Scurtu, true friends in need.
- Danuta and Constantin Bolintineanu, Andreea and Dr. Augustin Iuoras, Violeta and Dumitru Gheorghe Sdrulla, Dr. Andrei Vladimirescu, Ileana and Dragos Constantinescu, for helping the flame to stay alive on this side of the Pond.
- Mrs. Juliana Werner, my wonderful home teacher, for constant encouragement on both sides of the Pond.
- Many of the members of the *alt.usage.english* newsgroup on the Usenet, for help in mining the riches of the English language and of many literary works. Especially, but not only: Charles Bellemare (CDB), Donna Richoux, Professor John Lawler, Don Phillipson, John Dean, Robert Lieblich, Peter Duncanson, Frank ess, Ross Howard, Mike Lyle, Cheryl Perkins, Jerry Friedman, Mark Brader, Eric Walker, David (the Omrud), Iain Archer, James Silverton, Ray OHara, Lars Eighner, Raymond S. Wise, John Varela, Irwell, Robin Bignall, James Hogg, Stephen Calder, Cece, Isabelle Cecchini, Leslie Danks, Athel Cornish-Bowden, Derek Turner, UC, Tony Cooper, Adrian Bailey, Peter Moylan, Skitt, Horace LaBadie, Nick Spalding, Django Cat, Harvey Van Sickle, Pat Durkin, Harrison Hill, R H Draney, Ian Jackson, Laura Spira, Katy Jennison, Roland Hutchinson, Glenn Knickerbocker, Snidely, John Holmes, Aokay (David G. Bryce), Evan Kirshenbaum, Carmen L. Abruzzi, Stan Brown, Joe Fineman, Don Aitken, John O'Flaherty, Alan

Jones, Charles Riggs, Martin Ambuhl, Maria Conlon, Jonathan Morton, Arcadian Rises, Mike Barnes, Prai Jei, Steve MacGregor, Bob Cunningham, Guy Barry, Matthew Huntbach, J. J.Lodder, R J Valentine, Lewis, Whiskers, GordonD, Pierre Jelenc, Dr Nick. Sorry if I missed anyone. You have all been great.

- My critique partners, especially:
  Mooderino, Toddkonrad, Gaelle, Cheeno, for sharp eyes; Victorine and Jeannet, for their advice on indie publishing.
- My longstanding Japanese friends.

The errors are all mine.

Comments and suggestions are welcome at simonandhiroko@gmail.com. I am sure there will be corrections coming from both sides of the Pacific, and I commit to do my best to incorporate them in the next edition. However, I am sorry I cannot commit to providing replies to everyone.

37351417R00199

Made in the USA
Charleston, SC
06 January 2015